The Legions of the Sun

THE LEGIONS
OF THE SUN

A Novel about Ambrose Bierce

Jason C. Eckhardt

Hippocampus Press

New York

Published by Hippocampus Press
P.O. Box 641, New York, NY 10156.
www.hippocampuspress.com

Hippocampus Press logo designed by Anastasia Damianakos.

First Hippocampus
1 3 5 7 9 8 6 4 2

ISBN 978-1-61498-445-0 (trade paperback)
ISBN 978-1-61498-457-3 (ebook)

This is for
Sam Gafford, who started it all,
George Arnold, amigo and co-conspirator,
Fred Padula, profesor y amigo,
and
Rick Szatkowski, who always liked a good story

absent friends

Dark hills at evening in the west,
Where sunset hovers like a sound
Of golden horns that sang to rest
Old bones of warriors under ground,
Far now from all the bannered ways
Where flash the legions of the sun,
You fade—as if the last of days
Were fading, and all wars were done.
                    —Edwin Arlington Robinson

LOOK!
The eagle and
tiger princes
are dressing themselves
for war
                    —Ancient Mexican song

—Te digo que no es animal . . .
                    —Mariano Azuela, *Los de Abajo*

PART I

EL NORTE

1.

It was a cold and monotonous day in late autumn, 1913. Outside the windows of my flat, Washington was wrapped in wool and furs and bustled to its many destinations; but not I. I had not heard from my employer, Mr. Bierce, for several weeks and was beginning to miss even his caustic type of conversation. That was when the telephone rang.

"Mr. Littlefield?" came a direct, mannish voice over my telephone.

"Little*fault*," I corrected automatically. A common error, one I had long gotten used to correcting. "May I help you, madam?"

"Yes, you may, Mr. Littlefault. This is Helen Bierce Cowden. My father is the author, Ambrose Bierce. You are his secretary."

This was a statement, not a question, but an inaccurate one. Mr. Bierce— more journalist than author now, more retired than anything else at the moment—had a secretary, the very competent Miss Carrie Christiansen. I was his assistant in non-literary matters. However, both the nature of those matters and my not wanting to alienate the great man's only surviving child made me hold my tongue.

"Yes, Miss Helen," I said as smoothly as I could. "And how may I help you?"

"I need you to—that is, I would like you to look into the whereabouts of my father."

This was alarming news indeed. That I should not have heard from Bierce in weeks was no great cause for concern. I knew he had taken himself on an extended railroad jaunt through the Civil War battlefields of his youth by himself. But though he was old (seventy-one the previous June), he was still relatively fit, ambulatory, in full possession of his ever-astringent intellect. A stranger regarding the lives and persons of the two of us, side by side, might be forgiven for having more concern for me, twenty-seven years Bierce's junior and far more sedentary in my habits than he. But for Bierce's own daughter, one of the few members of his family with whom he still conversed, to have lost contact with him was cause for worry. However, my association with Bierce had taught me discretion and tact, and these I now employed so as not to increase the woman's anxiety.

"Your father is a man of many resources, Miss Helen. If he has chosen to seclude himself, I'm sure that he has both good reason and an eye to his own security. I really—"

"No, no, no," she chided me in a tone I knew well from her father, as if I were a forward child. "I am fairly certain I know *where* he is—at least a good general idea. But as for his 'eye to his own safety,' I think you have a more optimistic sense of it than is warranted."

"Really, Miss Helen? The last time that I saw him he seemed in reasonable health and spirits." *No worse than usual*, I might have added, but thought better of it.

"Then your senses are inadequate, Mr. Littlefault," she said with some asperity. "Father has been getting more and more morose of late, and his asthma has become a caution. Whatever possessed him to come to this—this pest-hole of a city, I'm sure I cannot say."

Again I held my tongue. In fact it had been the order of his then employer, William Randolph Hearst, that had "possessed" him to move to Washington, D.C., from his longtime home of San Francisco, to report on the capital's antics and to train his unerring wit and venom upon the worst rascals there. The move had increased Bierce's fame tremendously, and he had recently been putting in order his *Collected Works* for Walter Neale, Publisher. But it was also true that the dampness of the capital had aggravated Bierce's asthma. That, added to his age and a string of personal tragedies and public battles, had worn down the once "Almighty God" Bierce.

Long contact with a person can blind you to the incremental changes that come upon them. Such was I. His daughter's concern was a clarion call to me. For the first time I had a tragically clear picture of the man Bierce had become: a sick, weakened, bitter and vindictive septuagenarian. Now I began to worry.

"He has surely contacted you since his departure," I said into the 'phone.

"Of course. Postcards, mostly. Virginia, Tennessee. The battlefields of his youth." You could taste the disdain with which she regarded this most pointless of pursuits. "Most recently it was Texas, but I assume that by now he has reached Mexico."

Mexico! Now I really became alarmed. Mexico had been in the throes of a revolution for three years now and showed no signs of settling down. The lives of hardened revolutionaries were routinely snuffed out in that meat-grinder of a war. What it would do to an old gringo like Bierce didn't bear thinking about.

Again I summoned up tact.

"Do you know why your father should want to go to Mexico, Miss Helen?"

"I cannot be sure but—well, he has given some hints. I will read to your from one of his latest postals, this one sent from San Antonio on October 30th, in which he says"—here Mrs. Cowden cleared her throat, and when she came back on I could hear an imperfectly covered hitch in her voice. "He says, 'I'm going to Mexico to see if those devils can shoot straight. If you hear of me being stood up against a wall and shot to rags you will know that I went with a smile upon my face.'"

We were both silent then. Poor Bierce—and poor Helen. To receive such a message and not be able to do anything about it . . .

"So you see, Mr. Littlefault," she said with more resolve, "that is why I require you to find my father and bring him back. Whatever the intentions behind this juvenile adventure of his, it must end now. He has obligations back here, not least of all to me. I will research the necessary travel arrangements and cover your expenses as far as Texas. Beyond that, you must draw upon your own resources."

"But, Miss Bierce—"

"Cowden," she said, and hung up.

Well. I sat staring dumbly at the 'phone a good minute after she rang off. As little as she might like to admit it, I thought, the woman had inherited her father's commanding, peremptory air. Go here, do this, tell me what happens . . . Hadn't I been playing this game with Ambrose Bierce for more than twenty years now, all across the continent? And now to get the same treatment from his daughter—outrageous.

But my pride quickly faded before the very real peril Bierce could be in. It was more than just the Mexican Revolution, if the word "just" can be applied to that bloodbath. In the two decades of my association with Ambrose Bierce, I had come to learn that behind the veil of the everyday world (and oh, how thin that veil sometimes was) there lurked worlds and beings inimical to our stratum of existence. When that veil was rent and these Beings came through, then Bierce and I were called upon. For in addition to his well-known careers as journalist and fictioneer, he conducted a semi-secret career as investigator (and combatant, when the need arose) of outré phenomena. But for those poor souls who had recourse to Bierce's talents in this realm, I was the only one to know of these incursions into our universe; and since 1892, I had been privileged to aid him on these adventures.

It was with this latter possibility in mind—that Bierce was either in danger from such entities or on their trail—that I resolved to help Mrs. Cowden and find him as quickly as I could. In this I must needs work alone. Even Helen Bierce Cowden did not know of this aspect of her father's life and she had no need to know of it now.

Even if she could believe it, which I doubted. The world would be astounded to know the weird truths behind many of Bierce's so-called "ghost stories." But to present them as fact would invite ridicule and a dampening of our secret effectiveness against these incursions from "beyond the borderland of conjecture," to quote the great man himself. So we worked alone and in the shadows.

I went about putting my affairs in order as quickly as I could. Being a bachelor with few connections, this was easily done. Bierce kept me on a generous retainer, and what that didn't cover I eked out through some small writing of my own. I made arrangements for the rent to be paid on my apartment through Bierce's monthly payments. Beyond that, all I had to concern myself with was what to pack. It was December and cold, even in D.C., but I was headed south—deep south. So I threw together an assortment of heavy and light clothes, more light than not. Into this motley I placed a compact volume of Shakespeare, a Spanish grammar to brush up my rusty street-Spanish, and lastly, the gunbelt and Peacemaker revolver I had taken to wearing under Bierce's tutelage. Supernatural threats or not, there would be ample human threats along the way.

2.

Helen Bierce Cowden was as good as her word. The tickets for my journey arrived the next day by messenger, along with a schedule of trains headed south. I never saw the woman herself. On a brisk, clear Washington day I boarded a long, dark southbound at Union Station and settled myself in for the extended journey into my next adventure. Mrs. Cowden, for all her curtness, was not a niggardly woman. I was given a Pullman compartment and all the meals I could stuff down. So it was that I sat in comfort with my coffee and the latest newspaper, watching the famous names and places of the Civil War drift by my window. Manassas, Knoxville, Chattanooga . . . they rolled by in winter shades of brown and gray. It was already fifty years since the Great Rebellion, yet the scars were still fresh on every hand. Here were ruined warehouses in Richmond; there, a half-burned plantation-house among fields gone tall with weeds, or worked by drudge-like "tenant-farmers," Negroes who straggled behind the same plow their grandsires worked under the more honest name of "slavery." Sometimes the battlefields of the war spread out on either hand, peopled only by the statues the aging survivors of those battles had put up in memory of their fallen brethren. It was easy to see why the South didn't forget. I was from Pennsylvania originally, and we have only Gettysburg; and we don't forget.

Nashville, Jackson, Memphis. And the grand spectacle of the Mississippi, Old Man River himself, rolling sullenly through the heart of the continent. The deep woods of Tennessee were replaced by the flat patchwork of Arkansas. Poor farms, lean, angry faces. The Ozarks rose up and the piney woods were a relief to both my vision and my soul. The woods crowded close all the way down to and across the Red River; and then we were in Texas.

Texas. The very name conjured up visions of cowboys and Comanches; the Alamo and armadillos. It wasn't quite that anymore in the Year of Our Lord 1913, but wild enough for an Eastern boy like me.

And land . . . Lord Almighty, so much land, and all Texas. It stretched away to the horizon as if waking from a long nap. Dallas and Fort Worth, aptly known as "Cow-town," stockyards still jammed with bawling cattle; the lush, high grass of the prairie, and the false snow of cotton-bolls caught in the furrows of the Blacklands. In Waco I caught glimpses of the Brazos River, the "Brazos de Dios," the Arms of God that wrap their protective, brawny curves around the city. Later Austin rose like a dream from the flat haze. O. Henry's "City of the Violet Crown" itself, and the state's capital, planted opportunely between Spanish South Texas and Anglo North, in the crook of the land where flatland rose westwards into the Hill Country and the Edwards Plateau. Live oaks dotted the plain like giant toadstools, spreading welcome pools of shade. The new Texas capital bulked up majestic and insolent into hot Texas skies. They tell me it's just a little higher than the U.S. Capitol, and I could believe it. Across the sleepy, winding Colorado, where I longed to cool my traveling feet. Then south, ever south. New Braunfels—a whiff of streudel and polka music from that old German enclave. Finally a blue-jacketed conductor calling, "San Antone, San Antone!" My ticket had run out.

I detrained in the city's station and stood stretching while the cavalcade of Texan life boiled around me. Here were Mexican *abuelitas* in their black rebozos, dragging recalcitrant children; there a pair of cowboys, genuine cowboys you better believe it, ten-gallon Stetsons set securely on fence-post heads and lugging intricate saddles onto the train; here a young couple in the latest fashion, she in long, flared dress and extravagant garden of a hat, he in striped jacket and straw boater. They noodled together as they walked, and when they passed me I think they were speaking German. As I was of Pennsylvania Dutch extraction myself, it gave me a comforting feeling of connection to this vast, strange land.

Once I had gotten my bearings I carried my luggage to the street and hailed a taxi. The sophistication of the old city of San Antonio de Bexar, once a lonesome Spanish outpost, was evident in the tall buildings and swarm of smoking, chugging automobiles that met my gaze. "The South will rise again," they say. In places like San Antonio, I'd say it already has.

"Where to, bud?" asked the taxi-driver once I had clambered in.

"The Menger Hotel, if you please."

"Yes, sir, the Menger it is."

Helen Cowden had told me that her father had boarded at the Menger when he came through there in October. It seemed both the best place to start my enquiries and the easiest way to find lodgings. The taxi eased into traffic and rolled on. Under the eternal Texan sun the crowds in the streets strolled easily, slowly. As vital as San Antonio clearly was, it had the same somnolent pace of the other Southern cities I had seen. Here was none of the noisy hurry of New York or Boston or Chicago; here none of the self-important bustle of Washington. A hint of Latin "mañana" had crept into business as usual. Things clearly got done, but it didn't do to attack them too precipitately. Especially in that Southern heat. Even in December I could feel it bearing down upon the roof of the taxi.

A momentary vista of the dreaming San Antonio River in its ancient flume between crowding buildings; then we swept into Alamo Square. The Alamo itself was anticlimactic. For all the vaunted heroism of its defenders, slaughtered by the despot Santa Anna's troops eighty years before, the Texans had allowed the old mission to be turned into an agglomeration of cheap shops and attractions. Far more impressive, to my eyes, was the big, square, solid building to its right. MENGER HOTEL it proclaimed itself across its front, as if daring the passerby to refute it.

The taxi shuddered to a halt before the hotel. The cabbie helped me extricate my luggage from his vehicle, I paid him a bit more than he asked, and with a tip of the hat he boarded his vehicle and chugged off.

I entered the hotel and was pleasantly surprised at the sumptuousness of the interior. I suppose I still had some of the Northerner's ignorant disdain of anything south of Baltimore. The Menger cured me of that. I checked into comfortable rooms, secured my luggage, and in a fresh suit went out to find food. I had had breakfast on board the dining car on the last leg of my trip, but that already seemed days ago. When I asked for directions to an eatery, the comely *Fräulein* at the desk pointed me toward the Menger bar as the closest and best choice.

The bar was not large. It was dark with polished wood and glimmered mysteriously with brass appointments, bottles, and a large mirror behind the bar itself. When I asked the barkeep about options for meals, I was delighted to find they served summer sausage. I hadn't had any real German summer sausages since I had visited home in Pennsylvania two years previously; and this, accompanied with eggs, toast, and respectable coffee, made up my meal.

As I was finishing up I noticed that I was not alone there. My hunger must have been extreme indeed for me not to have noticed that old campaigner at the far end of the bar. There could be no mistake about his former occupation, for he still wore a soiled Army tunic and sweat-stained campaign-hat, the brim pushed up flat in front. A pair of dungarees and sandals, of all things, completed his attire. From the cut of the military garb and his grizzled, unshaven face, I guessed him to be a veteran of the Spanish-American War of the '90s. His age might have been forty; it might have been sixty. Drink and hard living had weathered him sorely.

I recalled that President Roosevelt's "Rough Riders" had met at the Menger before descending upon the Cubans in the Spanish-American War, and still had reunions there. That Bierce had hobnobbed with them, old soldier that he was, was more than likely. The opportunity seemed too good to pass up. Taking my coffee, I sidled over to where the veteran sat.

"Hot one today," I ventured. Weather was a cheap way to open a conversation, but I had little else. The veteran turned a sly, half-asleep eye my way and grunted.

"You ain't *seen* hot, mister," he said, and took a drink from his glass. I couldn't hide my accent, and he couldn't hide his contempt for this soft Yankee. All right—another tack.

"Pardon me," I said, "but I couldn't help noticing your uniform. Were you in the Cuba campaign?"

He sat up straighter and turned his full, wobbly gaze on me.

"I weren't just *in* the Cuba campaign, boy," he said. "I danged near *was* the Cuba campaign. Me 'n' Colonel Roosevelt, we kicked the dons from Havana to Matanzas, back into the sea."

"A Rough Rider?" I tried to strike a note of curious awe without fawning. It worked.

"Dang right, younger. 'Ninety-eight it was, and I still remember, 'member it like it was Tuesday. Up Kettle Hill, 'Damn the Dons!' we yelled. Even coloreds fightin'." He stopped to wet his whistle. Then, turning his unsteady gaze approximately on me, he said, "An' where did *you* serve?"

"I didn't," I said. "Too young for Antietam, too old for Havana." I shrugged, smiled, and hoped that would satisfy him. It did not.

"Too young, my foot," said he. "You're younger'n me. What're you, a coward? An' what's that yer drinkin'—*coffee?*"

Good grief. I flagged down the bartender and ordered a beer for myself. After the heat of the cab ride, it would go down well anyway. While I was at it I ordered a refill of the veteran's bourbon. When it came he mumbled "'Preciate it," and drank deeply. I slaked my own thirst and put out my hand.

"Amos Littlefault," I said. At first he didn't seem to understand exactly what that was, so I added, "It's a pleasure to meet a real Rough Rider."

"Sergeant Lucius Birkenhead," he said, and took my hand in a firm enough grip. With the mention of the Rough Riders he again straightened himself up and looked me square in the face. Poor devil, I reflected, once a war hero, now just a lush living off his past. In the dim light of the bar and with his newly upright posture, I could see a little of the man who had run up Kettle Hill with Colonel Roosevelt into a hail of Spanish bullets. The bony shoulders filled out, the stubbled jaw squared; the eyes cleared for a minute and he scrutinized me as a sergeant would a new recruit.

"Pleasure," he said. Then the shoulders sank, the eyes clouded. The sergeant was gone.

"As I say," I said, "you're the first real Rough Rider I've met."

"'S true," he said, nodding. "Ain't many of us around here anymore. Most've gone home, Chicago, Michigan, Hartford . . . I'm holding down the fort." He favored me with a smile that said volumes. I suddenly felt certain that the poor fellow had no home to return to. It was implicit in his every wrinkle and nod. I resolved to help him in whatever way I could.

"Say," I said, remembering my mission, "I'm looking for a friend of mine. Older gent, white hair, mustache, ex-military like yourself. His name's Bierce, Ambrose Bierce, and I heard he came through here."

Birkenhead swallowed his bourbon and nodded vigorously.

"Oh, sure," he said. "Pierce, nice guy, square fellow. Bought us all drinks.

Ninth Indiana Volunteers, Chickamauga, Shiloh, 'Lemme tell you how I got this scar,'" and he drew a shaky finger across his temple into his hairline, closely following the bullet-scar I knew Bierce had borne since a bad day at Kennesaw Mountain, Georgia, in 1864. Whatever else the campaigner had forgotten, he remembered Bierce. My heart leapt—I had seen that selfsame scar myself many times.

"Do you remember when you saw him?" I said.

"It was a month ago."

I started at this new voice. It was the bartender, a man of about thirty with slicked, black hair, curled mustache to match, and the blocky build of a farmer. Or a roustabout. As I watched him he turned to the shelf of bottles behind him and pulled out a paper from between a pair of whiskey quarts. He walked over to us. When he got closer I saw that it wasn't a paper; it was an envelope.

"He left this for someone he said would follow," the bartender said. He was looking at the front of the envelope, that side turned away from me. "Said not to give it to anyone else. What'd you say your name was?"

"Littlefault," I said, barely able to hear my own voice. "Amos Littlefault."

The bartender's eyebrows shot up.

"Well," he said, "can't be two with a moniker like 'at." And he handed me the envelope.

I looked greedily at my own name written in Bierce's neat hand on the front, then tore the envelope open, unmindful of the curious looks from the other two men. Within was a single sheet of paper printed with the words "MENGER HOTEL San Antonio, Texas" for a letterhead. Written beneath it in more of Bierce's strong handwriting was the following:

Amos—   Novr. 1

Meet me Borderland Hotel, Laredo. Frayser on the loose—

AB

That was my boss—brief and to the point. And there, in the comfortable safety of the Menger hotel bar, in the baking December heat, I shivered. "Frayser" was a code-word between Bierce and me, a reminder of a particularly disturbing case we had handled. We had since used it only when great danger threatened, and I could count on one hand the times we had used it in twenty years of adventures. For him to employ it in this note implied he was on the track of something very important, and consequently I must hasten to join him.

But November first. Ye gods, already a month . . .

"Ever'thing all right?" The bartender was looking at me with concern. I saw that Sgt. Birkenhead was watching me closely too; so I quickly folded the letter and stuffed it back into its envelope.

"Yes," I said. "Everything is fine, just fine."

"Don't look fine," said the veteran. "I seen that same look on men right before the charge."

"My—friend," I said carefully, "may be in need of assistance." Turning to the barkeep, I said, "Would you happen to know the times of the trains for Laredo?"

He scratched himself behind the ear.

"Not off the top o' my head," he said. "You in some hurry?"

"Yes, I'm afraid so." I regarded those two men and their earnest looks and made a decision. "Mr. Bierce may be in some danger."

The barkeep nodded once.

"Your Mr. Bierce was a straight-up feller," said he. "Bought a round for the whole passel of Rough Riders, and gave me a beaut of a gratuity on top of it. Lemme see what I kin do."

He walked to the back of the bar.

"Don't you fret, youngster," said the veteran. "Ernst'll set you up fine."

Ernst was speaking into a candlestick telephone so softly that I could make out nothing of what he said. He was writing as he spoke. When he was done he hung up the 'phone, returned to where we sat, and set a sheet of paper on the bar before me.

"Give this address to the cab-driver," he said. "When you get to where it says, tell 'em Ernst sent you."

I looked at the paper—"Caswell Field" was all that was written upon it. I frowned and said, "I don't understand. This isn't the address of the train station."

"No, sir, it isn't," said the barkeep. "I'm sure there's a train headed to Laredo sometimes soon, but I can guarantee you these folks'll get you there quicker."

I rose and shook his hand.

"I appreciate that very much."

"Anything to help Mr. Bierce. He was all right."

"Good luck, youngster," said the veteran, wringing my hand. "An' thanks for the drink."

I followed the barkeep over to the till to settle my bill. After I'd given him the money for food and drink, I handed him a dollar in thanks. Then, turning so that the veteran wouldn't see or hear (although he was already too submerged in his drink to really notice), I handed Ernst a five-dollar gold piece.

"This is for Mr. Birkenhead," I said, *sotto voce*. "Please give it to him after I leave."

Ernst turned the coin in his meaty hand, thinking.

"He don't cotton to charity," he said, moving to hand the coin back to me. "'Sides, he'd just drink it all up."

"Then put it toward his meals," I said, pushing his hand back. "He doesn't have to know where it came from or even that someone's footing the bill."

Ernst seemed to like that better. He nodded and put the coin in the till.

"You're a good man, Mr. Littlefault," he said, shaking my hand again. "I hope you find your Mr. Bierce safe and sound."

Amen, I thought, *for all our sakes.*

I checked back out of the hotel (to the perplexed expression of the pretty clerk) and retrieved my bags. The cab, a near twin of the chugging contraption that had brought me to the Menger, whisked me out of downtown San Antonio and southwards, out into country. We passed a couple of the city's lesser-known missions, sleeping a noble decay among their overgrown demesnes. I wished I had had more time to explore this ancient, fascinating city.

But Bierce's words weighed heavily upon my mind (*Frayser*) and fired me with impatience. I wondered what manner of conveyance good, honest Ernst was sending me to. A faster automobile? Back in those days the average automobile could only manage a sedate forty miles in an hour, and that at the risk of blowing a gasket or tire. Daredevils like Barney Oldfield were tearing up the tracks at dizzying speeds of seventy or even eighty miles an hour, but that was in rare and expensive machines. Could we be going to the home of some wealthy rancher who could afford such a machine? And would I be up to traveling in such a juggernaut?

The houses thinned, the last Mission was passed. Fields dotted with those vast, umbrella-like live oaks sped by us. I began to get a little nervous. Surely good, honest Ernst wasn't sending me out to be robbed—or worse.

Then we came clear of the trees and a wide, bare field opened up. There was a single shack on one side, outside of which a couple men in overalls sat and talked.

"Caswell Field," said the cabbie.

"Are you sure this is it?" I said, looking at the emptiness.

"Sure am. Ain't but one."

I dug the fare out of my pocket and paid the man. When I stood with my bags alone upon the edge of that field, the cabbie flicked the brim of his hat and said, with a grin, "Hope you enjoy your ride." And he drove away.

I stood irresolute upon the dirt. The heat seemed to press me to the ground. I took off my hat and with my handkerchief and wiped the perspiration from the inner band, knowing it would be soaked again within minutes. Across the field, the two men watched me in the flat light, curious and incurious at the same time. They could have been wooden props on a stage for all their reality to me.

Well, I thought, *this is absurd,* and took off my jacket. At least there was a slight breeze out there in the open. A high, droning hum curved in and out of the air—cicadas or some other insect, singing for rain in the trees. Except there were no trees nearby. Puzzled, I looked up—and beheld the biggest dragonfly I had ever seen. "Everything is bigger in Texas," came the cliché to my mind.

But even the inventor of that phrase didn't have this creature in mind. The white, glaring sky threw off my sense of distance and proportion; I thought of Poe's "The Sphinx," of the insect transported to monstrous dimensions by perspective. This, though, was quite the opposite. Details formed—struts, guy-wires, the shimmer of a propeller. In a moment my "dragonfly" had resolved itself into an aeroplane. The two men waiting by the shed were watching it, too, and now rose and ambled out onto the field. How wonderful, I thought—and then, *Oh, no.* They can't mean for me to—

The thought hung unfinished in my mind as the aeroplane, an intricate kite of fabric, wood, and wire, wobbled down toward the ground. It slowed as it came, graceful in the way a child on a bicycle first finds his balance. A tip of the wing here, a tentative dip at the earth—and it touched earth and rolled across the field toward me. The two men continued their easy stroll up to the machine.

Leaving my bags, I too walked over to the machine. Its twin propellers spun and twitched to a stop. Silence rushed in. The two men were helping the pilot out of the inner tangle of the machine, a courtesy I thought gallant if a little excessive. Why, any man could have just stepped down out of the thing. It wasn't until I got closer that I noticed how the pilot's overalls swelled at the hips and chest. And when he took off his goggles and helmet, I found that "he" was a "she." Dark hair was wound tightly in a coif around her head, and sprightly green eyes looked at me with curiosity and some amusement. Despite the raccoon's mask of dust on her face, she was clearly a pretty woman.

"Good morning," I managed, tipping my hat.

"'Tis, isn't it?" she said, smiling. Then she turned to the two men and said, "Hap, that right aileron is a mite sticky. Would you get some graphite on the linkages, please? And a couple of these guy-wires are loose, Lamar. I don't feature having to set down in the chaparral."

The two men touched their hats, said, "Yes, Miss Avis," and shuffled off to their respective tasks. Miss Avis turned back to me with those frank green eyes.

"And what may I do for you, sir?" she said.

Her frankness was something new to me, used as I was to retiring Eastern females, and put me off some. But I had a duty to perform and replied, "I was told to say that Ernst at the Menger sent me. My name is Amos Littlefault, and I need to get to Laredo as quickly as possible."

"Well, isn't that a whole burrito to digest," she said. "Old Ernst—well, you come with good recommendations, anyway. Ernst serves the best boilermakers I've ever encountered. My name is Avis Smalls, Mr. Littlefault, and why on earth do you want to go to Laredo?"

She proffered a small hand palm down and I gripped it briefly.

"It isn't that I want to go to Laredo, Miss Smalls, but that I must go there. A good friend of mine may be in danger there and I need to assist him in any way I can."

"You're a good friend yourself to make the effort, I'll tell you what. I expect *everyone* is in danger in the Valley these days, Mr. Littlefault."

"'The Valley'?"

"The Rio Grande Valley. That's what we call it around here for brief. The Mexicans have worked up a regular *pachanga* south of the river, and you could throw a rock from Laredo and hit a *federale* without trying. It's not a place I care to visit, myself." She looked at me keenly. "Are you *sure* you need to get there?"

"Yes. My friend is aged and infirm. He is—well, he is one of my dearest friends."

"There's the train," she said, shrugging.

"Speed is of the essence, Miss Smalls. Believe me, if I could find another mode of transportation"—I looked at the delicate-looking machine beside us—

"I would. No offense meant."

She nodded but looked a little put out.

"Laredo's a fur piece," she said. "I'll have to fill 'er up with petrol, maybe even bring an extra can or two. Fuel, travel, a couple days of my time—fifty dollars should cover it."

I swallowed hard—fifty dollars was a good deal of money in those days—but I got out my wallet and handed her the bills.

"Then there's the weather." She squinted up at the sky.

"It seems quiet at the moment," I said, also looking into that bald, burning expanse.

"Nobody but a fool or a Yankee predicts the weather in Texas," she said. "No offense."

While she conferred with her mechanics, I walked back and got my bags. When I arrived back at her machine, Miss Avis threw up her hands.

"Whoa," she said. "Hold on there, bud. You're not fixing to drag all *that* aboard my machine, are you?"

"The mere necessities of travel," I pleaded, but I could see she was adamant.

"There are rules and there are rules," she said. "And the rules of aerodynamics are not open to debate. I can carry a couple hundred pounds on this craft, nothing more. The extra petrol is going to take up some of that, and you'll fill most of the rest. I'm sorry, Mr. Littlefault, but most of that's got to stay."

I looked at my two bags, alone and dusty, as if at two orphans I was about to abandon. All right, I thought—priorities. Mr. Bierce is in danger. No time to equivocate. One bag was all clothes—those could be replaced. I could buy more in Laredo, I assumed. I opened both bags, took some—all right, most—of the clothes out of the smaller one and put my Spanish grammar, undergarments, and gunbelt into it. Shakespeare would have to stay.

"You might as well strap on that iron, while you're at it," Miss Smalls said, hands on hips.

"Don't you think that would be rather—provocative?"

"Brother, where you're going, nobody will look twice at it. They'll be more likely to stare if you *don't* go heeled."

I dutifully strapped on my "iron."

"There," I said, handing her the bag. She lifted it once or twice by the tips of her fingers as if weighing a cut of meat. Pushing out her lower lip, she nodded.

"That'll do," she said, and carried my bag to the aeroplane. I took one last look at my larger suitcase, open and eviscerated all over the Texas dirt, and sighed. *This better be worth it,* I thought and walked to the flying machine.

The mechanics were finishing strapping in two jerry-cans of petrol symmetrically on each of the machine's lower wings.

"That was quick," I said to them. "Is there an automobile station nearby?"

"Naw," said one of them (Hap? Lamar?). "We got a pump, side of the shack."

I looked that way and could now see a pump standing like some ridiculous, mechanical sentry on the side of the shack that had been hidden from me before.

"Oil and petrol are easier to come by around here than good coffee," the mechanic smiled. "Between here and Victoria, must be a thousand pump-jacks. Y'all have a good trip, now."

Miss Avis had walked to the shed and was returning now with two pairs of goggles dangling from her hand.

"I don't have another helmet, sorry," she said, and handed me one of the goggles.

"This will be fine," I said. "Thank you."

She fitted her leather helmet back over her hair and put on the other pair of goggles. Then, with a gracious assist from one of the mechanics, she climbed back onto her pilot's seat.

"Where do I, um . . ." I said, looking over the craft for the other seat. She patted the section of wing behind her own seat.

"Pardon the accommodations," she said, smiling. With her goggles and helmet, she looked like a large, grinning insect. "I don't usually fly tandem. Oh, and here—you'll be needing this." She handed me a strap with a buckle on it, like a large belt such as is used to tie trunks to automobiles.

"What's this?" I said.

"You'll want to tie yourself to one of the bigger struts," she said, pointing to one on my right. "I'd hate to see you get halfway to Laredo and fall off. It's a long first step." Again that entomological grin.

I dutifully climbed up behind her and strapped myself around the middle to the strut. My bag, I noted, was already secured similarly nearby.

The mechanics each grabbed the tip of a propeller close behind me (very close, it seemed to me), and Miss Avis called, "Contact, boys!" Instantly they heaved the propellers around. There was a twin bang followed by stuttering mechanical coughs. The big propellers swung round, circled, spun, faster and faster, and the engines sputtered into life. Miss Avis pulled back on a knob among the controls set before her and the engines roared. Miss Avis whooped with glee.

"Dang!" she yelled at me over the noise. "It works!"

Great.

Hap and Lamar each took a wing-tip and gently turned us around back the way Miss Avis had landed. They stepped back, waved, and the engines roared even louder, if possible. The aeroplane began creeping down the runway, then rolling; then racing. The flat central Texas countryside sped by and I crushed my hat to my head in the rising wind. Faster now, and suddenly I felt the most amazing sensation of lightness, as if I had shed a hundred pounds in an instant. The dun-colored ground fell away—distant live oaks grew tiny and toy-like, each one hoarding its shadow beneath it like a dark rug. Higher, and the land resolved into a colored map of fields, long, straight roads and the collection of pale children's blocks that was the ancient city of San Antonio. I forgot to be afraid. It was marvelous.

Miss Avis pulled the steering wheel over to her left and the aeroplane obediently banked that way. For a few breathless seconds I was looking straight down at the earth, some hundreds of feet below us; then we leveled out, the sun had switched from our left hand to our right, and we were flying south.

Below us the vast landscape of southern Texas began to change from the leftover greens of summer to the browns of semi-desert. The verdure shrank to clumps dotting the dry earth; snaking mesquite and ocotillo; lime-green growths of prickly-pear, as big as house-lots. We crossed rivers and arroyos— the Frio, the Nueces. Now and then a wagon or truck crept along the white lines of roads, on their way from nowhere to nowhere. Ahead the desert sprawled back into blue-brown haze.

"How long will it take us to get there?" I bellowed at Miss Avis's back.

"Oh, a coupla hours or so, I 'spect," she called back. "We're making a good eighty miles an hour, near as I can tell. Did you notice our hitchhiker, Mr. Littlefault?" She pointed to the right. I turned and beheld a large, bronze-black bird sitting on the leading edge of the craft's lower wing. As I gaped it turned an angry yellow eye my way. I was so surprised I pointed at it, forgetting that I had been holding my hat to my head. Instantly it flew off. There was a quick *flup* from the propellers behind me and the hat was gone. I have sometimes pictured it, lying alone on the gritty earth somewhere east of Dilley, Texas; or perhaps picked up and dusted off and decorating the dusky pate of some vaquero riding the plains. I hope he appreciates this $3 gift from Heaven and Sears & Roebuck.

Miss Avis must have felt my agitation for she turned a goggled eye to me and said, "You'll have need of a comb, time we get to Laredo, Mr. Littlefault."

I smiled my thanks, not trusting to my words.

"What is it?" I said.

"It's a tool to straighten out your hair," she said.

"No—the bird, I mean."

"A golden eagle. He probably thought he'd hitch a ride with Mamá-bird." She smiled and waved to the bird. It looked magnificently unimpressed. It glared at us a moment longer, then put its head into the eighty-mile-an-hour wind streaming over it.

The rest of the ride was uneventful, if you can call flying over the south Texas wilderness on a box-kite "uneventful." A long, dark brown scar, running north to south, parted the landscape far ahead. As we approached it I picked out a group of buildings hugging both sides of the scar. Miss Avis anticipated my question and pointed at it.

"The mighty Rio Grande del Norte," Miss Avis said. "That gaggle of houses on the far side is Nuevo Laredo, Coahuila, Mexico; that nearest to us, Laredo, Texas. Hold on—we're going to drop in for a visit."

She banked the aeroplane slightly to the left, easing us down, and I saw a broad open patch of ground, largely denuded of the ubiquitous mesquite and chaparral, toward which she was aiming us. The eagle took this opportunity to leave us. He dipped his great head and unfolded his wings, and dropped in a stoop off the aeroplane's wing. The last I saw of him, he was curving gracefully off toward Mexico.

The grid of stucco and wooden buildings that was the city of Laredo rose up on our right. Up, too, came the ground. I gripped the spar closest to me, but Miss Avis was an expert. She adjusted the controls and the engines' drone dropped in pitch and volume. We sailed down and down, and at the last moment my pilot pulled back a hair on the controls, we nosed up, and settled as gently as you please onto the ground. The machine sped down the field, slowed, and came to a halt. The propellers gave a last revolution or two and then they came to rest.

After two hours of those engines the silence was thick. It pressed against my eardrums. I unsteadily unstrapped myself and my bag from the aircraft and climbed off. Miss Avis was already standing on the ground, stretching. I joined her, pulling kinks out and releasing the tension I hadn't realized I'd had while flying. My hands, especially, were stiff from gripping the machine's struts in a stranglehold.

"Well," Miss Avis said. "Time to get purty." She tugged off the leather helmet, fluffed out her hair, and began unbuttoning the gray overalls she wore. Embarrassed, I turned away.

"Don't worry," she said, laughing. "Ain't nothing you've never seen before."

"I doubt that," I muttered. But when I turned for a surreptitious peek I saw that beneath her coveralls she was wearing a white cotton blouse and gray skirt. Watching her step out of that dusty skin and stand revealed clean and fresh was like watching a butterfly emerge from the gross cocoon of a caterpillar. She pulled a pair of women's shoes from a pocket of the coverall, rolled up the coverall, and set it on the wing. Then she sat herself down and began unlacing her flying-boots to change into the shoes.

"You can stop looking now," she said. Her glance was sly, mischievous. I blushed.

"Beg your pardon."

But I did keep looking. In this more feminine attire, I could see that she was quite pretty. Her face had strength, mostly in the eyes; but baby-fat in her cheeks lent the outline of her face a pleasant, graceful roundness. The one mar on it all was the ghostly outline left by her goggles in the dirt of travel on her face.

"I know," she smiled. "Raccoon, right? You too, bud." I had quit my goggles as well and now rubbed at my cheek. Filthy. Avis had unstrapped a canteen from the spars of the aeroplane and unscrewed the top. She pulled out a handkerchief and put it to the canteen's mouth and tipped the canteen. She smoothed the wet cloth over her face and the "raccoon" vanished.

"Here," she said, holding out the moist cloth to me. "Make yourself presentable for the welcoming committee."

I looked in the direction of Laredo and saw a group of ten or twelve children coming toward us at a run. I swept the kerchief over my face; and as I did so I caught a breath of Avis's perfume; honeysuckle or something equally sweet and sentimental. I closed my eyes as I wiped away the grime, breathing in the scent as deeply but as quietly as I could. I was in love.

I looked again and the children were closer. The boys in the group worked their arms in the air and the girls' braids flew out behind them. They couldn't run fast enough. What a wonder this must be, I thought, for these children. A real flying machine. The first boys, not quite teenagers, thudded to a stop a few feet away.

"That your flyin' machine, mister?" the tallest boy said.

"No," I smiled. "It belongs to the lady."

Miss Avis stepped forward and said, "Now, isn't this *the* most brave-looking bunch of buckaroos you've *ever* seen!" She knelt before them and gave them a sunny smile grown men would have fought for. "I expect y'all have seen aeroplanes before, haven't you?"

"No'm! No'm!" came the chorus of young voices.

"No?" Avis said with exaggerated surprise. "Well, we'll just have to fix that, won't we?" She picked up a little girl—the smallest little tyke of the bunch—and carried her to the craft's pilot's seat. The other children followed in a trance. I was amazed. This woman definitely had a way about her—aviatrix and brat-charmer. She set the little girl, not more than three years old, in the pilot's seat itself to the girl's utter delight. In her flouncy white dress, the girl looked like a big carnation set among all those spars and wires.

"Me next! Me, please, ma'am!" The other children hopped and pleaded and Miss Avis put out her palms in a calming gesture.

"All right, all right," she said. "You'll each get your turn. But you must promise not to touch any of the controls."

"I promise, I promise! Oh, me next, miss, *please!*"

While she hoisted and helped the children take turns at being pilot, I glanced back at the town. A large group of adults was following in the children's wake; and in their van, two heavily armed men on horseback. One held a carbine upright against his thigh; the other had a long gun scabbarded on his horse's flank. Both carried more pistols than I had yet seen in the State of Texas, and they wore their wide-brimmed Stetsons flat upon their heads. There was nothing casual about these gents.

When they had gotten near they stopped and dismounted. Every move they made was slow and easy as oiled machinery, but filled with deadly purpose. I heard Carbine say, "'Least they're not greasers." The other pinned me with a pale, blue-eyed look as if I were something he'd scraped off the bottom of his boot.

"You the owner of this vee-hickle?" said the one carrying the carbine.

"No," I said, jerking my head towards Miss Avis. "It's hers."

"And *you* are?" said the other man. My hackles went up at his tone, but then I noticed the badges the two of them wore on their flannel shirts—a star within a circle. The local law, apparently, well met.

"My name is Amos Littlefault," I said. "I contracted with this woman to fly me here."

"And I am Avis Smalls." Miss Avis stepped past me with a train of children behind her. She extended her hand to the last speaker. He took it briefly in his own.

"Ma'am."

The two men tipped their hats, but otherwise remained as stone-like as before.

Carbine said, "Do you have a license to operate this vee-hickle, ma'am?"

"I surely do." Avis drew a folded paper from the pocket of her skirt. The man took her paper, unfolded it, and looked it over.

"San Antone," he said, not looking up.

"Born and bred." Miss Avis smiled.

The man nodded, handed the license back to Avis.

"Sorry for all the questions, ma'am," he said, tipping his hat again. "We've got to keep an eye out since the Mexicans started their ruckus over there." He jerked his head back in the direction of the border.

"We ain't forgot about Juan Cortina," said Blue-eyes.

Juan Cortina—I had read about him. He had raised a rebellion of Mexican *rancheros* in the 1850s and caused a lot of damage along the border before being suppressed by the Texans. Bad doings, for sure. But looking at these two hardcases, neither of whom looked older than thirty, I thought that their "memories" of Juan Cortina must have been inherited from their grandsires.

"That's all right, Ranger," Miss Avis said, and there was that smile again. "We appreciate y'all keeping us safe."

So these were the famous Texas Rangers. They fit their fierce reputations down to the ground. I don't think I would have sneezed in their presence without asking permission first. With another "Ma'am" and a touch of the brim, the two Rangers remounted and rode slowly back toward Laredo.

The crowd that had followed them had stayed back in deference to the Rangers; but now they surged forward with a hundred questions. Miss Avis calmed them as she had done the children.

"I would be more than happy to answer y'all's questions," she said once she got them quiet. "But really, after a dusty flight such as I've had, what I really want is to freshen up and get something cool to sip on."

"Be my guest, miss! Best sweet tea in town! We have the cleanest facilities east of El Paso!" The offers tumbled over each other in the dusty air.

"Oh," Avis said, looking at her machine. "And I need someone to watch over my aeroplane."

A skinny young man was "volunteered" with a shove to his back and took up his post by the aeroplane with a mixture of authority and confusion on his pale face. Miss Avis led the crowd across the field toward Laredo, the children at her heels and the adults in a large, inchoate mass around her, leaving me in blessed solitude but for the "guard." I was out of breath from the whole episode, and my ears and whole body were still vibrating from the aeroplane's engines. A few moments by myself was just what I wanted. Hefting my bag, I started after the crowd at a stroll.

The Borderland Hotel was not hard to find. Laredo was not a large town in 1913 and its hotels few. I asked directions of a young man in sombrero on what I took to be the main street, and he smirked.

"Right there," he said, and pointed to a two-story brick building just down the block from where we stood. I thanked him, he touched his sombrero, smirked again, and walked away. I wondered what that smirk was about until I passed a store window and saw the fright my hair had become. There was a pump and a trough nearby, and I set my bag down and worked the pump handle until the gush of water from the pump was good and cold. Then I ran water into my cupped hand and splashed it over my head. The water felt good under that insistent Texas sun, and I stood, face in hands, savoring the coolness for a delicious minute before smoothing out my hair.

"Well, it's about time."

I knew that voice—there could be no mistake. Slowly lowering my hands from my face, I looked down the block to the hotel; and there, seated at a table out front in the hotel's shade, was Ambrose Gwinnett Bierce.

3.

I'd raced across half the country, risking my life and spending fifty precious dollars on a flight across the desert—and here he sat, Almighty God Bierce, like the Grand Turk. I could have wrung his neck.

Imagine him as he was then, seventy-one and still straight as a gunner's ramrod. He was tall, just over six feet, and crowned with a cloud of perfectly coiffed curly white hair. With that waxed and curled brush of a mustache and the eternal challenge in his blue eyes, it was easy to see why he was occasionally mistaken for Mark Twain. But there was an iron in Bierce's character that Twain lacked. I always found it significant that, while Twain was piloting a boat up and down the Mississippi during the Civil War, Bierce was actually fighting in it.

I dried my face upon my sleeve, picked up my bag, and walked over to where he sat.

"You, Amos," he said, pointing a smoldering cigar at me, "are a sight for sore eyes. Or at least one's eyes would become sore just looking at you."

I ignored his jibe and said, "Where have you been?" I didn't like the shrill sound of my voice; I felt like some harried mother addressing an errant child. But there he sat, reclining comfortably in his summer whites upon a wicker chair, one long leg crossed over the other knee, cigar in one hand and a tall glass of what looked like cold beer, streaming condensation, in the other. I, on the other hand, felt like laundry left out on the line during a sandstorm. Damn him.

"Why," Bierce said, spreading his arms, "I've been right here. In the shade. Enjoying this excellent beer and a *puro,* courtesy of my friend Mr. Romero." He nodded to his right and for the first time I noticed that he had company at his table. Sitting across from Bierce was a young Mexican man—a very dark Mexican man, whose very darkness had made him almost invisible to my sun-bleached gaze.

"D'you do," I nodded to him. He smiled back, an odd white crescent of teeth that turned down at the corners and revealed one incisor framed in what looked like silver.

"Mucho gusto." We shook hands. I turned back to Bierce.

"That's not what I meant and you know it," I said. "Your daughter sent me after you. She's worried sick. And I've traipsed two thousand miles by train and"—I lost the word for aeroplane—"flying contraption to find you. And here you sit, smoking your damn *puro* and sipping beer."

"Really, Amos, what else should I do? It's nearly ninety degrees in the sun. I'm surely not going to sit out there. And the beer here really is quite good. Waiter?"

He called to a man in shirtsleeves and apron, who approached with molasses–like alacrity.

"*Otro cerveza* for my young friend if you please," Bierce said. The waiter nodded and slouched back into the deeper shade of the hotel.

Suddenly I was very tired—bone-weary tired. I dropped my valise unceremoniously onto the dirt and dropped myself onto a chair. Everything seemed to become very still around me, and I took a good look at my quarry. Bierce appeared in top shape, younger somehow than I remembered him from Washington. He sat straighter, his smile spread more naturally beneath the great white mustache. His eyes, of an Arctic blue, *twinkled* at me, for God's sake. Whatever he had been up to down there, it agreed with him. I rubbed my face with my hands.

"We've been worried sick," I said between my fingers. "You head off on some holiday to the battlefields of your youth, send your poor, fretting daughter cryptic postcards full of suggestions of death . . . What were we to think?"

"That I could take care of myself, as I always have."

I looked up at him again and recognized the old Bierce—tough, immovable, confident in his own holy opinions if not in anyone else's. "Bierce," I said, pleading. "You're seventy-one years old."

"And you, Amos, are a mere lad of forty-eight, if my math is correct. Far too old to be flitting about heaven in an aeroplane. Although I commend your resourcefulness in finding one to get you here. I shouldn't have liked to wait for you *another* day."

The man was beyond exasperating. Fortunately my beer arrived just then and I plunged myself into it, body and soul. It was frosty-cold and was as good as Bierce had promised; and after being sandblasted across South Texas and walking a mile in that infernal heat, I swore that beer had never tasted so good as then.

The waiter was standing expectantly nearby. I began to dig out my wallet but Bierce waved me back.

"On my tab," he said to the waiter. The waiter still stood there, waiting.

"*En su cuenta, por favor,*" Romero said, pointing at Bierce. The waiter nodded, muttered "*Gracias*" to Bierce and faded away.

"Thank you, Juan," Bierce said to Romero. "Mr. Romero has been very helpful while I get my Spanish back to speed."

I could have laughed, if I had had the energy. Bierce's Spanish was a crude hodge-podge of instructions to maids and waiters, and the sort of comments one hears in certain streets—comments one doesn't repeat within the hearing of ladies. It didn't surprise me, for example, that he knew the word for "beer" (*cerveza*) but not the word for "bill" (*cuenta*). My Spanish wasn't exactly academy caliber, but would at least be understood by the average *mexicano*.

I sipped my beer and attempted to collect myself. In the nearby street the life of Laredo passed like a carnival in the white heat: trolleys clanged and rumbled; ox-carts, led by sombrero-shaded *campesinos,* rolled by; women in white shirtwaists and broad, flowery hats glided. Among the bowlers, boaters, and fedoras of the men were a fair sprinkling of cowboy hats. I noticed more Rangers with their silver badges—a lot of Rangers. They walked an easy, unhurried menace down the city streets. At least half, if not more, of the faces I saw looked Mexican.

The trolleys reminded me of San Francisco, where Bierce and I had met and worked for many years; and that, in turn, reminded me of the note he had left me at the Menger Hotel in San Antonio. I set down my beer.

"I got your note," I said.

"Obviously."

"So Frayser is on the loose."

Bierce took a deep breath and sighed.

"Frayser has gone into Mexico. And he is not alone. He has, in fact, many confederates south of the border. I am hoping that Juan here may be able to aid us in tracking him down."

I looked at Romero. Really looked at him this time. The crescent of teeth flashed out again in reply. He was probably about thirty, I estimated, of middling height. Neither heavy nor thin, with straight black hair and a threadbare mustache above that white grin. There was the suggestion of a scar beneath the mustache that I could not quite make out, like the trace of a mended harelip. His eyes, surprisingly, were green, and friendly in an eager-to-please way. I wondered how much Romero knew about Bierce's and my pursuits, and how much he could be trusted. If my calculations were right, Bierce had been in Laredo only a couple of weeks. Not really long enough to make the acquaintance, let alone to ensure the trustworthiness, of a stranger, I thought. The fact that Bierce was using the minor deceit of "Frayser" in the man's presence told me that he did not trust the Mexican completely, and this reassured me.

Bierce's implication was clear: we were going to Mexico. Bierce suffered stupidity in his fellow men with bad grace, which was a recurring personal problem as Bierce was smarter than most people he met. So rather than say something inane such as, "Are we going to Mexico?" I nodded to Bierce and just said, "So when do we leave?"

He nodded back approvingly and gave me a grim smile.

"Tomorrow."

Good. At least I'll have time to bathe, I thought, and had another pull of my beer.

"Why, Mr. Littlefault, I didn't take you for the drinking kind."

The voice was like dark honey and cut right through the noise of the day. We all rose from our seats at the sound of it, and I turned to regard Miss Avis Smalls, fresh in her white blouse and gray skirt, her face dimpling mischievously and her hands clasped primly over her skirt. She looked, if possible, even more radiant than before. Amazing what a little soap and water can do.

"Miss Avis Smalls," I said, reaching for the hat that was somewhere between San Antonio and Laredo. "May I present my good friend Mr. Ambrose Bierce to you?"

Bierce had undergone a change and looked even younger than he had just two minutes before. Women did that to him—when they did not drive him to drink. "Women is pizen, Amos," he liked to say to me, "but not necessarily fatal." In Miss Avis's attractive presence, he fairly throbbed with gentility and graciousness. Had he been a tom-turkey his tail feathers would have been spread in full display.

"My dear," he said, taking her proffered hand to his mustached lips. "I had no idea that when I aimed for Texas, I should arrive in heaven."

Oh, *brother*.

Miss Avis did nothing to stem this gush of flattery.

"Why, Mr. Bierce," she said. "Your fame precedes you, but is dimmed by your person."

He bowed graciously, hand to his heart.

"I understand you write stories," she said.

"Sometimes, yes."

"Sometimes I read them."

"Thank you, my dear."

"Stories—not necessarily yours."

Bierce stared at her as if hit by lightning. Then he burst out into a colossal laugh that tumbled into a coughing fit.

"Forgive me," he said, gasping his way back to the conversation. "My— asthma." He coughed forcefully a couple times into his handkerchief, shook his head and smiled.

"A real prize, Amos," he said. "Beautiful *and* she can quote my own scribbling to me. 'The Damned Thing,' Amos. You remember?"

"Of course, Bierce."

"Please, Miss Avis, won't you join us?" He offered her his chair. She sat and Bierce pulled over a chair from another table. We all sat.

"It was in Miss Avis's aeroplane that I came here," I said by way of introduction.

"Truly?" Bierce looked at her with admiration. "Then angels really do have wings!"

If I could have vomited discreetly, I would have just then. Miss Avis laughed like a song and touched the back of Bierce's hand. The man positively glowed.

"May I order you a refreshment, Miss Avis?" I said, partly to derail this monstrous flirtation.

"You certainly may," she said. "It's nice to see you found your manners, Mr. Littlefault, if not your comb."

I quickly ran a hand over my windblown locks. No good—I'd have to find a comb. Instead I flagged down the waiter.

"What would you like?" I asked Miss Avis.

"A beer with lime would be sufficient, Mr. Littlefault."

"Una cerveza con lima," I told the waiter. *"Para ella."*

"And another *cerveza por me, per favor,*" Bierce added, pronouncing *"favor"* as one would in English. The waiter nodded and vanished.

Bierce said, "Where are my manners? Miss Avis, this is my associate, Mr. Romero. Juan, Miss Avis."

Romero half-rose and said, "Señorita, a pleasure."

"'Lo." She blinked at him. Cool, I thought. No flirting there. "Well," she said taking a deep breath. "We are fairly met here in the metropolis of Laredo. And what are you gentlemen doing here, pray tell?"

Bierce and I exchanged quick glances.

"Mr. Bierce is here on an extended holiday," I said. "And I have come to assist him."

She considered this a moment and said, "You appeared to be in some hurry to get here, Mr. Littlefault. I thought your urgency was for more than just to 'assist' a friend on holiday."

"Mr. Bierce is not—in the best of health," I said, thinking furiously. "As you saw. His daughter Helen was concerned when she hadn't heard from him for some days, so I was dispatched to make sure he was all right."

So far as it went, all true. I caught Romero look a question at Bierce, who gave him a quick shake of the head. Miss Avis, watching me, saw none of this.

"You are a good friend to come so far to his aid," she said.

"I like to think so, Miss Avis. Mr. Bierce and I have known each other these twenty years and more and it has been my honor to assist him on many occasions." This was completely true, if, again, not the whole truth; and I was pleased to see Bierce give me a paternal smile of approval.

Just then the beers arrived, to everyone's relief.

"To our intrepid aviatrix," Bierce said, raising his glass.

"And to good friends," Avis added, and we all drank.

*

The rest of the afternoon—what little there was left—passed in small talk and more of Bierce's saccharine flirting with Miss Avis Smalls. At some point Romero got up, made his excuses, and left for his quarters.

About three o'clock, Miss Avis looked at the watch on her wrist and sighed.

"Well, Mr. Littlefault," she said, "Mr. Bierce, I hate to break up our little *tete-à-tete,* but I am losing daylight."

"You don't mean to fly back to San Antonio today," I said.

"I'm afraid I do, Mr. Littlefault. This little jaunt has been very agreeable"—she batted her eyelashes at Bierce, who looked ready to swell out of his suit—"but unexpected. I hadn't thought to bring the necessaries for an overnight stay."

"We can certainly provide whatever you need," said Bierce. "It is the least we can do for your assistance."

"Really, you are too kind. But the trip here also cut into my schedule and I need to attend to business back home." She stood up and we, ragged gentlemen that we were, stood also.

"My many thanks again for all your help," I said, taking her hand.

"Likewise." Bierce bowed.

"It was worth it, if only to make the acquaintance of two such gents as yourselves."

She turned to leave, but stopped just short of the sunlight. She made a very comely silhouette, I thought.

"Oh," she said. "If you need my services again, I can be contacted through Ernst at the Menger. It's probably the surest way to get a hold of me."

She graced us with a smile one more, delightful time. Then she walked away down the dusty street.

"A remarkable woman," said Bierce.

"That she is," I said, thinking of the way she had said "get a hold of me."

Bierce settled up his tab with the waiter, I helping sort out his execrable Spanish. Then I went into the hotel, got a room, and put my valise away. I rejoined Bierce, who was standing out front and watching the populace of Laredo as they went home to their suppers.

Supper—what a wonderful word. My stomach gave a petulant rumble.

"Any restaurants you would recommend?" I said as I came up to Bierce.

"Several," he said, still watching the crowds. "But if you can rein in your animal needs for a brief time, I need to talk to you alone."

The timbre of his voice was flat serious. Gone was the gushing boyishness of his flirtations with Miss Avis; gone even the clever irony of his usual speech. I looked at him, the proud profile set like the stone face of an Egyptian statue, and knew that we were headed for serious straits.

"Walk with me," he said.

We walked a little ways down the worn streets, then cut left down a side street. Laredo was bigger and busier than I had pictured it. A mere dot on the map, I thought, but this was no ramshackle border-town, haunt of rustlers and bandits. It lived up to its self-styled appellation of "The Gateway to Mexico." At this hour and in some side streets, however, it was pleasantly quiet. The whole, dizzying spectacle of my day stretched behind me—had I really been in San Antonio just this morning?

With that thought came the memory of my last meal, way back in the Menger Hotel bar. What with lack of food, the heat, and two beers under my belt, I was getting pretty wobbly. Despite Bierce's complaints, I grabbed a few tamales at a stand we passed.

Bierce led us all the way down to the river. There, on a bluff overlooking the Rio Grande and the whitewashed jumble beyond that was Nuevo Laredo, Mexico, we set ourselves down on a crude wooden bench. For a couple of minutes I ate and Bierce enjoyed one of his cigars. When I had finished the tamales, down to the last crumbs on my fingers, I took a deep breath.

"Okay," I said. "Now I can listen to you without fainting."

"A common complaint," Bierce said archly. We looked back across the river and contemplated the Mexican city, turning shades of blue and pink in the light of the setting sun.

"'Poor Mexico,'" quoted Bierce. "'So far from God, so close to the United States.'"

"One of your own?" I said.

"No—the late, lamented Mexican President Porfirio Díaz, who would know such things better than I."

"*'Mexico lindo y bravo,'*" I countered. "'Mexico, the beautiful, the wild.'"

"And never so beautiful nor as wild as now, Amos," he said with a dreamy air. We watched the river roll slowly past, and an eagle—my eagle? I wondered—wheeling over the stucco walls. It was such a peaceful scene that I had to remind myself that it was a country in the throes of war.

"We are embarked upon a dire mission, Amos," Bierce said. I looked at him, but he kept looking over the water. "You and I have seen some things, things that the average person would not credit, even if they had seen them themselves. Believe me when I say that it is no stretch of hyperbole that what we now face is far more evil and potentially destructive of our world than anything we have faced before." Here he reached into the inner pocket of his jacket and produced an envelope. He held it before him in both hands, considering it.

"I received this a month ago," he said. "Its author is genuine—I had him researched by the Pinkertons—and his statement . . . Well, I think it best if you read it in his own words."

I took the envelope from him. It was good paper, if thin; the economy of the genteel. Bierce's name, care of Hearst's Newspapers in Washington, was written in a neat, almost ornate hand upon the envelope; and the return address said simply, "T. Navarro M., Mexico, D.F."

I pulled the letter from the envelope and unfolded it upon my knee. This is what it said:

> Teobaldo Navarro M.
> Departamento de Antiguidades
> Universidad Autónoma del Estado do México
>
> 7 Sept. 1913.
>
> My dear Mr. Bierce,
>   I was given your name and address by a mutual friend of ours, Señor Gallego, to whom you rendered aid several years ago. Your fame as a writer and journalist has reached us here in Mexico, of course; but Sr. Gallego told me of your experiences with more obscure matters; matters concerned with the supernatural—and it is on this subject that I write to you. Believe me, I would not presume to contact you, but that the nature of the situation here is so terrifying that I will try any possible avenue to remedy it.

I paused and looked to Bierce. But he still looked out into the setting sun, the ruddy light making him look like some wind-sculpted monument of the West. I continued reading.

> You probably know something of our Mexican history, but it would not be out of place to give you here a *précis* of our conquest, the painful birth of our nation.
>
> In 1519, Hernán Cortes and some 600 Spaniards landed near modern-day Veracruz, and, through determination, clever alliances, and luck, within two years had conquered the great Aztec Empire. This was no mean feat; the Empire then contained a million people, and every healthy adult male Aztec had to undergo military training. Some few, more brave men could rise to become *tlacateccatl* or even *quauhpilli,* equivalents of our colonels and generals.
>
> But then there were those whose rare heights of bravery—and bloodthirstiness—raised them into the very elite of the Mexica forces. These were the famous Eagle-knights and Jaguar-knights; warriors so fierce that they could not be trusted with mere leadership. It was they who caught the captives whose hearts would be offered up to feed the sun-god Huitzilopochtli and ensure that he would rise again each morning.
>
> You will forgive my lecturing you on all this—the curse of a *profesor,* I fear. Its relevance is this: Someone, or some ones, have revived the Orders of the Jaguar-knights and the Eagle-knights in present-day Mexico. They are using the confusion of our present war as a blind, a "cover," I think you say in English, for their murders. The violence here in Mexico has reached such cataclysmic heights that these "Knights" can slay with impunity and in secrecy. When the countryside is strewn with the dead, who will notice a few more? The only clue to their killings is the state of the bodies they leave behind. The Knights remove the hearts. And even this is hard to discover when the slain are often so mutilated. If my contacts in the army are to be believed, the sheer number of these killings is staggering.
>
> All this is bad enough. But what they plan is far worse. These killings are a mere preparation for the advent of a new age—an age that will bring back not only the mass sacrifices of the Aztecs, but *the very gods they worshipped.*

Again I put the letter down.

"Really, Bierce," I said, but he cut me off.

"Continue."

Please understand that I am no *pagano* to believe in tree-spirits and fairies, Mr. Bierce. In fact, my Catholic faith is stronger now that I can see the evil these men are feeding. But there are forces walking abroad today in Mexico that would try the faith of the most devout. Gods or spirits, manifestations, call them what you will. Already the efforts of the Knights have altered the very reality of our lives here. And if left unchecked, I fear what kind of reality it will lead to.

So I am writing to you. Sr. Gallego spoke very highly of you and your abilities, and I beg you to consider this letter seriously. I may be reached at the address at the top of this letter. The telegraph office still works, for the moment, and that may be the quickest way to reach me. When we can coordinate our plans I will send a man I trust, Juan Romero by name, to guide you here to Mexico City. In these days our country—our poor, precious, suicidal Mexico—is no place for a *norteamericano* to be wandering alone.

Yours in complete sincerity,

Créame, por Dios,

Teobaldo Navarro y Morero [signed]

"Well?" said Bierce.

"Well," I said. I returned the letter to its envelope and gave it back to him. We stared across at Neuvo Laredo and its rising black blocks of shadow.

"It's a lot to accept," I said.

Bierce nodded.

"That is why I put the Pinkertons onto him, to verify his identity. It's fantastic"—Bierce turned a conspiratorial leer my way—"but we have seen the fantastic before, Amos, have we not?"

"Indeed we have, Bierce. But the potential scale of this thing . . ." I shook my head. "And to traipse into the heart of a revolution, all on this man's word . . ."

"'Heart' is an appropriate choice of word," Bierce said. "And you are right. It is a lot to ask. And that is why I have asked you to accompany me."

I was touched by this. Ambrose Bierce was not one either to scatter compliments or to ask for help. That he should do so spoke volumes about his regard for me. It also, I reflected sadly, said something about Bierce's acknowledgment of his own age and weakness. The time was when he would have blustered off into any adventure, dragging me along mostly to carry his equipment and record his victories. Now, looking at him, I saw the wrinkles around the ice-blue eyes; the great head of blond hair gone white as snow; the slight tremor in the hand that held the cigar. And how many times in recent years had I helped him through an asthma attack, dragging over a chair for him to hang himself over like some worn old suit until the fit passed? Helen was right: Bierce should never have taken his scarred lungs to a damp swamp like Washington, D.C. At least, I thought, looking at the brown land stretching beyond the border, we're somewhere dry now.

"All right," I said. "What is our next move?"

Bierce beamed at me.

"First," he said, like a general mapping out his strategy, "we go to Chihuahua."

"Chihuahua?" I gasped. "But the border is right there, Bierce. Why not cross here?"

"Because the forces of General Huerta are in control here. My coming to Laredo has been something of a bust, I'm afraid, though I did have to come here to rendezvous with Juan. But crossing at Laredo would be suicide. So Chihuahua it is. Pancho Villa is holding court there, and for the moment he is in good odor with our government. Also, if we are to discover any of these so-called Eagle-knights, I have a feeling that we will find some of them among his forces."

"But shouldn't we be going straight to Mexico City? Navarro seems pretty worried about this, telegrams and sending Romero to guide us and all."

"And we shall. But I want to test this Navarro's statement first. If there is some place where bodies can be disposed of easily, it is upon the battlefield; and if there is such a conspiracy as he claims there is, it must be insinuated among the combatants. What better way to gauge their strength?"

Oh, great, I thought. *I'm accompanying a septuagenarian asthmatic into a battle. Two tickets to hell, please.*

"Bierce, "I said, as reasonably as I could, "I really don't think—that is, to run into the clash of two armies . . ."

"Precisely," he said, and I could see a ghost of the old Lieutenant Bierce of the Grand Army of the Republic glaring out at me from beneath those shaggy brows. The Civil War was a long, long time ago, and no one, I think, would have considered it a "good time" in their lives. Yet there had always been something, some edge of excitement and vitality that crept into Bierce's every fiber and action when he thought on those days. He had seen some terrible fighting, I knew—the slaughterhouse of Shiloh, the bloody rout of Chickamauga—and suffered more than his share from the incompetence or outright barbarism of his commanding officers. And yet, and yet . . .

And this was surely part of his plan to go to Chihuahua. One last leap into the cauldron of war, if only to prove he could. And I knew, too, looking at that straight-spined old man, that no argument on earth was going to dissuade him. The least I could do was go with him and try to deflect as many Mexican bullets from him as I could.

"Do the trains even run to Chihuahua City?" I said. "We should at least be ready to get to Mexico City as quickly as we can, once we have reconnoitered."

"Just so. They do indeed run from there. The Mexicans, in fact, use the rails extensively to move their troops around." There was approval and admiration in his voice; Lieutenant Bierce approved. I knew Pancho Villa would be thrilled.

4.

The following morning I rose early and found a clothier that was just opening. Bierce had checked the train schedule from Laredo, and our train to Minero, Texas, our first leg on toward El Paso, did not leave until ten. Thus I had time to outfit myself properly for this expedition and to replace the clothes I had left upon the airfield in San Antonio. A good thing we were in the land of early-rising ranchers in need of new chaps and shirts, I reflected; I found an open shop and was fully accoutered by 9 A.M. When I walked back out onto the fabled streets of Laredo, I prided myself that I fit right in. Stiff new dungarees stovepiped over calf-high boots; a chambray shirt edged in scarlet stretched across my chest, flashing into view when my new gray corduroy jacket parted in front; and a charcoal gray Stetson of medium brim kept off the already powerful sun, and completed a picture of frontier sartorial brilliance.

"You look like an Eastern rube."

Bierce was always at his encouraging best in the morning. I found him seated in state at the same table where we had met the day before, a newspaper in his hand, coffee cup half-drained before him on the table, ashtray cradling a smoldering cheroot. He surveyed me with amused contempt.

"Thanks a lot," I said, ruffled. "I spent a good twelve dollars on this rig."

"'Costume' would be more accurate. And at twelve dollars, you was snookered."

He lifted the newspaper and glowered at it. I seated myself opposite him, dropping the sack of my old clothes onto an empty chair. The tortoise-swift waiter materialized nearby.

"Café," I said. *"Y migas con tocino, por favor."*

He nodded and slumped back into the shadows.

"I'll have the same," Bierce called after him.

"I thought you didn't like scrambled eggs."

Bierce stared at me, then shrugged.

"Is that what I ordered? Well, never too late to try something new."

I sighed.

"Really, Bierce," I said. "You should make *some* effort to learn the language."

He flapped a liver-spotted hand at me.

"Many of them understand a little English anyway," he said. "What they don't I can convey in what Spanish I have. Beyond that it's unimportant."

I thought again of the journey ahead of us—several hundred miles to Chihuahua, then another thousand south through a country tearing itself asunder in revolution, all to face some unknown terror—and wondered what part of what we'd encounter would qualify as "unimportant." Bierce must have seen me roll my eyes, because he said, "Besides, Amos, that's what you and Juan are here for. I will have more pressing matters to occupy me than mere translation."

That, at any rate, was probably true. I just hoped that my rusty *castellano* was equal to the task; that I had a vocabulary encompassing the outré as well as the everyday. Mentally I began compiling a list of words of possible use— *"fántoma," "espitiru," "desconocido," "cementario," "monstruo"* . . . Not a cheery list.

Our breakfasts came and we set to. For what the hotel lacked in prompt service, it more than made up for with the quality of its food. The *migas* were as soft as whipped cream, buttery and golden; the bacon delightful, midway between crunchy and yielding; and the toast perfect. When we were done, there was scarcely a crumb to offer the scrawny stray cat that came by to beg. Nonetheless, Bierce offered the creature his plate to lick clean, and even ordered another round of bacon to give to it.

"You're just encouraging it," I said, as Bierce hand-fed the bacon to the cat.

"I am *feeding* him Amos," Bierce said in a stern voice.

I felt ashamed. Bierce may not have had much love to spare his fellow men, but the dumb brutes of field and forest received plenty. They sensed this, too, in their simple souls, and would come when he called. His rapport with them was almost eerie. For a while he had had a squirrel, of all things, haunting his office; and I had seen wild birds alight on his outstretched hands when he cooed to them.

"Good lad," Bierce said as he scratched the cat's ears. The cat replied by purring and pushing into Bierce's hand. I wondered when it had last received such tender attention. Yet when it became clear that there was no more food forthcoming, it backed out of Bierce's reach, goggled its eyes all around, and trotted away down the sidewalk; in search, no doubt, of more handouts. Bierce sighed.

"So they leave you," he said quietly, "one by one." I was not so cruel as to point out that he himself had driven many of his loved ones away, from his wife to his friends to his own brother; but I knew it. As contrary and difficult as Ambrose Bierce could be, I resolved not to be another stray, deserting him for finer handouts. I was all he had left.

We still had a while before we departed; so rather than brood on my employer's shortcomings, I started our conversation on a new track.

"So," I said, sitting up, "what are we heading into, exactly?"

"'Exactly' is a poor term for the current state of affairs in Mexico," Bierce said, putting down his fork and assuming the Revered Sage posture I knew so well. "An educated gent name of Francisco I. Madero got the ball rolling in 1910, calling for a more democratic government than that of dictator Porfirio Díaz. Díaz, the old scoundrel, rightly tossed him in jail; but Madero fled into exile in the States and continued to foment rebellion. When it became clear that more Mexicans agreed with Madero than with Díaz, the old plutocrat took a long-overdue retirement overseas.

"All would have been well if Madero hadn't been such a good chap. The good ones never last, at least in politics, Amos. All Madero had done was clear the way for a worse monster than Díaz, and that monster is the current Hellion-in-Chief, General Huerta. Madero turned to Huerta to calm some restive locals, and Huerta returned the favor by arresting—and shooting—Madero and his vice-president. He's been shooting ever since, operating under the theory that fewer citizens means fewer problems. I have known some of our own generals to think the same of their troops."

He ran an absent-minded finger across the white scar at his temple. "Anyway," Bierce continued, "General Huerta's presidency has stirred up a true hornet's nest in Old Mexico. Villa is rampaging through the north, Zapata leads the peasants in the south, and Carranza directs from the wings. Huerta's reign may not last out the year, but in the meantime he is working hard at reducing the population to a manageable level."

"So we are going into Villa territory."

"Hopefully."

"'Hopefully'?"

"Villa has taken Chihuahua City and bids fair to push Huerta's men across the border or into oblivion. Hopefully, as I say, he will have done so by the time we cross the Rio Grande."

"And you have an introduction to the man."

"None at all."

"Then we are going into a war cold?"

"Hardly that, my boy. We are informed and intelligent."

"We're also both gringos, Bierce. Who would miss two crazy *americanos* who happened to stroll into some bullets?"

"By the same token, who would even notice two crazy *americanos* in all the sound and fury?"

I mulled this over, little mollified. Bierce sat back and lit up the morning's second cheroot.

"To be a gringo in Mexico," he quoted himself, smiling. "Ahh, *that* is euthanasia!"

"You're not reassuring me, Bierce. Your daughter thinks—"

A white light went off in my brain. His daughter—Helen—I hadn't contacted her since I had found her father. I got up and began gathering myself together.

"Off to Mexico so soon?" Bierce said. "I admire your enthusiasm, if not your common sense."

"No," I said, irritated. "It's your daughter. I told her I would notify her as soon as I found you."

"Sit down," Bierce said, patting down the air by my seat. "Helen's a big girl. She can wait."

I stared at the man.

"Don't you think that's a little thoughtless?" I said. "She went through all the trouble and expense of sending me after you. The least we can do is put her mind at ease."

"I will send her a card when we get to Mexico. Now sit down—you're making me nervous."

Me—making *him* nervous! I stood a moment longer, staring at him. I could have written an entry in his "Devil's Dictionary" at that moment: "'Infuriating,' adj. Content in one's own folly. A virtue common among the very old and very cantankerous. Cf. BIERCE." But neither clever retort nor argument, I knew, would budge the man. And Helen was his daughter, after all. I would just have to notify her when I got the chance.

"So we have no introduction to General Villa," I said, sitting back down. "No business to be there at all, really, stumbling around his maneuvers. Why, in God's name are we going there?"

"To verify Mr. Navarro's claims, Amos, as I told you. They are, as you noted, rather outlandish—a cult of death-worshipping Aztecs in modern-day Mexico? We have, of course, seen just as strange phenomena before—if not on this monumental a scale—thus it still bears investigation. If he's right, however, the proof should be easy to come by. With Chihuahua in his hands, Villa will be going to Ojinaga to finish off Huerta's northern troops, whither they have retreated. With luck we'll arrive in time to see the fireworks."

That slow, devil's smile again: "And maybe make some of our own."

5.

Bierce sent for Juan Romero and gave him instructions to meet us at the station well before ten.

"I thought the train didn't leave until ten," I said.

"It doesn't," Bierce said, straightening the brim of his hat. "But Juan operates under what we may charitably call 'Mexican standard time,' which is to say, chronically late. *'Mañana'* is one Spanish word I do know well, Amos, and it is employed mercilessly in the Mexican vocabulary."

"That seems a rather broad and unfair generalization, Mr. Bierce. Clearly the Mexicans live with some sort of punctuality; else they would not have so vibrant a civilization. Imagine General Villa considering the siege of a city and saying, *'Mañana, mañana . . .'*"

"Nonetheless, I do not intend to miss our train due to our Latin friend's dilatory habits. We'll lose a couple days just getting to El Paso, and thence to Chihuahua City will devour another day."

As it turned out, Juan was at the station before we were. He stared wildly around the famous streets of Laredo, an inconspicuous figure in neat dungarees, cotton shirt, and old, dark jacket. The shade from his hat, a less outrageous form of the classic sombrero we would soon see many of, cast his face in shadow; but when we spotted each other, that bright crescent of white teeth flashed out of it like a semaphore from a friendly port in a storm.

"*¡Finalmente!*" he exclaimed, putting out his hand in welcome. "I thought maybe I find the wrong *estación*."

I looked at Bierce, but the chagrin in his face was too dangerous to tempt.

"We had last-minute preparations to see to," I said, taking Romero's hand. He removed his sombrero to wipe perspiration from his forehead with his sleeve. In the plain sunlight I got a better look at his face and there was indeed a scar, like the souvenir of a hairlip, pale under the center of his mustaches. His green eyes slitted against the bald sunlight and looked inquiringly at us.

"*¿Listos, amigos?*" he said.

"Yes," Bierce said. "We're ready."

The first leg of our journey was a short one. We took the train just thirty miles to the small border town of Minera. Bierce had gotten the name of some-one in Minera who could take us overland to Eagle Pass, where we could get the train again to El Paso. The alternative was to ride the rails north back to San Antonio and thence out to El Paso; probably faster, in the long run. But both Bierce and I wanted to get a look at the border, and, if possible, find a quicker way into Mexico. Besides, the idea of backtracking was anathema to Bierce, re-gardless of efficiency.

Minera was as small as it sounds—dirt streets, the station, enough houses and a couple of stores to qualify as a town, but that was it. We followed the in-structions the hotel manager in Laredo had given Bierce, and found a livery sta-ble just a couple of streets from the station. A large, wholesome smell of horse greeted us as we walked in, but nothing more.

"Arnold!" Bierce called into the horsey darkness. Somebody snorted, wheth-er equine or human, it was hard to tell. But slowly a figure moved out of the gloom toward us. It was a man, a bit above average height, solidly built; white beard, Stetson, and, oddly, a pair of dark tinted glasses hiding most of his face.

"I'm Arnold," he said. "Who the hell are you?"

"Mr. Flanders of Laredo sends his regards," Bierce said, "and indicated that you might be available to take us to Eagle Pass."

Arnold turned his head and spat tobacco-juice into the dust.

"Christ on a biscuit," he said. "Ain't you the one. *Mister* Flanders got his head on backwards. I might be available—then again, I might not."

Bierce sighed and dug out his billfold. He fished out a few bills and held them out to Arnold.

"Might you be available now?" He raised an eyebrow at Arnold. Arnold stared at the bills—then took them.

"Might."

Arnold—I never did learn if it was his first name or family name—left us without another word and returned in ten minutes with a buckboard led by two sturdy and well-groomed horses. Just like Bierce, I thought as we put our grips into the bed of the wagon. Likes his animals better than his humans. The two older men, in fact, hit it off, if a mutual, grumbling lack of outright hatred could be considered "hitting it off." Bierce and Arnold sat up on the seat together while Juan and I were relegated to the bed—not as uncomfortable as it sounds. We padded our seats with old horse blankets and our bags, and jolted out of Minera into the desert afternoon.

As we rode north toward Eagle Pass, we kept an eye on the border. The Rio Grande rolled quiet and peaceful off to our left. I was seated against the right side of the wagon, so had a view of the river and Mexico beyond. When I offered to trade places with Juan so that he could enjoy the view, he shrugged: "I seen it."

Up on the seat, I noticed Bierce kept turning to look across the river. He, like me, was scouting for a possible crossing-place. Arnold picked it up quickly.

"If y'all're fixin' to cross the border," he said, "I don't recommend it."

"Which?" said Bierce. "Fixing or crossing?"

Arnold leaned over the side of wagon and spat.

"You wouldn't last a minute t'other side of that water, amigo. *Bandidos*, *federales*, Colorados, you name it. I wouldn't give a *cucaracha's* chance in a dance-hall to anyone who set foot over there."

I scanned the far shore for the murderous hordes, but saw only mesquite trees, the rocky soil, prickly pear cactus, and brush.

"Looks a lot like Texas to me," I said.

Arnold turned in his seat, looked at me, and snorted.

"I 'spect that sort o' ignorance from a Yank," he said.

That ruffled my feathers.

"Then tell me," I said. "What makes this side of the river any safer?"

For answer Arnold leaned over and pulled an enormous pistol from under the seat.

"Mr. Colt, Mr. Walker, and me—*that's* what makes it safer over here. This yere gun'll knock a bandido out the saddle at twunny yards."

Bierce chuckled.

"That's quite a piece," he said. Arnold handed him the pistol. Bierce turned it over in his hands and hefted it with an expert's touch. "I expect it would knock over the horse he rode on, too. Not many shots to stop all those *bandidos* and *federales,* though."

"I'm still here, ain't I?" And Arnold turned back to his horses and said no more.

We made good time that day and slept under a sky glittering with desert stars. It was a strange but welcome idyll in our odyssey, those three days along the border. Arnold became more voluble, if not more welcoming, and we learned about the various flora and fauna of the area. On the second day we spotted a pack of javelinas, the wild spotted pigs of Texas, trotting down an arroyo as if they were late to some important piggish meeting.

"Good eatin', them pigs," said Arnold. "Like bacon and jerky put together. Better eatin' than pets, though. Bastards'll clean out your garden in nothin' flat."

That same day we saw a troop of horsemen across the river in Mexico. They kept pace with us for several tense minutes; but when Arnold tipped his hat to them, they returned the gesture, put spurs to horse and galloped away without incident.

"*Tole* you," was Arnold's only comment.

It was two days more along the border before we raised Eagle Pass—little more than the metropolis of Minera, but our return to the comfort of the railroad. Arnold brought us right to the station itself. We all got down and he helped us with the bags—or rather, he helped Bierce with his bag. Bierce gave him a silver dollar and the two men shook hands.

"You're ever back this way," he said to Bierce, "you look me up. Leave the chirrun at home next time, though."

The "chirrun"—Juan and myself—obtained the tickets and loaded the bags into the train while Bierce had a smoke.

Our path lay due north to Spofford where we changed to the Galveston, Harrisburg & San Antonio train to El Paso. Thence it was a long stretch into the "wide open spaces" you hear about in song and story; six hundred miles of them to El Paso, and all within the great State of Texas. Despite having crossed the continent not once but several times, I still had the easterner's awe of large states. In the miles I had crossed since entering Texas just a week or so ago, I could have gone from Maine to Virginia, crossing the borders of ten states in the process. I began to see why Texans were so fiercely proud of their state, and why they stubbornly refused to forget that they had been a sovereign nation for nine years—even though that had been most of a century ago.

The change in countryside became plainer after we changed in Spofford. The heavy black locomotive chuffed and churned its wheels and linkages, and with a sudden jerk began its slow, inexorable drag forward. Our pace grew and grew, the modest houses of Spofford slipping by faster and faster until we were a juggernaut charging unchallenged into the enormous West. For a while we kept close to "the Valley," as Miss Avis had called it, with its ranches and fertile fields. But after passing over the Pecos near its confluence with the Rio Grande, the tracks carried us away from the river and out into the parched lands of west Texas. The colors changed, faded. The greens retreated to the horizon or shrank to the lime-colored clusters of prickly pear cactus. The sun shone on it all as if it always had and always would, but mercifully it was a cooler day than before. I was comfortable in my new western clothes, as was Bierce in his usual black suit and overcoat. But I was amused to see a couple of our fellow riders, locals from the broad accents, ask the conductor for travel-blankets. They may have had the better of me in a gunfight, I thought smugly, but my thick Yankee blood would give me the edge in a blizzard.

As the miles unspooled endlessly to the horizon, I filled the time with thoughts on the border. Borders are strange places; manmade and artificial, yet strong in meaning. There is a consistency to them, I thought, even between states; remembering a night long ago spent wide awake in a dodgy hotel room in the border town of Bristol, Virginia/Bristol, Tennessee. I could not now tell you which side of that rough-shod town my hotel was located, but I can still hear the muttered scheming and threats of a conversation I half heard through the thin lath walls that night. At first light I settled my bill and left whichever Bristol it was, and I haven't been back since. Just by establishing a barrier between people brings out impulses to break those barriers in whatever way possible, I mused, whether just sneaking a bottle of bust-head from a wet county to a dry, to the vicious bandit-raids the Rio Grande Valley saw for many years. On one side of this Texas/Mexico border the Mexicans appeared meek, subservient, ready to please the anglos in charge. Yet I knew that just across the river were men like Villa and Huerta and Obregón, men of pride and stature and strength, with armies of similar men at their backs. I glanced at Juan Romero, sitting serenely beside Bierce, and wondered how he would change once we crossed into his country. The change would be for the better, I hoped. Thus far I wasn't impressed with the man. He didn't offend me, but he didn't present much of a character to me at all either. His value to us lay in his acquaintance with the unknown Professor Navarro and his knowledge of Spanish—and, of course, of Mexico. Was he handy with a gun? That, too, could prove useful in the right situation. I supposed I should just trust Bierce's judgment of the man. It wasn't as if I had any choice anyway. I resumed my watch on the desert and my musings on the paradoxes of man.

The towns clicked by outside my window—Kinney, Pinto, Standart, Amanda. I borrowed part of Bierce's newspaper and read a bit, then dozed. More dry, hardscrabble towns—Del Rio, something of a metropolis among these border towns; McKees, Devil's River, Seminole, Feely, Cobra, Comstock. We crossed the wide Pecos outside of Viaduct. At Langtree, famous (or infamous, depending on which end of the rope you were) for Judge Roy Bean, we brushed the Rio Grande. After that we swung inland, and it was desert. I suppose there is a certain beauty to the desert, but it escapes me. I like green. I grew up in the fertile fields of Pennsylvania, and despite my travels I still consider that the norm. The monotony of the landscape told on me. Plus our train was the so-called "Sunset Route," a name it lived up to admirably as the shadows lengthened and deepened across the wide lands. Lights came on in the car, but I was spent. I made my excuses to Bierce and Juan and shambled off to my Pullman berth.

6.

"Rise and shine, little one."

I opened bleary eyes on the avuncular face of Ambrose Bierce. He smiled at me through the curtains of my berth like Old Scratch himself.

"What—" I said. "Why—?"

"El Paso awaits you, though not forever."

I rubbed the sleep out of my eyes and parted the curtain on my window. The Texas landscape had stopped, and was very different. Buildings crowded near the train; mountains rose in rugged splendor above and behind them. And the sun—it was behind us now. I had slept through the night, and we were in El Paso, Texas. End of the line.

"Good God, Bierce," I said, throwing off the covers and grabbing my clothes. "You could have awakened me sooner."

"To what purpose? You clearly needed the rest, even though I, some years your senior, did not. And you missed nothing but a lot of desert. Grandiose in its own way, but also monotonous as church music."

Juan's silver-edged smile came around the curtain too, along with something wrapped in a napkin.

"Got you a taco," he said. I took the napkin and unwrapped it. Spicy, savory vapors rose from within, and I felt my stomach rumble.

"Muchas gracias," I said. "Now you gents will excuse me while I make my toilet."

Once I had put myself together I joined Bierce and Juan and we exited the train. We were presented with a bustling town that reminded me of Laredo, if larger: a rough frontier burg putting on the bangles of the new century, but still a rough frontier burg. An imposing courthouse, theaters, saloons, stores, liveries, and garages; hyperventilating automobiles and their explosive farts and smoke; the glory of the railroad station. But behind and beyond it all, campesinos in white pyjamas leading ox-carts, the ubiquitous Rangers and soldiers with their guns and wary eyes; and the vast emptiness of the desert threatening to swallow it all.

Bierce said, "Well, gents, I suggest we find a cozy corner in which to reconnoiter. Any suggestions?"

I pointed across the busy street.

"That café should do the trick," I said. Bierce nodded. We hefted our bags and walked across to the American Café.

Our train had gotten in to El Paso at 8:30 A.M., so much of the breakfast traffic was still in the café. Even so we found a table where the three of us could squeeze in away from the draft of the front door. A waiter brought us menus and we ordered coffee and breakfasts. By unspoken consent we waited until the coffee arrived before discussing our next step.

"Whoa," said the waiter. "Hold on—I didn't see *he* was with you."

He aimed a curt jab of the thumb at Juan.

"Is there a problem?" said Bierce.

"Yeah—we don't serve greasers here."

I could see Bierce's color starting to rise. I mentally began preparing to calm him down, knowing that a scene here and now could do nothing either to get Juan a breakfast or to aid our mission. But it ended up being Juan who defused it all.

"'S all right," he said, raising his hand as if in surrender. "I will go find *comida* in a friendlier place."

He rose and Bierce rose with him. Bierce walked him to the door. They spoke in low voices for a minute. I saw Bierce hand Juan some money and point to his watch. Juan nodded and left. Bierce returned to our table.

"An unfortunate contretemps," said Bierce. "But one I hope to turn to our advantage. I have instructed Juan to find us a guide—after he has eaten, of course. From the looks of the soldiers around here, I'm sure they are not handing out invitations to cross the border."

Our breakfasts came and we dug into them in silence.

Afterwards we went back to the station, where we found Juan waiting for us with a smile.

"I find something," he said. "It's in a hotel, *no muy lejos.*"

Bierce waved to one of the waiting taxis.

"Where to, boys?" said the cabbie as we crowded inside his vehicle.

"Hotel Benito Juárez," said Juan, and we were off. Within five minutes we came to a juddering stop before a modest two-story building.

"*Ho*-tel Benito Juárez," the driver proclaimed. He leapt out and began unstrapping our baggage from the rack in back. The three of us unlatched the doors and got out. Bierce paid the driver and we carried out luggage into the Hotel Benito Juárez.

The lobby was only half-lit, but cozy in the quiet way a provincial hotel can be. A stout, balding white man in a vest and string-tie stood up behind the counter as we entered. He tugged the vest taut over his belly and said, "Welcome, ginnlemen, to the Hotel Benito Juárez. Rooms for three?"

Bierce doffed his hat and approached the counter.

"Yes, lodgings for three, my good man—one room for my associates and a room for myself. There will be no problem with my associate, will there?"

Mine host looked blank at us. He glanced at Juan and snorted.

"Think not," he said. "Hell, I *married* one of 'em. Just sign in here, gents."

He pushed a broad guest-book and pen toward Bierce. I couldn't help but notice the paucity of guests listed. On one hand I felt for the innkeeper; but on the other, we weren't inviting scrutiny from others. Having the hotel to ourselves suited us perfectly.

Bierce proceeded to scratch his forehead and winked at me from behind his hand. I understood. I watched as he signed "Halpin Frayser, St. Helena, Calif." in the book. I followed with "Peyton Farquhar, St. Helena, Calif." Juan merely signed his own name with no hometown beside it. The innkeeper turned the book around and I could see his lips move as he read our names to himself.

"We will pay now for the one night," Bierce said. "We will be up and out early, so I shan't want to bother you then."

The innkeeper stared at Bierce for a moment with his dull, slightly wall-eyed gaze. Then intelligence crept into it, he smiled and said, "As you wish, Mr.—*Frayser.*"

Bierce had taken a gamble that the innkeeper hadn't read his story "The Death of Halpin Frayser," as I had in signing the name from "An Occurrence at

Owl Creek Bridge." But looking around the modest lobby it didn't seem much of a gamble. There were only a couple of well-thumbed newspapers lying upon tables by the threadbare easy chairs, and no books at all. If the proverbial push came to shove, we even had illegally obtained passports in those names. Still, the innkeeper seemed to know that we weren't exactly what we presented ourselves to be, and clearly had no problem with that. I mused that he must see much of such traffic in such a place so close to the border.

The innkeeper grabbed two keys from the complete array on hooks behind his counter and led us up the stairs. Our rooms were adequate; more than that I couldn't say. But more than that we didn't really need. The innkeeper stood shifting on his feet at the door to Bierce's room.

"If there's anything y'all need . . ."

Bierce smiled. He dug a coin out of his pocket and placed it firmly into the innkeeper's thick, waiting palm.

"A bit of privacy," he said.

The innkeeper nodded and waddled back down the stairs.

"I suggest we take advantage of our time here to rest as much as we can," said Bierce. "I expect we will be on the hoof at some ungodly hour." He turned to Juan and frowned. "And where is this guide of yours, Juan?"

Juan smiled.

"*A ver,*" was all he said. *You'll see.*

*

The rest was welcome, even after my sleep in the Pullman. I lay down on the narrow bed and read a little in the El Paso paper on the bedside table. News of the Revolution so close across the river, advertisements for Crouch's Cure-all Remedy for Diphtheria, Croup, The Grip, Maiden's Problems (ye gods, what *didn't* it cure?), the new Ford sedan, a Resistol dealer . . . It all began to run together, and when I next opened my eyes it was getting dark. I could hear Juan snoring quietly in the other bed.

I found that I was ravenously hungry, so went back downstairs to find some food. The innkeeper was still at his counter, listlessly turning the pages of a newspaper. He looked up at me and smiled.

"Get yer some good sleep?" he said.

"Yes, thank you, I did. I could do with some food now, if it's no problem."

"Just so, sir. *Juanita!*"

The man turned toward the doorway behind him. A young and harried-looking woman, clad in a spotless white dress and featuring long, black hair caught up in a bun, came out of the door wiping her hands upon a towel. Despite her dark coloring, I noticed that her black eyes had the same dull, wide gaze of the innkeeper, and I placed her as his daughter.

"Food for the jinnlemen, dear," he said to her kindly. "And perhaps that new Chopin tune you've been learnin'."

"*Sí, papá,*" she said, made a quick half-curtsey, and disappeared back into the back room. Pans and plates began clattering out of sight.

"Right through that fur door, sir," the innkeeper said, pointing to the door opposite the counter. "Juanita will serve you directly."

I thanked him and walked into the next room. It was the near twin in size and shape to the room we had just quit, minus the sadly aging wing-chairs and plus several square tables and attendant wooden chairs. The room was deserted—except for Ambrose Bierce. He had chosen the table farthest from the door. I came over and sat by him, and we huddled together like the most devious of smugglers.

"You slept well, I hope," I said.

He seesawed his hand.

"Sufficient for the purpose," he said, and I knew that he probably hadn't slept at all. "I took advantage of the time to reconnoiter some." He leaned toward me.

"Crossing the border," Bierce said in a low voice, "won't be easy. The whole countryside is crawling with spies, the military, what-have-you, and without a clear purpose I can't see the border officials letting us across."

"Journalists reporting on the Revolution?" I suggested in the same, low tones. Bierce shook his head.

"Journalists least of all, I should think. No doubt Mr. Hearst and his ilk have plenty here already. Moreover, Villa may not want over-careful observation of his methods. He is, let us say, less than gentle with his detractors." Bierce raked the room with his gaze. "And I have yet to see this guide of Juan's."

Just then Juanita, the innkeeper's daughter, came in. She bore in her hands a tray upon which were three smoking plates. She looked at us with some confusion.

"Where is your other friend?" she said.

As if on cue, Juan came through the door behind her.

"Ah," he said, stretching like a cat. "I see you meet our guide!"

We looked at him—and at Juanita.

"You?" Bierce and I said together. The girl set the plates down on our table and shrugged.

"You want to get across the border, I'll get you across."

We looked at Juan then.

"She come with good recommendations," he said. "*Very* good."

Bierce sighed.

"I suppose, given the state of things, that we have little choice." He turned a stern gaze on Juan. "We are trusting your knowledge of the situation, Juan. I cannot over-emphasize the importance of this."

Juan smiled and gave a mock-salute.

"*Siempre a sus órdenes, Señor!* Now, what about that food?"

What about it, indeed. There were enchiladas with green sauce, rice and beans, and tortillas to mop up the whole mess. We set to like true trenchermen while Juanita sat at an upright in the corner and serenaded us with a Chopin prelude.

And again. And again. By the fifth time, Bierce sighed, stood up, and walked over to the piano.

"You play beautifully, my dear," he said, closing the keyboard cover. "I should like to remember your playing—in silence, if I may." He smiled at her, and the old Bierce charm worked its magic once again. Juanita smiled back and blushed as if he had given her a standing ovation.

"*Gracias, Señor,*" she said. "I will collect the dishes when you are done."

She rose, bowed, and left the room. Bierce returned to us. He scowled at Juan again.

"You're sure about her?" he said.

Juan chewed and made the sign of an X over his heart.

"Cross my heart."

When dinner was done, Juanita returned and cleared the table. At our request she returned with coffee.

She also returned a different person. Gone was the virginal white dress, replaced with dark brown corduroy trousers and what looked like a man's western shirt of green chamois beneath a canvas coat. Tall boots encased her calves, and she carried a wide-brimmed black hat in her free hand. Her hair, which had been done up in a simple but elegant bun before, was now pulled back severely and tied into a ponytail with a plain black riband. A handkerchief of blue was knotted at her throat. She regarded us with a cool intelligence I hadn't seen before. We all rose without a word.

"Before," she said, "I was just Juanita. Now, *soy la coyote*."

Bierce and I bowed. Juan just grinned.

"Your pardon, miss," said Bierce. "Clothes make the man—as they do the woman, apparently. Your knowledge of the area is, no doubt, unimpeachable, and your spirit is to be admired. But a young lady, on the war-torn border in these times . . ." He spread his pale hands.

Juanita gave him a black look. She reached into the wide pockets of her coat and drew out two pistols and a long, wicked-looking knife in a leathern sheath. She set them on the table with scarcely a sound.

"Jim Bowie married a *mexicana*," she said, and unsheathed the knife. "Did you know that? So did Papá. This was his, back in his wild days. You are right, Señor 'Frayser,' or whatever your name is. It is a dangerous place, *muy peligroso*, especially for a 'young lady' such as myself. Which is why you learn to use such tools as these at an early age. And," she said, giving Bierce a look of daggers, "I *do* know how to use them."

Without another word, she sheathed the knife and replaced it and the pistols in her coat. Then she picked up one of the coffee cups and sipped, as neat and dainty as any Washington City debutante.

Juan chuckled and I joined him. Change was sweeping over the world with the new century and Bierce, child of the frontier, veteran of the Civil War, and thoroughly nineteenth-century man, resisted it tooth and nail. He made a *harrumph!* and tugged his vest and jacket into place.

"Next thing you know, she'll want the vote," he said *sotto voce*, although not so softly as not to be heard around our table. Suffragettes were a favorite target for Bierce's vitriol in his newspaper columns, which is all very well and good in the papers: if you didn't like his opinions, you could turn the page. But here, trying to cross into Mexico with little more than our good looks, I was afraid Bierce would talk us out of a guide.

I shouldn't have worried.

"*Calma*, Señor Frayser," Juanita said with a laugh that lit up the room's dark corners. "Why should I want the vote? There aren't any *women* to vote for!"

Another chuckle from Juan and me, another earnest *har-RUMPH!* from the old man.

"Besides," said Juanita in a more serious tone, "we need the money. Look around you—you see how many guests we have? Papá doesn't know I do this. I slip the extra *dinero* into his cash-box when he ain't looking, and keep a little for myself."

Bierce put his hand to his chest and gave a slight bow.

"I bow to your superior wisdom, Señorita," he said with affected grace. "So—when do we leave?"

"Two o'clock. I need to arrange the horses and boat. *Pero, primero el dinero.*"

Bierce looked confused.

"The money," I said. "She wants to be paid."

"Oh," said Bierce. "Of course."

Juanita named a price and Bierce dutifully took out his billfold and laid the bills in a neat pile upon the table. It seemed a reasonable fee, but what did I know? Considering that Juanita was putting her own life and liberty in peril, I expected to pay more.

"Is that sufficient?" I said. Bierce turned a glower my way but I ignored it.

"Sí, basta," she said, gathering up the bills. "It shouldn't be too hard. Most people are trying to get *out* of Mexico these days. Only a fool or a gringo would want to get *in.*"

Judgment of our character aside, I hoped she was right.

7.

After our dinner group split up, Juanita disappeared to make her arrangements and we returned to our rooms to try to steal a little more sleep. I would need it, I knew, for the crossing would require us to be awake and alert for I knew not how long. Perhaps it was the excitement, perhaps the coffee at such a late hour, but I could not sleep for the longest time. I lay awake watching the squares of light thrown by the streetlight outside my window upon the splitting wallpaper of our room. That I did finally fall asleep I knew only when Bierce came to wake me. One moment I was staring at these pale parallelograms above me; the next, Bierce was standing at the bedside, lamp in hand, looking for all the world like my long-dead German *Grossvater*, all white hair and curled mustachios. He was shaking me gently by the shoulder and had a very ungrand-fatherly glint in his eye.

"Rise and shine, boy," he said, and for one brief, frightening moment I thought he really was my old Opa, back from the grave. Then he said, "Mexico awaits," and I threw back the covers of my bed.

Two A.M. is a mean hour, a sneaking, stealthy, dishonest hour. Despite what sleep I had stolen, my eyes burned and my muscles were stupid with fatigue. Juan looks as tired as I felt, but Bierce, damn him, looked as fresh as the month of May. Juanita met us in the lobby in the same clothes we had seen her in last—a little dustier, I noticed. Had she even slept, I wondered. Of her father there was no sign. When I stumbled into the front desk, she turned on me like a rattlesnake.

"*¡Silencio!*" she hissed. "*Caramba*—you're like to alert the whole Mexican Army, you stagger around like 'at."

"Sorry," I mumbled.

She led us out a back door into a dark alley. Five horses awaited us there, attended by a Mexican so dark that he appeared to be just a pair of eyes suspended in the gloom.

"Gentlemen," said Juanita, "this is Eufémío. He will help us tonight."

We mounted and rode slowly out through the dark streets toward the west.

Once clear of the town, we were suddenly in desert. It was cold—not the chill of the last evening, but a true, iron cold that gripped the skin. I was glad I had thought to wear my old shirt over my new one, and I pulled my hat down further, wishing for something to cover my ears. Our horses clopped slowly onto the hard sand; then, safely away from the town, Juanita urged us into a gallop. It was exhilarating, and not a little unnerving. What if we should hit an arroyo in the darkness and crash to the earth? A horse with a broken leg is a worthless horse, and then we'd be on foot in the desert at night—if we didn't break our own necks in the bargain. I could scarcely think of a worse situation. Then.

But Juanita and Eufémío proved as knowledgeable about the desert as Juanita had said. They led us out and away from El Paso in a wide arc that would, I assumed, ultimately bring us to the river. Never did they pause and never did the horses stumble. Tall shapes swept up out of the darkness; but they were nothing more than cacti and Joshua trees and ocotillo. I tipped my head sideways and looked up, and gasped at the dazzling array of stars above us. From horizon to black horizon they glittered and blazed and sparkled, and I swore I had never seen so many stars before in my life. I felt as if the normal skies had opened and left us bare and exposed to this vast and unknown universe. When my eyes had adjusted I realized that the landscape was not completely dark; that starlight itself painted the desert floor a soft blue and cut the crazy figures of mesquite and cactus sharp and clear. It took my breath away.

After what seemed like a long time jouncing up and down on that horse's back, Juanita put up a hand and we slowed to a canter. She brought us down to a walk and I wondered what was happening.

"We're close to the river," she whispered to us. "Sound carries a long way in the desert—we'll have to dismount soon and walk the rest of the way." Then she spurred her horse back up to Eufémío.

A couple minutes later she motioned us to stop. We dismounted. Juan and I took Bierce's bags and, bidding farewell to Eufémío, who stayed with the horses, we walked into the desert. I looked around and could just discern two faded glows over the horizon to eastward—the paltry lights of El Paso, Texas, and Ciudad Juárez, Mexico, looking tawdry and pale next to the magnificence spread above us.

On we walked. There was no need now for Juanita to tell us to be quiet; the towering, ancient silence of the desert loomed all around, and would brook no disturbance. Our boots made little noise on the packed earth. In the starlight I saw that we followed a well-used path. Yet I knew that if I were dropped into that spot, even in broad daylight, I could never have been able to find it. Juanita walked it without hesitation. We followed.

A murmur came to us out of the blackness ahead—the conversation of many an aimless multitude. After a moment I realized it was the voice of the Rio Grande. It sounded for all the world to me like the voices of the hundreds—thousands?—who had dared and drowned in that river over the centuries. As the sound of the water increased, Juanita's pace slowed and became more cautious. Now I could see a wide black line bisecting the landscape ahead—the Rio Grande del Norte itself, deep in its bed of stones. We came up to the lip of the river's gorge and followed Juanita over and down. Careful as we were, we couldn't keep from sending a cascade of pebbles down the steep slope; but the voice of the river covered all.

At the bottom of the gorge Juanita motioned Juan to follow her and they disappeared behind a large clump of bushes. I stood looking at the river, thinking how cold that water must be, and how, without our horses, we would have to wade across it.

A scraping over rocks, grunts of effort. Then he and Juanita emerged from the buses carrying a small boat—a very small boat, I reflected, thinking of the four or us.

They set the boat gently on the edge of the running water. Juan pulled two oars from out of the boat while Juanita held it steady against the current.

"*¿Señores?*" Juan said. He stepped back and offered us the boat. Bierce stepped gingerly in.

"In for a dime," I said, climbing in behind him. The boat rocked sickeningly while I tried to make myself comfortable. It rocked even more alarmingly when Juan and then Juanita got in; and once all four of us were within, the gunwales of the boat were scarcely six inches above the water.

But as Juanita pushed us off from the land the current seemed to steady us. Juanita pointed to an invisible spot on the opposite shore while she and Juan spoke in quiet Spanish. Juan put the oars to the oarlocks and began rowing. It looked as though his efforts were less to propel us across than to keep us from being swept away downstream. He did a good job of it, though, strong back and arms working the oars smoothly as we angled across the stream. The reflections of stars joggled and danced in the dark waters. A minute passed. The water gulped at the oars as Juan rowed, rowed. Another minute passed—and suddenly the bow of the boat scraped onto rock. We were in Mexico.

Juan and Juanita leapt out to secure the boat. Bierce and I, unregenerate landlubbers, toddled out holding our meager baggage. Before us stood a black wall of earth where it rose up to meet the desert floor, and up this we now scrambled as quietly as we could. Once atop the bank we waited while Bierce caught his breath. The dry desert air agreed with him, but it had been a night of tension and exertion. It told on his old frame.

There was a quiet rustling, nothing more, and suddenly a man stood before us holding the reins of four horses. Like Eufémío, he was dark and dressed in dark attire. A glint of starlight picked out watchful eyes beneath the rim of his sombrero.

"Davíd," Juanita said by way of introduction. There were murmured "Mucho gustos" all around. Then I noticed that there were one too few horses.

"Who gets to walk?" I said.

"Nobody," said Juanita. "I have to get back before Papa wakes up. Y'all are in Davíd's hands, now—Bienvenidos a México, amigos." And with a tip of her hat, she turned and was gone.

We strapped our baggage onto the horses, mounted, and turned them away from the river.

"¿Quién anda?" shouted a voice out of nowhere. From the left? The right?

"¿Quién anda?" roared the voice again. "Somos el División del Norte—alto!"

"Vámonos, amigos," said Davíd, and we didn't have to be told twice. The Division of the North—Villa's men. Probably border patrol. We put spurs to horse and lit out of there at a flat gallop. A gunshot banged out of the dark. Fast upon it came the sharp crack of the bullet speeding by my head. Later I would take off my hat and see the crease the bullet left along the brim. It was that close. We hunkered down in our saddles and urged the horses on with our knees, spurs, and profanity. A couple more shots came after us, but they seemed half-hearted; and in a minute they stopped altogether. I gathered that night-patrol in the desert was not a favorite duty among the *soldados,* and having discharged their firearms at the unknown *criminales,* they felt their duty done. I prayed that our escape would mask Juanita's own return across the river. She had done well by us and deserved a kind fate.

Following Davíd's lead we did not slow down for several minutes. Onward we thundered across the desert. The warm smell of horse was in my nostrils as I crouched low over its neck. "Good horse," I said into its ear. "*Brave* horse—please don't fall." By the faint smear of the lights of Ciudad Juárez off to our left, I knew we were headed south or southeast. After a time David slowed us to a walk and turned us toward those lights. Without the thunder of the galloping horses the big quiet of the desert swelled back around us. I listened, as I'm sure we all did, for the clatter of pursuing horses. But there was none.

We continued on this way for half an hour or so before Davíd raised a hand and brought us to a stop.

"We wait here," he said in Spanish, pointing at the ground. "Just before dawn I'll take you to Juárez."

"Can you take us to the railroad station?" asked Bierce when I had translated Davíd's words.

"*Sí,*" the *campesino* said, with a noticeable accent of doubt in his voice. "*Pues,* sure I can take you to the train. But it means I can't get home to milk the cow, chop the wood . . ." He gave an eloquent shrug.

"What does he say?" Bierce said.

"He says he needs a little more money to get us to the station," I said.

"Why, this is piracy!" said Bierce. Even in the dim light I thought I could see Bierce's cheeks go purple with rage. "Highway robbery! I won't *have* it!"

"Look, Bierce," I said. "One: we could wander all over Juárez until we either find the station or get stood up against a wall and shot for asking directions to it. Two: this poor fellow is probably putting his life on the line for us, and I'm sure he honestly needs the money. And three: it's just how things get done here."

"We call it *la mordita,*" said Juan. "'The little bite'—better than the big bite, Señor."

Bierce grumbled some more about burglars and footpads, but he dug out his wallet and gave Davíd a couple bills.

"Muchas gracias, Señor," the Mexican said, carefully folding the bills and stashing them in his shirt. "I will be happy to lead you to the *ferrocarril*."

"What now?" grumbled Bierce. His tone was less than amiable.

"He said he'd be happy to take us to the train."

"Well, I'm so happy that *he's* happy," Bierce said, and stumped off into the darkness.

We settled onto the desert and waited. A fire was out of the question, what with patrols roaming around, so I pulled my coat tighter around myself and tried to conjure up warm thoughts. To think that I had been grateful for that cold beer at the Menger Hotel just a few days before, feeling the sun press down upon San Antonio's colorful streets . . . Naw, didn't work. I hugged myself and tried not to think.

8.

We waited there for better than an hour, when the eastern sky over Ciudad Juárez began to pale and the everlasting stars faded, dwindled, and disappeared. We rose and stretched cold-cramped muscles. I had to help Bierce get on his horse. As much as he fumed and fussed for me not to, he was as stiff as a scarecrow, and about as pleasant.

Mounted again, we rode east. Ciudad Juárez seemed to echo the town of El Paso at first. The same adobe hovels, the same fine houses, the same ornate and ostentatious façades on the downtown buildings. But as we got closer the resemblance to El Paso crumbled. In the middle of the first street we came to, there lay the body of a man. That he was dead was plain to us in a second; he lay sprawled in the middle of a wide black stain of his own blood. There was a terrible, quiet symmetry to the figure. I thought of Leonardo da Vinci's drawing of a naked man within the circle that proscribed his proportions: *Ecce Homo—Behold Man*. Da Vinci's grace and beauty transformed into something sad and brutal. I remember that the man's feet were bare. That seemed important, somehow.

There were other corpses, too, although by the time we got deeper into the city people were up and set to disposing of the bodies. Juárez awoke and rumbled and then shouted. Gone were the tense but orderly streets of El Paso, replaced by a city at war. Gunshots sounded blocks away—one, two, three-four. The stoic, blear-eyed *campesinos* and women we saw trudged on without stopping to listen. It was just another day in a country that was tearing itself apart from the inside. There were a few automobiles, horns squawking to get through the crowds; but mostly there were horses and mules and carts. A truck passed, overladen with *soldados* in vast sombreros, rifles hung from their shoulders, looks of pride, excitement, and boredom on their faces.

"Villa took Juárez a month ago," Bierce lectured as we clopped along. Then he chuckled. "The devil packed a captured Federal train full of his own troops and sent them in to take the town. A Trojan horse—the oldest trick in the book."

In the new light I glanced at Davíd, our guide. He had the face of an Indian, long nose and slightly undershot jaw, chin tucked into his neck in an attitude of strength and resignation. A thin mustache had made a foothold on his upper lip. His sad, tired eyes watched the milling crowds with seeming disinterest; but I could tell that little escaped his notice.

In twenty minutes' time we came to the railroad station. My first impression when we got there was despair: it looked as if everyone else in Juárez—in all northern Mexico, for that matter—was there to catch a train. But Davíd calmly dismounted and bid us do the same.

"*Síguenme,*" he said, and we followed.

We walked the horses around the side of the great station, rounding the crowd, trying to get through it. We emerged by the tracks where two trains sat side by side, the engines huffing out great clouds of steam that rose lazily into the morning air. If I had lost hope at the sight of the station, now I absolutely despaired: not only were there people filling the trains, there were people crowding *atop* the trains.

"They ride up there 'cause the horses ride in the boxcars," said Juan, following my gaze.

"Easier to replace a soldier than his mount, I expect," said Bierce.

Juan nodded. "These days . . ."

The pale blue sky threw into silhouette a multitude sitting atop the cars' roofs, even huddled on the coal in the tender. Most of them looked like soldiers, armed men, at any rate; but I also got my first glimpse of the famous *soldaderas,* the women-fighters, who carried the fight to Huerta with as much bravery and gusto as their male equivalents. Many carried a child in one arm and a rifle in the other. They met our gaze eye to eye. They looked a formidable lot.

Davíd, meanwhile, had approached the foremost train and was speaking with a man in a dusty conductor's uniform. The noise of the station drowned out their conversation, but I saw the conductor shake his head and I could see his mouth shape, *No, no, no*. Davíd continued with intricate motions of his hand and head, but the conductor shook his finger at him—then his head—and then his head and his finger. Davíd, to his credit, didn't give up. His motions became more vehement, fist slapping into palm, a forefinger jabbed southward (toward Chihuahua City, I assumed), hands clasped in prayer.

"Time to oil the wheels again," I said to Bierce. He nodded, handed the reins of his horse to me, and stepped forward. As he approached the conductor he put up his white, liver-spotted hand as if to say, "It's all right—somebody responsible is here now." He cut quite a figure, I'll give him that—tall, pale, dressed in his impeccable black suit. The two *mexicanos* turned to him and ceased their arguing as he approached. The din of the crowds still drowned out their speech, so it was a dumb-show to Juan and myself. But eloquent in its way. Bierce's head nodded emphatically as he spoke—God knows what he said in his miserable Spanish. The conductor now wagged his finger at Bierce, now threw his hands up toward the overladen train as if to say, "Look at it! Just *look* at it!" Davíd tried a flank assault with more prayers, accusing jabs of the finger, beseeching looks to heaven.

At last I saw Bierce reach into his inner pocket and produce that magic item, the wallet. Suddenly the conductor became still. He watched as Bierce carefully removed one, two, three bills from the wallet, fold then neatly, and stuff them into the conductor's pocket with what looked like irrefutable force. The conductor looked down at the tips of the bills projecting from his pocket, then at Bierce. Clever, Bierce—now the conductor would not only have to re-fuse the money, he'd actually have to take it out of his own pocket. I saw the man rub his lower face, look up and down the train—then nod like a chicken pecking corn. He pulled several bits of paper out of his other pocket—old tick-ets, I assumed—and handed them to Bierce. Then he waved at the coach steps behind him and moved away quickly, as if to distance himself from his own per-fidy. Davíd returned to us and took the horses. Bierce grinned and waved us forward. Juan and I unstrapped our luggage from the horses.

"*Muchas gracias,*" I said to Davíd, palming him another coin as we shook hands. He nodded and said, "*Ígualmente, amigo. Y que vayan con Dios.*"

And may you go with God—I earnestly wished he were right. Davíd took the reins of the horses and faded into the crowds.

Juan and I ran to catch up with Bierce. He, not wanting to tempt fate, or the *villista* guards responsible for who boarded their trains, was already up the steps into the car.

We clattered up behind him and came to a halt. The train was more than packed—it was a solid mass of humanity, luggage, chickens, even a wall-eyed goat who regarded us with aloof interest. All right, then—we'd sit on our luggage.

"Just how far is it to Chihuahua City?" I asked Juan.

He shrugged. "Two-hunnerd, two-hunnerd-fifty miles, *tal vez.*"

"And how often does the train stop—to let passengers on and off, I mean?"

Juan rubbed that scar on his upper lip with one finger thoughtfully.

"It don't. There ain't really nothing between here and Chihuahua."

"*¡Viajeros al trén!*" somebody shouted outside. A couple of *soldados* shouldered past us, muttering, "*Permiso, lo siento,*" in quiet, surprisingly polite and deferential voices. Once they were past, the train gave a lurch; the engine resumed it chuffing; and we began the long roll toward Chihuahua City.

It wasn't as bad as it sounds. We sat on our bags in the entryway at the head of the coach where we came in and benefited from the fresh desert air pouring in the doorway. I looked at the crushed mass of *campesino, soldados, soldaderas,* children, starch-collared officials, and what even looked like a couple of gringo reporters filling the seats, and thought myself lucky. The heat was growing, and so was the smell of humanity in a crush. Again I was grateful for that open doorway.

A young *soldadera* was seated facing us at the end of a seat nearby. Across one breast she wore a bandolier glittering with long bullets; at the other breast, let out of her *blusa,* a tiny baby suckled. Such a sight, I reflected, you would never see in the States outside of, perhaps, the Indian reservations. Yet she showed no embarrassment, no concern. Like everyone around her, she jarred and rocked with the motion of the train, and uttered not one word of complaint. I recalled the crowded trolleys of Washington City, but the comparison was lacking. No Yankee would deign to sit in such proximity to his fellow human being. He'd wait for the next car. Perhaps because there was no "next car" here and they all knew it, everyone faced life with such stoicism. I wondered if that stoicism was an inheritance from the Mexicans' Indian ancestors. Most Mexicans, I had read, were at least partly Indian, Aztec, Maya, Zapotec or what have you. I wondered if we white men could learn such patience.

The *soldadera* caught me looking at her. I tipped my hat, said "*Buenos dias,*" and she dimpled a smile at me. Then she turned to look back out the window.

Bierce, surprisingly, looked the most comfortable of the three of us. Of course he had the seat of pride, his suitcase, while Juan and I squatted upon our valises. But more than that he just looked alive, more pink and vibrant that I had seen him in months. Even in Washington the northern winters can drag, and the colossal stupidity and greed of the Capitol had worn even his once-indomitable wit down to a fare-thee-well. Here, going somewhere, actually doing something, I could see him revive. His blood fairly thrummed in his veins. Sitting on his suitcase, knees akimbo, one hand braced on his leg and the other holding aloft a smoking cigar; the wind ruffling his white mane under his hat rim; his face set resolutely toward the future, he was the picture of resist-less Spirit. He had a future again, and he was plunging headlong into it.

And Juan, for once, was wrong. I should have known: a train laden with hundreds of passengers, running for four hours or more, had to stop once in a while. There were *sanitarios* at the ends of the cars, but they were little more than closets with a chipped porcelain bowl opening onto the speeding tracks below. A couple of stalwarts or those too desperate to wait did wind between the passengers and chicken-crates and baskets to use the facilities. But most waited in that ancient, patient silence.

Their patience, and ours, to be honest, was rewarded an hour or so into the ride, when the train began to slow. The yellow-white light outside the train showed the rough terrain slowing, slowing. Dun-colored sand, earth, rocks, and startled-looking thickets of Spanish dagger and blue-green agave. To the west was the high, dull wall of the Sierra Madre Occidental, like the rampart of giants. The only sentient thing I could see was a lone bird riding waves of heat far above. An eagle? My golden eagle from the aeroplane ride? When the train had stopped, the conductor (our conductor, studiously avoiding our eyes) came through, calling, "Fifteen minutes, fifteen minutes." Fifteen minutes—it hardly seemed long enough for the needs of those multitudes.

Yet it was. The people moved with courtesy and care, but they moved. Our position by the door showed its advantage again, as we preceded most of the people off the train. It felt good to stand and stretch after the rocking ride. I looked around.

There was a water-tower to service the train; several leaning shacks that clear-ly served as outhouses; and the wide sky. It wasn't quite the "nothin'" Juan had said it would be, but it was close. Looking back to earth, I watched my fellow pas-sengers. The women, for the most part, formed lines before the outhouses, but the men found whatever cover they could. I saw one beefy *soldado* with his pants already halfway down his wide buttocks, waddling as fast as the encumbrance would allow him toward a massive stand of organ-pipe cactus. We did what we had to, as discreetly as we could. Then we returned to stand beside the train.

While Bierce puffed away on the next cigar of the day and Juan rolled a cigarette, I surveyed the scene some more. People were coming back in twos and threes to the train. Now that they were alone or in small groups, I was able to get a clearer idea of each as individuals. The more formal gentlemen, like Bierce, stuck out like black-suited trees among the white and off-white cotton of the rest. Women in *rebozos* and sombreros chatted and laughed like pretty birds. Most of the *soldados* looked excited, and why not? They were speeding toward the heart of Pancho Villa's empire. They were champions of the North, and they knew it. We exchanged tipped hats and *"Buenos días"* with them as they clambered back on board.

"How much land does Villa control?" I asked my companions as another clump of soldiers, giggling like schoolgirls, passed us by.

"Almost all Chihuahua," Juan said. He waved at the landscape with a broad gesture.

"Since the seventh, when he took the City," Bierce continued, "he's become de facto governor of the state."

"And it's a big state, Señor—one of our most big."

"'Biggest,'" corrected Bierce with a fatherly smile. Juan nodded his thanks. Looking around at that ragged landscape with its spiny growths and the looming wall of the Sierra, I could well believe it. There may have been "nothin'" between Juárez and Chihuahua City as Juan said. But there was plenty of it, and it was all Chihuahua.

I leaned against the coach while Bierce and Juan smoked. It was a welcome moment of rest in all that wild travel. The fifteen minutes must almost be up, I thought. Most folks had already ambled back on board. I watched them through eyes slitted against the desert glare. More soldiers—Criminy, how many *were* there?—the pretty *soldadera* I had said hello to. Bierce lent a gentlemanly hand in helping her up into the coach. Her child rode upon her hip as if it had grown there. Another couple of *soldados,* quieter now, talking in muttered tones as they passed. One, a handsome fellow with a long scar down his left cheek, looked at us keenly as he passed. We must have presented a sight, even among that motley populace: I in my dusty, store-bought western rig and Bierce in his black suit and Homburg—more like something off the streets of New York than the Mexican desert. We nodded to them as we had the others, but they just kept looking and walking.

A conductor by the head of the train leaned out and yelled, "*¡Viajeros al* *trén!"* again, and we climbed back in. A couple of latecomers pelted across the dirt before they missed their ride. One was that hapless *soldado* I had seen disappear behind the organ-pipes. Poor fellow, he still had his pants halfway off. He yanked at them as he came panting up the steps. The train was already moving. Inside he was greeted by a loud chorus of jibes and comments from his fellow soldiers. Good sport that he was, he grinned, buttoned his pants, and squeezed through the crowd to his seat—*con permiso, lo siento, gracias.*

There isn't much more to tell of that part of our journey. We set ourselves back down on our luggage as comfortably as we could. Outside the open door the vastness of Chihuahua rolled by in brightly lit monotony.

Bierce was immersed in another newspaper he must have saved from the States. It ruffled and snapped in the wind from the doorway, but he resolutely read on. Juan took an impromptu siesta. Just when I was thinking I might as well do the same, somebody called out, *"¡Sí, sí, canta por nosotros!"* Sing for us! Intrigued, I looked back down the long coach-full of dark faces and saw a young *soldado* at the far end, smiling to beat the band. He reached back behind him and produced what looked like a small guitar. He tilted his head to the neck of the instrument and began plucking and tuning it. At the sound of the first rough notes, silence descended upon the entire car. Everyone watched rapt as he tightened the strings to their clear voices. Then smiling again, he strummed a cheery chord and launched into a song.

> *De la sierra morena,*
> *Cielito Lindo,*
> *Un par de ojitos negros . . .*

Even I knew this one—*"Cielito Lindo,"* "My Beautiful Little Heaven." By the second word everybody was singing along. I hummed along and tapped out the beat, not knowing all the words but not wanting to be left out of the beauty of it. When the soldier came back to the chorus, the crowds fairly shook the coach to pieces with their voices:

> *Ay, ay ay ay,*
> *¡Canta, y no llores!*

Sing, don't cry! What plain joyful, practical advice. Here these people were, riding from one battle to another. Many may have been widows, widowers, orphans; many certainly were. But they would sing and not cry. You couldn't help but admire them. I bellowed along with the rest on the chorus, and even Juan awoke and joined in. Bierce lowered his paper and glowered at us.

"Go on," I said to him. "Sing, you old buzzard!" I laughed and slapped him on the knee. If looks could kill . . . He retreated behind his paper with a *hmph!* Juan and I laughed all the more and shook our heads and sang along; and the train rocked and clacked and swayed across the desert.

9.

Chihuahua City. After the quiet tension of El Paso and the half-mad provincialism of Ciudad Juárez, Chihuahua City felt like a metropolis. The place was alive, moving, too busy for your petty complaints. Motors sped down the *avenidas:* squadrons of *villistas,* proud and silent and draped with mustachios and bandoliers, cantered by on their big horses. We detrained amongst the confusion of our fellow riders, made our way away from the crowds and looked about.

"All right, Bierce," I said. "What now?"

"You're familiar with the city, Juan," said Bierce. "Aren't you?"

"Pos, sí," he said slowly. "Some familiar."

"Good. Then I should like to meet with General Villa."

Juan and I looked at each other and burst out laughing.

"Christ Almighty!" I said, wiping my eyes. "Look around you, Bierce. You might as well ask for an audience with the Pope!" The comparison was so absurd that Juan and I guffawed again. It had been a long night and a long day, and we were punch-drunk. Bierce took off his hat and ran a hand over his face.

"If you gentlemen have exhausted your amusement," he said in quiet, level tones, "then perhaps you, in your infinite wisdom, would tell me how I could arrange such an interview."

"It's impossible!" I said. "Honestly, Bierce, the man is the *power* here in the north. Do you think he cares a whit about three vagabonds such as we?"

"¡El Centaur!" said Juan, gripping imaginary reins.

"You said it yourself," I said in more sober tones. "Villa is the de facto governor of this state, General of the Division of the North. What possible use or interest could he have in the three of us?"

"I'm a well-known author and journalist." Bierce tugged at his lapels.

"North of the Rio Grande," I said. "And besides, there are plenty of other journalists here already."

"Ah, but how many of them have the ear of William Randolph Hearst?" he said with a smirk. Even that I doubted; he had worked for Hearst's newspapers for twenty years, but the relationship had been stormy at best; acrimonious at worst. Bierce had burned a lot of bridges before heading off to Mexico.

But he didn't need to hear that now. I liked the new fire I saw in the man and I wouldn't be the one to dampen it. Instead I said, "So that's our story, now is it? Our disguise? Our 'cover'?"

"Precisely. I still have my card from the Hearst organization and somebody in this place has to have heard of me." He stopped to straighten his tie. "Besides, I should like to review his military operations."

Bierce's self-regard really knew no bounds. Of course General Villa was waiting on pins and needles for the approval of brevet Major Ambrose G. Bierce, Grand Army of the Republic, Ret.; there could be no doubt. I sighed and picked up our bags.

We flagged down a taxi. Yes, the *taxista* knew of a fine hotel for the *gentil-hombres,* and he would take us there *muy rápido y muy barato*. We agreed to the cheap fare and tumbled in. We had scarcely gotten seated when the car shot forward. To his credit, our *taxista* did bring us to a good hotel. The rates were very affordable (at least to our gringo sensibilities) and the linen clean. More than that we didn't have energy to ask for. We took turns in the communal bathtub down the hall; then all turned in for a welcome siesta.

That was about noon. We awoke around four to find the rest of the city taking siesta as well. Shops were closed, restaurants, too, so we rose and dressed and just strolled around the city. Not everyone was sleeping or resting; soldiers still patrolled, and a few *campesinos* ambled along at a glacial pace. The quiet was welcome, soothing.

We saw the cafés, the Governor's Palace (where, no doubt, *el Generalisimo* Villa lay sleepless in anticipation of the arrival of Señor Bierce), and the cathedral. It rose from the dusty streets like the face of an ice-cliff; white, towering, intricate, and cold. At its base, to the right of the doors, sat a lone figure. He was scrawny, dressed in brown rags, and one of the thin legs he had sprawled before him ended at the knee. He was sawing on a venerable, battered violin and quietly singing to himself. The violin's case was open on the sidewalk beside him; a few centavos glittered lonely upon the faded blue velvet lining.

As our shadows seeped across the dust toward him, he tilted back his head to look at us. The face the hat's retreating brim revealed to us was wasted to the bones. His cheeks and upper lip were sparsely shadowed with fine black hairs. Where his left eye should have been was a puckered hollow. He could not have been more than fifteen.

Yet the mouth surrounded by that pathetic beard and the remaining eye both smiled up at us.

"*Muy buenos días, Señores,*" he said with a touch of the bow to his ragged hat. "*¿Qué les gustaría oir?*"

What would we like to hear.

"Whatever you like to play, *varón*," said Juan, tossing a couple coins into his violin case.

The boy nodded and bent to his fiddle. He played with an easy grace born of many hours' playing, I could tell. And if the instrument wasn't equal to the playing, it couldn't harm the music either. The boy joined in after an introductory measure or two, singing in a clear, thin voice, the human equivalent of his fiddle.

I wish I could remember the whole song he sang. It was a *corrido* about General Villa, one of many such laudatory songs, springing up like May flowers in the wake of Villa's career, extolling this or that virtue of the man. The boy's song had something to do with Villa meeting the Devil in Juárez—my translating from song has never been good—and besting the old scoundrel in some game. I do remember, though, that it ended in the hopeful lines:

> "*Y porque encontró a Pancho Villa,*
> *El Diablo nunca volverá a está tierra.*"

"*And because he met with Pancho villa, The Devil will never return to this land.*"

With a final ta-tum on the fiddle the boy finished. We applauded with gusto—even Bierce, who was not what you would call a music aficionado. The boy grinned up at us and took off his hat to release a mop of lank black hair.

"*Gracias, muy generosos señores, muy valorosos señores.*"

We all dug into our pockets and dropped a shower of coin into the case. The boy bobbed his head, "*gracias, muchas gracias.*" I could see Bierce looking at the boy thoughtfully.

"Ask him," he said to Juan. "What happened to his leg and eye."

Juan asked him. The boy replaced his hat on his head and touched the dirty pants leg above his abbreviated leg. He seemed embarrassed, but when he looked up at us again there was pride in his eye.

"I was a soldier in General Villa's army," he said. "I got these wounds defeating the criminals who fight for *el Chacál.*"

"*El Chacál?*" I said. "Who is 'the Jackal'?"

"Huerta," spat Juan. "Huerta is *el Chacál.*"

No love lost on the President of the Republic, I thought. The boy spat too and dragged his hand across his mouth.

The Jackal. Such was the infamy of Villa's primary opponent, Victoriano Huerta, murderer of President Madero, traitor to the Revolution, and until recently overlord of northern Mexico. It was not the last time I would see this deep-seated hatred of the man.

Bierce was still looking at the boy. He leaned over to me and whispered, "How do you say, 'You're very brave. As soldier to soldier, I salute you'?"

I whispered back the words and Bierce leaned over toward the boy. He extended his hand to him.

"Tienes mucho coraje," he said. *"Como soldado a soldado, te saluto."* If his accent wasn't academy, his heart was clearly there. They shook hands, the boy looking up at this great, ancient gringo in his black suit and fierce mustachios, the *gringo viejo* looking back fondly at the crippled hero. Bierce straightened up to his full height, gave the boy a crisp salute even General Sherman would have approved of, and the boy returned it. I could see tears starting in the well of his one eye. With a muttered "What the hell," Bierce pulled out his wallet, dug out a couple of bills, and dropped them into the violin case.

"Que vayan con Dios," the boy said, and wiped away a tear.

"Y contigo, también," I said, and we walked away.

Bierce was quiet—exceptionally quiet, for him. Juan and I let him lag behind. When he was out of earshot, Juan said to me, "What bothers *el señor?*"

"Mr. Bierce was a soldier in his youth," I said. "More, Bierce had two sons who died. One son was named Day, Day Bierce. He was Bierce's pride and joy. He killed himself over a girl when he was about that boy's age."

"*Ay, que triste.* An' he never forget."

"Would you?"

I turned to look back at Bierce, no longer Bierce the Scourge of the West Coast, no longer the hero of Shiloh and Chickamauga, but just an old man; a wanderer and a mourner at the graves of two sons. He paced down that dusty Mexican street like a long black shadow.

We meandered. None of us knew the city, so we just let our feet take us where they list. First was the downtown, businesses lining broad streets. But here the heavy hand of Revolution was evident in the boarded windows; glass crunched underfoot. Villa had let his men loose here to "gather" whatever they could and the ruin of many was the result.

"*El General* have no love for *los gachupines,*" said Juan as we passed yet another boarded storefront.

"'*Gachupines?*'" said Bierce.

"E-Spaniards. He take their businesses, tell them to get out of Mexico."

"That seems a trifle extreme for people you just don't like."

"*¿Y qué?*" Juan shrugged. "They are just *señores,* not *hombres* like us Mexicans."

Gentlemen, not men—a clear distinction.

We wandered into a residential street. Heavy adobe squares, pierced by deep windows and doorways hung with age-hardened plank doors; block upon block of white adobe, relieved by the occasional robin's egg blue or yellow-ochre. Here a *curandera* had put out her shingle, advertising herbs and simples for anything that ailed you; there a cobbler advertised with a comically large boot hung from the front of his store. In the near distance, a burst of male laughter—harsh, forceful. I heard the surprised squawk of a rooster. Cockfight? I remembered reading that General Villa himself was an avid cockfighter. More pleasant, the sound of a Victrola playing some maudlin, sentimental song in Spanish—eternal pleas of love, promises of fealty, wails of regret. Glasses clinked and quiet voices exchanged easy small-talk. And all invisible behind those weathered walls and windows. Not a soul did we see abroad, only the attenuated shadows of the afternoon.

Eventually our meandering tread led us to nicer streets, among more grandiose and well-kept residences. Palms and other trees nodded their heads over massive garden-walls; there were tiled roofs, there were tall, polished windows showing hints of drapery, ornate furniture in European styles, wall-sized paintings of frowning paterfamilias. Through iron gates and over the smaller walls we sometimes saw lone *peones* in their white cotton, tending the flower-beds or raking the walks with careful slowness. Like an oasis in the heart of the desert, peace reigned here in the heart of the war.

At one particularly fine *casa,* a small, neat woman was tending to her plants just within the gate. Her long, blue, well-fitting dress and arranged coif of black hair showed her to be no *peon.* Probably the *señora* of the *casa,* I thought. Behind her in the perfumed shade of the garden, two small girls in white frocks tended the flowers in careful imitation of the woman.

"*Perdóneme, Señora,*" Juan said, tipping his hat. "Can you tell us if *el General* Villa lives near here?"

Two soldiers in spotless khakis and vast sombreros materialized on each side of the gate. Rifles were slung from their shoulders, and they looked like men who knew how to use them.

But the woman laughed—a clear, light sound, the jingle of gold in the heavy air.

"Pues, sí," she said. "He lives very near here. In fact . . ." She waved a small hand back at the grand stucco pile behind her. "I am Señora Villa."

We all doffed our hats.

"Your pardon, ma'am," said Bierce. *"¿Habla Usted inglés?"*

It never ceased to amaze me how Bierce's knowledge of Spanish miraculously reappeared just when he wanted it to—conveniently, and often, in the presence of women. And the tone of his voice, too, the voice of the soldier replaced by that of the lover. Honey for gunpowder. The Bierce charm engaged in full.

"Sí," said the Señora. *"Un poquito."* She held up her thumb and forefinger scant centimeters apart.

"My name is Ambrose Bierce, and these are my associates, Mr. Littlefault and Mr. Romero. I am a writer and journalist from the United States, and I have come a very long way just to meet *el General*. But they tell me"—he darted a glare like a sliver of ice at Juan and me—"that he is unapproachable."

"Qué," started Sra. Villa with a frown. Juan translated. Bierce nodded his thanks.

"Exactly," he said. "May I ask you, *beg* of you, is there any way that I might meet with *su esposo famoso?"*

At that moment the two little girls ran up to the Señora. She gathered them close to her. They peeped around her skirts at Juan and me as if we were wild beasts; but to Bierce they gave shy smiles. They looked up at him as if he were a bright angel. The older of the two, I could swear, was flirting with the old soldier.

"Your daughters?" said Bierce.

"Sí."

Bierce tugged his pants legs and squatted before them.

"Hello, my beauties," he said softly. Big, dark eyes regarded him from the safety of their mother's shadow. The girls did not come any closer, but neither did they run away. One of them giggled. The guards came closer to the iron gate when Bierce approached, but now they set their rifles at parade rest and smiled at the old gringo and his young admirers.

"They are lovely girls," Bierce said, straightening up. "You are blessed."

"Thank you," said Sra. Villa after Juan had translated. She put her hands gently on her daughters' heads and looked at the girls, considering. Finally she looked back at Bierce.

"My girls are, *¿cómo se dice?* Good at people. Good judges, *¿es verdad, mis hijas?"*

She looked at her girls. The older one said, *"Es muy guapo, el abuelo,"* and plunged her face into her mother's dress. The grandfather is very handsome, she said. Bierce didn't need to translate to know when he was complimented. Sra. Villa laughed again.

"I will try to get *el General* to see you," she said with a slow nod of her head. "More than that I cannot do. But he does trust the word of his two *diablitas.*"

She ruffled the girls' heads and they ran laughing and screaming back into the garden.

Bierce said, "I am forever in your debt, madam." He put his hand to his heart and bowed low. He took a pen and notebook from his inner coat pocket and began to write.

"I and my associates may be reached at this hotel in the city," he said, tore the page from the notebook, and handed it through the bars to the Señora. "If there is anything that we may do for you in return, do not hesitate to ask."

The lady nodded her thanks when Juan had translated.

"Just write something nice about my husband," she said. And with that she gathered her skirts and strolled back into the green shade of her gardens. After a look of warning at us, the guards followed her.

*

"Well, Bierce, you've done it again."

We were walking back toward our hotel in the falling dusk. The quiet of the day had infected us all as we walked; but once away from General Villa's mansion, I had to say something.

"Don't give me credit yet, Amos," Bierce said back to me. "We haven't gotten an audience with the great man yet. His wife seems a congenial woman and has her charms. But she is, withal, just his wife."

It seemed a cold thing to say. Bierce's own marriage had been a recurring disaster toward the end, and it surely colored his view of all such unions. Yet Sra. Villa had been so gracious to three strangers such as we, that I couldn't let it pass.

"I think you underestimate both her influence and his respect for her," I said. "He clearly cares much for her and his children. Witness the comfortable, nay, luxurious situation he has put them in."

"Confiscated by *force majeure,* no doubt," snorted Bierce. "Still, there is something in what you say, my boy. We will hope for the best."

Back in the heart of Chihuahua City and just as it was awakening from its siesta. The custom was strange to me, but it made more sense the longer I was in Mexico. During winter it was less obvious; but during the warmer months it was foolish to work—or even be abroad—in the heat of the day. And contrary to the stereotype we had of "the lazy Mexican" back in the States, the folk returned to work after their siesta and sometimes worked until eight or nine o'clock of an evening. Then came *la cena,* the evening meal, with drinks and possibly cigars for the men. Here in Villa's capital doors were opening; men in suits and work-clothes and women in long cotton dresses and shawls were emerging. Taxis and trucks swerved around one another and the ancient ox-carts lumbered. Street-vendors resumed their monotonous calls of *"¡Refrescos! ¡Mangos! ¡Tamales!"* The great machine of society had reawakened.

We grabbed a light dinner from some of the vendors and took it to the city plaza to eat. The cool of evening did nothing to discourage the Chihuahuans from taking the air. To the contrary: groups of young men and young women moved around the plaza's perimeter, flirting and posturing as they passed each other. *Abuelas* in black herded gaggles of children, their hair so black and straight and their eyes so tilted that they looked almost Chinese to me. An impromptu band of guitar, trumpet, and bass lumbered into a march back among the trees. We sat and digested and enjoyed the scene, Juan especially.

"You have seen *'México bravo,'*" he said. "'Wild Mexico.' Now you see *'México lindo,'* beautiful Mexico. Is for this that we fight."

I nodded. It was worth the fight, I could agree. Yet where did the revived Aztec knights fit into all this? There was harmony here, peace. A lull between battles, it was true, yet this was surely the norm, not the wanton slaughter that shook the country. Could these self-styled Eagle-knights and Jaguar-knights really feel that they could offer something better than this? A child's laugh hiccoughed up into the night sky; the band played, and a couple that looked old enough to have known the French invasion of the '60s danced vigorously to the music. I looked across at Bierce, he caught my eye, and I knew he was thinking the same thing. For all his cherished military past and the memories of glory on the battlefield; for all his wanting to see if those Mexicans could shoot straight; for all that, I could see that he knew the value, the inestimable value of an ordinary, quiet evening such as this. This is why we had come to Mexico. He blinked acknowledgment at me; I blinked back.

The party was still going—just getting started, really, as people emerged from their jobs—but by eight o'clock we were weary and ready for bed. We turned tired feet back toward our hotel.

Once back in the hotel, we were crossing the lobby to the stairs when we were surprised by a messenger who came at a run. He was dressed in the worn khaki that passed for a uniform in Villa's División del Norte. He looked about thirteen.

"¿Señor Beer?" he said breathlessly as he ran up. Bierce raised his hand. *"Un mensaje par Usted."* The boy handed him a folded piece of paper, saluted, and ran off again out into the night.

"Why walk when you can run?" I said, looking after the boy, suddenly envious of all that energy.

"I expect he was under orders," Bierce muttered. He unfolded the message, scowled at it, and thrust it as me. "Read this, please."

"'De la Oficina de General Francisco Villa,'" I began. *"'El General les pide—'"*

"No, no, no," Bierce said. "In English, you fool."

I smiled. It wasn't often I got one over on the old man.

"'The General asks you to meet with him at his office in the Governor's Palace at ten o'clock in the morning, December fifteenth. Please be on time.' I take that last to be an order, not a request."

"We will regard it as such, at any rate."

10.

We received a further surprise on the morrow when, exiting the hotel to keep our appointment, we were greeted by a soldier in uniform so clean it looked *pressed*. He saluted us smartly and held open the door of a long, dark motor.

"The general gives you greetings of the day," he said in Spanish. "And requests you make use of his automobile."

Bierce turned to me and raised those extravagant eyebrows.

"Will wonders never cease?"

We entered the automobile, large enough to seat all three of us side by side. The soldier shut the door, got in the front passenger side, and we were off.

It wasn't a long ride to the palace. Even so, I was still recovering from the previous day's exertions and welcomed the luxury of the ride. Then, too, I cannot deny that I enjoyed the honor given to us by the general. It was a fine motor, putting to shame anything else on the road. The seats were leather, the appointments brass and a dark wood I thought might be teak. In short, it was a conveyance someone such as myself would never have been able to afford. I sighed, sat back, and surrendered myself to my own vanity and comfort.

The motor swung off the main avenue and curved smoothly around front of the Governor's Palace. This great edifice stood like a square rock upon which the tides of war and revolution might break with little effect. Bullets had chipped it here and there, and one or two windows were patched with wood; but it still stood solid, an image of the permanency of order and authority. I knew a little of General Villa's personal history and wondered at the one-time mountain bandit, now ensconced in this palace, the ultimate power in that part of the world.

Our escort leapt out of the car and opened the door for us with a soft, *"Con permiso."* We followed him within the vast arched doorway into a courtyard, across and up a sprawling staircase one would never expect to find in the northern Mexican desert.

Down a hallway where the clack of our footsteps was the only sound; down another; and finally to a door with the simple sign, EL GOBERNADOR. Two soldiers flanked the door just as they had at Villa's casa. They held rifles at parade rest and looked as natural in their uniforms as wolves in sheep's clothing.

Our escort knocked on the door. From within came a raspy *"Pásele."* The escort opened the door and stood back to allow us in.

I'm not sure what I expected to see when we went in—a roomful of burly, drunken *mexicanos,* a lair of deadly killers—but it wasn't what I saw. Instead, we entered a large, quiet room dominated by a hulking cliff of a desk of some dark, carven wood. On the left, a large map of Mexico was pinned to a rolling stand. Chalk lines and colored pins made it bright with color. Windows in the wall on either side of the desk gave a glare that made the environs of the desk dim, but clearly someone stood behind the desk; someone with that indefinable quality you might term "presence." Bierce had it in spades, and so did this fellow. He was a solid man of middling height, short, dark hair, wearing a hunting-jacket of the usual khaki but of much finer cut than what the *soldados* wore. He was bent over a paper on the desk that he seemed to be trying to scowl into submission. From this angle I could tell little about his face except for the usual Mexican mustache. Occasionally he would write something or cross something out with quick, angry motions. He deigned a quick glance up at us.

"Vengan," he said, waving us forward. *"Siéntense."* There were chairs before

the great desk but none of us sat. Finally the figure at the desk capped his pen and set it down with a slap, ran his hands over his short hair, and stood erect to face us.

The first thing I noted about General Francisco "Pancho" Villa was his eyes. In stature he wasn't large; at five foot nine I was close to his height, though he was much deeper in the chest than I—the build of a boxer. And his face, while handsome, was not one to stand out in a crowd. But those eyes . . . They were as dark as the desert night, profound with unknown depths that drew you in. Wrinkles, pale against the sun-darkened flesh of his face, radiated from his eyes like sunbursts. Direct, unswerving, shrewd, calculating. One look into those eyes and you understood immediately the history of this man, killer at sixteen, bandit chieftain, general, and revolutionary. He exuded a feeling of great strength that would serve a friend or a cause unflinchingly. But God help you if you crossed him.

Villa strode directly to Bierce. He thrust out his hand and said, "Pancho Villa, *a sus órdenes.*" Bierce gripped the other's hand and said, "Ambrose Bierce. It is an honor." Juan and I might as well have been furniture. The two men held each other, hand to hand, eye to eye, for a long moment. They were sizing each other up, gauging strength and weaknesses. More, each was clearly relishing the contact with a fellow man, a real man of power and decision. I was reminded of Juan's critique of the Spaniards: *"señores, no hombres"*—they were "misters," not men. Here were two men who had come by their high status in life not by birth or privilege, but by the hard work of life itself. Without knowing the details of each other's lives, they recognized a fellow *hombre* when they met him.

(For the sake of my patient readers, I will omit the back-and-forth translating that Juan and I performed at the meeting of these two great men, and present their words in English.)

At last Bierce and Villa released their grip on each other.

"Please," Villa said, waving again at the chairs. "Sit and be comfortable."

Bierce sat and, taking our cue from him, so did Juan and I.

"So," said Villa with a slow smile, "I am informed by 'the boss' that you wanted to see me."

"Your wife is a most gracious woman," Bierce said. "I should not have presumed to bother her but you are reputed to be a hard man to see."

Villa waved at the map of Mexico.

"I'm busy, if that's what you mean. Huerta still pesters me. The little drunkard doesn't know when he's beaten."

Villa's nickname for Huerta—"*el borrachito*," the little drunkard—was surprising at first. To look at Villa you would assume that he could hold his own in any cantina where the tequila flowed like the Rio Grande. But I later learned that he was, in fact, a teetotaler. Nights when Huerta had to be half carried to bed (and it was rumored that that was most nights), Villa enjoyed a tall, cold glass of . . . *milk*. It was probably this clear-headedness that helped him hold together those wild-riding *campesinos* of the north into a successful army.

Villa continued.

"I take a city, he takes it back. I fix a railroad, he tears it up. *Cabrón*." He sighed and shook his drum-like head. "I take Chihuahua, and what does he do? His troops retreat to Ojinaga, of all places—a dog-piss of a spot on the border where they stand and yip at me. They might as well jump the river and call themselves gringos and be done with it." He grinned at us like a wolf. "No offense."

"None taken," Bierce said, readjusting himself in his chair and crossing his long legs. "I assume you'll follow and finish the job."

Villa shrugged eloquently.

"What else can I do? Leave them to plunder the countryside? I could be on my way to Mexico City, but not with those dogs at my back. *Caray*."

Bierce nodded thoughtfully. Then he got up and walked to the map of Mexico. He clasped his hands behind his back and leaned forward to stare at it.

Villa rose, too, and joined Bierce.

"You know maps?" he said to Bierce.

"Mm. I was a surveyor for General Hazen in our own War between the States." He said this as though it were an afterthought, but I could see it struck a chord with Villa. Clever Bierce.

"Here's Chihuahua," Villa said, pointing a thick finger at a large dot on the map. "And here's Ojinaga." He pointed to a much smaller dot on the double-line indicating the border between Mexico and the U.S. Bierce gave a curt nod.

"About a hundred and twenty miles," he said. "And the rail line doesn't go there, I see."

"No, *claro que no*."

"Pity. You did so well using it at Juárez."

Villa puffed up a little at this. "It's a different battle," he said. "Juárez was dumb luck, us getting that Federal train. Here there is no surprise. It's going to be a siege."

"And your approach?"

Villa shrugged again. "Same as the old days—horses, foot, wagons, caissons, and howitzers drawn by horse."

Bierce rubbed his jaw. "You have an opportunity here. If you can get there in time, on these three sides, with the Rio at their back, Huerta's troops will be trapped."

"Trapped except for the United States."

"And if they cross, so what? They'll be locked up in a military prison and out of your game."

Villa grinned like a cat. "That's what they said about me back in '12. Huerta would have had me shot as a horse-thief, but I ran to the U.S. *Adios, Pancho.* Then I crossed back into Mexico early this year with six men—*six men,* Señor Bierce. Have you seen how many I command now?"

"Yes, but I dare say that none of Huerta's officers is another Pancho Villa, correct?"

Villa laughed and slapped Bierce on the shoulder.

"*Como no,*" he said. "There is only one Villa."

"Even so," Bierce said, scrutinizing the map, "I should like to see a more detailed map of the area to be sure."

Villa led Bierce back to this desk. He pulled open one of the drawers and produced a roll of paper, which he then spread upon the desk, anchoring the curling corners with paperweights and his pistol. As Bierce leaned down to look at it, nearly head to head with the revolutionary general, I caught a slight shifting of the shadows to our right. A man materialized out of the darkness. A shiver ran down my back—had he been there all along, but we—or at least, I—hadn't seen him? As with Villa, the glare from the tall windows had hidden him, and even now obscured his features. Seeing him now, if dimly, I though in many ways he was just another *villista* soldier, if taller and narrower in build than some, clad in nondescript clothes, jacket and hat. But the darkness that hid his eyes held mystery—and menace.

"Fierro," Juan whispered to me, never taking his eyes off the figure. "El General's bodyguard. *El Carnicero*—the Butcher."

Now I really shivered. Villa had his savage side, there was no doubt. He once shot a fellow officer in the face to settle an argument. But the stories told about Fierro chilled the blood. Here was a heartless brutality that existed just to feed itself. When a shift of those hidden eyes caught a glint of sunlight, I was reminded of nothing so much as of a spider lying in wait in some dusty hole.

Villa and Bierce, however, seemed immune to this evil scrutiny.

"No, *here*," Bierce was saying as he poked at the map on the desk. "If you position the howitzers there, they won't have as much effect."

"Mm." Villa, hands clasped behind his back, studied the map.

"Bring your troops up this way and you can't lose." Bierce gave the map a final poke and straightened up. Villa continued looking at the map for another few seconds, nodded once, and straightened also.

"Excellent," he said and shook Bierce's hand again. "I am in your debt, Señor Bierce. None of my officers have seen it quite that way. I have no doubt now that we will flush those *fulanos* out of Ojinaga."

Bierce graced the general with an avuncular smile.

"Really, General, it was nothing at all—a fresh perspective—"

"No, I insist! You have helped me immeasurably."

"Well," drawled Bierce, looking at us, "we have an obligation in Mexico City. Perhaps the General would be so kind . . ."

"Consider it done."

"And a look at your troops."

Villa chuckled. "*¡Por Supuesto!* I'd be honored. Come, gentlemen."

Villa strode to the door and we all followed. Fierro, like the shade of Death, fell in behind us. I knew this less from sight than from the feel of the man behind us, like the chill off a large cake of ice.

Villa led us back down the halls and out through the courtyard to the street. All along the way soldiers snapped to attention and threw smart salutes his way. Villa, distracted, waved half-hearted salutes back.

When we got to the street Villa led us to his big motor, still waiting in front of the Palace. The driver, ever in attendance, saluted and grabbed open the car's rear door—just in time for Villa to plunge through it. Villa plunked down on the seat.

"Come, come," he said, waving us in. We piled in back onto the tonneau's bulging leather seats. It was a big car but still a tight fit. I was wedged between Villa and Bierce. Juan perched on the fold-down seat opposite. Funny the things one remembers. Off of Bierce I caught a whiff of lemon hair-cream, cigar smoke, and cotton fabric warmed by the sun; from Villa, leather, horse, and, curiously, mint. Bierce's arm against my side was long bone and muscle like corded rope. Being pressed against Pancho Villa was like being packed in with a side of beef. Fierro sat up front but hooked his arm over the back of his seat so that he could watch us with that wolf's smile. How nice. How cozy.

Still I wouldn't be honest if I said that I wasn't honored by the company. I was seated in the middle of an historic moment, and I knew it. In that sense it was a very comfortable ride. The driver ran around front, gave the automobile's crank a hard turn, and when it fired, he ran back and jumped in the driver's seat. We set off at a brisk but steady pace. The driver knew his job and the importance of his charges. If the ride from our hotel had been slightly hurried, it was now smooth as glass.

But as we moved off, I must admit I felt a trifle nervous. Part of it was the chilling presence of the silent Fierro, but part of it was Villa himself. Villa had been, if not welcoming, at least pleasant. But I had heard enough about his infamous temper and seen enough bullet-pocked walls to set my imagination going. It was hardly eased when Villa barked to his driver, *"Al campo, Chucho"*—to the countryside, Chucho. What was out in the countryside? Where *were* we going?

We left the ostentatious buildings of downtown behind and passed through the humble streets we had negotiated the evening before. Further, out into the countryside. Here was erected another city, I saw, a sprawling landscape of white tents and thrown-together *jacales*—the home of the Division of the North. The driver slowed the car and eased it up one of the broad rights-of-way between the tents. Where the tents petered out he pulled to one side and killed the motor.

A rolling cloud of dust caught us up and tumbled slowly over us. We climbed out of the car; and when the dust settled we found ourselves surrounded by soldiers, campesinos, their wives and even children. All eyes were on the general, but it was a more casual mood than the formality of the Governor's Palace. Soldados ambled up, tipped their outrageous sombreros, and greeted Villa with a companionable *"Buenos días, General."* Easy smiles all around. Somebody handed Villa a mug of steaming coffee.

"Gracias, Chuy," Villa said and patted the fellow on the back. These were not just Villa's soldiers; these were his men, his *compañeros,* with whom he had shared victory, hardship, defeat. If he had wanted us to be impressed, it was working. The crowd increased, a dozen, a hundred, a couple hundred; but never did I feel threatened. We were the guests of the general—show some respect. They adored this man. They would fight for him—die, if need be, for him. Revolutions and plans and ideas were all very well and good, but they didn't lead you into battle or look after you—or your widow—when you were hurt in his service. All the trials of war would be worth it if one day, as a white-mustachioed *abuelo,* you could tell your grandchildren with pride: *Yo fuí a batalla con Villa*—I rode with Villa.

For the moment, though, all was good humor. A cool, sunny morning in the desert; the low murmur and laughter of the *tropas,* the ticking of the automobile's cooling engine, the hale-fellow-well-met words of General Villa. Juan, Bierce, and I watched from the sidelines. You might have thought that Bierce would resent the lack of attention, but you would be wrong. Rather, he was admiring the way Villa connected with his soldiers. Bierce had had his share of commanders, good and bad, in the Civil War, and he could appreciate one who genuinely cared for his troops.

Villa ended a conversation with a loud laugh. He turned to us.

"Gentlemen," he said, Welcome to *la División del Norte,* the finest fighting outfit in all Mexico!"

This drew a ragged but heartfelt cheer from the assembled crowd. *¡Viva Villa! ¡Viva la Revolución!* Villa beamed at them. He walked to one soldier who leaned a rifle across his shoulder.

"*Dáme el fúsil, amigo, por favor,*" Villa said. The soldier obligingly handed him the rifle. Villa snapped back the bolt, checked for a bullet in the chamber, snicked it back, and thrust the weapon at me.

"Here," he said. "I don't take bad shots in my army. My soldiers hit what they aim at. Hit *that.*"

He pointed and the crowd separated like the Red Sea before Moses. I looked down the path made by his arm and saw a large clump of prickly-pear cactus, maybe three-hundred feet away.

"*That?*"

"That."

Well, in for a dime, in for a dollar. I hefted the rifle to my shoulder—heavier than I expected—and steadied it as much as I could toward the distant cactus. The assembled *soldados* were silent with anticipation. The end of the barrel wavered more than I wanted; the smallest twitch of my arms translated into wide sweeps at that end. But I finally got a bead on the cactus; took a deep breath; and as I breathed out, squeezed the trigger. A loud band, the rifle bucked back into my shoulder, and . . . Dust spurted up in the desert. Not even close.

"*¡Ay, que lástima!*" The crowd erupted into laughs and cat-calls. Villa chuckled and took the rifle from me.

"Maybe *el mexicano* can show you how it's done," he said. He handed the gun to Juan, who hefted it easily and with familiarity. Then he seemed to become conscious of all the attention focused on him and gave a sheepish laugh.

"I'm not used to this," he said. He raised the rifle to his shoulder, aimed, and fired. He didn't seem to take much care in it; yet when the smoke cleared we could see his bullet clipped the very outmost paddle of the cactus.

A cheer rose up. A dozen men came forward and shook Juan's hand, patted him on the back, offered him praise and tipples from surreptitious flasks.

"Beginner's luck," he shrugged as he passed me.

The rifle was given to Bierce. He took it and examined it with a keen eye. The actions clicked and clacked as he made sure of it; he lifted the gun to his shoulder and sighted down the barrel at the offending cactus.

"*¡Socorro!*"

Everyone turned toward the yell. It had come from the tents to our left and was followed by a young soldier running flat-out in our direction.

"Escaped!" he said, breathless as he pounded to a stop before us. Then, seeing just who he was in the presence of, he doffed his hat and saluted. He gulped and gasped.

"*Perdón, mi General,*" he said. "One of the Federal *hijos de perra* has escaped."

Villa's good-natured grin curved down into a dangerous glare.

"How did this happen, *varón?*" he said.

The youth swallowed again.

"He grabbed a knife, *mi General,* no one knows where from, and killed two guards."

Villa was still glowering at the youth when another cry went up to our left.

"There he is!"

A hard tattoo of hoofbeats and more cries of alarm. We turned to the left again and beheld a man on horseback break from the tents and race out into the desert. Shots rang out, but for all Villa's vaunted soldiers who "hit what they aim at," none of them hit this target. The fugitive was hatless, wore the dirty uniform of a Federal, and was crouched low over the neck of his stolen steed. He was perhaps fifty feet from us when he left the camp, but was elongating the distance between us in a hurry.

"Take this."

Bierce thrust the rifle at me and I took it. A few soldiers near us were unslinging their rifles or pulling pistols from belts and holsters, and a couple had already sent wild shots after the fugitive. But with the press of the crowd they had to dance around to avoid hitting their companions.

Then there was Bierce. In one smooth, swift movement, he swept his Colt from its holster, leveled it out toward the rider (now just a diminishing toy in the distance), and squeezed the trigger. The Colt roared out like a lion among the lesser barks of the other guns. Suddenly the Federal jerked upright in the saddle. For a second he held a pose of surprise, arms held up as if in surrender, before tipping sideways off the horse. He fell full into the clump of prickly pear that had been our target.

For a moment, all was awestruck quiet. Then another cheer roared up into the desert sky. The crowd pressed around Bierce—handshakes, slaps on the back, ¡Increíble! ¡Que tirón! The great man himself calmly lifted up his pistol and blew smoke from the barrel of his gun.

Villa just stared at where the *Federal* lay among the wreckage of the cactus.

"*Hijo de la Chingada,*" he breathed. "Welcome to the *División del Norte, amigo.*"

11.

We did not know at that moment just how literally Villa meant that. In our minds it was just an honorary title; but to Villa we were truly his soldiers now, and subject to his orders. The first indication of this came soon after Bierce's moment of marksmanship glory, as we walked back to Villa's car.

"So, General," said Bierce, "we would be greatly obliged if you would arrange our travel as soon as may be."

Villa smiled a secret smile.

"*Mañana, mañana,*" he waved it away. "Today I am busy. Go rest, now—tomorrow *you* will be busy."

Busy we were, but not in the way we had hoped.

Bierce's gambit had worked too well. He—and, by dint of our knowledge of Spanish and by association, Juan and I—were called upon to inspect and advise upon Villa's troops. A harried-looking *soldado* would appear every other day or so and ask, "With the general's regards, if we would be so kind . . ." Our transport to Mexico City kept getting put off—a *mañana* that never came—and if there were any doubt that we were unwitting "protected guests" of the general, we had only to look around. There always seemed to be two or three fellows, armed, nonchalant, and always present, whenever we thought of slipping away. We had no doubt that they were there to protect us from the perils of freedom.

Christmas arrived, and Chihuahua City bloomed like a desert flower. It was an odd beauty for me, used as I was to northern snows and evergreens at that time of year, but beautiful nonetheless. The people arranged their *posadas* and wandered amiably from house to house, their faces rubicund and bunched in smiles in the light of the paper lanterns lining the walkways. Bierce, Juan, and I exchanged *regalitos,* little presents obtained in town.

About this time Bierce composed what at the time seemed a minor note, but which ultimately had historic poignancy. He had been carrying with him some unanswered correspondence, and by Christmas it had nagged him long enough. I came across him, wrapped in a wool poncho and seated against an abandoned ammunition case. He was frowning down upon some sheets of paper propped on a book in his lap, where he was writing with what looked like measured fury.

"Who are you writing to?" I asked as I came up to him.

"Blanche Partington," he said without looking up. The pen continued to tear across the page. I knew Miss Partington to be an admirer of Bierce's, but why he should be writing to her now and there puzzled me.

"Do you think that is wise?" I said.

Bierce looked up from under his frosty brows.

"Wise? I should think it neither wise nor foolish, Amos, merely a response to an annoying letter. It has been eating away at me through my saddle-bag for days now. I grow tired of its teeth."

"But you are revealing our location. I thought this was something of a secret mission."

Bierce sighed in that tired way that signaled his weary patience with a stupid world.

"There is little chance, given the haphazard running of the trains these days, that this will even reach her in the next week. By then we should be away from here. Anyone besides Miss Partington who reads it will be deceived into looking for us here, should any such curious individual exist. Besides, I am forwarding it through my niece Lora to confuse the trail. Obfuscation through obviousness—satisfied?"

I was not satisfied, at least not completely, but he returned to the letter with the posture of one who will not be disturbed again. We might indeed be leaving Chihuahua in the next few days—in fact, given recent events to the north of us, it seemed very likely. Yet a determined investigator would find our trail there and follow it. I didn't know at the time that that was to be the last written word to the greater world from Ambrose Bierce; and I wonder whether he knew it either.

Our enforced stay in Chihuahua had had the unforeseen benefit of gaining us new friends, and a more welcoming and devoted bunch you couldn't ask for. There was Augustín, one of many refugees from the haciendas Villa had closed down in the north; Gordito ("fatty" in Spanish—the others used the nickname so consistently that we never did learn his real name), the heavy sergeant who almost missed the train from Juárez due to his bowels; and Chino, a full-blooded Indian from the mountains of the north, a man of few words but a boon companion. On a whim I went back into town and retrieved Diego, the one-legged, one-eyed teenage veteran we had met on the cathedral steps, and his fiddle became an instant "hit" with the men. Lacking anything better, the camp became his new home. Of a sudden Juan Carlos, the *guitarista* from the train, would appear, and he and "Dieguito" would thump and saw their way through some ballad that was old when Padre Hidalgo raised the call for independence from Spain. Bierce splurged and bought a case of tequila for our new campfire friends. The tequila and *ron* were passed 'round and the night became joyous and ridiculous with mirth. Juan, I noticed, had his own bottle and guarded it jealously. I hoped that his taste for the liquor wouldn't become a problem. At one point he retired "to see a man about a horse," as the saying goes; and Bierce, his own bottle exhausted, picked up Juan's. He uncorked it, tipped it, and took a pull. It must not have been his vintage, though, for he held the bottle out and stared at it as if it had insulted him. Finally he just set it back on the ground and went in search of something better. To each his own, I thought.

Not all members of the Division of the North were so friendly to *los gringos locos,* though. There was one group of junior officers especially who loitered around the artillery and leveled hard, amused stares at us when we passed. Our new friends told us they were members of the "Dorados," Villa's special elite. One of them in particular caught my attention—a thin, handsome young fellow, an unsheathed sword of a man with a long scar down the right side of his face. His ball-bearing gaze said volumes that his smirking mouth did not. A query to our friends revealed his name as Lieutenant Bendiga; we were told that he was not a man to cross. He looked familiar, too, but I couldn't place him until one day as we passed and yelled out, "*¡Abordo, cabrónes!*" Then I knew him for the same scarred man from the train from Juárez. He and his amigos would lean on the field-pieces and watch us pass and trade comments about us just on the edge of audibility; but I never felt we had anything to fear from them. It was commonly known that we had the protection of General Villa himself, and this alone was enough to keep us safe. Still, I wouldn't have wanted this Bendiga and his friends at my back in a battle.

One morning, after a night of one of our campfire fiestas, I awoke on the ground. A blanket had been thrown over me but my legs, draped over the log off of which I had fallen the night before, were numb with cold. My mouth tasted like the floor of a distillery, and somewhere deep inside my head some idiot was pounding on the walls. I opened my eyes, rubbed the sand out of them, and froze. A scorpion sat not a foot from my face. I had known in an academic way that the creatures existed in that part of the world, but had never supposed I would actually meet one. It was small, half the length of my thumb, was a pale shade of green with white legs, and poised with its stinger arced high above its back. Its claws were leveled ready before it; and before I could release the yell building up in my throat, the scorpion darted forward and grabbed a beetle that was walking by. Its tail shot down once, twice, three times while the claws held the poor brute helpless.

That released me from my paralysis. I threw off the blanket and lurched backwards and upwards, gasping out calls for help, getting tangled in my own useless legs. I managed to get halfway to my feet before thumping back down on my backside, a whole yard from where I had started. Reaching back my hand, I felt something under a blanket—another sleeper. I jerked myself around to rouse him, get him to stomp the horrid thing out of existence, help me flee—when I saw the sleeper's face. It was Bierce. He was lying on his back, as still and white as marble, his head cushioned on his nearly crushed hat. The image was completed by his usual black suit and the two ghastly, liver-spotted hands folded on his breast. He was so still. He had died in his sleep.

In one of the more maudlin, tequila-soaked pockets of the night, Bierce had told me that Christmas had been the anniversary of his wedding to Mollie Day. "Forty-two years," he'd said. "Forty-two years . . ." He'd stared off into the fire as though down a long, dark corridor through which he could never return. Now here he was, no more words. Poor Bierce, never got to see his last, big battle . . . My throat clenched and I felt tears well up in my eyes, breaking the old man up into a quivering jumble of prisms.

Then his eyes opened. I blinked and tears spilled down my cheeks.

"Amos," he said quietly. "You look as if you had seen a ghost."

"Damn sand." I drew my sleeve across my face. "There was a scorpion—" I pointed vaguely. A few yards away I saw the creature, bearing the dead beetle back to whatever miniature hell it called home.

"Yes," Bierce groaned, sitting up. "You have to watch out for such dangers."

"Which reminds me," I said. "This—all whatever this is, this army life, singing around the campfire, what are we doing here, Bierce? Professor Navarro——"

"And what, pray, do you *think* I've been doing, Amos?"

I looked at Bierce closely then. He leaned upon his two, thin arms like a weather-worn lean-to on a pair of saplings, but those eyes still burned into me with a white light.

"You've been consorting with the soldiers——"

"And?"

"Gaining their trust."

With a final glare he nodded at me, reached back, grabbed up his hat, and began poking it back into shape.

"I have been making the best of our enforced stay here," he said. "Juan," he added, looking around for the absent Romero, "is a good fellow, but I prefer my information at first hand. If I learned nothing else from my forty-odd years of journalism, some odder than others, it was to 'consider your sources.' I prefer not to get all my information through the filter of that honest but simple Mexican guide of ours."

"And what do your 'sources' say?"

He held up a warning finger to his lips. "Soon."

The camp was just coming to life. Pale, young sunlight spread over the tents, dyeing them pastel oranges and pinks. Soldiers emerged from those tents in assorted stages of dress—no hat, no tunic, no weapon. But all wore their boots. I remembered my morning visitor and judged them wise to keep their boots on.

Bierce and I got up (he refused my offer of a hand up) and surveyed our campsite. In the center was the black and gray wreckage of the fire, with the sleeping bodies of our companions radiating away from it as if the party had exploded from the center. While I brushed dust from his back, Bierce scowled down at the sleepers as if at deserters.

"Amateurs," he said. Gordito snored at the skies. Bierce sighed and said, "I will return presently."

Bierce was too genteel to say it, but I knew he was going to the latrine. While he was gone I did what I could to clean up the campsite, returning our possessions and putting empty bottles—every one of them—back in the case they had come in. It appalled me to see just how many of them there were, and that they were all empty. And any time I bent down to pick one up, that idiot deep inside my head hammered another crack in my skull to remind me that I had helped empty them.

As I was putting away the last of the bottles, Juan Romero walked up. He looked more fresh and awake than he had a right to.

"Muy buenos días," he said, flashing me his lopsided smile. "I hope you had a good fiesta."

"Mm," I said. "Where did you sleep?"

"In the tent, *por supuesto.*" His smile widened. "The ground was comfortable?"

"Shut up, Juan."

Bierce reappeared then. His unspoken trip to the latrine had done wonders for him; he stood straighter, seemed more alert, even his clothes looked newly pressed. He must have found water somewhere to wash the grease of sleep off his face and smooth back those silver waves of hair that women seemed unable to resist.

"Good morning, Juan," he said. His voice widened a crack in my skull.

"Señor Beer." Juan touched the brim of his hat. "The *soldados* say we march to Ojinaga soon."

Bierce nodded approvingly.

"A delay will only allow the enemy to entrench himself more securely," he preached. "I approve."

I sat on one of the logs and cradled my aching head in my hands.

"I'm sure General Villa will be glad to hear it," I said. Though I couldn't see it through my hands, I could feel Bierce's glower on me.

"I am sure the general has better things to do than concern himself with the opinions of two gringos," he said.

That awoke something in my memory. I jumped up and immediately regretted it.

"Helen," I said, then clutched my head. "Jesus, Mary, and Joséph."

"I do not usually group my daughter with such company," said Bierce as he pulled out the first cigar of the day.

"No," I said, struggling to hold onto the thought. "I—you need to write to Helen, I need to write to Helen, tell her you are all right."

Bierce sighed dramatically; his breath smoked up into the cool morning sky.

"Amos," he said with exaggerated patience, "I did write to Helen, from El Paso. Perhaps you recall—there was a very irritating gadfly there that looked a lot like *you.*"

"That was weeks ago. It's after Christmas. She's your daughter. Augh . . ."

I sat back down to nurse my head.

"All cogent arguments, I concede. If it will make you feel better, I will write when we get back to town. Does that make you feel better?"

"Ouch."

"Now clean yourself up. We have preparations to make."

I didn't argue, not even to point out that it had been I who had straightened up the campsite while he attended to his toilet. Besides, he was lighting his cigar and I was certain that the smell of its smoke would destroy any last equilibrium my head and stomach retained. I rose and stumbled off to find the latrine and a water-cask.

Chihuahua City was a thrumming hive of activity. Cars, trucks, and wagons hurried around each other in the dusty streets; soldiers in everything from serapes and sombreros to peaked caps and Sam Brown belts double-timed alone or in squads down the sidewalks; a mounted squad of *Dorados* thundered down the street. Civilians clapped their hats to their heads and dodged into stores and cafés to avoid being trampled. The great mobilization was on.

It impressed me greatly, more so in retrospect years on, when Ojinaga was relegated to a footnote in histories of the Mexican Revolution. Juárez, Torreón, Zacatecas—far greater battles had been and would be fought. Yet here was a population on its feet and armed, all to take a piddling little border town that would be forgotten in years to come. The decorations of Christmas were discarded, trampled. Looking down, I saw something caught on the toe of my boot. It was one of the *farolitos*, the paper sleeves that held candles during *las Posadas*. Christmas was truly over and, it seemed, so was the era of goodwill to all men.

We were nearly run down by a howitzer drawn by a frothing team of horses, but managed to get back to our hotel in one piece. Back in our rooms, I took a bath while Bierce sat down to call in a breakfast for us.

Back from the bath, cleaned, scrubbed raw, and decked out in clean duds, I felt like a new man. I came in and found Bierce addressing himself to a large omelet and a steaming cup of coffee. Seating myself opposite him, I took the coffee-pot and poured myself a cup. The coffee did wonders in clearing out the last of the cobwebs in my head. I was just pouring a second cup when Juan burst in the door.

"*Caballeros*," he said between gasps. "We are ordered to leave."

La División del Norte in motion was a stupendous thing to see. And yet we were just a reinforcing expedition, not even the main force. As if by magic the tent-city without the city's borders had folded like so many morning-glories and disappeared. In its stead appeared an army: files of infantry; regiments of horse; and the tag-along parade of cannon, caissons, supply-wagons, and camp-followers. Among the female camp-followers were those who were "no better than they should have been," as the saying goes; but there were also the wives and sweethearts, doing what they could for the war effort by keeping their husbands and boyfriends fed and comforted. Bringing up the rear was the largest assembly of cattle I had ever seen. Someone had told me that Villa and his army had "liberated" 60,000 cattle from northern *haciendas,* and it looked as if they were taking the whole blessed lot with them to Ojinaga. The cloud of dust they raised up blotted out the sun. The whole shebang was part military maneuver, part pioneer wagon-train, part gypsy parade.

One look at the troops, however, would have disabused anyone of the idea that this was all play. These were disciplined troops, marching in precise order; the cavalry units, some in uniform, many the wild caballeros of the desert in catch-as-catch-can and their massive sombreros (how they made those absurd headpieces look not only good but respectable was beyond me—I tried it and looked ridiculous), walking an easy but rigid parade. And all faced the road north with rock-hard resolution.

We had been issued horses and rode among the less orderly troops behind the main cavalry. We walked the horses up the road to Ojinaga (it wouldn't do to tire them so early on the journey), and before long we were coated from the billows of dust our predecessors churned up. Still, the sun shone and the mood was one of suppressed excitement. Jokes and bottles were passed around. I turned back the latter with a smile and a *"No, gracias."* I had never been one to subscribe to the healing properties of "hair of the dog." And Bierce, too, politely passed on the bottle untouched. I knew in recent years he had been cutting back on the alcohol, but this seemed to be something more. We were going into battle, and for all his jests and sometimes boyish glee at the prospect, when it came down to the actual day of battle he was all business. At one point a wave of cheers, yells, and even the patter of gunshots swelled out of the ranks behind us. It grew and grew as it came closer, an irresistible current of excitement. Beneath it all was the staccato fusillade of hoofs; and there rode General Villa, hell-bent for leather on his white steed, racing down the length of his army.

"¡VIVA VILLA!" went up the cry from the Mexicans, and we yelled with them. *"¡Viva la Revolución, hijos de la chingada!"* From the hilarity of our companions you would think we were going to another fiesta.

We were not.

We camped that night some twenty-five miles north of the city. The army moved well but not quickly. Organizing and setting the whole mess in motion must have been long work for Villa and his generals, but they did it handily.

We settled into our own corner of the encampment. After the day's ride and a quick "bath" of cold water splashed over my dusty face, the campfire felt good, soothing. Our usual gang was necessarily dispersed to their respective units, but a couple still remained. Augustín and our maestro, Diego, crouched with us by the dancing flames. It was after dinner, and the sun had gone down in brilliant shades of victory behind the mountains of the west. We stared into the fire, each lost in his own thoughts. Diego drew the bow over his fiddle softly, thoughtfully, wandering after a song he hadn't yet found. The mood was mellow.

"Tell, me Augustín," said Bierce, apropos of nothing. "You have been with General Villa a long time, ¿verdád?"

Augustín nodded.

"Desde el primero," he said. "Right from the beginning, after he came back from his exile. I have fought with el General from Juárez to Tierra Blanca." He leaned sideways and pulled up his shirt on his left side, exposing smooth brown flesh scored by a long white scar. "Torreón," he said proudly. "A pinche Federal shot me there. He won't shoot anyone anymore."

Bierce nodded and removed his hat.

"Kennesaw Mountina, '64," he said, running a finger along his right temple. "A lucky Rebel shot. My brother Albert tended to me." He stared into the fire. He hadn't spoken to Albert in months.

I looked away. I was out of my league here. What would I do, pull up my sleeve, point to the white hairline there and say, "Harrisburg, '71. I got it falling off a carousel"? Augustín spared me the embarrassment.

"It is good to have brothers," he said. "In battle you have many brothers. A mis hermanos," he said and raised up the bottle he had been drinking from. We raised our tin cups of coffee and clinked with his bottle.

"To brothers."

We sipped our coffee and Augustín took a long pull from the bottle. After a silence Bierce said, "General Sherman had it right, gentlemen—'War is all hell.' None knew it better than he, the old barbarian."

"De verás," said Augustín, staring into his own memories in the flames. I watched his face, so still and bronze in the firelight. He was more Indian than Spaniard, and like his indio brethren he had no fear of silence. When the quiet had stretched for a couple minutes, Bierce leaned forward.

"You have seen terrible things in this war," he said. It was not a question.

"Sí," said Augustín. *"Muy terrible."*

"In Tennessee once," said Bierce, "after a battle, we saw wild pigs eating the corpses of our soldiers."

Augustín gave Bierce a troubled look. Bierce didn't look back. I kept my silence; I knew what Bierce was doing.

"Pigs are bad enough," said Augustín. "But men are the worst animals."

"Amen," said Bierce, and nodded.

Silence. I could see a story working its way up through Augustín's soul. He was debating whether to tell it to us. What would these good *gringos* think of the Mexicans if they heard it? What would they think of good Augustín? He licked his lips—he had made a decision.

"Once," he began, "outside Tierra Blanca. We had conquered, *los huertistas* were beaten, on the run, surrendered, dead. I was with a patrol, going around the countryside, looking for enemies . . . ?" He looked a question at Bierce.

"Of course," Bierce said. "On patrol, mopping up, as we say. I have been on such sorties."

Reassured, Augustín continued.

"We found them in an arroyo, way back from the battle. It was getting dark, we were alone, just four of us. And there they were, the *federales,* lying in a neat row in the arroyo. Twenty of them. Somebody had found them before we did." He clamped his lips between his teeth, then said, *"Les faltaron las cabezas y los corazones."* And he made a hurried sign of the cross on his breast.

Bierce frowned, puzzled. His Spanish was better than it had been, but there were still gaps in it. He turned to Juan and me.

"¿Les faltaron . . . ?" he began.

"He means their heads and hearts were missing," I said.

The silence that descended then was far deeper than those before and felt as if it had come from the ancient night at our backs. I shivered and saw Diego put down his fiddle to pull his serape close around his skinny frame.

"An atrocity," Bierce shook his head. "War is a great, sleeping beast. You release it and think you can control it, but after a certain point you cannot." Augustín listened to this statement in English, nodding but clearly not catching it all. Bierce must have seen this for he added in Spanish, "Who would do such things?"

Augustín looked away. *Aha,* I thought. So comes the moment Bierce had been grooming him for these past days. His question could have been taken as rhetorical—what *kind* of person would do this?—but Bierce let it hang in the air to make it specific. I pretended to take interest in my coffee-cup; Bierce listened with feigned casualness. But I, who knew him, could see the tension like wound springs in his neck and back.

Finally Augustín shrugged as if it were no big deal.

"Men," he said. "Just . . . some bad men."

Bierce said nothing, looked intently at the campesino before him. Augustín licked his lips, sipped from the bottle, turned his head to look over his shoulder into the dark. Then he looked straight into Bierce's eyes, leaned forward and said one word, softly:

"Fierro."

Fierro. Villa's bodyguard and one of his generals; the man history would remember as *"el Carnicero,"* "the Butcher." It made a terrible sense. He not only possessed the brutality and resources to do such things, but the authority to get away with them. Any question, if one was even dared to be raised, would be met with the catch-all excuse for savagery in every war—"It was for the good of the Cause."

But I could see Bierce still frowning.

"I have heard stories about him," he said, not wanting to repeat the man's name aloud. "He is a monster; I can believe it. But if I heard correctly, he does all his killing with a gun, *¿no?* And he is only one man. Hard to imagine him 'getting the drop' on a whole platoon of *Federales.*"

"Sí, un pistolero, and only one man. But he is deadly, Señor. He shot three hundred men once." Again he crossed himself.

Bierce and I exchanged looks. *Three hundred men?* It beggared understanding. But even if it were true, something still nagged Bierce.

"So, Augustín," he said, "these *Federales* you found were all shot, then cut up?"

"No, no, not shot. Only . . ." He moved his hands in chopping motions.

"I can't see how only one man—"

Augustín sighed. "Not one man, Señor Bierce. Some men—*many* men. *El Carnicero* has many friends in the army. He is just their commander."

That gave us pause. Professor Navarro had intimated that this movement, cult, or whatever had spread across the country. But "many men" within Villa's army? And among his elite as well? How to tell the good from the bad? We could be sitting in a veritable nest of them right that second. It was my turn to pull my blanket closer around my shoulders.

And my heart went out to Augustín. There, with the firelight flashing gold across the flat planes of his broad Indian face, his soul branded with the knowledge of this atrocity. And what could he do? Who could he tell? No one. Just some old gringo and his tenderfoot friend? Fierro, or one of his lieutenants, would have him dead in some ditch within a day. Villa was brutal, but Fierro was savage. I hoped that, at the very least, telling us would lighten the burden on Augustín's soul.

Then I saw something amazing. Bierce, tentatively at first, then with bluff resolve, reached out and patted Augustín on the shoulder. Bierce was not a demonstrative man, at least not in the department of affections. He could work himself into a righteous fury over the railroad barons or the duplicity of politicians; but expressing closeness to others came hard for him. I could count on the fingers of one hand how many times Bierce had comforted me so, and I had known him those twenty years and more. On the other hand, a lot was at stake here; and empathy aside, Bierce simply recognized that he must maintain and support his source of information. Or so I comforted myself.

"It's all right," he said to Augustín. "We all have our crosses to bear."

Augustín looked at Bierce. I tried unsuccessfully to read something, anything in that flat gaze he gave.

"*Tengan cuidado, las águilas,*" he said, and pointed to the crook of his right elbow. The gesture was foreign to me. It resembled the "*codo,*" a touch to the elbow the Mexicans employ to indicate a cheapskate. But this was different. Augustín upended his bottle, draining away its last amber dregs; rose, and walked off into the night.

Be careful, he had said. *The eagles.*

12.

The next couple of days passed in an endless monotony of dust and discomfort. It was amazing how quickly the enthusiasm of our departure changed into this endless, gritty, noisy slog over the desert. As I've stated before, I find little of interest in desert scenery. This being winter, there was not even the relief of cactus blooms or other colorful highlights. I spent the hours thumping up and down on my horse by telling and retelling myself stories, conjugating verbs in Spanish (in present, preterite, *and* subjunctive tenses), even reviewing multiplication tables. Bierce and sometimes Juan offered conversation, but it was limited by the clatter around us and the dearth of inspiration.

Bierce and I had known each other forever, it felt; so, like an old married couple, we had little fresh to share between us. Juan quickly exhausted the saga of his simple life—born to poor-to-middling parents in Malinalco, southwest of Mexico City, grew up doing whatever, finally settled as a carter driving produce into the city from the gardens of Xochimilco. How he gained the acquaintance of Professor Navarro was a trifle more unusual and interesting. The professor had ordered fruits for a fiesta he was throwing in honor of a colleague. Juan had delivered them and the two began talking. The professor had expressed interest in Juan's home in Xochimilco, which, he explained, held the last surviving *chinampas* or floating gardens the Aztecs had built centuries before. Juan knew all about that; didn't his *arroz* and *frijoles* grow on such swampy mats? So had begun the acquaintance that flowered into an unlikely friendship between professor and carter. Juan beamed with pride over it; proud, too, he told us, of how he had known all about the *chinampas* before *el Profesor* had explained them to him.

"You should see them when *las calendulas* are in bloom," he said, dreamy-eyed.

"'*Calendulas*'?" both Bierce and I asked in unison.

"*Sí, calendulas, como se dice* . . . What you say in English gold-flower, many-gold——"

"Marigold," I said, snapping my finger.

"Ah, *sí*, marigold. When they bloom, the *chinampas* are a field of gold and orange and yellow. We also call them *maravillas*, and truly, it is a *maravilla* to see them all glowing in the sun."

"Your English is admirable," said Bierce. "I wonder that you learned it so well, working as a drayman for fruit vendors."

I could have slapped Bierce. He meant no disrespect, I knew, but the bald way he said things sometimes left something to be desired. Fortunately Juan didn't feel any belittling.

"It's the professor," he said, nodding. "He teached me much about English."

"'Taught,'" Bierce said with an avuncular smile.

"*Sí*," Juan smiled sheepishly. "'Taught.' You have many irregular *verbos en inglés*."

"No more irregular than those who speak it," Bierce muttered.

Our ordeal ended—or rather, changed—when we approached Ojinaga. It was somewhere around the New Year (the momentous year of 1914 arrived without fanfare or even notice for us) when we rode into sight of the small plateau upon which the town sat—if I may employ so grand a term as "town" for that low, crumbled assortment of adobe buildings, sitting alone between the desert and the Rio Grande. We heard the battle at the same time that we espied the town, a distant rattle and crackling of gunfire. Bierce straightened in his saddle at the sound like a hound catching scent of prey. Smoke from the guns drifted slowly up into the desert sky all around the village. Villa had it surrounded with the river at its back. Bierce surveyed the scene with the clear gaze of the topographical engineer.

"I'm surprised Huerta's men haven't surrendered already," he finally opined. From his tone he was clearly not disappointed that they hadn't.

"There are five-thousand *federales* in the town, Señor," Juan said. "General Villa's men have tried, but, *pues,* they are not General Villa."

In the general's absence, his commanders had initiated a siege with an occasional assault for variety; but a month's work had done little to reduce the town. We were among the reinforcements, fresh bodies to replace those laid low by Federal bullets, I guessed. The prospect didn't thrill me.

So we played cards and waited while the generals sorted out their strategy, and watched the battle pop and smoke from safe and distant prominences. At least we weren't being jostled atop a horse all day. Sitting was still a careful experience.

One day during this interlude I left my companions to find water. Villa's supply officers were well trained, and tanks of potable water had been distributed throughout the camp. I walked to the closest and filled our canteens. A tin tub had been set on the ground in front of the tank, and a man was stripped to the waist and bending over the tub, throwing sprays of water over his dark head and shoulders. Something about him, his narrow build, was familiar to me. I filled my canteen at the tank but kept watching the man. He finished his ersatz bath and stood with hands braced against the edge of the tub, letting the excess water rill off his head into it. There was a mark on the inside of his right elbow, right at the crook of it. It could have been a bruise, or a thumb-print—it was the right size—but was neither. It was a tattoo of an eagle, done in a highly stylized and geometric style that I would later recognize as Aztec. He must have felt me staring, for he raised his dripping head and glared at me. It was Lieutenant Bendiga.

"What you lookin' at, *cabrón?*" he said.

"Nothing," I said, swallowing. "Nothing. Sorry."

Be careful—the eagles.

I capped our canteens and walked back toward our camp as casually as I could, all the time feeling the heat from Bendiga's eyes upon my neck. Had he seen that I'd seen? It was hard to know. The man had already formed an antipathy for me. Perhaps that was all. How stupid, I thought, to be discovered by the enemy at the moment I should discover him. I walked on, expecting every moment a bullet between my shoulder blades.

I arrived back at our camp, shaken but whole, and finally dared look behind me. No Bendiga; just the usual slow bustle of the camp. Bierce emerged from our tent and took one of the canteens from me.

"Careful," he said. "You'll spill that water. Are you all right, Amos?"

To my embarrassment I saw that my hands were shaking.

"Let's sit inside," I said, and we entered the tent together. Our cots were there and a camp-stool. I sat on one of the cots—Bierce took the stool.

"What is it, Amos?"

I was pleased to see and hear concern in Bierce's demeanor; it put me at my ease again. I took a deep breath.

"I have seen one of the eagles," I said.

Instantly Bierce was rigid with attention. "Where?"

"Just now, at the water-tank. It was Bendiga."

I had told Bierce about my discomfort around the lieutenant, but he had discounted it as "jitters." Now, I was gratified to see, he took it more seriously.

"Was he alone?" he said.

"Yes. He was bathing and had his shirt off. The eagle, it's a tattoo, right here." And I pointed at the crook of my arm, just as Augustín had indicated some nights before.

"Hmm," Bierce mused, smoothing his moustache. "It's not the most obvious sign, but it's something."

"We can hardly walk around camp, asking people to roll up their sleeves."

"Of course not. But it's a fair guess that if Bendiga is one of them, then some or all of his companions are as well."

"The gang he pals around with around the guns."

"Just so. You were right, Amos, and I stand corrected. Could you recognize any of Bendiga's fellows?"

"Two or three, I guess. Everybody here has that same damned moustache . . ."

"A sin I approve of, you'll understand. Besides, you sound like a bigot. Think hard, Amos—our lives quite literally may depend upon it."

I pondered, watching the soldiers at their chores.

"Yes, I could certainly identify three of them, four if I saw them in Bendiga's company."

"Good. Your pistol is loaded and primed?"

I had to smile at Bierce's antique question: pistols hadn't needed to be "primed" in a long time. Still, I unholstered mine and spun the cylinder to make him happy.

"Six cylinders full," I said, reseating the gun in its holster. "And yours?"

"Amos," Bierce said, looking reproachfully at me. "The very idea—to go unarmed into this hornet's nest."

"Right, sorry. What do we do now?"

"'Hide and watch,' as the Texans say, 'hide and watch.' For the moment there is really nothing more *to* do. We have a villain and we have a tattoo, but no crime. Drilling Señor Bendiga now would be tantamount to murder, and I don't think even General Villa would approve right when he needs all the troops he can muster. Let us hope that the advent of battle unleashes the eagles in our sights."

"And not at our backs."

The following couple of days were nerve-wracking for me. Before I had seen Bendiga's tattoo, the whole notion of a wide-spread cult of Aztec warriors was hypothetical, a fairy tale of ogres. Now . . . I still had trouble countenancing the more fantastic elements of Navarro's tales, such as the revival of pre-Colombian gods; but to see evidence of the cult, and some thousand miles from its supposed fountainhead in Mexico City, made it all that much more real and frightening. Bendiga had transformed in my mind from nuisance to threat. I found myself glancing behind me often, especially in crowds where I couldn't see more than three faces back. To minimize our exposure, we employed Juan to procure us our food and water. His relative anonymity and honest Mexican looks allowed him free passage through the camp without, it seemed, any risk. Augustín and our other campfire friends stopped by, concerned about our reclusiveness; but I put them off with excuses of "*el gringo viejo's* poor health" and how I must act as his nursemaid.

The truth of it was that the old buzzard was better off than I. I was feeling the first creakings of middle age, aggravated by days in the saddle and nights on the flimsy army cot. Bierce, by contrast, was in his second flowering, hale, upright, and with a new flush to his cheeks that made him look like the bridegroom awaiting his bride.

But the bride was a terrible one: war. She flirted with Ambrose Bierce across the rocky, cactus-dotted plains of the desert. Just over there, up that plateau, where the ground smoked with the incense of sulphur and death, she clicked her castanets and bared her bloody bosom to him. She beckoned and he chafed to be with her, embrace her as he had done once as a tow-headed twenty-year-old from Indiana. She was back, big and full and irresistible, and Bierce re-awoke in his desire for her.

Fortunately—or not—his wait for her company was short. It seemed like dragging weeks but was in fact only a couple more days until Pancho Villa, frustrated at his army's inability to dislodge and destroy the enemy, arrived in person with the rest of his considerable force. It was the seventh of January, 1914, and battle was about to be really and truly joined.

The way it came about was thus:

On January 5, the Federal troops had sent a cavalry sortie out from the town to capture one of the *villista* batteries. Communication was poor in our camp, and what started as "an organized withdrawal" (God forbid Villa's army *retreat*) became a rout. The resultant panic was such that it was upon us before we knew what was happening. Bierce, Juan, and I were in our tent when there was the growing thud and patter of many feet, like a rainstorm approaching fast, and the silhouettes of running men sweeping over the canvas of our tent like figures in a mad shadow-show. We grabbed up what we could and joined the rout. We all came to rest a half-mile back from where we had been— without our tent. It made for cold nights, but fortunately only a couple.

When word got back to Villa about this reversal, he was wroth. In two days he was in Ojinaga himself at the head of the bulk of his army, and there was no question that he would leave that field in victory.

I had never been in a battle before, and earnestly hope that I never shall again. Oh, there had been fights, certainly, and the many encounters with the supernatural Bierce and I had had over the years. But not this concentrated man-on-man violence, not this overwhelming noise and fury and confusion, as if the world itself were shaking itself apart.

Then, too, there is the terrible feel of violence between human beings. It had been far easier for me to aim a gun or one of Bierce's anti-manifestation machines at things from Beyond than to level that heavy Mauser rifle at the dusky faces peering over the crude battlements of Ojinaga. I felt alone in my hesitation, too. Juan, caught up in the revolutionary fervor of the country, had no qualms about killing *"los demonios malditos,"* and Bierce took to it with a cold efficiency that scared me. It reminded me of the one conversation I had had with my father about his own adventures in the Civil War.

"We had a job to do and we did it," he had said with Teutonic brevity and finality. There was no further discussion of the matter. Bierce had the same unflinching drive. I would have dreaded to be in the path of that energy.

For us it began on the eighth, the day after Villa arrived and mobilized the troops on the ground before the town. Unofficial "guests" that we were, we were swept up in the assault, charging across the stony hillocks and hollows with everyone else toward where other men were setting their sights on us. Villa held back nothing. I got the feeling that he had thought, after Juárez and Chihuahua, this would be a cake-walk, something he could clean off his boots on the bootscrape of history. The fact that not only had the siege stalled, but that *los pinches huertistas* had actually had the temerity to throw an offensive maneuver at *his* troops, must have sat badly with him. The resultant storm of infantry, cavalry and artillery tore across the desert toward the sleepy little town without mercy.

And yet it held. Ground was gained, the bodies accumulated, and still the crumbling walls held. Clouds of adobe dust flew off the riven walls, rifle-smoke still puffed from behind them, artillery shells hammered down in towering plumes of flame and smoke; but the town held.

Bierce and Juan Romero and I ended up in a hollow, a natural foxhole in the desert, wrapped in our serapes and clutching our weapons as the shells screamed overhead and men yelled and howled and died in the distance. Other groups huddled in similar bowls in the earth nearby, pinned down by the storm of lead flying overhead. It's odd what details one remembers from times like that. I remember the mixed smells of wool and gun-oil as I crouched there. I remember a flat stone on the ground near my head, shaped exactly like my home state of Pennsylvania. Idly I pushed a tiny pebble across it surface until it sat where Harrisburg, the capital, should have been. Smoke blew by. Sometimes it was the pungent smoke of gunfire. Sometimes it was the stomach-churning reek of burning flesh and cloth. A panic rumor of *"el tifus"* spread through the troops, and the dead were being burned outside of camp. Bierce was contentedly smoking; Juan appeared to be asleep. I have heard that a common saying in the Army is "hurry up and wait," and here was the proof. The last couple of days had been long hours of waiting, cleaning our weapons, and attending to our physical needs, punctuated by calls of *"¡De pié, muchachos! ¡A Victoria o muerte!"* Then we heaved our stiff bodies to our feet again and followed the charge across the desert.

The one advantage to this hectic period was that I didn't have time to worry about Lieutenant Bendiga and his gang. They might be stalking us and they might not—there was nothing I could do about it either way. I had no idea where they were stationed (as regular army, they had more exact assignments than we), and if by some chance he should get an opportunity to put a bullet in the back of my skull, so be it. I had as much chance of meeting a Federal bullet head on anyway. Bierce would not leave the battlefield, and I would not leave Bierce.

Then came the big push. Again it seemed that General Villa had had enough of dithering about (if sending thousands of men and women into the hell of battle could be called "dithering") and launched a massive assault on the town. We had just settled down to warm ourselves and devour a quick tamale or two. The evening was clear and bitter cold, I remember. Even near the campfire I pulled my wool poncho tighter around me. Sparks flew up from the fire to join the stars. It was, ironically, peaceful.

Then the air erupted in explosions. They were in ones, twos, then in crazy syncopations one on top of another in a crush of sound. We jumped up, food and campfire instantly forgotten, and looked around us. On either hand in the distance Pancho Villa's howitzers were pounding Ojinaga. Their muzzle-flashes lit up brief scenarios like photographs: gun crews, stripped to the waist even in the winter cold; men standing at attention, men crouching; stretches of bleak, scrub-grown earth; cactus, cannon barrels, and wheels in black silhouette. Suddenly men, officers, and sergeants were running among us.

"¡De prisa, cabrónes!" they shouted. "Get moving—attack in an hour!" So while the howitzers shredded the desert night and sent shell after shell into the town, we were herded and bullied into a loose line of battle. We were not, thank God, and despite Bierce's pleas, in the front line; but it was hot enough where we were. I am no military historian, nor even a former topographical officer like Bierce, so I can't tell you exactly where we were in the battle line. We ran northeast: of that I am fairly sure. After a certain point there was only one direction—"Forward." It was the chilly night of January 10, 1914, and though we didn't know it, Ambrose Gwinnett Bierce was about to leave the realm of the Known and cross into the borderland of Conjecture.

The pounding of the guns made it seem more than an hour. Standing still in the cold didn't help, either. Juan shifted from foot to foot until Bierce turned to him and barked, "Oh, for God's sake, Juan. If you have to urinate, go ahead and do it. I'm sure General Villa will wait."

Juan ducked his head thankfully and ran out into the darkness. When he returned, the cannons ceased. After that barrage the silence rang like crystal. Then came the orders—"*¡Adelante! Victoria pa' la Revolución!*" And in a wave of yells and cheers that dwarfed the banging of the howitzers, we were swept forward.

We trotted over the hard-pack and stone, Juan, Bierce, and I among our loose company of *villista* infantry, lit by the fading campfires behind us. The way ahead was hillock after hillock, what we could see anyway, rising slowly to the eminence of Ojinaga. Hunched backs of men heaved and rocked in front of us, beside us, all around us. My middle-aged lungs rasped painfully as I ran. The Mauser grew heavy in my hands. With a whoop a troop of horsemen, Villa's dreaded Dorados, thudded by on the right at full gallop. The distant crackle of gunfire ahead of us was growing louder, closer. Machine-guns, then a novelty but soon to be the scourge of the Great War, chattered somewhere like idiot skeletons. Individual shots whip-cracked close by us. A Mexican running beside and a little ahead of me stopped suddenly, stood for a moment as if trying to decide which way to go, and then fell onto his face. It was that quick, that random; that meaningless. He just died in front of me. I must have stopped to stare at him, for I heard Bierce yell, "Amos! For God's sake get your head down and *run!*" I didn't need to be told twice.

It wasn't the last death that I saw that night by a long shot. At least the pause had allowed me to catch my breath. But the men were falling more frequently now; that one in the dark sombrero, that poor fellow twenty feet off to the left, this boy—this *boy*—just ahead of me. Darkness and smoke hid the land. Bodies appeared on the ground before me like the reaping of Death. I leapt over them, dodged around them, stepped on them when nothing else would do. An artillery shell hit a hillock to the right, shook the earth and showered us with dirt. I followed Bierce's lead as he ducked behind a rocky mound. Our momentum was broken. Now it was dodge and drop, jump up and charge on again. Bullets razored the air, spat up fountains of dust. A soldier nearby rose to charge, clutched his chest and said, "*Ay, Diosito mío, valga—*" Then a second bullet hit him in the forehead. I turned my head away, sick.

Over the hill, down a gully, up another hill. The air grew thick with dust and smoke and the mingled curses, cries and prayers of men. Someone shouted, "*¡Viva Villa, compañeros!*" and we all took it up. I didn't even realize I was yelling it, too, until my throat began to hurt. We charged on—how far had we run? How much farther to go? I felt the ground tilt forward in our headlong run. Nothing could stop us, now, nothing . . .

And suddenly we were at the walls of Ojinaga. They came up out of the smoke and darkness so abruptly that we stumbled to a stop. I was glad for the reprieve, but Bierce, damn him, looked as if he were going to a party. By the light of burning buildings he was bright-eyed, panting like a hound upon the scent, smiling a slightly unhinged smile—the very Devil himself.

"Pat yourselves on the back, boys!" Bierce said over the popping of gunshots. "You survived your first charge!" A bullet pee-whanged off the stone wall Bierce and I leaned upon. "Why, you ungrateful . . ." he said, shouldering his rifle and charging off into the dark. I sighed. Juan and I exchanged shrugs and followed Bierce into the terror-shot chaos that was Ojinaga.

Later we learned that most of the Federal troops, those who could move, anyway, fled across the Rio Grande—and into the waiting arms of U.S. soldiers from Fort Bliss, Texas. That was yet to come, though. Right now they were doing a damn good job of defending this miserable pile of bricks. As we darted down this street and that, following the old man, we could hear the ragged clatter of the main battle off to our left. At one corner, while we waited to see if the coast were clear, I saw a *villista* standing over a fallen *Federal* in an alley. The *Federal* was badly wounded and was trying, first one arm, then the other, to push himself off the dirt where he had fallen. All the time he was repeating, *"Por favor, por el amor de Jesús . . ."* The *villista* seemed not to notice any of this. Instead he calmly inspected the cylinder of his pistol. When he was satisfied that it was loaded, he snapped it back into place, pointed the pistol at the *Federal*, and shot him in the face. Bierce, mercifully, took that moment to prod my shoulder and lead us away.

I was beginning to feel a deep fatigue take a hold of me for which I could not account. The run across the battlefield had winded me, for sure, but this ran far deeper. It felt as if a lead weight dropped down, down, down through a well in my heart. So much killing, I thought, and it wasn't over. It wasn't even that large of a battle, relatively speaking. As I said before, Ojinaga is barely a footnote in U.S. histories I've read since, sometimes not even mentioned at all. It certainly didn't stand comparison to the bigger battles of the Revolution. Yet it was important because it broke, finally and decisively, President Huerta's power in the north. And it certainly was important to us.

And a lot of men died there—a lot. Every street, every mean, dusty *callejón* we trotted down, was strewn with bodies. We did our best not to become three more of that grim company, but Bierce wasn't making it easy. Being in the battle wasn't enough; he was intent upon our being in the thick of it. There were close calls; once a shot rang out from a rooftop and a bullet chipped the wall near Bierce's head. I, following behind him to protect him, threw up my rifle and squeezed off a shot back at the sniper. The rifle barked, kicked back into my shoulder, and when the smoke cleared, the sniper was gone. My first killing? I don't even know.

No time to ponder it, though. Bierce, too, was gone, running those long, black-clad legs down the next street. Juan stood at the corner, frantically waving me on. I caught up and we jogged after Bierce.

And then we met the enemy. There were four of them, in dirt-smudged khaki of the Federal corps, and they looked as shocked to see us as we felt to see them. We literally ran into them as they came out of a side street. There were even muttered *"Perdónames";* in the shifting dark, it was hard to tell friend from foe. Then we disentangled, stood back—and the guns began their racket. One Federal came at me swinging his rifle like a club. I ducked the blow, kicked him back with a foot to the midriff, and shot without aiming. The soldier cringed, folded, fell. More shots, a cry, thuds of flesh on flesh, and it was over. Three bodies lay at our feet. Bierce stood panting and wild-eyed as ever. His hat was askew, but otherwise he looked unharmed—untouched, even. Juan had a swath of blood across his forehead, but it wasn't his own.

"All right?" said Bierce. We nodded. "Good." And on he went.

At the next intersection Bierce stopped to let us catch up.

"That way," said Juan, pointing to the left. "That way the plaza, the church."

"No," Bierce said slowly. "No—*this way.*" And he turned right and loped away. Juan looked nonplussed, even angry, that his advice hadn't been taken. I could see his reason: men and women *villista* troops were pouring into the town and most of them were headed to the left, toward the plaza and the center of town. The Federals had begun their exodus across the Rio Grande and Villa's troops were hot after them. It made sense to go where the numbers were.

But Bierce had an intuition about some things. I had seen it often enough, and seen it proven right often enough, that I didn't hesitate to follow. I clamped my hat to my head and followed. Juan, after a brief, muttered condemnation of all things *yanqui,* lurched after us.

We came back together again a couple blocks on when Bierce pulled up beside an abandoned cantina. When we reached Bierce he held up a hand—

wait—silence. Without the racket of our own running, we could hear hoof beats approaching. We flattened ourselves against the wall, rifles held cocked and ready, and waited. On they came—more than one horse, but not a charge. Four, five . . . they broke from beyond the corner ahead of us, big and unstoppable, five *villista* troopers in sombreros and bandoliers. They were riding hard for the plaza. At first I wondered at our hiding from them. They were on our side, after all. What better escort could we have? Then I saw the leader's face, in shadowed profile against a burning house; and even in that moment's glimpse I knew he bore an eagle tattoo on his inner arm. The faces of the men who followed him were familiar to me, too. I held my breath as they thundered past, and even after their hoofbeats had faded away in the distance.

Bierce looked after the troop for a good while before he said, "All right. Come on, boys."

We followed him around the corner whence Lt. Bendiga's troop had come and down into a quieter, poorer part of the town. None of the adobe houses in Ojinaga would have been what one would call "palatial," but at least most had been neat and cared for. Here the adobe had fallen away in big patches from the mud-brick beneath, doors leaned in their frames or lay in the street, windows stared glassless at us with idiot emptiness. We went down one street, between a pair of bullet-pocked *casas*, emerged in a smaller street, and stopped. We were facing a short row of houses near the edge of the town. They seemed to quiver in the orange glow of fires. Between and beyond them I could see the stars and the glare of the campfires in Villa's camp against utter blackness. I could hear the raucous shouts of victory, the chatter of the machine-guns and bangs of individual pistols and rifles. But it all seemed so far away. Here there was a silence so solid and so grave that all those noises came to us muffled. It was as though we stood in a rock-walled tomb, listening to the gaiety of the living beyond our reach. Directly ahead of us was yet another gaping doorway; but while the others we had passed had offered only emptiness and a dirty abandonment, this one gaped with a concrete blackness. Smoke from the battle blew across it. I swear that the passing vapors were *reflected* in that blackness. And did I see three, small, pale figures also reflected there, three small, mortal men daring to face that more than night?

Bierce looked back at me.

"You look slightly green, Amos," he said softly. "I assume you feel it, too."

I shuddered a breath and nodded. "How could I not?"

It was something that we sometimes called "the Hand." After so many brushes with the supernatural, both Bierce and I had developed this sensation, something like a hand being placed on the back of the neck. Most people have it to a degree; the writer's "hairs standing up on the back of the neck" feeling, that sense that something is off, wrong. On this cold, catastrophic night in January, we felt "the Hand" distinctly, and it was warning us about that doorway.

Bierce nodded and strode straight to the door. As I moved to follow, I could see that it was now just an empty doorway. Beyond would be just another poor room, a few pitiful sticks of furniture, the humble clay *comal* where meals were cooked . . .

The blackness swallowed Bierce. I followed upon his heels and immediately lost all sight. It's just the drop from firelight to shadow, I told myself, pushing panic down, it will all clear in a second. Even so I bumped into Bierce, who had come to a halt only feet into the building.

"Excuse me" I said, and stepped back.

"Shh."

That was when I felt it, and smelled it. Death had walked big-booted into this room. It was a different feel entirely from the quick, violent, anonymous deaths of the battlefield, dreadful though they had been. This was a heavier death, and more intent. Ceremonial, I thought. Something sacred—or abominable—had happened here. And Death sat here, and you were quiet before him and you showed some respect.

And the smell, that rich, cloying, insinuating mixture of excrement and decay, that smell that takes one days to be rid of. That haunts the nose and saturates fabric. Neither the clergy's "odor of sanctity" nor the novelist's "sickly sweet smell of decay." No: the smell of Death. I tried to swallow again and again.

Bierce, now faintly visible to me though barely feet away, moved slowly around the edge of the room. Juan had come in behind me and I heard him gasp.

"*Ángeles me protejen,*" he whispered. He circled around to the left, leaving me alone in front of the doorway. There was something sitting in the middle of the room. I was blocking my own light from the doorway, so I moved to one side. The sitting figure grew from the darkness into a pile of stones, a rough pyramid of stones and crude clay bricks, maybe four feet high. What could be so terrible about a pile of bricks, I have wondered since. What subtle arrangement of its parts, the dim, hesitant light on its rough facets, a trick of proportion? To this day I cannot say; yet the vision of that pile, years old now in my memory, still has the power to terrify me. It stood in that awful room like the last pylon of the world; or the first sign of the next. *Beyond this, Mystery.* As my eyes grew used to the dark, I saw that the cairn was stained with black, running in thick lines and pooling in its dust-choked corners. Beneath the latrine-decay stench of death I smelled the iron tang of blood.

Then my clearing vision picked out the bodies around this horror. There were four of them, dressed in what remained of the slate-gray uniforms of the *federales.* There was something wrong about them, their proportions. Their shoulders looked too high, too broad. They had no heads. And their tunics had been pulled up to disclose gaping incisions just beneath their ribcages. From the cuts blood had flowed freely and stained the figures' brown skin slick and red.

"Dios," Juan gulped and ducked into a doorway beside him. I could hear him wretching. I staggered to the wall and studied myself against it. Everything was spinning, lurching in sickening, monstrous swoops. Only Bierce appeared solid, stable, immovable. He had his rifle at his side and he stared down at the carnage before him.

"You will notice," he said in thick tones, "that the bodies are arranged according to the cardinal points of the compass."

"Bierce," I said, barely keeping myself upright. "For God's sake—"

"This is significant," he said. He was pointing at the body nearest him, but looking at me. His tone was not quite that of the impatient professor now, but more of the sage who needs to impart something vital to his acolyte. I straightened myself up as best as I could to reply.

At that moment the light from the doorway was eclipsed. Juan had emerged from the other room and the three of us looked at the newcomer. He was bulky, and his big sombrero cut the light like a demon planet. At first he was just a silhouette, but a familiar one at that. His head swiveled toward me and he said, "Ah, Señor Littlefault. *¡Qué chiste!"*

It was Gordito, *compañero* of our campfires. But what did he mean by "what a joke"?

His silhouette changed again. He lifted up his right hand and pointed a pistol at me. From this foreshortened point of view, it was nothing but a gray-rimmed hole pointed at my face, the bottomless hole into which I was about to plunge.

Gunfire erupted all around. Flames shot out from the shadows and lit up the doorframe and bodies in heartless relief. Gordito flashed into view in staccato flashes, a nickelodeon film of shock. He jerked and crumpled, shuffling a step or two back toward the doorway, and dropped like a bag of cement. Waving the gunsmoke out of their faces, Bierce and Juan approached the body, holstered their smoking pistols. A thudding of retreating hoofs came from outside.

"Damn," Bierce said. "He had company. Quick—get him inside." I helped him drag Gordito inside by his feet. From his slack weight I knew he was dead. We dragged him into a corner away from the doorway so that he wouldn't be readily found.

"The rest will be back soon," said Bierce. "We have to get out of this place." He wiped his hands on his handkerchief as if to wipe off all the killing.

"Amen," I said. Then: "Wait." I bent down, took out my pocket knife, unclasped it, and stabbed it into Gordito's right sleeve. I yanked the blade down and tore open the sleeve all the way to the wrist. In the fleshy hollow of Gordito's elbow, an Aztec eagle spread its wings.

"'By this sign shall ye know them,'" I quoted as I stood up. Bierce and Juan leant down to examine the tattoo.

"Just so," said Bierce. He leaned out the door a little and looked up and down the street.

"There's another horse there," he said. "Our erstwhile friend Gordito's, I have no doubt. How inconsiderate of him to have left only the one."

I looked out across Bierce's shoulder. There was the horse, pawing nervously at the dirt street. Beyond it the scene of cracked adobe walls shifted in and out of smoke like cheap stage sets. In the murky depths of the streets between, things may or may not have moved like creatures at the bottom of a well; things may have walked on two legs or four, padding slowly, purposefully toward our hiding place.

"There's more than that horse out there," I whispered.

"A *lot* more," said Bierce, and we withdrew into the hovel again.

We had the advantage of the besieged, but for how long?

"If we can get to the corral," Juan said, and left unfinished what we all were thinking.

"'If' being the operative word," said Bierce. "It's a long walk back to our camp." He looked around the room. "Juan," he said, "was there any egress from that other chamber?"

"'Egress'?" The Mexican wrinkled his brow.

"Una salida," I said. "A way out."

"No, no, nothing, no way out."

Bierce ducked quickly through the doorway into the other room anyway, and we followed. We didn't have many options at that point. Within this room it was even blacker than the first, yet a cleaner blackness somehow.

"There," he said. He pointed toward the base of the room's back wall. A few points of flickering light shone through the wall there. When we looked closer we saw that the wall had been partially dismantled.

"To make the *pirámide*," said Juan, pointing back to the other room.

Bierce scratched a match into fierce light and we went at the loose bricks and mortar, digging with hands, knives, and finally feet, kicking the rough bricks into the night beyond. When a hole big enough to admit a man had been opened, we stood back from it.

"After you," Bierce began, but I shoved him toward the hole. It wasn't a time for niceties. When he was through I pushed Juan in, and with one final look at that awful house I followed.

The ground fell away from the back wall of the house and down toward the lights we had seen flicker through the gaps in the wall, and we half tumbled out into the dirt. We twisted as we slid down, keeping one eye and our guns trained on the crumbled building we had just quitted. Off before us, the barely audible rumor of our camp. Its lights looked impossibly small and distant to me, like the mocking glint of unreachable stars.

We kept to the shadow of the buildings as far as we could. Beyond that, the firelight from the town threw and jerked our shadows out into the desert before us. It faded in a few yards, but we took no chances and ran, expecting at any moment to hear and feel shots at our backs.

Away from the town and the light of destruction we picked our way among the hillocks and thorny desert growths. Our night-vision returned maddeningly slowly; but the starlight, much stronger here in the rare desert air, helped. Before us the slope spread out in silver-blue with the dark, fantastic shadows of each cactus and creosote bush, standing here and there like dumbshow spectators to the town's destruction. Beyond these, the campfires of Villa's army. And away to the left of these, the low, evil lights where the dead were being burned.

Once or twice a lone soldier ran by us on toward the conflagration in Ojinaga. Another time it was a man on horseback, and by unspoken consent we hid from them all. Seeing Gordito revealed as an agent of the Eagle-knights had shaken our confidence in our safety and anonymity. If the jovial, harmless Gordito could be among the enemy, anyone could.

"Our enemies will send out patrols," said Bierce after the horseman passed. "The camp will be too dangerous."

"But we have to get our horses," I said.

"We have to get *some* horses," Bierce corrected me. I looked at him in the darkness.

"That sounds suspiciously like horse-thievery," I said. "The general himself was once accused of it—"

"Probably with good reason."

"And almost shot for it. He won't take kindly to someone stealing his army's horses, Bierce."

"He won't care if he doesn't know."

We were getting closer to the camp now. We had intentionally strayed farther toward the corpse-fires, hoping that there would be fewer passers-by and patrols there. We got as close as we dared and hunkered down behind a sprawl of prickly pear to plan our next move. When the wind shifted, a thick, greasy, stomach-wrenching pall of smoke drifted over us, bearing the perverse smell of roasting pork.

"It's all academic," I whispered to Bierce. "The camp is like a hive that somebody has kicked. We wouldn't survive getting to the corral."

"Then we'll have to go dead."

I aimed a puzzled look at him, but he pointed out toward the fires. A pair of *campesinos* had appeared near the fires. They were walking in a stilted way a constant distance from each other, one after the other like two parts of the same wind-up toy. When they passed in front of one of the fires, we saw that they bore a stretcher between them. Upon the stretcher was what looked like a very dead soldier.

We exchanged glances, nodded, and I jerked my head at Juan to follow us.

Bodies were not hard to find. Though the taking of Ojinaga appeared total, it had come at a cost. The landscape through which we had snuck was littered with fallen *villistas*. Some hugged the ground as though asleep; some gaped up at the starry heavens as if in wonder. None would miss their clothes. Still, it took a little looking to find both the right fit and something not too badly stained. I found a sombrero that fit near a fallen caballero, and an unstained white cotton blouse and calzones—the ubiquitous white peasant pyjamas—on one poor devil who had been shot through the head. These I put on over my own garments, not relishing the touch of dead man's clothes, but grateful for the extra warmth and disguise. Across the blouse I hung two bandoliers. With the application of some soot from an abandoned campfire, I thought I made a tolerably convincing *campesino,* as long as I stayed in the shadows.

"Well?" I said, standing up to let Juan inspect me. And he said the strangest thing. Looking me up and down with an expression of amusement and wonder, he said, "Sheep."

"'Sheep'?"

He shook his head.

"*Nada,*" he said. "*Nada,* no, nothing. You look good, *puro mexicano.*"

It puzzled me, but we had little time for puzzles. From the body of a tall *soldado* who appeared to have walked into a storm of machine-gun bullets, we took a blood-soaked shirt. Bierce was more fastidious than I, more fastidious than anyone I had ever met, really. But he was also a brutal realist when the situation demanded it, and with a grimace he pulled the bloody shirt on over his own. For good measure he rubbed his black jacket in the dirt before putting it on over the shirt. Then we went in search of a stretcher.

We had made it almost all the way back to the camp and were despairing of finding our prop, when we stumbled across one leaning against a bush. Juan and I laid it upon the ground and opened it. Bierce hesitated.

"It's now or never," I said. "You're the one who wanted to come to Mexico to die. Now's your chance."

"All right," he grumbled. "It reeks of cowardice, though."

"It reeks of common sense and desperation," I said, "unless you want to shoot your way through the whole blessed Mexican army."

With a sigh he walked the length of the stretcher, sat down upon it and lay back. Those long legs reached just beyond the canvas. God, I thought, he looks seven feet tall. It would be a stretch—no pun intended—to convince anyone he was just another dead *mexicano.*

He closed his eyes and took three, deep breaths. He grew terribly still. And when he lay his hands at his sides, I had a premonition. This is another of those intangibles, like "the Hand," that many will write off as superstition or a misinterpretation of the ordinary—"more gravy than grave," to quote Mr. Dickens. But men in an occupation such as ours—men such as Britain's John Silence or the irrepressible Carnacki, or Germany's Dr. Hesselius—can't afford such vagaries. Our lives depend upon "intuitions" of this sort, and we take them very seriously. Consequently, when that feeling of premonition swept over me, I shivered. There's nothing I can do, I thought, bleak and alone; there's nothing I can do, and my friend Ambrose Bierce will die.

Bierce's eyes opened.

"Well?" he said, pinning me with that gaze. "Do I have to lie here all night or are we going to the party?"

"Right, Bierce. Sorry."

Juan and I bent and grabbed the handles of the stretcher. We raised Ambrose Bierce into the air and began shuffling into the camp; and I put my premonition away into a dark corner of my mind. But I did not forget it.

We came over a shoulder of the land and of a sudden we were in the life of the camp once more. Soldiers, *soldaderas,* and camp hangers-on bustled about, gathering up ammunition and weapons for the front, helping the wounded to the medical tents, praying over the dead. We moved among it all as unobtrusively as possible. Just another poor *muerto* being brought back to burn. No one gave us a second glance.

Until we had almost reached the fire-pits. "Pits" was a euphemism for shallow trenches gouged out of the sand, into which were thrown the dead and a covering of cut brush. The whole mess was then set alight. We had smelled the greasy smell of it before. Then it had been an annoyance, a note of disgust to add to the symphony of fear around us. Now it was overwhelming. The pits were a hellish place.

Just short of the pits a horseman rode up. He clattered out of nowhere so fast I thought he would run us down. When he had reined in, he looked down at us. I recognized him as one of Lieutenant Bendiga's pals, a sleepy-eyed brute who had once shot a man for laughing too loud. He had his rifle out.

"*Órale, chamacos,*" he said to Juan as we set our burden down. "Who you got there?"

We set the stretcher down. I moved off a few paces where the light was poorer, tilted my sombrero to shade my face, and pretended to fuss over a nearby body.

Juan, bless his heart, played his part well. He pushed his hat back on his head, squinted up at the *caballero* and smiled.

"*El gringo viejo,*" he said. "The *federales*' machine-gun stitched him a new shirt. At-at-at-at," and he swept the night with an imaginary Maxim gun.

From where I stood the bloodstains on Bierce's shirt were plain to see. But the horseman seemed dubious. He leaned over in the saddle and pushed back Bierce's jacket with the rifle barrel. I put my hand to my Colt.

"*Caray,*" said the horseman. "They really chewed him up."

Bierce never twitched. Even when the *caballero* dismounted and drew a long, wicked-looking knife and bent down toward him. I saw Juan tense, and under the cover of the crackle of the fires I thumbed back the hammer of my pistol.

But the horseman merely set the blade of his knife over Bierce's mouth and nose. He was checking for the telltale fog of breath. There was none; the blade remained clear. To be sure, he even bent down and put his ear to Bierce's chest.

"Bueno," he said, straightening up and shoving the knife back into its sheath. "That's one. You see that *gringo pendejo* friend of his?"

Juan shrugged broadly.

"¿Quién sabe? We found *el viejo* up that slope——" He pointed into the darkness, back whence we had come. "You're welcome to look."

The horseman regarded Juan for a long few seconds. Juan just smiled that idiotic smile back. Finally the horseman snorted, pulled his horse around, and galloped off. I let the hammer back down on my Colt and rejoined Juan at the stretcher.

"Good," I breathed. "Let's get Bierce out of the light."

We carried Bierce off through the inferno of the burning-pits, the mean, crackling glow of burning bodies, the oily smoke, and past into the night. Around at the backside of the camp stood the corrals and lines where the horses were kept. While still out of the light we set Bierce down on the ground. I leaned down and put my hand to his heart.

"Bierce," I called softly. "Ambrose Bierce. Come back, now." The body beneath my hand was a still and cold as stone. Not a beat, not a breath.

"Come back, Ambrose Bierce," I repeated. Was that a beat, a faint tick as of an insect's step in that old chest? It was, and another. Bierce's eyelids fluttered and he took a long, deep breath. His heart gave a lurch beneath my hand. He brushed my hand away and sat up, looking around.

"I assume we have eluded capture," he said.

"By the skin of our teeth," I said. "I thought one of Bendiga's thugs was going to cut you a new windpipe."

Bierce looked up at me with interest.

"Really?" he said. "You'll have to tell me all about it—some other, more opportune time."

I wasn't arguing. We had dodged a bullet, real and metaphorical, back there at the fire-pits. I'm a believer in luck, but not in pushing it. While Bierce stretched and completed reawakening his old body, Juan and I snuck up to the nearest horse-line and liberated three strong-looking beasts. They were horses, but, as Bierce observed, not our horses. Looking for those especial creatures would take too much time. And I reflected again on the irony of our making our escape on stolen army horses. Such a crime had once nearly earned Villa a visit to the firing squad. It would surely do as much for us if we were caught.

With that at the front of our thoughts and the fall of Ojinaga at our backs, we turned our new horses south, and rode off into the night.

PART II
Desesperados

1.

The sun rose as bright as a marigold upon a field of blue. It dyed the desert a soft salmon, purple shadows stretching from the spiny clusters of cactus and scrub.

We had ridden all through the night; but exhausted as we were, we would have ridden longer.

Once, late, we heard the oncoming drumbeat of hooves that we had dreaded, and we rode quickly behind a rise in the land. We had little hope of outrunning our pursuers; we hadn't the energy. But we could show them a good fight, and dismounting, we prepared to do just that. Once ensconced behind some rocks with our guns drawn, we sat and waited as the hoofbeats thundered down toward us.

We didn't have long to wait until we saw our pursuers. I counted three men on horseback as they broke from the chaparral and charged into the open, a quarter-mile off.

But these weren't Villa's men. These wore the peaked caps and gray of Federal troops, recognizable even at that distance in the hard starlight. And hard upon their heels came . . . *something.* It was late, mind, and we were exhausted by all that we had been through. If I say that it resembled a large, running cat, a man on all fours *imitating* such a cat, and a flow of viscid waters, I will not be unfaithful to the nature of the thing. As I say, it was some distance away and we were tired enough to have been hallucinating. Suffice it to say that something large was in pursuit of those *federales,* and was gaining at a terrific pace. We watched the panicked parade race through the vale and disappear behind the next hillock. It was unreal, dreamlike; yet like a dream, it stayed in the memory. I wondered why the riders hadn't just shot the thing. But fast upon that thought came the response, *Maybe they had.* The hoofbeats faded, and, as if reading my mind, a gun was fired twice. Then all was silence again.

This, to say the least, gave us all pause. We had all seen it, yet none of us could agree on just what we had seen. A jaguar? I had some idea that they didn't roam that far north. A puma, then? Bierce was surprisingly silent on the whole subject.

Tired and stunned as we were, we rode hard the rest of that night. At first light, however, I looked down and saw that I was still dressed in a dead man's clothes. It hadn't even occurred to me during our flight, but now I couldn't bear the thought of another mile in them. Bierce was in agreement. We halted and peeled off the offending raiment, burying it where we stopped and muttering a thanks to the dead men who had lent it to us. May they rest in a peace ignorant of the inconceivable deaths of others.

I felt more comfortable after quitting the disguise, more comfortable still when the sun rose higher and burned off the chill on the desert. This is not to say it was warm, but it was tolerable. Our mounts were fine beasts. They trotted easily along, galloped when we judged the terrain safe for them, and gave as smooth a ride as possible given the conditions. Somewhere, I mused, three very angry *caballeros* were cursing us to *el Diablo* and back. I might have felt bad about it if I hadn't felt relieved just to be alive. Our lives were worth their inconvenience.

We were safe but tired—very tired. We had been awake and going for twenty-four hours, hours that included a major battle, a discovery of dreadful murder, and a hair's-breadth escape from remorseless enemies. I was dog-tired, so tired that I rocked in the saddle, faded in and out of a half-dream doze, and didn't care whether I fell off or not. Some instinct of preservation must have persisted, though, for I urged my horse on unconsciously to keep up with the others.

But if I was tired, Bierce looked exhausted—completely spent, a shadow on a shadow horse. The great energy that had fired him and carried him through the days before was gone. In its place was a frightening void; not even lassitude or resignation, just—nothing. His asthma was back, too, I saw with concern. I had hoped that the desert air and the rising altitude would have held it back, but he slumped in his saddle and coughed.

More, though, he was an old man, and the night's exertions had told on him. I knew they did on me, aching in every joint and too tired to lift my canteen to slake the thirst that made my throat raw. It must have borne down upon Bierce terribly.

But we still had a job to do. As weary as I was, I recognized that Bierce needed to be reminded of this, to know that he still had a purpose. I prodded my horse up beside his.

"How far have we come, do you think," I said.

"Thirty miles, perhaps . . . little more." He stared straight at the horizon.

"How much farther do we need to go? To be safe, that is?"

He was silent for so long I thought he hadn't heard me or had forgotten the question. Then he mumbled something.

"Beg pardon?"

He drew a breath as if he were pulling it from the bottom of a mine.

"I said . . . never."

I felt as empty as he looked. I suppose I had assumed that once we were clear of Villa's forces . . .

"Huerta, you mean," I said. "And the Colorados—"

"No. Not . . . *them*."

We rode in silence. Day bloomed around us. The spiky, inhospitable plants of the desert took shape, defined and bristled. Away to the west the Sierra Madre Occidental spread its folds in purple, sand, and rose.

"Torreón," Juan said abruptly. "Torreón, maybe?"

Bless you, Juan. I took heart.

"Torreón, you think? And how far is that, Juan?"

He shrugged.

"Two, three hunnerd mile, *más o menos*."

Más o menos. I looked out across the uncaring miles and thought *más o menos* could spell life or death for us. Consider: we were in the heart of the desert, on three stolen horses; we had no food, but for a lucky stash of jerky found in one of the stolen saddlebags; and no water but what three not-quite-full canteens held. And most of that must of necessity go to our horses, for without them we wouldn't reach more water anyway. That pitiful tally had to support us over three hundred miles of wilderness, *"más o menos."*

Still, the alternatives seemed worse—at the moment. To return to Villa's forces meant either a frightful death at the hands of our enemies or, if we were lucky, a quick trip to the firing squad. Before us, the questionable safety of Huerta territory. So we kept to the desert, moving just east of south, paralleling the National Railroad line between Chihuahua City and Torreón but far enough out into the waste that we wouldn't be spotted. We hoped.

By late morning we had had all we could take. I called a halt and we dismounted in a small depression that would shield us from the casual view of any potential pursuers. Bierce was all in. I helped him down off his horse, something I had never had to do in twenty years of adventures together. He let me do it, too, which was even more unprecedented. Afterwards I guided him to where I had draped my serape over a Spanish dagger bush to give him some shade. With my hand on his elbow he felt like a walking skeleton, weightless, insubstantial. Now and then he gave a short, wheezy breath. And he said nothing. I was very worried.

Juan, meanwhile, undid Bierce's saddle from his horse and set it under the bush as a pillow. As I eased Bierce back onto it, he said something so low I couldn't catch it.

"Pardon, Bierce?"

"So many deaths," he said in a voice scarcely breath. "So many . . ." And he fell asleep.

Once I had Bierce comfortable under the serape, I turned to Juan. He had hitched the horses to a log of deadwood and was standing, fists on hips, surveying the countryside.

"You want to rest first or shall I?" I said.

"You rest," he said. "I wake you in a while."

I was too tired to argue.

"Thanks," I said. "Just give me a couple hours." I trudged off to one of the less uncomfortable corners of our hollow and dropped myself onto the dirt like a marionette whose strings had been cut. After settling in and wrapping my coat around me, I lay back and looked up. High up in the middle of the sky was a bird, a mere black cross, circling. It was a dark bird, and so high that I couldn't gauge its size. My eagle, I wondered. Then I slid into sweet sleep.

2.

When I awoke the sun was already in the western half of the sky. I sat up, gritty, groggy, face smarting from sunburn. I got up and walked to where Juan was sitting on the ridge enclosing our camp.

"Thanks, Juan," I said. "What time is it?"

"Three, four, ¿quién sabe?"

I started.

"That late? You should have awakened me. You must be exhausted."

"You needed sleep, I can watch. It's okay."

"Well, no, it's not okay. You've got to sleep too, and then we have to get going."

He pointed down to where Bierce still lay, fast asleep on his saddle.

"Señor Beer, he need sleep—mucho sleep. Un viejo like him, he thinks he's tough, but he can't go like a couple chamacos like us." He grinned at me. "Let him sleep—Pancho Villa can wait."

Like it or not, I saw the wisdom in this. Bierce really did need the rest—

anyone could see that. I could only hope that Villa and his minions were too busy mopping up the Federal nest at Ojinaga to bother with three horse-thieves like us. As for the Eagle-knights, we'd have to trust to luck.

Juan stood up, stretched. He walked down into the hollow where Bierce rested beside our horses. I kicked a couple of rocks aside and sat down on the hardpan. I took out my handkerchief, unscrewed the cap on my canteen, and dampened a corner of my handkerchief. I dabbed it at my face. It felt good, cool on the sunburn, and pleasant to clean the charcoal and dust of the trail off my face. I knew it was probably the last such wash of any kind I'd have for a good stretch, and I relished it. When I was done, I took a sip from the canteen, but just a sip. It only took a glance around to remind me that it was not a place to be wasting water. I screwed the top onto the canteen tightly, rested my elbows on my knees, and settled in to keeping watch.

The sun rode its slow path down into the west. Night spread over us, cold and aeon-deep. The heat of the day was leaching out of the ground into space, and it wasn't long before the cold found its way through my clothes and through my skin into my very bones. I stood it as long as I could; then rose and walked down into our hollow. My serape was still pinned to the Spanish dagger, but the old man it had been rigged to protect was gone. Where had Bierce gotten to, I thought as I wrapped the serape around me. I was pleased, on one level, that he felt well enough to get up on his own. But to be wandering alone in the desert . . .

I saw him as soon as I climbed out of the hollow. He was standing to the east, a cut-out silhouette of a famous man against the spangle of stars and the last glow upon the mountains. At a glance he appeared as still as one of the cacti that loomed in unearthly shapes around him; but then I caught the faint wisps of his breath dyed blue by the starlight. He might have been praying; I knew he was not. He had his own personal pantheon of ghosts, and more than likely he was communing with one or another of them. Slowly, and scuffing my feet a little to announce my presence, I walked over to him.

"A lovely night," he said as I came up to him. "For all its barrenness, the desert does offer this inviolate silence as recompense." He drew a deep breath (for which I sent up a prayer of thanks) and stood listening.

"Juan tells me that we're headed into a place called '*la Zona de Silencios*,'" I said. "The Zone of Silences. Perhaps we are already there."

I saw Bierce's shadow-head nod.

"Juan has proved an asset indeed. And you, my lad. I must thank you for tending to me in my weakness." There was a coloring of shame in his words that went to my heart. I shrugged as nonchalantly as I could.

"We all need an extra hand now and then," I said. "That's what friends are for."

"Indeed. But I look forward to the time when I may return the favor."

I could have reminded him of the countless times that he had done that already; of the dangers and wounds and sickness that he had pulled me, his so-called "assistant," through twenty years of association. But it was too much. Between two men in that place and time, such tendernesses weren't spoken. They were understood.

"Well," I said, a trifle too loudly, "I'm sure the Mexicans will give you the opportunity ere long."

Bierce grunted.

"No doubt they shall. Speaking of which, and with Señor Villa in mind, perhaps we should break camp and proceed."

"Juan lay down to rest just a short while ago, Bierce. I'd like to give him a little more time."

"Just so. Then let us join him, shall we?"

We walked back into the hollow and found places that weren't too uncomfortable. I lay back and pulled the serape close up under my chin. And looked up at the black sky and its spray of stars. So many, I thought, more than even in the country back home. It was as if I looked into a new sky entirely, looked into a thousand unknown and unnamed constellations. And the silence was enormous. It was the hush of respect for the great church of night.

It was with these last ruminations that I must have fallen asleep, for when I next was aware of anything Juan was gently shaking my shoulder.

"Señor Amos," he said quietly. "*Despiértate*—wake up. We gotta get goin'."

I blinked and started to unravel myself from my serape. It was still dark, and the stars still stared down at us with timeless patience. Across the hollow the deeper shadow of Ambrose Bierce was standing by the Spanish dagger.

"Three A.M.," he said. "Time to leave." The click of his watch-case shutting put a period to his statement.

In five minutes we were mounted and headed south again. We hadn't dared light a fire this soon after our escape, so the ride was a cold and stiff one. Again we saw the sun rise over the mountains to the east; again, the desert reformed itself around us. The landscape was rumpled in places and made the going slower. Somehow we managed to gather the miles behind us. The hours passed in silence.

But when the sun had risen a hand's-breadth into the sky it thawed us out, and we began to chat. It must not have been important talk—mere-chatter—for its content is long lost to me. But it kept our spirits up and held the monotony of riding at bay. Now and then one of us would twist in the saddle to look back the way we had come. There was a tacit expectation in each of us, I think, of seeing a troop of devil-horsemen riding down upon us. But they never came. Only the triple trail of our horse's hooves, stretching over the still landscape back to scenes of slaughter.

The next few days passed in near identical simplicity; the clop of the horses' walking, the idle banter between us, the unrolling landscape of sand and rock and desert growths. I learned, under Juan's tutelage, the different flora of the region. There was the organ-pipe cactus, tall and formidable, often used as a very effective fencing around haciendas; a large, dangerous-looking bush of bayonet-like spikes called, of all things, *"lechugilla,"* "little lettuce"; the ubiquitous prickly-pear, old friend from Texas, with its many-faceted arrays of lime-green paddles, a handy source of nourishment and water in a pinch; and barrel-cactus, squat and round and looking for all the world like the Devil's footstool. Juan assured me that in the infrequent rains of spring the cacti would bloom.

"Such blooms, *que hermosas son*," he said. But even without the blossoms I acquired a new appreciation for the plants' beauty. This was enhanced when I leaned the culinary benefits of prickly-pear, or *"nopalito"* as it is known in Mexican kitchens.

Overall it wasn't the ordeal I had feared it would be. The cold was intense at night, but after that first night we deemed it safe to light a campfire. And during the day it warmed to a pleasant temperature. We often rode in our shirtsleeves. We were spared, at any rate, the annihilating heat of summer.

Food and water remained our primary concern. The former was supplied, when the jerky was gone, with the rare game we encountered. One day it was a javelina, one of the fierce desert-pigs. One day it was a rattlesnake, stupid with cold, that Juan surprised from under a rock. The creature had barely begun its terrible rattling when Juan drew his machete and swiped off its head—*snick*. The cut was so quick and so clean that the snake's head dropped from it body as if by magic, still hissing and snapping.

"Good food," Juan said, holding up the snake's body to our dubious gaze. "The *aztecas* ate many *culebras* like this one. Made them *muy fuertes, muy machos*." The headless body twisted and coiled in his grip. I had my doubts, but beggars can't be choosers, as the saying goes. What does rattlesnake, grilled over a campfire taste like? Another cliché says that it "tastes like chicken." I suppose a certain kinship between bird and reptile exists, to believe the latest archaeological findings. But to me it just tasted like snake.

Water was a more pressing concern. Our canteens emptied alarmingly quickly, mostly into our hats to serve the horses for troughs. One morning we awoke to a dusting of snow, and this we scrambled to scrape up before the day's warmth melted it. By our third day the need for water had passed from pressing to dire. The few drops we allotted ourselves made no dent in our thirst; our lips split; we thought about water constantly.

"The Conchos is only miles that way," Juan said, pointing westwards.

"So is the road to Chihuahua," Bierce said, "and perhaps Huerta's troops."

"We have little choice," I said. "Perhaps there is a section of the river less frequented . . . ?"

"Might could be," said Juan. "But we can try."

We rode westwards into the afternoon sun. The ground grew hillier as if waking up, and our passage slower.

But luck was with us. Just before sundown and somewhere, we figured, not five miles from the Conchos, we smelled the clean, young, and welcome scent of water. Then we heard it, running down out of the hills, a tributary of the Conchos. The busy noise of it clapping over its rocky bed was music to our ears, and at sight of it we had to keep out mounts from running down the scree to plunge in. As it was, it became a contest between who, men or horses, would get to thrust their dry faces into it first.

After we had slaked our thirst, filled our canteens, and let the horses drink and wallow to their hearts' content, we turned back southwards. Night was falling, but it was still too close to the haunts of men for our liking; so we rode on until it was full night and we were sheltered beyond the hills again. There we lit a fire and ate our cooked rattlesnake and were content.

South again. The sun curving its way across heaven, the nights star-shot and still. Then late one day, we heard a new sound in the long distance. Campfire stories of *"La Llorona,"* the phantom mother who haunts the empty spaces, searching for the children she murdered, came to mind—and, from my companions' expressions, came to theirs as well. It brought us to a startled halt; but in a moment we recognized that long, musical wail for what it was.

"A train whistle," murmured Bierce as if it were the most wonderful thing in the world.

It was indeed a train whistle, and soon, low upon the southern horizon, we saw a line of smoke prolonging itself out east to west over the land. It was coming from the direction of a dull, brownish sierra—nothing new there. We had passed hills, rises, and sierras to last us our lives through already. But now we looked more closely. Smoke rose in a few pale threads from its slopes.

"A town?" I asked Juan.

"Puede ser," he said.

In another hour we were riding west of the sierra, skirting its dark rumpled slopes until we hit the rail-line. The train was long gone by then. We followed the rails back into the cut in the slope, hoping that the dying of the light and the long shadows would hide us from any prospective snipers. We wouldn't have dared it except it had been one of Bierce's bad days, and I wanted to get him a few moments of rest and civilization before we went on. Our water was low again, too. We counted on the famous Mexican hospitality to provide us with both and save us from whichever army was ascendant in the area.

So we approached the town slowly and carefully. It sat in the lap of the Sierra; a small, flat Mexican town with little to differentiate it from those we had already seen except its curious location out in the desert. A sign on the train station reading SIERRA MOJADA—"Wet Mountain"—both explained the town's location and encouraged our thirsty souls. Streets of humble, whitewashed buildings, the quiet sounds of a town settling in for the night. The church tower, predictably, was the highest structure in town.

After replenishing our canteens and horses at the town fountain in the plaza, we stopped at the first café we came to; for all I know the *only* café in that sleepy town. Bierce irritably waved away my attempts to help him dismount, but allowed me to guide him to a table inside with my hand on his elbow.

It's amazing to think what this little interlude inspired. In our brief time in Sierra Mojada , no more than half an hour, I should say, we set in motion one of the great theories about the fate of Ambrose Bierce. The café owner and one weary-looking patron were the only residents of the town we met, so it must have been from them that set the ball rolling. They saw Juan and me carefully guiding Bierce to a chair and they saw us help him outside again when we had finished our tortillas and coffee; and by the time a *gringo* investigator came through some years later, we had grown to a squad of soldiers escorting *el gringo viejo* as a prisoner to a firing squad. Perhaps there was another *gringo viejo,* for surely *somebody* is buried under the plaque to Bierce this investigator put up. But it isn't Bierce. He was pretty worn down that night, but he walked out on his own legs.

Similarly I've always wondered about our escape from Ojinaga and its consequences. That friend of Lieutenant Bendiga who questioned Juan when we were carrying Bierce on a stretcher must have told others about the "body" we were bearing to the burning-fields; and no doubt, passing soldiers noticed us, too. In years since I've heard the competing theory that Bierce was killed at Ojinaga and his body shoved into a common grave with the other fallen *solda-dos*. What a laugh Bierce would have had over these "deaths" of his. It saddens me to think I cannot share that laugh with him.

Refreshed and a little nervous about the possible presence of soldiers near-by, we put our backs to Sierra Mojada and cantered out into the desert. Ironically, it was a relief to get away from civilization again, even the diminutive civilization of that place. It smelled of men. And our time in the desert hadn't been all bad. After the bustle of Chihuahua and the chaos of Ojinaga, the over-powering quiet of the desert spaces was balm to our nerves. Even the struggle to keep ourselves warm, fed, and watered rendered our senses keen, gave us a sense of mastery over our lives, that had been lost in the tide of revolution. A rattlesnake might bite you, a scorpion might sting you; but these things they did out of defense and their nature. Men just seemed to like to inflict pain for the pleasure of it. Being clear of such monsters for a while was a relief.

3.

After Sierra Mojada the way became easier. The landscape became greener, the vast wall of the Sierra Madre Occidental galloped out of the west until we were almost among its skirts. And we had decided to wander back to the world of mankind. Even with the nightly stops, I could tell that the journey was wearing on Bierce, both physically and mentally. His temper grew shorter—a sure sign that he was getting bored.

"Damn it, Amos," he said one overcast day as we clopped along. "I came to Mexico to be where something—*anything*—was happening. And for the past two weeks all I've done is ride."

"You must have been lovely company between battles in the war."

This earned me a smoldering look.

"Don' worry, Señor Beer," Juan said. "There is plen'y of war to go 'round."

"'*A*-round,'" Bierce said and retreated into a merciless study of the de-sertscape.

Juan's words were prophetic. Three days south of Sierra Mojada we came to a road; and two miles down the road, a telegraph pole with the bodies of three men hanging from it. We smelled them almost as soon as we saw them. The sun had baked their skin to leather; their six feet pointed straight down as if trying to reach the ground they'd never know again.

"Plen'y of war," Juan said, and crossed himself.

There were tilled fields along the road now. The spiky brush of the desert withdrew behind us, to be replaced by gentler bushes and deciduous trees. It was a pretty country, less demanding on both the body and the soul than the desert had been. My eyes were fairly thirsty for green and I stared at the thickening plants with relief.

And there were houses, too, or the ruins of houses. Doors stood ajar, windows gaped black and empty. I began to wonder where everyone had gone, but stopped myself. I knew where they had gone.

But the houses of the living increased as we went along as well. A huddle, a village, a hacienda where men in chaps circled wild-eyed horses; nearby, a pergola hung with the sad remains of last year's vines.

In the early afternoon, in the heat of the day, I decided we needed another halt and water. Bierce said nothing, but the wheezing undernote of his breath was eloquent enough. We approached a fence of towering organ-pipe cactus, broken only by a gate. Beyond it, across a bald yard maybe fifty feet deep, was a house; no hacienda, but neat in its borderline poverty.

Juan had barely reached the gate when two men came out of the house. They came closer and resolved into a man of middling age—a few stray strands of gray in his thick, black hair—and a tall, gangly boy. Both carried rifles.

"*¿Qué quieren?*" asked the man from halfway across the yard. "What do you want here?"

"We've ridden a long way, amigos," said Juan in Spanish. "My friend"—he pointed at Bierce—"is very sick. We'd like to rest, eat, have some water for ourselves and our horses, if it doesn't trouble you."

The man and boy stopped several yards short of the gate, close enough to look us over but far enough back to get a good shot if needed. Finally the man came forward and looked through the bars of the gate at Bierce. Bierce returned his look—and wheezed. He couldn't have chosen a better moment for it. The man nodded and began unlatching the gate.

"I'm sorry," he said. "In days like these, you can't be too careful."

"We're very grateful," I said, tipping my hat as we walked our horses in.

"Much obliged," breathed Bierce.

"*Muchisimas gracias,*" said Juan.

Our prospective hosts stepped aside to let us pass, but I noticed that the boy kept his rifle at the ready, his finger on the trigger. The man re-latched the gate and led us to a rude shack off to the right of the house. Within its scant shelter an aged and swayback chestnut chewed hay. He gave us one glance, snorted in equine derision, and resumed munching. We dismounted and led the horses in, and the man threw down some hay for them as well. They attacked it the same way I'm sure I would have attacked a steak just about then.

"I am José Martínez," the man said, and put forth a strong hand. We shook it in turn.

"Amos Littlefault."

"Ambrose Bierce, your servant."

"Juan Romero, *a sus órdenes, Señor.*"

Martínez turned with a smile to the boy.

"And this is Ernesto. Ernesto! Lower the rifle, now!"

Ernesto had brought his rifle to quarter-arms. At his father's command, though, he dropped it completely in the dirt.

"*Ay, caramba,*" sighed Martínez. "It's always a lesson with this one. Pick it up, Ernesto, and go tell your mother we have guests. *Vengan, Señores.*"

The boy did as he was told and ran to the house. We followed at a more sedate pace.

The house's interior echoed its exterior in mood—everything worn, many things patched or glued, yet all neat and clean. It was lit with a scattered array of candles and a kerosene lamp. There was pride in this house. We all removed our hats upon entering. Juan closed the door behind us. A large, plain table, attended by a diverse assortment of chairs, dominated the center of the room.

"*Mi casa es su casa,*" José said with a slight bow. In the light we got a better look at José and his son. José was a little shorter than I but equipped with the sturdy body of a farmer. His black hair was short, almost shaved on the sides in the style that was becoming more popular. His eyes were black as sloe but filled with a wary kindness. He had the requisite mustache and wore worn blue overalls over a flannel shirt of faded green. Ernesto had his eyes but little else. He looked fourteen or so, and his loose frame loomed at least an inch over his father's. Hair as thick and lank and blue-black as a Chinaman's flopped over his forehead and half-hid his sullen, curious gaze.

We stood like earnest schoolboys, hats in hands, until a woman came in from an inner room, wiping her hands on her apron and looking as us as if we were bears loose in her house. She was pretty in a solid, no-nonsense way, long brown hair pulled back in a bun and sharp, brown eyes. A younger, thinner version of herself followed, trailed by a boy of six or so.

"*Señores,*" José said. "Let me present you to my wife, Ángela, my daughter Araceli, my second son Benito. Ángela, these men rode from far away and come in need of food and shelter."

"Oh no," I said, putting up a hand. "We won't impose upon you. We only need to rest a little and we will go."

"No," said José and waggled a finger at us. "No, you are my guests. You will stay here tonight, I insist."

I was amazed at this generosity. So, it seemed, was Ángela, who, as José passed her on his way into the house, said, "But José, *¿dónde . . . ?*"

"*Calma, calma,*" he said and ushered her into the other room. The kitchen, I assumed. The most amazing aroma was issuing from that door, and my stomach growled royally in response.

"Sit," the girl Araceli said with a nervous smile and a wave toward the table. Juan and I sat, but not Bierce.

"I should like to freshen myself before dining," he said with polite gravity to the girl, who wrinkled her faultless brow and looked to us.

"He would like to wash before eating," I translated. The girl's face reformed into a laugh. It lit up the room.

"Of course," she said. "Follow me, Señor." She led Bierce back out through the front door. In a moment we heard the squeaking bray of a pump in the front yard.

Martínez and his wife and younger son reappeared from the kitchen bearing plates, forks, knives, and a large steaming clay pot of whatever was giving off that heavenly aroma. Benito bore a platter of tortillas behind his mother with all the dignity of a ring-bearer at a royal wedding.

The table was set, Bierce reappeared, miraculously groomed, and we all set to the feast. José led us in a brief but solemn grace. We all finished with "amen," all except Bierce, atheist or agnostic or whatever he was that week. Even he, though, nodded politely at the prayer's conclusion. He may have had no respect for organized religion—"a gross paradox," he liked to say—but the rules of courtesy were sacrosanct to him.

Ángela ladled out bowls from the pot. When mine came around the table, I saw that it was a thick stew, floating with carrots, potatoes, onions, and bits of spice. I speared a bit of the meat in the mixture and looked at it. Not beef, not pork . . . The smell of it was pungent, gamey, familiar.

"*Cabrito,*" José said with evident embarrassment. "It is all we have."

Goat—of course. The odor had reminded me of *chevre,* goat-cheese, that same peculiar scent. I put the meat into my mouth and chewed.

"Delicious," I said, and meant it. Both José and Ángela looked pleased, almost relieved. Bierce leaned over to me.

"What is this?" he said quietly.

"You've often said you were hungry enough to eat a goat," I said. "Well, now's your chance."

He frowned at his bowl, shrugged, and dug in. From the avidity with which he devoured it, I'd say he enjoyed it very much. It may also have been that two weeks' diet of jerky, *nopalito,* and snake had honed his appetite to a fare-thee-well.

Dinner done, Ángela and Araceli cleared the table and politely but firmly refused our help.

"Women's work," said José with a happy shrug. "Ernesto," he said to his son. *"Las copitas, por favor."*

The boy rose, said *"Sí, papa,"* and walked to a sideboard painted in red with busy floral designs crawling all over it. From the top he removed a bottle and several small clay cups, fired a deeper, earthier red than the sideboard. While he placed these on the table I admired the honey-gold of the liquid in the bottle. José spread the cups in a row, uncorked the bottle, and tipped some of the liquid into each of the little cups.

"*Con permiso,*" said Juan, rising. "Been a long day. I think I'll stretch my legs before catching blinks."

"'Winks,'" Bierce and I said together. Juan gave us a weary wave and stepped out the door.

"Well," José said, recorking the bottle, "more tequila for us." He pushed a cup to each of us, raised his own and said, *"Salúd."*

Bierce raised his on high and said, in his most official voice, *"Salúd, dinero, y amor, y el tiempo para disfrutarlos."* Then he upended the cup into his mouth.

We stared at him in amazement. "Health, money, and love, and the time to enjoy them." He had repeated the traditional Spanish toast without a hiccup or a pause. He finished his cup with a smack of the lips, set it down on the table with a *thunk,* and looked around at us.

"Where on earth did you learn that?" I said.

"Don't look so surprised," Bierce said. "I had weeks in Laredo, waiting for my lackadaisical assistant to show up. Do you think I wasted all that time?"

I raised my own cup to him.

"Leave it to you, Bierce. You couldn't translate your way through a greeting card, but where drink is concerned . . ."

He crumpled a frown at me, but next second laughed. I raised my cup to him again and sipped. As a rule I do not care for hard liquor. Dutchman that I am, beer is my drink of choice. But I have to admit that I did like this. It was smooth and slightly smoky in character. When I had finished it, I joined Bierce in requesting *"un otro, por favor."*

Full, relaxed, and pleasantly inebriated, we all settled in to our chairs.

"So," José said, "if it doesn't bother you, tell me where you are from."

Bierce and I exchanged glances, but I felt we had no choice. This man had trusted us enough to welcome three filthy, armed men into his house. The least we could do was return his trust—albeit with a certain lack of detail.

"From the north," I said, and pointed to where I hoped north was. "The United States."

"*Sí*, of course. I knew you were *grin*—*norteamericanos*—the moment I saw you." His quick correction from the slightly pejorative "gringos" to the more proper *"norteamericanos"* reassured me. He sipped his tequila and added, "And where do you go?"

"Mexico City." From the edge of my vision I saw my companion look at me, but I ignored him. José sipped, nodded.

"*El De Efe. Qué padre.* I've never been there. They tell me it is grand, beautiful. I went to Chihuahua City once, when I was a boy . . ." He smiled sleepily at something far back in his memory. "This is a great country," he continued. "You must not judge us by today. These are evil days, dangerous days." He shook his head sadly. "These *revolucionarios, Constituciónalistas,* whatever you call them—Madero, Obregón, Villa, Huerta. It isn't like the old days of the *Porfiriato*." He shook his head again and drank again.

"And thank God it isn't."

Our heads all turned as one to the new voice. It was Ángela, fists on hips in her kitchen doorway. From the look on her face, I'd have sooner charged the guns of Ojinaga again than confront her. Bierce and I rose as one.

José turned in his chair.

"Ángela, *querida* . . ."

"No, José, don't you remember? President Díaz was a vampire"—she actually used the word *vampiro*—"sucking the life out of poor people like us, supporting the *hacendados* and making them all rich."

"But, *querida,*" José tried again, "he brought us the trains, the telegraph . . ."

"And when was the last time you used either a train or a telegraph, José Martínez y Torres? Hmm? Never, that I've seen. *Muchisiams gracias, Presidente Porfirio Días,* and good riddance."

José looked chastened but muttered, "He brought order."

"So does Don Máximo," Ángela said, raised her eyebrows significantly, and strode back into the kitchen.

José sighed.

"Your pardon, gentlemen," he said. "An old argument."

"And not peculiar to your good house," I said. "Governments fall over this question: order or freedom?"

"*Exacto.* And this freedom we have now, the freedom to be conscripted, to be tortured, to be hanged. President Díaz wasn't perfect, but he brought order, peace. These *cabrónes* we have now, they let loose something terrible on the countryside, something . . . *animal.*"

When I had translated this to Bierce he sat forward eagerly. He put a hand on my wrist and said, "Translate for me, if you please, Amos." He licked his lips.

"Tell me," he said to José through me. "You speak of something *animal* loose in your country. May we take this figuratively—or literally?"

My Spanish may not have rendered every word exactly, but the meaning clearly got through. José looked at Bierce in an odd, unreadable way for a few long seconds, twirling his little cup between his fingers. Finally he put the cup down and leaned across the table towards Bierce.

"*Fíjese,*" he said, raising a forefinger before him. "Fix this in your mind, Señor Bierce. There is something, some *things,* that are killing our animals and our people around here. Few have seen it, and no one can stop it. It tears out of the night and kills and maims and eats, and no one—*no one*—can stop it. We have told Don Máximo about this, pleaded with him to stop it, but he . . ." José threw up his hands. "He cannot stop it. Or he *won't.*"

"And who, pray tell, is Don Máximo?"

"Don Máximo Golón y Alvarado. He is our *patrón,* our *cacique.* How do you say it in English? 'The Boss'? He owns our town of San Andrés Tecolotzán. He says who stays, who goes. He buys the grain we plant, sells what we harvest, runs the *fábrica* de tequila where your drink was made, and he keeps the bandits away."

"Seems there are bandits, and then there are bandits," said Bierce sidelong to me.

"But surely you have the Rurales, the rural policemen, for that?" I said.

José barked a laugh.

"Don Máximo *is* the police. Or his *pinche* nephew, Rodrigo, is." He snorted. "Rodrigo is the lieutenant of the Rurales around here. I think he got the job only because the uniform wouldn't fit Don Máximo's fat sons, *que el Diablo les tomen.*"

Bierce said, "You sound less than pleased with this Don Máximo, José. Why don't your townsfolk get rid of him?"

"Because, who holds the guns? Don Máximo. And besides, we'd only be trading him for a worse evil."

"That animal, you mean."

"Yes, among other things. Another *cacique,* maybe more brutal than don Máximo. It's order versus freedom again, *¿ya ves?* El don and his family take what they want around here, money, food . . ." He trailed off and looked toward the kitchen door, beyond which his wife and teenage daughter were settling the kitchen for the night. At that moment Araceli herself came in with a stack of plates. We watched silently as she lay the plates upon the sideboard. She was so young, as graceful as a gazelle—not a day over fifteen, surely. What a weight for her parents to bear, that the local strongman's sons could swoop down upon their farm any day and . . . And nothing they could do about it.

I looked at Bierce. I knew this was a tender point for him. His relations with women had not always been chivalrous, let us say, but he would abide no violence against the fair sex. His eyes glared blue-white beneath his shaggy brows, and his mustache bristled like the whiskers of a cat on the prowl.

"Ask him, Amos," he said in a chillingly quiet and even tone, "once more about the animal."

José considered while he poured us all another round of tequila.

"It comes at night, as I told you. And it's *big.* The old people call it *'la onza,'* and its papá was a tiger and its mamá was a lion. But it's greater and more powerful than either of these. Some say it runs like a beast, some say it flies like an eagle. They also say it is a *brujo,* a sorcerer, a man who can turn himself into the onza at night and back to a man during the day."

Bierce and I exchanged a glance.

José continued: "Men from Torreón, from the city, we have told about this creature, but they laugh at us. *'Demonios,* ghosts,' they say. *'Cuentos de hadas*—fairy tales, amigo. You've got a rogue puma on your hands, nothing more.'"

José swallowed a mouthful of tequila.

"Not so, *Señores*," he said, wagging his finger at us. "The puma we know and he stays away from our guns. He doesn't like our smell, ¿*m'entienden?* But this one comes right into the village as if it knows it well. It lives here as a man, have no doubt.

"But who? This is a small town, everyone knows everyone. Unless it's some old man out in the *monte* . . ." He pondered this through alcohol-thick eyes.

The tequila was getting to us all. For me it induced a cozy languor. For Bierce I had thought it had been lulling him to sleep—until the subject was changed. Now he looked as if all the fumes of alcohol had been blown away by a cold wind, leaving him alert and energized.

He said, "Is there a particular time or night when this *'onza'* roams abroad?"

"Dark of the Moon," said our host. "A night or two, more or less."

"A couple nights hence," mused Bierce.

At that moment Ángela came back in, herding her children. We all got to our feet, unsteady but polite.

"Time for bed," Ángela said. "Kiss your papa now."

Araceli, little Benito, and Ernesto all dutifully came forward and kissed their father, who embraced each one as if they might fly away from him at any moment. Bierce watched this, swaying a little on his long legs, and I watched him. Two boys and a girl; the ages and order of the children were a little off, but Bierce could not fail to see the similarities. Especially when Ernesto came up, and José shook his hand, hugged him, and kissed his cheek. The first-born, so full of promise, so like his father. Bierce quietly coughed into his fist and cleared his throat.

As Ángela herded them back out, she turned to us and said, "There are blankets that can be spread upon the floor here. *El Viejo* may have Ernesto's bed—he will sleep with his brother. *Buenas noches.*"

We all muttered *"buenas noches"* in return.

"Well," Bierce said when they were gone. "A most illuminating evening. I must thank you again, Señor Martínez, for your hospitality. We are in your debt, and"—he coughed, *abrup-brup-brup*—"and anything we can do for you and yours, we most assuredly will." Cough again—*wheeze.* "Amos," he said, arching his finger at me. "Your company, if you please."

He opened the front door, exited, and closed it behind him. I moved to follow but José grabbed my arm.

"Tell me," he said. "Your friend is very sick. What is it that ails him?"

"*El astma*," I said. "He is stronger than he looks, but sometimes the asthma is stronger. That is why we took a chance, asking for your shelter."

José cupped his chin in his hand.

"Hmm," he said. "I think I know of someone who can help him."

"Really? We would truly be in your debt, if that were so. He has tried many doctors, many medicines. Mostly he just suffers through it."

"Ah, but he has not met Mamá Huitzil."

I left then to join Bierce. I found him on the house's creaking front porch. He was looking up into the skies with perfect attention. The moment I approached, though, he snapped back to earth and faced me.

"Amos," he said, his voice taut with excitement, "this is a great discovery—what the scribblers call 'a scoop'!"

"I had the same thought, but I have my doubts, Bierce. I'm inclined to believe what the men from Torreón said—a mean catamount, nothing more."

"Oh, come now, Amos. This bears many points in common not only with our shape-shifting friend in the desert, but with the Marlowe case as well. Surely you cannot have forgotten that."

Surely I could not. It had been one of our more poignant cases; a beautiful young woman accursed before birth with an animal possession. Bierce had turned it into his celebrated tale, "The Eyes of the Panther," but I knew it was no fiction. I still awoke some nights in a sweat, seeing Irene Marlowe's wide, green eyes staring into mine.

A word or two on the entity known as the shape-shifter. Among the zoology of the outré that Bierce and I had compiled over the years was the shape-shifter, a being that could change itself from its natural state to that of another creature. The popularly known entity called a werewolf is one such being, but the choice of animal is not restricted to just the wolf. Factors such as the skill of the shape-shifter himself or herself, and the patron-animal of the person, determine the shape-shifter's form. Sometimes, as with the doomed Miss Marlowe, the change involved is involuntary. Sometimes the change is voluntary. Such skill bespeaks a great talent in the Black Arts. Eagle-knights, Jaguar-knights . . . could it be?

"There are similarities, I'll grant you," I said. "But even if this were another such case, it isn't our concern."

The big cat's whiskers bristled again.

"Is it not?"

"No, Bierce, it isn't. It's a distraction from our primary mission. Surely you haven't forgotten that."

"No, young man, I have not. And I will beg you not to lecture me upon my responsibilities again. And further, the tequila must have dulled your senses appreciably for you not to see the connections here. The two cases are one in the same."

"Shape-shifters and Eagle knights? I fail———"

"Yes, you fail. Moreover you fail to connect it all to our near confrontations in Ojinaga and beyond."

The smoke-draped streets, the shapes that may have walked upon two legs, may have walked upon four . . . Something that ran like lava across the desert floor . . .

"But," I said weakly, already knowing I had lost the argument, "we are still far from Mexico City."

Bierce smiled.

"Ojinaga is farther." The smile faded. "We are well on our way and can afford a slight delay. What is more, this is most certainly our concern. These people have shown us the utmost courtesy and generosity from their limited means. If I can aid them in any way, I shall. That young girl . . ." His gaze was far away and achingly sad.

I could have argued against a vain chivalry; I could have argued against a transposition of affection from Bierce's own shattered family to this poor Mexican one. But I did not. The alienists whose theories Bierce himself had used in his fiction would, I have no doubt, have supported me wholeheartedly. But they could not see that empty, searching look in Bierce's face; could not hear the tenderness in his voice, a tenderness his legions of enemies would never have recognized. In the end this was Bierce's show, for good or ill, and I must stand by him.

"All right," I said. "José has indicated that he knows someone in town who can help you with your asthma." Bierce started to fuss, but I cut him off. "You want to play Sir Galahad for this family, have at it. But I won't have you galloping off to battle with half a lung. Those are *my* terms. Besides," I said to ameliorate him, "it will be the perfect excuse to go into town to reconnoiter."

He looked askance at me for a moment, but finally nodded. I knew he'd like the military lingo.

"Excellent," he said. "We think independently, it seems, but not at least at cross purposes. Did José indicate the nature of this treatment or its practitioner?"

"No. Someone named Mamá Wistful, I think."

Bierce chuckled.

"Well, there's no denying that the expensive medicos back home have done me no good. Might as well try the local witch-doctor. Now, Amos, you will excuse me briefly before we retire."

"Of course, Bierce."

He stepped off the planks of the porch and crunched across the dirt yard until he faded into the blackness. Juan took that moment to materialize out of the night and stand by me.

"The beds are all ready," he said. Then, squinting after Bierce, he said, "I have seen him do this before, in the desert. Where does Señor Beer go?"

I took a moment before answering. Bierce had stopped at the far side of the enclosure; no more than a blacker shadow against the bristling wall of organ-pipe cactus. We could just hear his voice coming softly through the silence.

"Mr. Bierce," I said slowly, "sometimes needs time alone to think and to—commune."

Juan turned a shadow frown at me.

"No te entiendo," he said.

"Here," I said. "Let's sit."

We sat in a pair of weathered chairs and looked out across at the old man's silhouette.

"Years ago," I said, "Mr. Bierce had a family, a family much like this one—a wife, two sons, a pretty daughter. He loved them dearly, but his other duties kept him away from them. His elder son, Day, especially, was the hope of Bierce's future. He was blond and handsome like his father, and like his father, headstrong and impulsive."

Juan snorted.

"Claro que sí," he said. "Señor Beer, he has a head like an ox."

I smiled at the comparison.

"Day fell in love with a girl," I said. "The girl ran off with Day's best friend. He followed them, shot them both. Then he shot himself. He was sixteen years old."

I let the statement hang in the air. It was so simply stated, so bald in its tawdry particulars; yet it held so much importance to understanding who Bierce was, his priorities, traits, and actions.

"Caray," Juan swore softly. *"Qué horror.* And the other son?"

"Leigh was an aspiring writer, again like his father. And like his father, he drank too much. He passed out on the street one New Year's Eve, got sick, and died." Again, a pause in deference to the dead. "Bierce divorced his wife over a trifle. She's dead now, too. All that is left is the daughter, Helen. It was she who sent me after Mr. Bierce, to make sure he was safe."

"Araceli," Juan said, and nodded.

"*Eso*. And for that reason, we may be staying here for a few days."

Juan nodded again.

"*El Mayor* is a man of honor. I respect that." He tucked a nod at Bierce. "And he goes to pray alone. So he is a religious man, too."

I choked back a laugh.

"No," I said, wiping my eye. "No, no, no, ye *gods*, no. He is most certainly not a religious man. He goes alone to speak with his son, Day."

"*¿Qué?* Then, he is *loco?*"

"Well, I'm sure there are many who would agree with that, but no. Ambrose Bierce is one of the sanest men I have ever met. I don't know whether he hears his son answer him, or believes the boy's shade watches over him, but it soothes Bierce to talk to him. Even if it's only in his mind."

Juan nodded. The hidden creatures of the night scuttled and sniffed and clicked around us; and across the poor yard, the great man spoke with the ghost of his son.

4.

Ernesto led Bierce to his bed, and Juan and I settled into the impromptu pallets laid out for us on the dining room floor. In the morning we awoke to the children stepping over and around us on their respective chores.

"*Buenos días,*" Ernesto said with a broad smile. It seems our value in his eyes had gone up overnight.

"*Buenos días,*" I croaked. I could still taste tequila, and from beneath my blankets came a ripe smell of unwashed man. Good God, I thought with horror. And these good people let us in to their house, smelling like this? The cold of the desert and just plain familiarity must have dulled our senses to it over the past days. Aside from a quick, frigid splash in that tributary of the Conchos days ago, I couldn't recall when we had last had a proper bath. I sat up against the wall and drew my legs up to get out of the children's way.

"Ernesto," I said in Spanish. "Is there somewhere we could take a bath?"

That smile again.

"*Por supuesto, señor.* I will show you the tub."

The tub was outside; in its own enclosure, tacked onto the back of the house, it's true, but still outside. And when Ernesto handed me a bucket and pointed to the pump in the front yard, I knew I was in for another cold dunk.

While I pumped and lugged water back to the tub, he brought me a bar of hard, yellow soap, a threadbare towel, and his father's razor (mine having been lost with everything else in Villa's camp).

It was as cold as I had anticipated. I washed quickly and donned my clothes. I shaved using the same yellow soap and, lacking a mirror, managed it by sense of feel. It wasn't the Ritz, but it made me feel a whole lot more human. Lastly I dumped out the water from the tub and went in to apprise the next victim of his bath-time.

"Good morning."

Bierce was already sitting at the table with a large mug of what I hoped was coffee steaming before him. He sat straight, his white mane was combed and brushed into its usual waves, and his suit was so neat it looked almost pressed, for God's sake. I knew that he could spend as much as two hours on his personal toilet in the morning, even camping in the Sierra Nevada back home; and it must have been as much of a relief for him as for me finally to get clean. Yet he looked as if he had just walked out of the Army & Navy Club in Washington, while I felt I must still look like a hobo. The one new feature about Bierce's appearance, and it was a surprising one, was the rough beard that still whitened his cheeks and chin.

"My God, Bierce," I said and rubbed my own newly scraped chin in sympathy. "You look like Father Time."

"I think it rather suits me," he said while gently smoothing the beard with the back of his hand. "Besides, a little disguise cannot hurt in this business."

"'Little' is right. You stand out among these people like a white birch among yews. If you were any whiter, you'd be transparent."

Bierce's inevitable retort was cut off by the arrival of Ángela and Araceli carrying plates of scrambled eggs, beans, and tortillas. More coffee appeared, too, thank the gods. The smell of it brought Juan, José, Ernesto, and Benito in from the front porch, and we all tucked in.

"We'll take the wagon," said José, obviously continuing a conversation from the porch. "I need to buy some supplies anyway, and I can drop you at Mamá Huitzil's."

"This Mamma Huitzil," said Bierce, making it sound like some German food. "She is a doctor?"

"No, not a doctor, really," said José, spooning up eggs and beans. "We have a doctor, Dr. Segovia, but he is mostly for Don Máximo's family. The rest of us, we can't afford him. Mamá Huitzil is a *curandera,* a healing-woman." He looked slightly embarrassed. "Back when we were *indios,* we always had a *curandera.* She knows a lot about healing herbs, illnesses, how to make a man more *macho*."

"But can she cure asthma?"

I was proud of Bierce for not dismissing the woman out of hand. He was rewarded with a vigorous nod of the head from José.

"She can cure anything, Señor. When our Benito had the fever and was like to die, she saved him even from the arms of Death." He turned and ruffled the boy's head. "And we pay whatever we can pay. Sometimes its money, sometimes it's a chicken or a goat or a bag of corn meal. She never turns away the unwell, bless her."

"The free market at its best," said Bierce. "Well, let's go see this wonder, then."

"Sí, vámanos ya."

Done with breakfast, we helped José roll his buckboard out of its shed and hitch it up to his lone horse. He left Ernesto and Benito with instructions for chores, then he and Bierce vaulted up to the wagon's seat while Juan and I hunkered down in the bed.

It was a slow, bumpy ride of several miles into town. But the sun shone and the chill had burned off, and the scenery was increasingly welcoming. Though it was still winter and the fields bare, it was a relief just to see healthy, tilled soil after the desolation of the desert. There were trees, too, real, blessed trees, some in scrappy-looking orchards and many backing the fields. In summer, I thought, their shade would be welcome. One immense field we passed was planted with blue-green explosions of agave. They stretched into a distance of blue haze.

"Don Máximo's *fábrica de tequila,*" said José, pointing to a cluster of shacks bordering the agave. "That's where they make it." My understanding of the word *"fábrica"* was of a factory, and I suppose that my *norteamericano* perspective envisioned tall, neat, brick buildings and smokestacks. But this, with its tin-roofed sheds and an ancient mill-wheel yoked to a discouraged-looking donkey, looked more like a farmyard to me. Still, we couldn't argue with the product. I rubbed my forehead in memory of the punch the tequila had given me.

We passed other *ranchitos* and stucco houses. They multiplied as we approached the town proper; spreading down dusty roads to left and right, peopled by housewives batting rugs, children playing in the dirt, and evil-looking dogs. One and all watched us pass with a bald curiosity. The road we were on became a street, and the street bore us down into the close-walled town of San Andrés Tecolotzán.

It lay in homey, semi-ordered, blocky array in a gentle valley. Most buildings only aspired to one story, but the town church stretched its white-washed tower at least three stories higher above them. People at their chores waved as we passed. It was a picture of bucolic peace.

But just shy of the town center we came across a thick wall standing alone to the right of the road. What building it had once been part of, we could not tell. Its fellow walls were gone, the stones hauled off, no doubt, to help construct other buildings. The rash of bullet-holes that pocked and pitted it, though, proclaimed clearly what its use was now.

"El paredón," José said, pointing to it. "Sometimes that's where the soldiers shoot their prisoners when they pass through. Mostly, though, it's used by Don Máximo."

We rode on down into the narrow streets. The town's houses and storefronts, often merging one into the next, defined the street with their straight, gaily painted walls. José reined us in by the second-to-last building on such a particolored row. The buildings to each side were ochre, sky-blue, yellow. Our destination was a deep carnation pink broken by a doorway and two windows, deeply recessed in the adobe and bordered by mustard-yellow shutters. Upon the pavement beside the open doorway stood a black sandwich-board lettered in chalk:

Mamá Huitzil la Curandera
Puede curar lo que quiera

_____

Té de Cedron
Para la comeson
También para la hinchazón
Y para ese barrigón

_____

Té de la ruda
Para el que estornuda
También para la Cruda

José led us through the open door and into a darkness heavy with the scents of drying herbs. It made my head swim, but it wasn't a bad smell. Rather, it was as if Summer herself had slipped in there and gone to sleep. As my eyes adjusted I saw the herbs hung in serried rows from the roof-beams; shelves groaning beneath the weight of ceramic jars labeled with this or that ingredient; a wall-board bristling with nails from which hung tiny silver effigies of arms, legs, hands, animals, and hearts; a workbench with knives, a mortar and pestle of volcanic rock, twigs of mint and rosemary, and what looked like an eagle's talon; and overseeing it all, a large, framed image of a Madonna with a decidedly Mexican face. The icon was next to a doorway hung with a Mexican blanket done in descending shades of blue and green. Before the doorway stood a table with two chairs, and upon one of the chairs sat an old woman. Like many older women in that land of sorrows, she wore a widow's black. But there was a hint of laughter in the wrinkles around her sloe-colored eyes that made the widow's weeds seem less dismal and more comforting. This was the black of sleep, of peace, not of death.

"Bienvenidos," she said in a cracked voice that reminded me, oddly, of that of an adolescent girl whose voice was changing rather than a voice eroded by age. There was surprising vitality in it for a woman who appeared to be on the shady side of eighty.

"Muy buenos días, Mamá." José removed his hat and stepped forward. "This friend of mine"—a nod to Bierce—"is troubled by a spirit in his lungs. Would you be so kind as to help him?"

She looked at Bierce; he looked back at her. Then her face crinkled up into the most impish smile imaginable.

"Como no," she said in that teenager's voice. "But I think Don Ambrosio here already knows a lot about spirits, *nó?*"

All this had, of course, wafted over Bierce in a soft, incomprehensible wave. At mention of the Hispanicized version of his name, however, he came to attention.

"What does she say, Amos?" he whispered to me.

"She says you are familiar with spirits—and not those to be found at the Menger Hotel bar."

"And how does she know my name?"

"Because you look like an Ambrosio," said the woman. Her English was heavily accented but sure. Her voice remained soft, but still it made us all jump to hear it. Again she graced us with that impish grin.

"I attended *el colegio* in my youth," she said. "Don't look so surprised, *mis caballeros*. Back then I was more interested in those handsome *catrines* and their flattering words. But I did pay enough attention to learn a thing or two."

My fascination for this woman grew by the moment. Where had she gone to school? How did she end up here, a *curandera* in a sleepy backwater town? I felt there were layers and strata to this woman, this Mamá Huitzil, that would take weeks or months to uncover.

Fortunately she brought us back to the matter at hand.

"I will be happy to examine Señor Ambrosio, José. What can you give to me in return?"

"A week's worth of firewood?"

Silence, and that tilted, sloe-eyed regard.

"And two chickens."

"Make one a *gallo* and it's a deal."

She extended an age-spotted but strong-looking hand from out her black robes. José shook it.

Mamá Huitzil nodded, put her hands to her knees, and pushed herself upwards. Bierce, seeing her effort, stepped forward and put a helping hand on her upper arm.

"Muchas gracias, Señor," Mamá said to him with a smile that held more of the coquette in it now than the imp. "I usually charge more, but José is a friend, and, well, I am still a fool for a handsome *caballero*."

Bierce grew an inch taller. His head fairly parted the hanging herbs and scraped the age-black roof-beams.

"Come," Mamá said. She parted the blanket over the door and held it while Bierce ducked in. "You all may return in an hour." She followed Bierce and let fall the blanket.

Back in the open air, wide and clean and thin after the fug of the shop, José hitched up his pants and said, "I'm going to the *mercado* down the block. You may come with me or stay here—I will return in an hour."

"We will stay, thank you, José," I said. I had every confidence that this Mamá Huitzil was harmless and, possibly, beneficial to the old man. But old habits die hard. I would stay close.

Juan sat on a rude log bench by the curandera's door, and squinted into the morning sunlight. I followed José a few steps to his wagon and touched his shoulder. He turned to me, eyebrows raised.

"Here," I said. I handed him a handful of coins and crumpled bills. "For your family."

He frowned and shook his head.

"No, no, Señor. You are very good, very kind. But we can buy our own food, thank you."

"Then buy ours," I said. "I don't know how long Señor Bierce needs to get better. We may be here a couple of days, and I—*we*—don't want to impose."

He looked at me as if for a different answer. I could hear his fingers juggling the few coins in his pocket. How few, he must have thought. And there was the payment he had promised to Mamá Huitzil. In the end he nodded. He held out his hands, I dropped the money into them and he mumbled *"gracias"* without looking at me.

While José continued down the street I returned to Juan. He was rolling a cigarette, pouring tobacco into a paper cupped in his palm.

"So we will stay?" He didn't look up.

"Yes, I think so. Bierce is concerned with what is happening here."

"Not our business."

"I made the same argument. But he is convinced that it does concern us, that it is linked with his mission in Mexico City. And you know how he is when he is convinced about something."

Juan turned a grin to me.

"Cabeza de buey," he said, and he held pointed fingers up beside his head in imitation of horns.

"Exacto."

We settled in to a companionable silence. Juan finished assembling his cigarette, scratched a match across the bench, and lit it. I sat back against the sun-warm wall, looked at the quiet house-fronts, wool-gathering.

I must have dozed off for a minute, for the next thing I knew was Juan jostling me with his elbow.

"Mira," he said. "Here comes the Prince."

I looked up and became aware of hoof-beats slowly coming our way down the street. There, one ahead and two behind, came three mounted men. The foremost was young, clean-shaven, and sleek in a way that connoted strength, not indolence. His pearl-gray suit was fashionably tight across his chest, arms, and booted legs. A matching fedora dipped at a rakish angle across his forehead, with the left brim turned up just *so*. His companions—bodyguards, from the look of them—were dressed neatly but nowhere near as nicely. Where he was sleek, they were bulky. Their pinstripe jackets and black pants jarred with the sombreros they wore; and their eyes and heavy mustaches were nearly lost in glutinous expressions of flesh. Juan had hit the proverbial nail on the head— here came the local "Prince," out to inspect his demesne. The effect, though, was more of a trio of gangsters, looking for a fight. All three wore gunbelts and pistols. Not unusual in that time and place, but the two thugs also carried carbines over their shoulders, and blocky bulges at their armpits hinted at yet more firepower. They came ready for a war.

As they rode abreast of us I got a better look at the leader. He was young—I would have put him at twenty-five years old at most—but his smooth face already looked freighted with evil.

What does evil look like, you may ask. There isn't a ready answer. With some it could be a certain cunning, in others even a craven smile. With this gay *señor,* it was his confidence, his arrogance. He looked at ease with anything he cared to do, and confident that he could do anything he wanted. From the heavy, arched black eyebrows to the straight nose, the half-smile on the full, almost womanish lips, and the way he regarded the world from behind half-lidded eyes, he was a cold prince of the world. Juan had pegged him right off.

This vision trotted and clopped across in front of Juan and me. I had no doubt that he had watched us all the way down the street, and that he watched us now. As he passed us, his smile grew a centimeter wider, and he tipped his hat to us. We tipped ours back. The henchmen followed like a storm-cloud, black eyes glaring and glinting at us from beneath the sombreros' shade like the eyes of spiders. They trotted by, rounded the corner. Gone.

"One of the Golón clan," Juan said. "One of Don Máximo's sons, I bet."

"I'm sure you're right," I said. "And now they know we're here."

*

When Bierce emerged from Mamá Huitzil's *tienda,* he looked like a new man—if that man resembled a ruddier, healthier, straighter Ambrose Bierce. Mamá rode upon his arm like a maiden at her first dance. They were laughing.

"How does he *do* it?" I whispered to Juan as they come into the sunlight.

"Corazón," he said and thumped his chest. "El Mayor has *heart.*"

"Really, Don Ambrosio," Mamá was saying, *"¡Que chistoso!* What a joker you are."

Bierce beamed beneath the brim of his hat.

"A joker trumped by a queen," he said, and patted her hand. "Ah, gentlemen—well met. And I see José is just returning. Good. Then we may be on our way."

Mamá Huitzil looked genuinely pained.

"So soon? Ah, well, men and their errands. But you will return to me tomorrow, *¿no?* It is important that we continue your treatments."

"Without fail, madam, without fail. I feel much improved already."

Whether that was from the woman's attentions or her skills as a healer, I let it slide. Just to see Bierce this jovial and strong again was worth it.

José eased the wagon up in front of Mamá's storefront and we clambered on. Just before we rode off, the woman came to José's side and touched his arm.

"Never mind the *gallo,* Josécito," she said kindly. "The wood will be enough. The company of this charming *caballero* is ample payment. " And she aimed a smirk at Bierce.

I waited until we were well on the road up out of the town before turning to Bierce.

"So, 'Don Ambrosio,' what did Mamá Huitzil do for you?"

"An' what did she do *to* you?" Juan grinned.

"And you to her?" I added. Juan and I burst into laughter.

Bierce turned on the seat and glared doom at us.

"Juan. Amos. Really. I expected better of the two of you. A gentleman neither takes advantage of a woman nor admits it when he does."

"Oh, come on, Bierce," I said. "The two of you came out of that shop looking like two newlyweds. At least tell us about your treatment."

He fussed and tugged at his lapels as if putting on his dignity.

"Well," he said, "at first she had me lie upon a cot and she rubbed an egg over me."

"An egg?"

"Yes, an egg, Amos. Let me continue. She moved this egg over my entire body with especial attention to my chest area. Then she broke the egg into a bowl and observed its contents.

"'Hmm,' she said. 'This demon has been with you many years.'

"'Seventy or so,' I said. 'My whole life.'

"Then she had me quit my shirt and—and gave me a vigorous massage."

He stopped to adjust his lapels again. I was shocked to see a blush rising under the scruffy frost of his beard.

"She used some highly aromatic salve—cedar, I should think. Finally she rummaged among her pots and philters and assembled a brew for me to take."

He extracted a small pouch from his jacket pocket and tweezed the mouth of it open to look inside.

"May I?" José held out his hand. Bierce placed the bag in his hand and José sniffed at it, peered into it.

"Cherry-bark," he said nodding. "Good for the lungs."

"So she tells me. I am to take this three times a day as a tea and return daily for treatments at her hands for the next four days."

We clopped down the road for a couple of minutes in silence.

"Bierce," I said. "We met someone in town."

He turned again to regard me.

"Did you indeed? Someone of importance?"

"Possibly." I looked at Juan. "We think it may have been one of Don Máximo Golón's sons."

I described the rural prince and his escort. José's eyes stayed trained upon the road ahead, but I could see the muscles of his face tighten.

"That would be Julio César," he said. "Don Máximo's middle son. Big trouble, him."

Bierce held me with his look before turning back to stare at the road ahead.

"Then we are discovered." He didn't look at me.

"Yes and no. He knows there are strangers in town, but not our nature, nor, you being absent, our number. Nor does he know where we are staying."

"*Gracias a Dios,*" said José, crossing himself.

"Then we will keep it that way," said Bierce. "But for my visits to Mamá Huitzil, we should all keep close to the Martínez ranch. With luck young Golón will think you two were just drifters passing through."

I nodded.

"Say, Bierce, if there had been any way to—"

He waved it away.

"You could scarcely have scurried out of sight at his approach. Nothing would have aroused his interest more, I'm sure. The balance of it is that now we know what he looks like as well."

"Hard to miss, with those two knuckleheads at his heels."

5.

Once back at the Martínez place there was a loud discussion that we weren't meant to hear. Or perhaps we were. It took place behind the closed door of José and Ángela's bedroom, but we caught enough words—words such as "strangers," "Araceli," and, most significantly, "Golón"—to catch the drift of it. Juan, Bierce, and I sat at the table, looking at our feet, our fingernails, that fascinating pattern in the floorboards . . . Three errant schoolboys awaiting the teacher's verdict.

At last we heard the bedroom door open and Ángela swept into the room.

José was right behind her. We stood for our sentence.

"Señores," she said, pushing a loose hair off her forehead, "I am sorry but we cannot let you stay in this house any longer."

Bierce stepped forward.

"It's all right, madam. We have imposed upon your hospitality too much already, and I personally wouldn't wish harm upon you or your family for the world. We shall seek other accommodations immediately."

But when I had translated this to her, her look softened.

"No, no," José said. "You do not understand: just not in the *house*. We have a granary shed on the land where you can stay, your horses, too, all out of sight." He looked apologetic. "I am sorry, Señores, but the three of you, our young lady . . ."

Bierce put up a hand.

"You needn't explain, José. We are in your debt already and will remove to the shed immediately. Boys?" He turned to us and we nodded and collected our things—such as they were. José led us out behind the house and across the scrubby property past the shed where the horses were lodged. We got our three mounts and followed to a larger, old adobe structure that looked as if it hadn't been used in years.

"In the days of my grandfather," José said, "we stored grain here and fodder for the horses. Now there are no cows, only our goats and the one horse, so we don't use it much." We reached the barn and José yanked on the door. It dragged open with a loud complaint. I peered in but hesitated.

I said, "There aren't any—insects in here, are there, José?"

"'*Insectos*'?"

"He means scorpions," Bierce said. "He had a memorable encounter with one in Chihuahua."

"Ah. Well, yes, there may be some *alacranes*. Just brush them away." He demonstrated with a few swift strokes on his arm.

"Bully," I said. "Just bully." Juan chuckled.

It wasn't as bad as I had feared. José and Ernesto made a thorough search and sweep of the place and reassured me that, for the moment, the place was clear of scorpions. There was a loft for hay where the three of us could bed down off the hard earth; and below that plenty of room for the horses. Bierce seemed recovered enough that he could stand the coolness of the place, given enough blankets, and it was really little worse than the accommodations Juan and I had had on their dining room floor. More than anything, it beat the desert.

José paused, hat in hand in the doorway of the barn.

"Again, Señores, I am very sorry for this trouble. You will join us for *la cena,* though, *¿no?*"

I translated, and Bierce stepped forward to clap the poor rancher on the shoulder.

"It is we who should apologize to you, José," he said in avuncular tones. "And we would be honored to join you for supper."

There were still hours yet until that meal, however. We passed the time as discreetly as we could, doing what chores José allowed us to do out by the barn. After José and Ernesto had dragged some timber in from the countryside, Juan and I insisted upon reducing it to the firewood that José had promised Mamá Huitzil. He protested feebly, mostly out of form, and looked relieved when we shouldered the axe and saw.

That occupied us for a good part of the afternoon. What Bierce was doing, I didn't know, and didn't think about until we had stacked the last of the split logs in José's wagon. The day had warmed marvelously, and Juan and I were perspiring even in our shirt-sleeves. I leaned upon my axe and looked around for Bierce.

"Where has that old buzzard gone to?" I asked no one in particular.

"I seen him walk out that way," Juan said, and pointed to the rolling, scrub-dotted countryside beyond the barn.

"'Saw,'" I said to Juan. "'Saw,' not 'seen.'"

Juan raised the tool he had been using.

"'Saw'?"

"*Sí,* 'saw'—no, not that saw. I mean—oh, forget it."

Bierce ambled into view not long afterwards. He walked upright and with purpose. He looked good. I told him so when he reached us.

"This country air," he said and filled his capacious chest. "And, of course, Mamá Huitzil's ministrations."

"I would have thought you had had enough of country air," I said, "what with crossing the desert and all."

"This is different, Amos—can't you feel it? Perhaps a tad more moisture in the atmosphere, and the breath of the trees." Another deep, noisy breath. "Delightful."

"Did you walk far?" I said.

"Far enough. I was reconnoitering"—he gave me a wink—"and got the lay of the land." He squatted on his haunches and picked up a stick. "We are here," he said, and made an X in the dirt. "San Andrés is here, to our southwest. And

La Hacienda Golón, seat of our enemies, is here, to the northwest of town."

I said, "You assume they are our enemies already."

"Until informed otherwise, yes, I do. They are at the very least in opposition to our most sacred values, I venture to say, and seem inimical to the good people hereabouts."

Juan, squatted nearby, shifted as if uncomfortable.

"Señor Beer," he said. "I still don't know why you are thinking 'bout *los Golón*. It ain't our fight."

"'*Isn't* our fight,' Juan, and in a way you are right. It isn't *your* fight. I know that Professor Navarro hired you to guide us to him, not to be a soldier in our adventures." Bierce looked down at his impromptu map. "Still," he said, scribbling in the dirt, "I had hoped that we had formed a certain bond of camaraderie in the recent past . . ."

Juan sighed.

"Of course you can depend on me, Señor. I never turned from a fight in my life, *jamás*. It's just I don't fight when I don't have to fight, *¿me entiendes?*"

"Understood. It may not come to that anyway, but I feel we must at least look into this '*onza*' business." He gave a straight, uncompromising look at Juan. "Are you game?"

"*Como no, jefe,* I am your man."

The iron gaze turned to me.

"And you, Amos?"

I shrugged.

"Of course, Bierce. What else do I have to do?"

"Good. Then I suggest we relax until supper."

We stayed outside as long as the sunlight and heat permitted. We sat against the back wall—the west wall, that is—of the barn, Juan dozing, me whittling, and Bierce, I was interested to see, writing.

"What are you scribbling at?" I said. He finished the sentence he had been writing in the little leatherbound book he held and stabbed a period at the end of it.

"Oh," he said, "just notes at the moment. Impressions of our journey, of the land . . ."

I was intrigued, but cautious. He hadn't written fiction in a long while and he wasn't one who reacted well to pressure.

"Are you planning a new story?" I said, trying not to appear too curious.

"A fiction, perhaps, or perhaps merely an account of our travels. It might make for interesting reading for the not overly discerning reader. Don't you think, Amos?"

"Most interesting, indeed," I nodded. "Especially phrased in Biercian prose."

He snorted and slapped shut the little book.

"Flattery, Amos, really. I should have thought you beyond that."

"There's flattery and there's praise, Bierce, not quite the same thing. Can't you accept a certain amount of praise? You've earned it, I dare say."

"In my experience, the problem with praise is it is often followed by expectations of recompense. Nothing for free."

I turned to face him.

"Do you really expect me, Mr. Bierce, *me,* to demand something in return? Why, look at what you've given me already." I waved at the dusty chaparral in the low, thick, yellow sunlight. "A free holiday in central Mexico! What more could a fellow want?"

He tried that practiced scowl at me—then burst into laughter.

"You're right, of course," he said. "My faithful Boswell, Sancho Panza, and Iago, all rolled into one." He looked into the sunset. "We have seen some things, haven't we, Amos?"

"That we have, Bierce, that we have."

"And I venture to say that we shall see more ere this drama is ended. Deep waters here, deep waters indeed. Frayser is not merely loose in this land; he is Legion. The fact that we can travel hundreds of miles and still encounter the same evil speaks to both its reach and its power. This war does more than hide it, Amos—it *feeds* it."

"I believe you're right," I nodded. "And there is a disturbingly human element to this adversary that frightens me. What was it José said? That the revolutionaries had let loose something 'animal' upon these people? Animal, yes, but terribly human, too, from our first ape ancestor who walked red-handed out of the jungle in an unbroken stride to today. I don't believe the revolutionaries are to blame, per se, but they had a hand in creating the circumstances amenable to this horror.

"And the war feeds upon itself, a self-perpetuating machine. With President Madero's murder and the ascendancy of Huerta, the war received new life—new blood, figuratively and literally speaking. Should Huerta be defeated, and Villa augers well to do it, there will no doubt rise another threat, another log to throw on this awful conflagration. A thoughtful manipulation of violences could extend this bloodbath for years."

"And all that blood feeding the cult of the Eagle-knights and their unholy aims . . ."

The sun was set and a cold wind had risen.

"Come," said Bierce, pushing to his feet. "Rouse Juan—it's time to go in."

Half an hour later, while we sat in the glow of the kerosene lamp José had left us, little Benito came into the barn at a run.

"Time for supper," he gasped, and ran out again. We dusted ourselves off, blew out the light, and followed him back to the house.

Within all was light and warmth and welcome. The lines of stress were gone from Ángela's face, and she welcomed us to her table with genuine friendship. Nothing was said, on either side, about our new accommodations; it was simply necessary. We all sat at the table and Araceli and Ernesto brought out steaming platters of meats and bowls of boiled potatoes, onions, and garlic. The meat was *cabrito* (goat) again, and would remain so for every evening meal at the Martínez house, for they were goatherds, after all. But Ángela fixed each meal with enough variety that, during our short stay with them, we never tired of it.

Afterwards, the women again cleared away the plates and the men again sat to their cigars and tequila. I could see that José enjoyed having other men around with whom he could mull over the events of the day. I had no doubt that he had friends in town; but that was a couple miles away, the Martínez *ranchito* was secluded, and I'm sure Ángela did not want her man out to all hours in some dark and evil cantina where no decent man would go.

So we happily passed the bottle (all but Juan, who, as in Ojinaga, had his own bottle), and Bierce smiled and pontificated and Juan and José and I laughed at it all.

"*Mire,*" José said, reaching to the back pocket of his overalls. "I got a paper in town this morning. There is news from the north."

We eagerly spread the paper out on the table and crowded over it. It was a copy of the Torreón *Día Especial*, a few days old, and printed in enormous black letters across the top were the words:

OJINAGA CAE

DERROTA Y MATANZA

"'Ojinaga Falls,'" I translated for Bierce. "'Defeat and Massacre.'"

"That much we knew," he puffed smoke at the ceiling. "What else does it say?"

"It says that the Federals abandoned the city, five thousand troops crossed the river, and are now in holding-camps guarded by U.S. Army troops."

"At least it was not the slaughter it could have been."

"Bad enough," I said, and saw headless bodies lying in an abandoned house.

José looked up at us from the paper.

"Then you were there," he said. There was amazement and something more in his voice. Bierce, Juan and I exchanged looks. In for a dime . . .

"Yes, José," I said. "We were there. We were with Villa's army from Chihuahua."

"Ay, Dios," he breathed. "Then, *revolucionarios . . ."*

I could see fear growing in his eyes, so I quickly said, "No, José, just— observers. We were on our way through Chihuahua and got caught up in it. As we said before, we are going to Mexico City. We aren't on any side of this war, neither Villa nor Huerta."

He seemed reassured by this, but still frowned at something.

"General Villa," he said. "They say he is a bad man, a good man. He kills the Rurales, he kills the innocent. Which is the truth?"

"The truth is both," said Bierce. "Señor Villa is ruthless in his tactics, but his aims appear legitimate. He speaks of better education and wealth for the common man, and he is no friend of the hacienda owners."

José nodded, absorbing this.

"Huerta is a beast," he said. "The Rurales work for him now, and they take men to fight their battles."

Bierce said, "Conscription, you mean."

It took me a minute to translate this sufficiently to José, who afterwards shook his finger vehemently at Bierce.

"No, not like in the army. He just takes them. Any man who resists, they hang. And I hear, too, *el Chacál* has soaked the streets of Mexico City in blood."

"La Decena Trágica," Juan piped in. "The Ten Tragic Days, when Huerta took power in Mexico. And *sí*, the streets were red with blood then. I remember." He crossed himself and, just to be sure, took another belt from his bottle.

Bierce squinted thoughtfully through his cloud of cigar-smoke.

"Tell me," he said, "Juan or José. If my grasp of Mexican history is correct, wasn't there also a 'Sad Night,' a *'Noche Trágica,'* in the colonial period?"

"Sí, la Noche Triste," said Juan, and I could tell he enjoyed correcting Bierce for once. "That was way back, Cortés and the Aztecs."

"A sad night indeed," said José, raising his cup, "for *los españoles.*"

"*No cabe duda,* a sad night for *los gachupines.*" Juan tipped his bottle to his lips and drank. "They were in Tenochtitlán then, where Mexico City stands now. They had the Emperor Moctezuma prisoner, so the Aztecs couldn't attack them—a ostrich, you say?"

"'Hostage,'" said Bierce. "Continue."

"*Eso,* hostage. But the emperor died. Some said it was Cortés and his soldiers what killed him, some said it was *los aztecas.* That he was a traitor, welcomed in the invaders. Anyway, dead is dead. Without him the Spanish had to run. They ran at night—"

"Cowards," muttered José around his cup.

"—but the Aztecs, they caught 'em on the bridge out of Tenochtitlán." Juan's gaze grew distant. "On that bridge they caught the *pinches españoles,* and there was a great battle. Men died, Spanish and Aztec. They fell on the bridge, they fell in the water. The Spanish cried out, but their metal armor dragged them down under the water. And the swords rose and fell and the stone-edged *macahuitls* swung and blood flew and the rain fell . . ."

We were all quiet, watching Juan. He kept staring away for another few moments. Then he blinked, shook his head, smiled sheepishly.

"All children in Mexico learn this story," he said.

"*Verdad,*" nodded José in agreement.

"You tell it well," said Bierce.

"Was the birth of our country, *Mayor.* I grew up near Mexico City, *el De Efe,* so it's all real to me, all true. You can walk the streets where walked the proud *conquistadores,* where the Aztec princes rode their boats on Lake Texcoco."

"What happened after *la Noche Triste,* Juan?" I said.

"The *gachupines* came back and they came back with many friends. Enemies of the Aztecs, people who sided with the Spanish instead of their own people. They fought their way back in to Tenochtitlán, block by block, canal by canal. Los Aztecas, they got the fever from the e-Spanish, and the dead lay thick in the streets. *Ay, que triste.* Tenochtitlán was a great city before, a jewel on the lake, like that Italian city, *¿no?* The one with all the canals."

"Venice," said Bierce.

"*Sí,* Venice. Tenochtitlán was like that. But when Cortés and his men came back, they tore it all down, and threw the stones of the temples into the canals and filled them all up." He shook his head. "Gone now, all gone."

"But the Aztecs had terrible sacrifices, as well," I said. "Those are gone, too."

"*Sí*, but the Spanish brought their own sacrifices to replace 'em—slavery, sickness, *la Inquisición*. The Church, she burned people, cut off their hands. All in the name of *Cristo Rey*, Christ the King." Juan paused and again the bottle rose and fell.

"You have to understand," José said, leaning toward us. "The Spanish brought civilization, learning, peace. But at a cost. I may have a Spaniard's speech and name, but when I look in the mirror? *Soy mestizo*. I'm a mix, we're all a mix, Spanish father and Indian mother. We're both, and we're neither."

"And proud of it," said Juan, and he and José clinked bottle to cup.

That was enough history for our tired, alcohol-muddled minds that night. We filled the rest of the evening with small-talk. The next day being Monday, José had to bring his children to school; he would take Bierce with him and drop him at Mamá Huitzil's shop. Juan and I asked about chores and José ticked off a list of things he had been meaning to get to but never had—greasing the wagon's axles, repairing sections of the ranch's fence, a leak in the roof. He had to tend to his goats and attend to business in town. Would we be so kind as to . . . ? We most certainly would.

Walking in the deep dark to the barn that night, we heard some creature wail in the distance. The cry rose from a high moan to a clear, hollow note held far into the sky. It sent ice-water down through my spine. Still the cry soared into the blackness, at once tragic, lonely, and triumphant. It reached a peak and warbled back down to silence. Its echoes winged away over the hills.

"*¿La onza?*" said Juan. His face was a pale blur in the starlight.

"Who can say?" said Bierce. "We have slipped into a realm of magic, gentlemen. Wherever there is a major cataclysm, such as an earthquake or war, the fabric of reality is shaken loose and tears appear. What comes through these rents is what we must face."

As we stood listening, the last of the echoes shrank into nothingness.

6.

The Rurales came the next day.

Bierce, José, and the children had rumbled off in the wagon, Ernesto was in the *monte* with the goats, and Juan and I had settled into our chores. As luck would have it, we were in the barn gathering up our tools when we heard the horses. It was a clear, still, blue morning, and the sound of the hoofbeats traveled far. The barn was situated far back from and to the right of the house. As such it afforded us a good view of the approach to the house; and across this now trotted three mounted men.

"Juan," I said. "The field-glasses."

Bierce had brought along a good pair of field-glasses, a gift from one of Villa's officers, and I now trained them upon the horsemen. They all wore matching gray uniforms and sombreros with tall, pointed peaks—the uniform of the dreaded Rurales. Many men could wear those enormous hats with ease and even style. I had never learned the trick and stuck to my Stetson. But these fellows wore them stiffly, like gigantic gumdrops on their heads. They would have looked ridiculous but for the sour look on their faces. I watched them until the house intervened between them and me. Then, turning to Juan, I said, "Juan, gather up the bedding and our gear. Load it onto the horses and lead them out into the *monte*."

As I helped him roll up our bedding, he said, "And what will you do, Amos?"

"I'm going to spy on these characters, make sure that they don't harm Mrs. Martínez."

"Three against one, if it goes bad. You handle that?"

"I'll have to. But hopefully it won't come to that. Now hide the horses before they come out here—*¡de prisa, amigo!*"

While he finished clearing the barn of our incriminating presence, I dodged out toward the back of the house. There was little cover, drat the luck, but no windows in the back of the house; and so far the Rurales must have been occupied at the front. I ran and ducked behind this bush, that barrel, until I finally threw myself against the back wall of the house. Breathless, I drew and cocked my revolver. Then I snuck in a crouch around the right-hand side of the house. I crept under the level of the windows up to the front corner of the house, where it met the porch. Voices came around the corner from not far off. Men's voices. Two voices? Three? I could smell cigarette smoke, too, pungent in the winter morning air. I took off my Stetson and, as slowly as I could, I put my face to the corner of the house until I could see around it with my right eye.

Two Rurales stood near their horses in the sunlight maybe ten feet from the front of the house. Chatting and smoking. Where was the third? As if in answer I heard a thud of moved furniture from the house. It was in the back—in the bedrooms? My worst fears for Señora Martínez's safety rushed up in my mind like attacking beasts. I quelled them as best as I could and snuck back to the rear window. Voices again, this time from within the house. A man asking questions in a casual tone; a woman answering shortly. Good—if they were talking, then the Rural wasn't attacking her. I risked a peek over the sill of the window. The rural policeman was standing not three feet from where I crouched, separated from me only by the thin glass of the window. I could have shot him in that broad, gray back as easily as talk about it. Beyond him, in the shadow of the room, stood Señora Martínez; and as I looked at her face, she saw me. Her eyes widened a fraction of an inch. I raised my eyebrows, but she gave the tiniest shake of her head. Then she focused on the lawman again and swept at her hair to hide her tension.

I put my hand up to reassure her and scuttled back around behind the house. The tone of their conversation had sounded informal, and I recalled José saying that the rural lieutenant was one of the Golóns' cousins. In a small town such as this, everyone probably knew everyone else, and I could construct a conversation between the *teniente* and Señora Martinez: Good morning, Ángela. Good morning, Ramon, what can I do for you? I'm sorry to bother you, Ángela, but we have word that strangers have been seen hereabouts. Strangers? My goodness, who are they? We don't know, but may I look around?, etc. I hoped this was the case. I hated to leave Ángela alone with that man, but she appeared at ease with the situation; as at ease as could be expected, all things considered, and more shocked by my presence than by the presence of the Rurales.

Back to the barn. Juan had done a good job in clearing away all signs of our habitation, even to scattering hay and other farm detritus across the boards where we had slept. Relieved, I went back to the barn door and looked out— and saw the three Rurales walking slowly across the ground toward the barn. One peeled away to check on the horse-shed near the house, but the other two walked straight toward me. They were all carrying carbines.

I ducked back inside, mind racing. There was one door and no way for me to exit the barn without being seen. I looked around, frantically searching the shadowy spaces for somewhere to hide. But for partitions for horses or cattle, the ground floor offered nothing. And the loft where we had slept was even more open, one wide shelf of lumber and hay.

Then I saw it. A window, a white square of sky up above the loft. If I could reach it and drop out to the ground behind the barn, I might have a chance to run into the brush before being spotted. I ran to the crude ladder to the loft, took it two rungs at a time. Onto the loft itself—the voices of the Rurales, the crunch of their boots on the soil, laughter—coming closer. To the window, jumped up, missed the sill. My boots made a hollow clump on the loft as I dropped back down. Hold still—had they heard? No—they still talked easily, closer to the barn door. I cast around for something, anything to stand on. Nothing, just the dusty boards. At last I took several steps back, and as quietly as I could (not an easy thing—you should try it sometime), ran toward the wall and leapt.

My fingers caught on the sill. Good, but not good enough. I knew that I would be silhouetted in the window, an easy, obvious target the second the Rurales entered the barn. With a heave I pulled myself up to the sill—and stopped. Lying on the middle of the sill was a scorpion—*blast!* Of all the things, of all the times and places . . . I muttered a few well-chosen words and felt cold flush through my body. The creature was not six inches from my face. But it wasn't moving. Was it dead, or just inert from the cold? Without waiting to find out, I drew my knife and flicked the horrid thing out the window with the blade. Then, knife still in hand, I clambered up onto the sill, swung my legs out before me, and dropped down, just as I heard the barn door groan open.

In my hurry I hadn't bothered to look where I was dropping. Probably a good thing; I fell into a large bush that broke my fall, but tangled my legs. I spilled head-first out of the bush onto the ground. Not the most graceful of getaways. And I was sure that I'd made the devil's own racket crashing down that way. But when I stopped to listen, all I could hear was the two Rurales still talking in low, casual tones, echoing in the barn's interior. My luck held.

I got up, wiped the gravel out of the palms of my hands and ran for the brush. This part of the Martínez property faded without visible boundary into the *monte,* that Mexican catch-all for wilderness, mountains, or countryside. I ran among the frequent bushes and agaves until I was over the first hillock. Then I turned, dropped down, and looked back. Nothing. Just the back of the barn in shadow. I kept watching, though, and sure enough, in a minute the Rurales came around both sides of the barn, hoping to catch any miscreants in their net. All three of them were there, two on the left and one on the right. That reassured me about Señora Martínez's safety, if not my own. Surely they would see the broken branches of the bush I had landed in, or my footprints in the dirt.

But apparently not. They may have been the terror of the countryside, but trackers they were not. I'm sure I left an utter mess of a trail, but they didn't see it. The three ambled around the barn, looking here and there, prodding the odd cactus with their gun-barrels. There were no *pinches gringos* here—what a waste of time. The three gathered at the back of the barn and conferred. I watched them talk, gesticulate to one another, wave at the barn, the brush, the sky. One flicked away a cigarette. Its smoke curved through the still air, hung motionless in the sunlight. Finally one, the Golón cousin I assume, turned and waved the other two to follow. The three strolled back around the barn, carbines resting on their shoulders.

When they were back out of sight behind the barn I waited a minute; then I followed them. It was a risky thing to do, but I had to see them off the property and see our hostess safe. From the corner of the barn I watched them walk back to the house; and from the corner of the house I watched them remount their horses. Señora Martínez, wrapped in a shawl against the cold, came out to see them off. I couldn't catch the lieutenant's words, but he touched the brim of his big sombrero to her while he spoke—a good sign. Polite, maybe a "Sorry to have bothered you, Ángela," or the like. He mounted and, with a *"Vámanos, chamacos,"* led the other two back out the front gate. They didn't shut it behind them.

When I was satisfied they wouldn't return, I rose and came around to the front of the house. Ángela was still standing, motionless as a statue, watching where the Rurales were dwindling into the distance.

"¿Está bien?" I said as I walked up to her. She jumped, peeped a little scream. Then she put her hand to her breast and said, "Oh, Señor Littlefault, you frightened me."

The idea that she had just successfully faced down or deceived three dangerous men, and was now startled by me, was almost laughable.

"I'm sorry," I said. "Are you all right?"

"Yes, fine. And you? I'm sorry, but I could not stop them from searching the barn. I hope you were able to hide."

"Yes, it wasn't a problem. I'm impressed at how you handled the Rurales."

She smiled, a rueful expression.

"El Teniente is an old—friend." I caught the pause and looked at her. She shrugged. "We all grew up together. Ramón is a Golón but not one of *the* Golóns. Bad enough, but *estúpido,* thick as a stone. A few words from a helpless *señora* and he was satisfied."

"'Helpless?'" I smiled. "You don't strike me as that, Señora."

She shrugged again.

"Men have their weapons, women have theirs. One of the best is man's pride: You can deflect a bullet with flattery as well as with armor."

My estimation of this strong, level-headed woman went up several notches. What a life, to be a woman in that country overrun by war-mad men. I had seen the *soldaderas* and their valor in battle; but here was another, equal if more subtle courage. I could see her shouldering a rifle if her family were threatened, but before that ever happened she would do whatever she could to redirect danger away from her family without violence.

"You are a remarkable woman," I said. "And we are, again, in your debt for our safety. *Muchisimas gracias.*" And I tipped my hat to her.

A smile, like the shadow of a little bird, flashed over her handsome face.

"No hay de qué," she said. "Think nothing of it. And forgive my bluntness, but please go away as soon as possible."

She gathered her skirts and walked back inside.

Juan had done an excellent job of hiding himself and the horses; so good, in fact, that it took me an hour to find them. I had almost come to the conclusion that he had run off with the whole outfit when I heard him singing over the next rise. Coming over the crest I saw Juan, sitting on the earth, a cigarette dangling from his fingers, singing softly to the horses, who were munching the tough, wild grass nearby. A more peaceful scene could not be imagined. He stopped singing and leapt up, hand to his pistol, when I came over the ridge.

"¿Está bien?" he said.

"Yes, Juan, all's well. The Rurales are gone, Señora Martínez is safe."

I took off my jacket—the morning was warming up as it advanced. Looking around at the jumbled landscape of browns and greens, I said, "You hid well. I was beginning to think you'd left us."

He dropped his hand from his pistol, shook his head, and chuckled.

"Naw," he said. "Traveling with you and Mayor Beer is too much fun. You're stuck to me."

"'Stuck *with* me,'" I said, and chuckled too. "Come on—let's get these horses back to the barn."

The rest of the day flowed by in a welcome peace. After the episode with the Rurales, a tension went out of the air; a tension that we could not have named or even admitted to ourselves before, but was certainly gone now.

Juan and I went back to our chores, replacing red clay tiles on the house roof, fixing a lame wheelbarrow, feeding the chickens.

Bierce returned to us late in the morning, so late, in fact, that we could not resist ribbing him about it.

"So," I said, "the doctor has increased her treatments, I see."

"Yeah," said Juan, stretching like a cat. "Man's gotta have 'treatments' now and then."

Bierce's face took on the dusky aspect of a thundercloud.

"You two *boys* are on a Pullman car to hell," he rumbled. "I will have you know that Huitzil is an accomplished healer and our sessions are purely— salutary."

We guffawed again as he fumed.

"I'm sure they are," I said, and gave Juan a wink. "And 'Huitzil,' is it? So we're on a first-name basis now, eh?"

"Yes, Amos, we are. Two mature adults. Huitzil is a charming woman and I will insist upon your not impugning her honor."

"It isn't *her* honor I'm worried about," I said. "Huitzil—an unusual name."

"It is," said Bierce in a softer, almost dreamy voice. "It means 'humming-bird' in the old Aztec tongue. A fitting cognomen, in my opinion."

I looked at him. Was he smitten? This old warrior on his last crusade, smitten like some callow farm-boy? And 'hummingbird.' It was hard to reconcile with the image of the impish old woman. Yet there was a certain appropriateness to it. I recalled seeing Bierce call the wild birds and seeing them alight on his outstretched hands. Had he charmed this frail old hummingbird as well? I said, "All right Bierce. I'm sorry. I'm not used to seeing you this, well, this—"

"'*Treated,*'" Juan supplied, and we unraveled into tears of laughter again.

"You people are impossible." Bierce stomped off toward the house and we resumed our chores.

Late in the afternoon Ángela asked if we could collect Ernesto, who was far afield with the goats. Bierce and I volunteered. I was pleased because I hadn't yet had a chance to tell him about the morning's encounter with the Rurales.

"You did well," he said as our horses clopped along over the rough ground. "I should hate to see any harm come to this family, the women especially."

We mulled this over for a minute.

I said, "Do you think we're in the clear, then?"

"If by 'in the clear' you mean that we have escaped detection and are free to gallivant across the countryside, I would say no. We have but deflected suspicion from the Martínez clan; I am sure that Golón and his thugs are still looking for 'the strangers.'"

"Do you still hold to the idea, then, of finding this onza creature, or somehow reducing Golón's power here?"

"I do," he nodded vigorously. "The former, at least. Breaking Golón is a much larger proposition, I feel, and sadly, not within either our means or schedule. We have yet to see Mexico City."

I really bit my tongue then.

"As for the onza," he said, "I have spoken to José about searching it out. We come at an opportune time, it seems. The creature has not been seen for a month or so, and often appears near the new moon. We are in that period now. I have convinced José to take us out tonight."

"Tonight? That seems abrupt."

"It does indeed, and allows for minimal preparation. However, our continued presence endangers the Martínezes, and my treatments with Mamá Huitzil come to an end in a day or two." He seemed to shrink in his clothes. "There will be no reason to linger after that."

"Bierce," I said, feeling my way, "I don't mean to pry, and all joking aside, but are you enamored of this Huitzil woman?"

He straightened in the saddle and looked at me sharply, but not, I hoped, without friendship.

"She fills a need in my soul, Amos," he said.

"That sounds rather clinical, if you pardon my saying so."

"Yes, but I fear I cannot elaborate. The constraints of being a gentleman prevent me from giving details of our relationship."

"That's truly none of my business, Bierce. But as a friend I am concerned about your heart and its integrity. Will you be able to leave her when the time comes? And at what cost?"

He drew a long breath (Mamá Huitzil was, at least, living up to her reputation as an excellent healer) and released it in a titanic sigh. He said, "Amos, I have asked myself the very same question. Huitzil and I are mature people and our expectations are free, I believe, of the tangled nonsense of youth. But I cannot deny a growing—*affection* for the woman, which she appears to reciprocate. I have spoken with her about our journey, not"—he raised an eyebrow at me—"going into too many particulars, and she understands that our sojourn in San Andrés is necessarily brief. However, I hope that, when our errand is done, we may return this way and that she and I many resume what we have started here."

"Does she echo that wish?"

"In all humility, I believe she does. Her life here is one of quiet study of herb-lore and healing-craft, and she submerges herself in it. Of true friends here she has few, mostly older woman like herself. And of acquaintances of sufficient intelligence to match and stimulate her own, none."

"That is where you come in."

"I like to think so."

"Do you think to settle here, then, 'when the great hurly-burly is done'?"

He smiled at me: he always did like Shakespeare.

"It isn't an impossible suggestion. And I must admit to having considered it."

"But if Mamá Huitzil finds intellectual stimulation rare here, what of you? Won't you miss the give-and-take of politics and society? The bustle of a Washington or Frisco?"

"To be brutally honest, Amos, no. I have been drifting away from all that for years now already. I have had my say and more, both in journalism and in fiction. With the Walter Neale edition of my *Collected Works,* any fool—and there are many—may delve into my brain for what it's worth without my having to be present. I have severed ties with many in my life; and as for the bustle of humanity, it makes me tired. Scoundrels will be scoundrels, regardless of my critiques. I suppose I had held out a hope that Man might someday somehow drag himself out of the reeking swamp of his own iniquities; but I can see now that that was a vain hope."

"You can't be completely without hope for our species, else we wouldn't be here, doing what we're attempting to do."

"I suppose," he said at last, "that it's a difference between preaching to the congregation and actually tending to them. My sermons in writing are done—time to do something concrete. And while I may despise the vain stupidity of humanity as a whole, there remain certain individuals who merit my salvation."

And he gave me a most grandfatherly smile. It touched my heart. Friends of Ambrose Bierce, those few who still survive and still consider themselves to be his friends at all, will tell you that he loved and valued them—but that he was exacting with his friendships. Quick to anger and slow to forgive, he could be a challenge to even his most devoted followers. I was fortunate not to have been a victim of the general purging of friends in which Bierce had engaged in recent months. I don't, however, credit my own sterling personality with this good fortune. Rather, I like to think that Bierce needed me in those final months, needed me for the great role he had taken on. As for those others, I feel that he pushed away his many loved ones precisely out of affection for them; that he knew he would be leaving "this veil of tears" soon, and wanted to spare them the heartbreak. All this is armchair psychology, of course, but it comes from my observation of the man at close quarters under a variety of circumstances; and during this period he never spoke ill of any of those old friends or relations—never. As for me, if I must play the Sancho Panza to his Don Quixote, so be it. It allowed me to protect him and, more importantly, to enjoy his odd, powerful, and always engaging company, one more time.

We rounded up young Ernesto and his contentious troop of goats and went back to the Martinez ranch. Dinner awaited us—*cabrito a la Ángela*—and afterwards, tequila and cigars and cigarettes.

"The onza comes from the west," José said as he put his drained *copa* down. "I think we will have the best chance to see it if we wait at that side of town." He looked around at us. "If you still want to do it, that is."

"Yes, we do," Bierce said through his own personal cloud of tobacco smoke. "It is important for our mission, I believe—an aspect of our enemy we have not yet seen clearly."

José nodded. "Very well. We will wait until it is late, then I will lead you there."

If was late indeed when we finally rode out. Ángela and her children all slept peacefully as we strapped on our gunbelts and gave a last check to our weapons. Bierce was a tyrant where the guns were concerned. He drilled Juan and me on the proper care and handling of them until we could field-strip and reassemble our Colts in the dark. I grew to know the feel of a hog-leg as well as I knew the feel of this pen I hold.

The four of us went out to our horses and mounted. José had muffled the jingling harnesses with strips of rag to lessen the noise we would make; and, each of us lost in our own private speculations, we rode in silence out of the ranch, down the road to San Andrés Tecolotzán.

Just shy of the town José motioned to a track splitting off to the left. We followed it in a wide arc around the village, crossing a larger road heading south toward Torreón, and onward into the *monte*. I was glad of José's leadership, for among the bushes, cacti, and ubiquitous agave we would have become quickly lost. After fifteen minutes riding away from town, he held up a hand for us to halt. We dismounted and tethered the horses to whatever plant we could find. Then José lead us on foot down an arroyo winding among the hillocks. Followed this for a couple minutes until it met a larger gully; then up the bank and hillside beyond. Just below the crest we lay on the stony earth and looked out across the landscape. The land rolled off to the north and west like a rumpled blanket in the dim night, dotted with the odd flora of the region. The great curtain of the Sierra Madre Occidental was drawn across the western horizon, its peaks just defined against the night's overcast. At the point where country-side and foothills met, lights burned yellow in a low line.

"Casa Golón," José whispered. "About three miles away."

"And this onza creature comes from that direction?" said Bierce.

"Mostly, *sí*. It's hard to tell sometimes—who would want to follow such a creature?"

Who indeed? And what sort of fools would actually pursue one? The minutes walked by into the night. I heard Juan shift, pull his gun free, and spin the cylinder. With no moon or even stars to reckon the time, I pulled out my watch and clicked it open. Two A.M. It felt as if time itself had gotten lost in this dim immensity and had left us behind.

Then a subtle shift in the air. Bierce was sprawled beside me and we looked at each other.

"Hand?" he said.

"Hand."

That tingling hand upon the back of our necks. Something wicked that way came. A vibration in the ground.

"*El ritmo,*" Juan whispered eagerly. "*El ritmo en la tierra.*" A rhythm in the earth, resolving into the thudding of hooves; and interwoven with the hoof-beats, a softer, rustling patter of nameless paws, galloping in syncopation with the horses. I felt the hand press more insistently upon the back of my neck. I drew my gun and felt the others draw theirs, too.

Silhouettes broke the horizon to the northwest. Three, four? It was hard to tell. They ducked and bobbed among one another like the several heads of a Hydra. It/they ran in an amorphous, shifting huddle, a sombrero here, shoul-ders there, a moving, shifting clutter of heads. It grew in size as it approached. Hammers were clicked back around me. Then the figures dipped down as they met the shallow valley below us. The thudding in the earth drew close, the black huddle of mounted figures moved swiftly down into the valley. Without the moonlight, our view as poor; yet even so I could tell that there was some-thing off about the group of passing horsemen. The legs of their mounts, churn-ing like the wheels and pistons of a locomotive, were obscured by something long and low that ran beside them. *The onza.*

Now the hairs on the back of my neck really stood on end. None of us said a word, none dared lest some trick of the night send it to those others' ears. But I saw the barrels of my companions' pistols and José's rifle slide forward over the rim of the hill. Had those horsemen and their unholy companion only known how Death tracked them across that little valley . . . But we suffered them to pass. The group rumbled through the valley, rose to its crest in the east, toward town, and sank again into the blackness of the earth. For just a moment the group was silhouetted against the lesser blackness over that horizon; and for just a moment we got a glimpse of the huge, loping, somehow *liquid* thing that ran with the horsemen.

"*Válgame, Dios,*" José breathed. I swallowed a hard lump. The hoofbeats faded with distance toward town.

And again we waited. Again without saying so, there was a tacit agreement among us to stay and see this business through. The seconds ticked by. Cold embraced me, and I pulled my jacket and serape tight around my neck.

A wail, neither human nor animal, but owning the quality of the former and the mindless hunger of the latter, spiraling up into the night from the direction of town. Shivers chased each other down my back. The cry cut off at its peak, there was a distant rending of wood—a snap. *Gunshot?* We waited.

After what seemed hours, we heard the tattoo of hoofbeats approach us again from the town. Over the same ridge to eastward the phantom patrol swept up and was cut in silhouette again. Sombreroed heads bobbed urgently, a cape or serape like an eagle's wings shivered out behind them. They descended, thudding and steaming, into the valley again; but before where they had passed us some hundred yards away, this time they angled up our side of the valley. If they kept to this course they would pass nearly under our guns. The black tangle of men, horses, and leaping, galloping Thing beside them swept up out of the valley's shadow toward us. The "hand" upon my neck grew and spread down and across my shoulders. The thin night air itself felt strained, taut as a piano-string. Any slight thing would snap it like a stroke of lightning, and onward came that pounding charge out of hell.

Yet the break, when it happened, came from the place I expected least. As the riders rose closer and closer to us, just discernible in the maw of the Thing was something white; something rippling in the wind of travel with the quality of fabric; something the size of a small child. I heard Bierce growl something that sounded like "Enough," and lurch to his feet. Both his guns were out, and he leveled them at the oncoming Beast and fired. The twin jets of flame from the guns lit in shocking detail the scene: Bierce upright and righteous, our fellows just rising and raising their own guns; and the startled faces of the riders, caught in the flash like the flattened denizens of a photograph.

And *the Beast*. Because of the angle of their charge, only the head and rolling shoulders of it were visible—but that was more than enough. Again I felt a pain and a nausea at the sight of it. A jaguar's mad face, striped and maculated but much larger than any natural jaguar; soulless feline green eyes glowing with reflected light; and gripped in its unnatural maw, a tiny form in a stained white nightdress.

The flash from Bierce's guns only lasted a second; but when our fellows' guns opened up, we saw the riders and Beast turning from their path toward us into an arc paralleling the ridge. Shots crashed in an avalanche of sound all around us. The muzzle-flashes lit the riders up in stuttering progress like the images in a nickelodeon—here, there, then there, cut-out figures between spaces of black. Caught up in the excitement, I joined in the firing. I'm sure I hit nothing, though someone caught two of the horsemen (there were four, it turned out). One jerked upright and slumped over his pommel; the other threw his whole body back and fell from the horse into the dust. Another scream tore the night. Someone had hit the onza. The next sudden glare of gunshots showed the creature had dropped its bundle and was limping off on three legs, racing to catch up with the retreating riders.

"Cease fire, cease fire!" bellowed Bierce. We all put up our guns. Smoke and the smell of gunpowder drifted around us. Ringing silence, and a good thing, too. Into that silence came a soft sound, a sad sound, the sound of a child crying. "Thank God," said Bierce, shoved his pistols back into their holsters and loped down the hill. We followed.

The little wrapped form lay upon the slope, motionless, accusing. The wrapping, it turned out, was a nightdress. It was torn and twisted around its contents, but there was no sign of blood. The dress was edged with lace and embroidery. From out of the tangle of it all, a girl's face stared, dirty, bruised, and wide-eyed with terror. Her long black hair was a bird's-nest of snarls, her pudgy little hands gripped the edge of the fabric as if it would shield her, and she looked from one to another of us with wonder and fear.

"Jesus," I said.

"Have mercy," said Bierce.

Beyond the girl lay one of the fallen riders. Bierce and I looked down at him.

"One of young Golón's thugs?" said Bierce.

"One of them."

"Then we're in the game for sure."

All at once the girl stretched wide her mouth until her eyes were mere slits, and emitted a howl of grief that cut to my heart. I was lost—what to do? Not Bierce. He gathered the girl into his arms and stood back up.

"Hush, child," he said, shushing and cooing. "It's all right now, all right. The bogeyman has gone away."

"Let's hope so," I said, scanning the darkness. Juan stood a little apart, José further back, just one more thorny shadow of the desert. I said, "What do we do with her?"

"Bring her home, of course." Bierce smoothed some of the girl's hair back from her face, and her crying dropped to a whimper and a hitch.

"That seems a little dangerous," I said, "especially for José."

"She hasn't seen him clearly, and I really doubt that she can understand English—can you, sweetheart?" Bierce smiled down at her and she looked up at him in pure wonder. "We'll circle back near the town, find out where she was taken from—it shouldn't be hard—and leave her nearby. They'll only know us as phantoms."

"Yes, the strangers the Rurales are looking for. They'll tear the place apart looking for us."

"No doubt, Amos. But would you have it otherwise?" He held the child out toward me. She gave me a long, doe-eyed stare.

"Of course not," I said. "I just fear the repercussions of this night's work."

"'Sufficient unto tomorrow are the cares of tomorrow,'" he misquoted in grand style, and began walking back to our horses.

Bierce was right. Long before we reached the village we could see torches and lanterns moving like a swarm of maddened fireflies in the northeast corner of town. Voices came to us, the cries of women, the half-panicked shouts of men. Rather than run the risk of riding right into a crowd of enraged villagers, we skirted the town and kept well out of the light. When we had reached a dark and lonely quarter of the village not too far from the crowd, Bierce dismounted with the girl in his arms. She had ridden in the crook of his arm the whole way, and after a minute of riding with this giant avenging archangel she had stopped sobbing completely. Bierce set her on the dusty street and straightened out her nightclothes.

"Go on, girl," he said, waving his hands at her as if to waft her homeward. "Go see Momma."

The girl looked at Bierce. Then she turned to face the light and clamor a couple blocks distant. She looked at Bierce again. He sighed.

"Go on, now. It's all right."

When she still stared at Bierce, Juan dismounted and squatted on his haunches beside her. He softly murmured a few Spanish words to her, sprinkled liberally with diminutives such as *"casita"* and *"sueñitos,"* finishing by pointing down the street toward the noise. She turned and looked down in the direction of the torch-lit street. Then, giving Bierce one more soulful look, she gathered her nightdress around her like the most proper lady and toddled off. We watched her until she was two blocks down and the first rays of light from around a corner limned her tiny form. For a moment she stood there, looking this way and that, and then there was a cry of surprise from beyond the corner. The girl looked that way, smiled, and disappeared beyond the building.

We remounted but waited another minute. Sure enough, cries of joy and amazement rose up in a chorus beyond the houses.

"We should go," I said to Bierce. He was still gazing after where the little girl had gone.

"How old do you think she was, Amos?"

The question threw me for a moment.

"Two, surely no more than that."

"Two."

"Come on, Bierce. They'll be horsed and looking for blood soon."

We rode quietly until we were free of the town's grid of streets, then put spurs to our mounts and galloped hard for home.

7.

The storm we had ignited broke in full fury over the town the next day. Rumors of confusion drifted across the countryside. From our refuge in the Martínez barn, we saw squads of horse go flying over the *monte;* murderous-looking men with big hats and big horses and long guns. José brought us a simple breakfast of *migas* (scrambled eggs) and chorizo sausage wrapped in tortillas. A platter heavy with thick, white mugs and a blue enamel pot of strong coffee completed the repast.

"They're using dogs," said José, pouring coffee. "The Golón's terrible dogs. They're tracking us."

In my mind I pictured mastiffs, the powerful war-dogs of the Conquistadors, and I shivered. "Good thing we didn't come straight back here," I said.

After leaving the town we had struck wide out into the bush, crossing and walking the horses down what streams we could find. That and the muddle the townsfolk's own horses made in looking for the girl—and her rescuers—completed the confusion.

"It'll put them off for a while," Bierce said between sips of coffee. "But they'll find us if they have to tear up every building in the state."

José nodded sadly.

"*Es verdad.* I'm very sorry, Señores, but you will really have to go now."

We all nodded gravely. It wouldn't be easy, either to get out of José's land unseen or to quit the town.

"We should give them a hint," I said. "Something to let them know we've left the town, draw them away from these good people"

Bierce nodded with enthusiasm.

"Agreed. We can't leave the Martínez family to the mercy of these devils. A last parting shot or two?"

"From a safe distance."

"If there *is* such a thing as a 'safe distance,'" added Juan with a morose look into his coffee mug.

But the opportunity didn't come. The minutes passed in slow procession in the musty dark of the barn, indicated only by the slowly moving shafts of sunlight through the cracks in the walls; and ever in the distance roamed clumps of armed men. We chafed at the bit, Bierce most of all.

"I must see Huitzil once more," he said. He fretted and paced and made us all nervous as cats.

"For crying out loud, Bierce, settle down," I said. "Unless you can figure a way to get out and away without alerting the enemy to who hid us, here we sit."

"The Martínezes are intelligent people. They could say we forced them."

"That's all well and good, until they put a gun to Ernesto's head—or Araceli's."

Bierce sighed. "We wait for dusk, then, and flee under cover of night."

I leaned back and looked at the one, square window above the loft, the same window through which I had evaded the Rurales the day before. It was now full of bright, peaceful morning sky.

"That's a long way off, Bierce. How long until they come here and search this barn again?"

He clapped his fist into his hand. He stalked back and forth.

"You have a plethora of objections, Amos," he said. "Would that you could, by some alchemy, transmute them into solutions."

"I say we watch until the next patrol goes by, then make a run for it. The chances will be better after they pass, don't you think?"

He massaged his new beard. "Could be," he said.

"And once we're away from here," Juan chimed in, "they have no way to know where we hided."

"'Hid,'" Bierce and I said together. Juan threw up his hands in an elegant gesture of *Who cares?*

"All right, then," said Bierce. "We wait until they pass, then run for the brush as fast as we can."

"Cut around town," I said, "and maybe shoot out a window or something in passing, get their attention."

"They will guard the roads," Juan said darkly.

"Probably," said Bierce. "So we keep quiet until we get to a roadblock and pass by guns blazing. That should get their attention."

I looked to Bierce. "Is that really the best we can do?"

"Short of riding right into Señor Golón's parlour and tying him up, I fear it is."

"If we're gonna ride," Juan said, getting to his feet, "then I gotta piss."

I felt my own bladder press on me at Juan's suggestion.

"I'll just be a minute," I said to Bierce. He nodded without comment. Ever the Puritan, he would not dignify bodily functions with words.

I emerged into bald, blue light of day. Juan was already returning from the "two-seater" behind the Martinez house.

"Watch out for e-scorpions," he said with a grin.

"Thanks a lot."

I had barely finished my own visit to the outhouse when I heard footsteps slapping hard and fast toward me from the barn. Emerging, I beheld Juan, wild-eyed and breathless, coming towards me at a run.

"Señor," he started, bent to lean on his knees and catch his breath. Then: "Señor Beer—he is gone."

*

"Curse that man for a righteous old poltroon!"

Juan and I were trotting back to the barn. Juan said, "Where you think—"

"Town," I said. "Mamá Huitzil's, I have no doubt." I could hear the anger in my own voice, making it brassy, loud, and mechanical. Damn Bierce—*damn* him! For all his fine plans to leave the town guns blazing, and then just deciding to see his lady love one last time . . . For a cynic, he could be infuriatingly romantic at times. At the worst of times.

"What to do?" said Juan.

"Why, we go after the old buzzard, that's what we do. We haven't a choice: they'll tear him to shreds. We can at least give him company in death."

We had reached the barn. We gathered up as much firepower and ammunition as we could, saddled our horses, and rode out into the day.

The problem now was to decide which route he had taken. He wouldn't have taken the road—that was too open, too obvious. But keeping to the brush presented several possibilities. Would he go by the direct route, daring pursuit and trusting to speed? Or would he circle wide, skirt the town as we had done the previous night, and come in from the north? Or west? I scanned the low hills and thickets, the blue agave, the green prickly-pears.

"Do you have any idea which way he went?" I said to Juan.

"No, no—maybe. Maybe I seen him go that way . . . ?" His dusky face brightened as he looked. "Yeah, look—there he is!"

He pointed northwest. I strained to see but saw nothing but the scrub.

"Are you sure?" I said. Juan looked unsure, squinting here and there.

"I thought . . . maybe it was—"

"All right," I said. "I'll go that way, you head straight to town. But take care, don't go directly in and keep your eyes open. *Buena suerte.*"

"*Igualmente, amigo,*" he said, and turned his horse west toward town.

I worked northward through the thorny landscape. If Juan had seen Bierce, he had better eyes than I; nothing but the brown earth, crisp verdure, and blue sky appeared before me. Juan's hoofbeats faded away in the west, and I suddenly felt very alone. For weeks now the three of us had ridden, fought, and bunked together. Now neither of the others was nigh, and while I usually liked solitude, it was a sad and hollow feeling just the same. I guided my horse over several low ridges, between the bristling thickets of cactus and shrub, looking left and right and all around. No Bierce, nobody. Nothing.

A flash. Was that a gleam of sunlight on metal? A gun-barrel? Caution and eagerness fought within me. It might be Bierce, it might be Golón's men. Down a gulley, followed an arroyo into a broad, open space, a natural dish in the land. There—that flash again, up on the next ridge.

And growing out of the ground beneath it, four men on horseback.

I reined in and kept my eyes on them. They stopped at the crest overlooking the bowl, just . . . watching. At that distance, fifty yards perhaps, I swore I could see one of them smile.

That was enough for me. I pulled the horse's head back around, put my head down, and put spurs to hide. The horse leapt forward as if galvanized. But now there were more men, and coming from back the way I'd come. Horse and I plunged down into the arroyo, heedless of the rocky bed. Some of the panic I was feeling must have translated to my good mount, for he put his ears back and his long legs shot out and devoured the distance as never before. A man and horse avalanched into the other end of the arroyo ahead. Trapped. I tried to head my horse up the far bank of the arroyo, dirt and pebbles and dust flying, but there was a gunshot, the horse screamed and pitched sideways toward the fast-flying earth, and, as the novelists put it, I knew no more.

8.

I was seated by a pool of still, black water. It was the dark of dusk around me; fronds of fantastic tropical plants leaned and drooped into the scant light around the pool. And figures sat there: grimacing stone figures, with obscene and unknowable decorations on their faces, sprouting like geometric leprosy from their limbs. They sat in a circle around the pool. They faced me. The nearest one, just across the obsidian water, began to move. It was carved into the likeness of a man, of a jaguar—of both. It spoke—horrible sounds, half-growl and half-whisper—and as it spoke it looked less like stone and more like a living creature. Its coat blushed from stone-gray to tawny yellow, bruised with the black dots and parentheses of the jaguar. Its upraised paws grew real claws. And from its mouth, its strange, downward-twisted mouth, the words of a language older than man poured in an unending stream. It pointed a claw at me; it pointed down into the black pool. I leaned over it, impelled by the spell of the jaguar-man, until I was looking straight down into the depths. From deep below, my face reflected pale and small back up at me, a mask of white-eyed surprise and terror. Then it wasn't my face at all; it was a Face from the awful deeps of Time, a Face only suggested by those Pre-Columbian artisans who worked the volcanic stone with crude tools; a Face rushing up toward my own as my balance shifted and I plunged head-first into the water . . .

Water shattered over my face. I gasped, coughed, snorted two jets of water from my nose. The water was cascading over my face and I was caught, something had caught my hair and I was stuck face up under the torrent. Water gushed down and down—and stopped. The catch on my hair was released and I jerked forward, sputtering out the last drops from my nose and mouth. Blinking the water out of my eyes, I inhaled deeply to catch my breath and looked around.

The black pool was gone, but the stern figures still ringed me round. When I had shaken the last drops out of my eyes, I saw that they were men— "just men, Amos," as Bierce had told me, and therein lay my fear. They were hard men all, men in the short *chaquetas* and chaps of cowboys, men in the uniforms of the dreaded Rurales, men in fine clothes of European cut. In my panic I couldn't count accurately, but there were perhaps seven of them. They all carried guns and long knives, and they were all looking at me.

Behind these desperadoes were the details of a fine, broad room: neat stucco walls painted a soft mustard, black exposed beams crossing the low ceiling, a fireplace and mantel to the right, upon which sat an ornate clock in dark, carved wood and against which leaned a well-dressed *catrin* smoking a cigarette. His suit of dove was marred by the bandages wrapped around his left leg and midriff, and by the crutch he leaned upon; and I suddenly recognized him as the arrogant young Golón we had seen in town. He glared a smoldering hate at me.

To my immediate left was a heavy table of age-darkened wood. Seated next to this and facing me was a broad, heavy-set man seated in an ornate chair that must have been a set with the table, and looked to have been an antique when Mexico gained its independence from Spain a century before. He was dressed in dark, tailored trousers, polished boots, a clean white shirt and a black vest that enclosed his wall of a chest like a coat of black paint. His black hair was parted neatly on the left and oiled back; the obligatory mustache was as neatly trimmed as a black hedge above his wide mouth. Something about his nose, straight and patrician, reminded me of something—young Golón, of course, leaning against the mantelpiece. But the eyes distracted from all else. They were black and lightless and set deeply in his healthy, abundant flesh, and they were turned remorselessly upon me. Don Máximo Golón y Alvarado, at your service.

He was smoking a cigarette. He took one long drag upon it, his eyes never leaving mine, and stubbed it out against my wrist. It was then I discovered that I was tied to a chair, and pull though I might I couldn't get my arm away from that bright pain. The water they had poured over my head had splashed onto my arms, and it lessened the burn. But it still hurt. It hurt a lot. Golón took his time with it, too; and when he was finally done, he flicked the butt across the room to land in the fireplace. A practiced move, a casual move. The butt flashed like a comet in the fireplace's black maw and disappeared. Don Máximo leaned toward me.

"Speak e-Spanish?" he said.

"*Un—un p-poco,*" I managed.

"*Bueno.*"

He leaned toward me further. Concern wrinkled his hard features. He was a favorite uncle, he was an old friend. *Digamos, amigo*—we're just going to have a little chat.

"*Mira,*" he said. "We have a problem, amigo. We live in a fine town here, full of good people. I do for them, they do for me—*muy simpatico, ¿ya ves?* But somebody—*somebody*—someone not so good came into *my* town and shot up *my* men. My *son.*" He threw his arm out at the man with the bandages, who still looked at me with level hate.

"My son," Don Máximo continued. "Can you believe it? Now: the people of my town would never do such a thing—they are good people. They care for their don and his family, always giving us things. We are all a family here. Who do you think would dare to shoot at my son, in this town, eh? Not a member of *my* family." He mused, struck out his lower lip in thought. "A stranger, I think. Yes, a stranger. Somebody like . . . like you, amigo."

All those eyes. I swallowed but said nothing.

He shot to his feet—shockingly fast for a big man—and slapped me. It was an open-handed blow (he's saving the fists for later, I thought, falling), but his hand was like a ham and it knocked me and the chair to which I was tied reeling over to the right. Two large, dark hands reached out of somewhere behind me and righted the chair before I could hit the floor. My head rang and the entire left side of my face stung. Don Máximo looked down upon me. His cheeks were dark with blood and his breathing heavy. With a visible effort he sat back down facing me. He unbuttoned the sleeves of his immaculate shirt with slow deliberateness and rolled them up just past his elbows. Was I surprised to see the small Aztec eagle tattooed there, just below the white linen? Not really. Again he leaned forward, but the favorite uncle was gone. He raised a thick, manicured finger before my face.

"*No te hagas guaje,*" he said. "Don't play the innocent with me, *cabrón*. We had peace in this valley until you strangers—*pinches gringos*—came here. Now, my boy here says that more than one *pendejo* shot at him and his men."

"More like five or so," young Julio Cesar squinted at me through blue cigarette-smoke curls.

"Five or six," said Don Máximo and waggled his head in an *"así, así"* motion. "My boy, he exaggerates sometimes. Makes him look *más macho, ¿sí?* But even two or three, that's bad enough. That's two or three more than should be in my valley. You wouldn't say, 'Oh, there's just three weasels in the henhouse, that's not so bad as five or six, let's leave 'em,' would you?"

I risked a wobbling shake of the head.

"Good. Then we are *de acuerdo,* in agreement." He looked around him, frowned under chairs, raised his black eyebrows at his men. "So where are these weasels, then? Do you see them?"

"No, Don Máximo," several men said, not quite in unison. The don turned back to me with the impassive face of an ancient god.

"So where are the weasels, amigo? Where are your friends? And who sent you here to trouble my valley?"

A voice similar to my own, but pitched higher and quieter said, "No friends. Just me."

Don Máximo looked at me a long time with no expression. Then his face stretched into laughter. It caught like wildfire in the old room and all the other men laughed too, and I felt my bowels turn to water.

"¡Que chignón!" chuckled Don Máximo, pointing at me. "A real 'tough-guy,' eh?"

Again his hand flew out of nowhere and hit me hard—harder this time, so I'd get the point. This time Amos and chair and all crashed unimpeded to the hardwood floor. My head struck with a stupid-sounding *bonk,* and the scene of hacienda, gunsels, and Don Máximo all faded into a swimming gray shot with sparks. Then the world began to tip, right itself. Gravity shifted like a huge wave washing over me. My head lolled, and with a clack of chair-legs hitting the floor I was set back upright. When I had blinked away the grogginess, Don Máximo was looking at me again, his hands on his thighs. There was a solid nothingness in those black eyes that was more terrible than his rage.

Voices raised in argument came through the hacienda's heavy oak door. Don Máximo sighed and pushed a hand through his oiled hair.

"Caray," he said. "Somebody see what all that noise is."

Immediately the two men closest to the door pulled it open. Their hands were already upon their guns; but when they had the door wide they relaxed. Past Don Máximo's shoulder I saw a rectangle of deep evening blue filling the doorway. Standing against the blue like actors against a backdrop were another Golón thug and a crouching form in ragged serape and stained sombrero. One ancient, wizened hand stuck out from the serape like the claw of a vulture, and a weak voice from the serape said, *"Por favor, por los santos, muy generoso gentil-hombre . . ."*

"A beggar," said one of the guards inside the door.

"I can see that, *fulano*," said Don Máximo. "Give him something and get him the hell out of here. *De prisa, cabrónes,* hurry up."

The man by the door dug in his pockets, brought up a couple coins, and threw them out the door. A whining *"Gracias, gracias, Señor"* was cut off as the great door was pushed shut.

Don Máximo turned to me again and leaned upon his legs. He sighed.

"Real tough-guy," he said again. The clock on the mantel ticked away the seconds. Through the door came the muffled voices of the guard and the beggar, quieter now. I felt blood crawling out of my nose, over my lips, down over my chin. Somewhere far away the burn on my wrist buzzed. Finally Don Máximo sat back.

"Chuy," he called over his shoulder. "Bring me the *joyero*."

Joyero, I thought through sluggish tides of pain. Like *joyeria*, jewelry. A jewel-box, that's it. One of the younger men present, a wiry teenager, said, *"Sí, papá,"* and walked to a cabinet against the wall away to my left. He reached up and lifted down a large, plain clay jar from atop it. He handled it as if it were rarest china. With exaggerated care he brought it to his don and set it upon the table beside him. The don stood up and lifted the jar a fraction of an inch and tapped it once, twice upon the table-top, as if settling its contents—*tock, tock.* Then he took a folding-knife from his pocket, unfolded the blade, and used it to pry up the wide cork stopper sealing the jar. With great care he lifted the stopper with the point of the knife and peered beneath it. Satisfied, he took the stopper out of the jar completely and laid it upon the table nearby. The jar he picked up and, turning slowly, sat back down with it and held before him. Every motion had been done as carefully as in a ceremony. He looked down into the jar and smiled.

"You may have heard how rich our country is, *gringo*," he said. "This is a land of gold and silver, of copper and many jewels. Here are some jewels we picked up just off the ground."

Slowly, slowly, he tipped the jar so that its opening was aimed toward my face. I blinked. At first it was just a solid circle of blackness. So black—it yawned wide like black glass, like a black mirror. Was there something, some *things,* reflected in it? Small pieces of light glittered and moved in its depths—

yellow, gold, green. I looked as close as my bonds would let me. Pale legs moved, segmented bodies and tails. The jar was full of scorpions.

"*Que bonitos, ¿no?*" Don Máximo grinned at me over the jar. "As a guest in my house, I offer you these jewels. Go on, take one—take as many as you like. Osito?"

The big brown hands that had righted the chair previously appeared from behind me again, this time attached to two forearms like oak limbs. One hand held a knife. I tried to yank myself free of my bonds but only succeeded in rocking the chair back and forth in sharp little jerks. Don Máximo and his troops watched without expression. Meanwhile Osito's powerful left hand gripped my right wrist while his right hand used the knife to saw through the leather thong binding it to the arm of the chair. Then both of his hands lifted my arm and began pushing my hand toward the open mouth of the jar.

At first sight of the scorpions I had drawn in a long gasping breath until I could take in no more air. Now it was stuck in my chest. I couldn't breathe. Nor could I stop Osito from pushing my hand into that nightmare black maw of shifting, glittering, clicking death. It was as if an alien spirit guided my arm and nothing I could do would stop it.

Yet even as my body strained with every ounce of strength against my restraints, my eyes were fastened upon the mouth of the jar. Each second the view within it became clearer; the pale, translucent legs of the horrid arachnids moved over and around one another, winking in and out; the barbed tails darted stings. The whole interior of the jar shifted and glittered and twitched in countless machine-like movements—the Devil's clockworks.

I couldn't move, couldn't breathe. Everything was vividly clear, painfully clear, as if for the first time in my life a filter had been removed from the light of the world. Bierce had written about this kind of preternatural lucidity in stories such as "An Occurrence at Owl Creek Bridge," but I had always taken it as a literary invention. Now, like one of Bierce's own characters, I saw that it was all too true.

The unseen Osito still pushed my hand closer to the jar-mouth, inexorable but with deliberate slowness. His grip was so powerful that I might as well have tried to stop the Earth turning as break his hold. My hand was going into that jar and that was that. At the last second I spread my fingers out like a starfish across the mouth of the jar. The fingertips just reached.

Don Máximo sighed. "Break his fingers."

Something soft and heavy thudded against the wall by the front door. Heads turned, hands shot to pistols, rifles. The big oak door flew wide, and framed in it was the beggar, but beggar no more; transformed into Ambrose Bierce, and Ambrose Bierce transformed into an archangel, not the gentle angel who had saved a young girl, but a grim and towering Angel of Death. The filthy sombrero was gone and in one sweeping movement like the rising wings of an eagle, Bierce threw back the old serape he wore and stood tall in his black suit and gunbelt. For a second he stood thus—white-eyed and terrible—and the room froze. Then, with a crossover as fast as a rattlesnake, he jerked out his pistols and began firing.

The room exploded. Men yelled, pistols crashed, and rifles barked. Smoke began filling the room, lit up by sudden jets of flame. Don Máximo stood and pivoted on his heel and set the jar on the table in one movement. He tore the pistol from the holster at his hip. But before he could even get off a shot Bierce leveled his big Colt at him, and the steel eye of the barrel burst forth in flame. I saw two sudden holes pop open in the back of Don Máximo's vest. The don bent double and crashed to the floor. Men were falling back from Bierce as before a strong wind; they cringed, they fell, they died. And careless and silent as if he were walking through a museum, Bierce came on, his guns roaring death. And when the hammers of his guns fell on empty chambers, Bierce dropped the guns and, smooth as a dancer, grabbed up the guns of the fallen. He didn't miss a beat. I saw young Julio Cesar, already bloody, snapping off shots from his pistol even as he slumped back against the fireplace. It was hard to tell through the blue smoke, but at the last he looked like a long, sinewy beast, trying to tear itself free of the bandages that wrapped it round. In the midst of the whirlwind, Bierce stretched his left hand out straight at Julio Cesar. The Colt banged, Julio Cesar bucked back and slid into the fireplace.

It was a hurricane of hellfire, a hailstorm of lead. Blood splattered the walls; a pistol went pinwheeling above my head. Terrified, I saw Bierce's clothing twitch from bullets striking him. But though he grimaced, he kept coming on and on.

A thick arm thrust over my shoulder. Osito again, and this time holding a pistol out straight toward Bierce. My right arm was free. Without thinking I grabbed Osito's brawny arm and shoved it straight up.

"Bierce!"

Bierce turned at my voice, seemed to aim at my face, and fired. His shot passed so close to me that I heard it *crack!* through the air and felt its heat sear my temple. Osito let out a surprised *"hunh!"* and his arm pulled back and away from me. I felt his body thud to the floorboards.

A stray shot hit the jar and shards of pottery and scorpions flew into the air. They scattered across the table-top. Pulling my arm to the utmost, I shoved the table over.

And then it was finished. Or mostly so; Bierce walked among the fallen army of Don Máximo Golón, kicking this body, firing a bullet into that. Smoke drifted.

"B-Bierce," I said. "Watch out—scorpions."

"Vicious creatures." He fired at something among the bodies.

But there was still gunfire. Slowly I realized that it was coming from behind me. It must have been drowned out by the calamity happening in the room before. It, too, seemed to be coming to an end. Another shot, two more, then silence.

Bierce strode over to me. He shoved Don Máximo's body aside with his foot as if it were dirty laundry, and knelt before me. His eyes were as clear and direct as I'd ever seen them, and he looked at me with concern. The Avenging Angel was gone, and in its place was again an angel of mercy. In its place was plain old Ambrose Bierce, my friend.

"Are you hurt, Amos?" He snapped out his clasp-knife to cut my bonds.

"No," I managed. "Nothing serious."

He helped me to my feet. Once I was steady I leaned against the upended table and forced myself to take several long, deep breaths. My hands were shaking. A scorpion went skedaddling past the toe of my boot—I didn't even have the heart to crush it. The real monsters were dead, all around me.

I glanced over at the chair where I had been bound. Behind it sprawled a hulking sandbag of a man, mountain-ranges of legs, belly, chest, chin. Osito. His black hair, cut so close as to be a shadow, grew low in a widow's peak on his brief forehead, and just below the peak was one black hole. He looked up at the ceiling in disbelief.

And then Juan Romero was there, and three other men I didn't recognize. All carried rifles; all walked solemn and silent through the wreckage.

"Juan and the boys from the village led the charge from the back of the hacienda," Bierce said, sliding home his pistols in their scabbards. "They waited upon the sound of my attack, then launched their own."

Juan and the other men surveyed the carnage.

"*Caramba,*" Juan said. "We killed some out back, but this . . ."

A sudden wave of fury swelled up in me. I pushed off from the table and walked to Juan and slapped him across the face. That odd smile of his had been forming as he saw me, but in the instant it disappeared. In its place was a look of cold emptiness.

"You son of a bitch," I said. "You sent me to these—animals. You son of a bitch."

What would have happened next I don't like to think about. Juan was shifting his rifle to his left hand, preparing, I'm sure, to pull out his machete. I was still in the lock of my own rage and not ready to back down.

Fortunately Bierce strode in between us.

"Easy, men," he said. To me: "He didn't know, Amos. He *couldn't* have known Golón's men were there. It was my fault for slipping out like that. My fault." He put his hand on my arm. "There's been enough bloodshed, son."

I wiped my hand down my face.

"Yes, you're right, of course. And I'm sorry, Juan. All this—I wasn't thinking straight. Please accept my apology."

I extended my hand to him. He just looked at it for a second, but finally took it in his own.

"'Course, amigo," he said, and the old, odd smile returned. But there was something missing from it, and I knew that I had lost trust with the man.

Then I remembered the details of the gunfight and whirled on Bierce.

"But you," I said. "They shot you. I saw it."

"Oh, yes." Bierce frowned down at himself and stuck a finger through a neat bullet-hole in his coat. "Yes, well, I had the foresight to stop at Mamá Huitzil's shop before coming here, and she gave me a treatment, shall we say, against such wounds."

He dug a finger into the watch-pocket of his vest and produced the flattened remains of a bullet. He turned it over in his palm. "Quite efficacious, it seems."

The open front door and whatever windows or doors Juan and his troops had broken down to gain ingress were allowing the smoke to drift away. The corners of the room, the fine mustard-colored stucco walls, now streaked and dotted with blood, came into focus once more. So did the carpet of dead gunmen.

And so did a lone figure standing back at the rear left-hand corner of the room. It was a woman, tall, stately, still as a painting. Her iron-gray hair was feathered up in a fashionable bouffant. From her chin to the floor she wore a long dress of a pale pink, almost white, speckled with some reprinted design in red. Her face was long, rectangular; hard, imperious, merciless. From the round bump of her chin to the lipless cut of a mouth, and especially the two black stones of eyes, she was the very portrait of authority. There was nothing of the "frail female" about her, nothing feminine about her at all. In her eyes, absolutely nothing human at all.

"La doña Inez," said one of Juan's companions, and slowly wiped the sombrero from his head. We all turned and looked at her; we, the killers of her husband and family. Now I could see a resemblance to some of the men who had fallen: a more delicate version of Julio Cesar's jawline, the original of another man's rectangular face. How many sons had they had? Five? Six? The bodies lay mute all around us.

The doña's gaze moved from one to another of us. Marking, memorizing. When her gaze alighted on me, a shiver went down my back. Her moving regard came to rest on Bierce. If that soulless stare troubled him, he didn't show it.

"Madam," Bierce bowed. She continued to stare at him as if she were stone. Bierce turned to us.

"Time to go, gentlemen."

We walked out through the tumbled bodies and the stench of death. I stopped to retrieve my gun, which Don Máximo still held in his rigid hand. At the door I took one last look back. The bodies still lay, the lady of the house still stood. I could picture that tableau lasting into the millennia to come, unchanged.

Outside the evening air was blessedly cool and fresh. I breathed in a long, reviving draft of it, and my hands stopped shaking.

Bierce stood at my side; he was holding the reins of two horses.

"Are you all right to ride?" he said.

"Quite all right, thank you. And you?"

"Never better."

9.

After the gunfight at Hacienda Golón, we stayed in San Andrés for only a couple more days. I was not quite as recovered from the ordeal as I had thought, and Bierce had his *despedidas* to make to Mamá Huitzil. Juan puttered about, helping the townsfolk bury the Golón gang and strip the hacienda of everything of value or use. He was civil to me but little more. I regretted having hit him, but damn it, he had put me in a bad spot. Because of his carelessness, I could have been killed, and not in a clean way, either.

But the demands of the day prevented me from ruminating on it much. We had to prepare to leave for Torreón. Fortunately the townsfolk were more than generous in their gratitude to us. I was given a fine mount from the stables of the *hacienda* to replace my poor, dead chestnut; and a pair of the men from the village would accompany us to Torreón, both to guard us against any surviving Golón partisans and to bring the horses back to San Andrés. A few of Don Máximo's henchmen and hands had escaped the massacre; and while we were pretty sure they wanted only to get away and wouldn't lie in wait for us, it was reassuring to have the extra guns with us.

As for Doña Inez Salazar y Golón, she was never seen again. I imagined her being given a horse and buggy and being shown the road out of town; but when the townsfolk returned to the hacienda later on the night of the gunfight, she was already gone. Some of the locals spoke of a white owl that had been seen flying over the abandoned hacienda, screaming as if to mourn her lost chicks; but who could believe such tales? Might as well believe that a man could change himself into a jaguar.

We left San Andrés Tecolotzán on a bright blue morning. Some of the villagers, including the whole Martínez family, came out to make their farewells. Bierce and Mamá Huitzil stood apart, her small hands in his great, pale old claws. I gave them their privacy, but even at a remove of twenty paces I could see the sunlight glint on tears in the old woman's eyes. She shook her head several times—it seemed more than her not wanting Bierce to go, more like a refusal to believe it. But he was adamant, as always, and with a last embrace he walked from her to where we waited with the horses. When he was mounted Mamá came to his side and put her hand lightly upon his boot.

"Farewell, my dear," Bierce said, and lifted his black hat. "*'Hasta la proxima,'* as you folk put it so melodically."

But the old woman shook her head.

"No, *querido*. I will not see you again. If you leave, this is *adios,* and *que los espiritus les cuiden*—may the spirits watch over you and yours." Then she took her hand from his boot, backed away, and stood with hands folded like sleeping doves against the black of her dress.

We rode south all that day and part of the next. That next morning we crossed a railroad siding, and one of our guards from the village pointed along the long tracks to eastward.

"Horizonte is that way," he said, "not far. There is a station there, too."

But Bierce preferred the anonymity of a large station, such as the one in

Torreón, to a parochial branch-line outpost where we would stand out.

We reached Torreón at midday, and it was as busy as Bierce could have hoped. Two major railway lines—the Mexican Central and Mexican International—met and crossed here, and the place was a hive of activity. Campesinos, businessmen, *indios,* and *federales*—lots of *federales*—milled and shuffled and called and hurried around the station, changing trains, escaping the north, coming in to trade. *Mecapaleros,* young men and boys with outrageous towers of goods on their backs, secured with a band across their foreheads, strode through it all on single-minded missions. Vendors had set up their carts along the track and called out *"Tamales! Sombreros! Joyeria de plata! Ahorre mucho!"* in an unending chorus in that sing-song accent of Mexico that somehow made it all harmonize. Overall there was a busy Oriental feel to the scene that reminded me of Chinatown back in 'Frisco. Even the faces and some of the straighter, thicker hair brought Asia to mind. I have since read that men of science theorize that the ancestors of all the native peoples of America had come from Asia over a land-bridge to what is now Alaska. How long had these people been here? Ten thousand years? Twenty thousand? And what secrets of the land had they learned in that time?

The *federales,* fortunately, all looked too harried and nervous to pay any attention to an ancient gringo and his ragged train. They were a mixed lot, those soldiers; hard-faced veterans laden with bandoliers; Indians in ill-fitting uniforms and hand-made *huaraches* on their mahogany-colored feet; and boys, mere boys, peering out from under the bills of their peaked caps. The presence of the boys—some as young as nine or ten or I'm much mistaken—gave credence to the rumors that Huerta's troops were on the ropes. It was reassuring to see the dreaded *federales* put to such extreme measures, but chilling to think of those boys conscripted out of their mothers' arms and going into battle.

Bierce especially looked long and thoughtfully at these *niños heroes.*

"They would have been given a drum back in Buell's army," he said with a sad shake of the head. "Not guns."

I said, "It's a different kind of war, Bierce. A revolution, more than a civil war."

"No, Amos," he shook his leonine white head sadly. "It's just war, and as General Sherman is known to have said, 'War is all hell.'"

So as not to attract any more attention to ourselves than necessary, we bade our rustic escort farewell some way from the station. As briefly as we had known these men, it was still an emotional farewell; because they were men, true men and good, and they had risked their lives alongside us. I gained a new appreciation for the nostalgia that Bierce held for his Civil War days. How clear and simple it must have been, to be young and strong and ignited with righteous fervor; and how fulfilling to throw one's self into dire danger alongside your brothers-in-arms. The bond one forms in such circumstances is hard to explain, but no less real for it. I would miss these good men of San Andrés. *Vayan con Dios, amigos.*

"Your carriage awaits," quoth Bierce with his arm outstretched. We hefted our belongings and trudged to the station.

After muscling through the crowds and the acrid steam gushed forth by the locomotives, we found we still had some time before the next train to the capital—the *"De Efe,"* as the Mexicans call it, for "Distrito Federal," their version of our Washington, D.C.

"I should like to find some new clothes," I said to Bierce after we had secured our tickets.

"I should like to see you find some new clothes," he replied, giving me a withering head-to-toe appraisal.

"All right, all right," I said. "So you're no Rose of Tralee, either, mister. Juan, do you know Torreón at all? Where can we find some *ropa nueva?"*

No, he said, he did not, but with some polite questioning of the locals we found what passed for "downtown Torreón," and a serviceable dry-goods store. Equally important, a public bath and barber. An hour later we three were all newly fitted with neat new togs and freshly shorn faces. I had gotten myself a new suit of charcoal-gray, topped with a black fedora that I flattered myself made me look dashing and slightly dangerous. Shiny new button-up shoes replaced the down-at-heel boots I had had since Chihuahua. Bierce, too, looked reborn. A new black suit, cravat, a clean replacement for his trademark black homburg, black shoes with white spats, and a white shirt so new it looked almost blue in the daylight. He was once again the dignified and intimidating figure of old. Juan, on the other hand, appeared to have merely replaced his clothes with less ragged version of the same.

Thus appareled, we retired to the train. Our money, that inexhaustible bank that Bierce wore around his waist, held up, and we treated ourselves to a first-class coach to the capital. Bierce purchased a bottle of whiskey from a white-coated *mesedora;* Juan opted for a bottle of his clear tequila gotten with a whisper and a coin from the conductor; and seated with our three glasses, we relaxed and took in the carnival flowing past the windows.

"Amos," Bierce said, licking stray drops of whiskey from his mustache, "your Spanish is a little better than mine. Would you clarify this, please?"

He held a newspaper out to me that someone had left on the seat beside him. I took it and read the headline from the left-hand column:

ESCRITOR NORTEAMERICANO PERDIDO EN MEXICO
AUROTIRDADES LE TEMEN DIFUNDO.

"'American Author Lost in Mexico,'" I read aloud. "'Authorities Fear Him Dead.'" Below this was a very faded half-tone cut of a familiar portrait done years before, and in the paragraph below this my eyes were caught by a familiar name—"Ambrosio Bierce."

"So you're 'Ambrosio' now," I said, returning the paper to him.

He screwed up his face.

"Never did like that name, and turning it into Spanish makes it no sweeter. However, at least I am dead."

I raised my whiskey.

"The King is dead," I said. "Long live the King."

We three clinked glasses and drank.

I glanced at the paper again and said, "It's not a very good likeness, Bierce."

"Thank God for small favors," he said. "That and the announcement of my recent demise should throw our enemies off the scent, I hope. The elimination of the Golón gang should help as well, for though a couple rascals may have es-caped our wrath, yet they did not know my name . . . I assume?"

I rubbed at the cigarette-burn on my wrist.

"Not from me did they hear it," I said. "And I suspect those men weren't so well read as to recognize the famous *autor norteamericano* in your guise as aveng-ing hobo."

Bierce smirked and took another jolt of whiskey.

"Still, a tall, fair-haired gringo tends to stand out," he said. I didn't correct the obsolete reference to his hair color; Bierce had a vanity streak a mile wide. His "fair hair" had been silver for years. He added, "We must maintain a dis-creet profile."

Juan was looking at each of us in turn.

"'¿Un perfil descreto'?" he said. "¿Que significa?"

"He means we still have to lie low," I said.

"'Lie low'?"

"HIDE," both Bierce and I said together in a voice that turned heads throughout the coach.

"Ah," said Juan, and sipped his tequila.

We were roused from our new-found indolence by voices—voices in English, no less, and female.

"I told you, Deliah, dear, that that was *not* our car."

As a man we three turned toward the voices. There, bustling though the doorway to the exit like a storm of bleached cotton and black taffeta, was a tall, well-dressed woman of approximately sixty years, carting bags and parcels and navigating a hat of manhole-cover proportions through the narrow entry. She had a large, long nose, a bit too much for her face. It appeared to have pushed her lower face into the neck, causing a pair of chins just above her high collar. A pair of wet blue eyes half-lidded from the habit of looking down on the rest of the world and a small mouth pursed at the revelation completed her appearance. Swept in on the draught behind her cumulus of skirts was a smaller woman in black; smaller in every way—form, face, and presence, but more focused somehow, more real. She was a pretty brunette with dark eyes of gray or hazel. Behind her in turn and almost lost in the miles of female fabric were two young boys, neat in their matching tweed jackets and knickers. And finally, behind these was a rumor of servants and porters laden with the ladies' impedimenta.

The procession came to an abrupt halt just within our car. The redoubtable dame in front raked the car with an imperious gaze.

"I *told* you, Deliah dear," she said as if addressing the DAR, "that *this was not our car.*" Her accent was pure New England; "not our car" came out as "nawt owah kaa." After weeks of Mexican Spanish, it was as refreshing as a glass of cold water. Her inspection continued round until it lit upon us, three freshly scrubbed *hombres* standing at respectful attention. I crushed my Stetson off my head. Immediately a light appeared to have been ignited behind the lady's features. Her eyes opened to their full extent and a smile curved open betwixt nose and chin like a crescent of pink darkness.

"My word!" she said. "Can you believe our luck? Deliah, dear, come!" And she rushed down upon us like a Yankee nor'easter. She went straight up to Bierce (of course) and hovered just feet away, her hands clutched together at her throat in a surprisingly girlish gesture. The crescent gaped in undisguised pleasure.

"Oh, sir," she said to Bierce, "you cannot imagine what a delight this is! To meet you, to actually *meet* you, and in such a Gawd-forsaken country as this!"

Bierce and I exchanged uneasy glances. We didn't really want his identity broadcast so, and other heads were turning our way throughout the car.

"You have the advantage of me, madam," Bierce said with practiced courtesy. The woman put a blue-veined hand to her mouth and giggled—actually giggled.

"Of course," she said. "Forgive me. It's just that it isn't every day"—she reached out and grabbed Bierce's right hand in a lady's finger-grip. Still, it looked painfully tight.

"I am Mrs. Ethel Gadbury of the Waltham, Massachusetts, Gadburys." She pronounced the town's name as WOLL-thim. "And I am a very great admirer of your books!"

This was a little more to Bierce's liking. I saw his back straighten a centimeter, and he replied, "My blushes, madam. You are too kind."

Mrs. Ethel Gadbury buried Bierce's hand in both of hers.

"Yes," she said, gathering steam, "you are one of my very favorite authors, I have always said, haven't I, Deliah dear?"

The petite brunette behind her muttered an uninspired, "Yes, Mother, you have."

"Yes, I have. That is why it is such a delight—a revelation!—to actually meet you here! Why, 'Huckleberry Finn' virtually changed my life!"

The smile on Bierce's face froze—then stretched into a painfully taut rictus.

"As it did mine, madam," he said, and shook both her hands in his. "As it did mine."

It wasn't the first time Bierce had been mistaken for Mark Twain. They were of an age and had actually known each other in the London expatriate community in the '70s; each was distinguished by manes of coifed, white hair, the outrageous mustachios of the previous age, and eyebrows to match. Add the cigar and many people couldn't tell them apart. Never mind the fact that Mr. Twain had been in his Connecticut grave for four years by then. Bierce usually bristled at the comparison, but today it fit his needs perfectly.

After that there was nothing for it but for the entire family to meet "Mr. Twain" and shake hands with the great man. Juan and I were introduced as well, though clearly as an afterthought. Mrs. Gadbury's eyes undeniably shone only for the celebrity in our midst. We were shuffled unceremoniously into the background while the Great Ones conversed.

But as it turned out, that was fine by me. It fell out that there were two Mrs. Gadburys—the indomitable senior, Ethel, and the diminutive Mrs. Gadbury, Junior, Deliah. Accompanying the latter were the two boys, the latter's two sons, Jerome III and little Harry. They wore not only matching tweeds but matching empty, hollow, brown-eyed stares, and each clutched a tin soldier in his hand. Napoleonic, or I was mistaken—shakos and tails.

"Hey, boys," Juan said to Jerome and Harry. "Wanna see some *real* soldiers?"

Four large, pleading eyes looked to Deliah.

"All right," she said. "Just stay in sight and out of trouble."

They bustled off after Juan, just down and across the car from us. And I suddenly found myself alone with Mrs. Deliah Gadbury. I offered her a seat, she took it, and I sat opposite her.

"A long way from Waltham," I said, pronouncing it as the elder Gadbury had done.

Deliah cringed.

"Wall-tham," she said, putting equal emphasis on both syllables. "Mother likes to put on airs. By Beacon Hill standards we haven't the right, but that doesn't deter her."

She shared a New England affect with the elder Mrs. Gadbury—elided r's, stretched vowels. But where it came out in a bray like a cold gale from the elder woman, from Deliah's mouth it was like a cool breeze off a cake of ice in the heat of summer.

"To Mother," she continued, "money, even nouveau riche money, is money. That we can't trace our ancestors to the *Mayflower* makes no difference to her. But it does to *them*."

"The Cabots and the Lowells, you mean?"

She raised dark brows in amused surprise.

"So you know of our local pantheon. No, we aren't nearly that high in the stratosphere. In Waltham, it's the Moodys and the Dennisons, families who got into the watchmaking game before Father did."

"Then your father made watches?"

She laughed like a flock of doves taking flight.

"Gods, no! He started the manufactory that produces them, Gadbury Timepieces. Have you heard of them?"

"I'm afraid not. I carry a Sears myself."

"I'm not surprised," she waved it away. "Still, he sold enough to make the scads of money that support us still. And he wasn't my father—he was my father-in-law."

"Your pardon, Mrs. Gadbury. I heard you address the lady as 'Mother', and . . ."

"A term of affection," she said and looked away. I was sure she had been going to say "respect," but changed her mind. I sought to turn the conversation.

"A fascinating business—making watches, I mean. So many parts, aligning them just so. Your husband must be occupied with a thousand aspects—"

"My husband occupies six feet of stony Chihuahua earth, Mr. Littlefault."

I was mortified. I should have known, of course, from the black dress and shawl, the sadness in her eyes and the gloom lying over her boys. For a long moment we looked at each other, the bereaved and the embarrassed.

"I'm terribly sorry," I said. "Both for your loss and for my indelicacy."

She smiled, sad and sweet.

"The latter is nothing, the former is—not. It is why we are here, running south to catch a steamer back home, away from all the killing." She reached into the jet-beaded reticule at her wrist, withdrew a hanky and dabbed at her eyes. It was her turn to be embarrassed.

"Then we have something in common," I said. "We were in Chihuahua weeks ago and have been running ever since. In fact, this is the first we have been able to travel south by train."

"Really?" She put away her hanky. "You interest me, Mr. Littlefault. I had thought you and your Mr. Bierce were traveling for pleasure."

I started, looked around quickly.

"Then you recognized him," I said. It seemed pointless and disingenuous of me to lie.

"Surely. He has neither the public presence nor the voluminous hair of Mr. Twain, whom I have seen read his works in Hartford." Then she leaned over to me and put a doll-like hand upon mine. "But don't tell Mother—this is the highlight of an extremely trying trip for her."

"I shan't say a word," I laughed, "if I may ask the same discretion of you."

She clapped her hands over her mouth, and we both had a real laugh.

It broke the ice, as they say. The details of her "trying trip" came out them, punctuated by tear-wetted pauses, and strung together with bits of biography and the history of the whole family. Succinctly put, it came to this:

Upon the death of his father, Jerome Gadbury, Sr., Jerome Jr. had sold off half of his personal shares in the family watch-making business to buy a ranch near Ciudad Cuahtémoc, some fifty miles southwest of Chihuahua City. When his family objected, he pointed to magazine articles enumerating the successes of Canadian Mennonites who had moved to that fertile region and who had prospered.

"'The watch-making business is a losing game,' he said." Deliah stared at something in memory's fields. "'There is too much competition,' he said. 'A man who has no land is nothing.' And so we went, five years ago. My younger boy Henry is technically Mexican by birth—can you feature it?"

I looked over at him, chatting in an excited voice with Juan in what sounded like colloquial Spanish without a hint of accent, and said yes, I could.

Five years had passed in peace and prosperity. Jerome Jr. was vindicated— the life of a *hacendado* fit him down to the ground. If it fit Deliah less than perfectly, well, she was adept at making alterations.

Then the Revolution came. The Pax Porfiriana was over, and bands of horsemen could be seen running the horizons at all hours. Was that thunder or cannon? The mountains held their secrets; the plains kept their silences.

One day a couple months past, one of those roving bands had come to Hacienda Gadbury. The Revolution demanded sacrifices, the People needed the land. Down with the dons! Long live *la Revolución!* Were they *villistas,* I asked her. She didn't know, didn't care. The family must leave, they must go *now.* The Quinto Flores was being appropriated for that unimpeachable god of fanatics, the People.

Jerome Gadbury was no don, but no coward, either. He emerged from the house with a rifle and a Yankee set to his jaw that said *This far and no farther*.

"They shot him," Deliah said. She said it simply and a little louder than she might have meant to. Juan turned a worried eye at me, but I gave him the okay and he nodded. "They shot him in front of me and the men, but not, thank God in front—" And she put her face in to her hanky. I put a hand out, hesitated, then set it as gently as I could upon her arm.

"I am so sorry, Deliah," I said. "I cannot begin—"

Her face came up out of the cotton, hard, resolute. I snatched my hand away. She said, "No, you really can't, can you? But thank you anyway. They gave us an hour to clear out the house and . . . Jerome. The men were wonderful. They had been with us from the start, Jerome had always treated them fairly and well, and they repaid it with their industry and faithfulness. We had all we needed and more packed and on the wagon at hour's end, and Jerome sleeps now under a favorite mesquite grove. Mother tried to, that is she wanted . . . but this climate, this heat . . ." Deliah waved and gave a mirthless, twisted smile at the sky as if the climate had been some cruel joke perpetrated upon her alone. "Anyway, I gave the men what money I could. They wouldn't take it at first, but I knew they had nowhere to go now, so I passed it to Rudolfo, the foreman, to give to them after we had gone."

She stopped and stared and shook her tear-stained face slowly back and forth. She looked drained of every reserve of strength, of everything.

"I cannot understand," she said. "All this—death, all this cruelty."

"The bleak face of war," I said. "It never changes. I'm sure our own Civil War was just as bloody, in its way."

"Do you think so, truly?"

"I have little doubt. You've read Bierce's work?"

"Only a few stories, 'Event at Owl Creek,' or something. Very disturbing, as I recall."

"He'd be pleased to hear you say that. But his Civil War reminiscences can be just as potent."

She nodded, still distracted. "In Massachusetts, we're brought up to respect the legends of the glorious Minutemen. You'd think the entire Revolution was fought and won on the fields of Concord and Lexington, without a moral blemish. Yet I've read of how the Minutemen shot from behind stone walls and loaded their guns with pocket-knives and nails for maximum harm. No one, it seems, is blameless."

We sat in silence, each wrapped in memories of war and loss. Then something, a passing church-tower or someone walking a burro along the siding, brought Deliah back to the present.

"We stayed in Torreón a month. Family friends, God bless them. I don't know how much further I could have traveled, being strong for the boys"—she smiled—"and being proper for my mother-in-law. For a woman who had just lost her son, she has betrayed very little emotion over it. And I know she expects the same of me."

A less rosy glance at Mrs. Gadbury Senior, busily telling "Mr. Twain" every detail of her fascinating life. Deliah sighed.

"The curse of the proper Yankee, which grows in proportion to the wealth you possess. Oh, I don't presume to claim the 'poor little rich girl' mantle; I'd insult every genuinely poor person I've ever seen if I did, and I've seen quite a few down here. But the Bennings, our hosts, were cut from the same old stiff cloth as we, and some days I'd just shut myself in my room at their house to cry and cry."

She looked at me then, searching, pleading.

"Do I strike you as spoiled, Mr. Littlefault? Should I bear up more gracefully under all this?"

"You bear up amazingly well," I said, "given the circumstances. Nobody could ask more of you, although I think you could ask more of the world."

"I lack for nothing, I assure—"

I batted the air in an impatient gesture.

"Wealth has nothing to do with it. What you possess in money doesn't balance what you have lost in comfort."

"I tell you that the Bennings were hospitality personified. If I couldn't find comfort there, then the fault was my own."

I smiled at her.

"There's that stiff-necked Yankee again," I said. "And you confuse the meanings of 'comfort.' I meant a friend to whom you could pour out your feelings rather than keep them crated in the attic of your heart. Someone who could help bear the burden for you."

"And what makes you think that I have not found such a friend?"

The tracks *shuck-shuck, shuck-shucked* beneath us. The Mexican scenery flashed by, greens, browns, ochres. Deliah and I looked at each other; we knew each other.

"As," I said slowly, "have I." And I again lay my hand upon her arm. She made no move to take it off, and in this pleasant, peaceful stasis, we sat and looked into the warmth of each other's eyes.

"Mother," Deliah said sotto voce. I didn't need to ask or turn to see; I slid my hand the long, weary three inches from Deliah's arm to the arm of my own wicker chair.

"Deliah, dear," Mrs. Gadbury boomed down the length of the car. Her accent made it come out "Delier, deah," and it must have been as deafening as a howitzer at close quarters. I turned to see her rushing down between the chairs with Bierce following at an easy pace. With her acres of white muslin and his black suit and cigar, they looked like a locomotive pushing an avalanche down a valley. I stood.

"Mr. Twain has generously consented to join us for supper!" the woman gushed. "Isn't that superb?"

"We wouldn't want to impose, Mr. Bi—Mr. Twain," Deliah said.

"The imposition is all mine," Bierce said. "The company of two such charming creatures as yourselves will do wonders toward brightening my day." I sent Bierce a look, the slightest twitch of an eyebrow. He caught it, understood, and added, "As it will for my companions."

Mrs. Gadbury Sr.'s elation dimmed a few watts.

"Why," she said, favoring me with a pasteboard smile, "of course. We would be delighted to have you join us—if you are not otherwise engaged . . . ?"

I ignored the hint. Damned if I would be thwarted from seeing Deliah again.

"It would be our pleasure," I said. Juan came up then with the boys. Mrs. G. looked at Juan with undisguised contempt. There was clearly a struggle going on inside the woman, whether it was worth the honor of dining with the famous "Mr. Twain" if it included dining with his swarthy companion. Finally, though, she took a deep breath.

"I'm so pleased," she said.

"Excellent!" Bierce rubbed his hands together with vigor. "My associates have accompanied me through many vicissitudes. I should hate to leave them behind when the harvest finally comes in."

Mrs. G. said, "Quite. Shall we meet in the dining room at, say, six o'clock? That should give you sufficient time to . . . freshen up. Henry, remove that soldier from your nose, dear. Deliah? Shall we?"

It wasn't a request. Deliah rose, smiled dutifully, and said, "Of course, Mother. Gentlemen?"

We bowed and the Gadbury clan left us for their own car, the next one forward.

"A remarkable woman," said Bierce, looking after them.

"Yes, indeed." I watched until the last shred of Deliah's black dress disappeared among the railway furniture and people.

10.

Supper was festive. Mrs. G. Senior, happily enveloped in "Mr. Twain's" oversized personality as she was, forgot about her dislike of us mere mortals. The rest of us peasants continued our own fiesta at the lower two-thirds of the table. The meal was *mole poblano,* the national dish of Mexico, or so the waiter informed us. I thought the combination of unsweetened chocolate and spices in the *mole* itself a savory, if unusual flavor; but the boys balked at the very idea of it.

"You must at least try it," said Deliah, holding out a forkful of turkey coated in dark mole toward young Henry. "You shan't get anything else."

"Chocolate on *turkey?*" said Jerome the Third, and made a face that was instantly mirrored by his younger brother. Deliah looked ready for a nap.

"Miren, chamacos," Juan said. He carved himself a neat oval of breast-meat, ladled mole all over it, and folded it into his mouth. His eyes closed; he chewed slowly, rhythmically, with almost obscene pleasure.

"Mmmm," he said, and swallowed. *"¡Es muy rrrrrrrrico!"*

His rolled Spanish "r" purred into the upper spaces. The boys, who had watched this fascinated, burst out in gales of screaming laughter. Mrs. G. Senior looked down from her Olympus at the end of the table and said, "Boys! Stop that cacophony right now!"

"DON'T YOU EVER TELL MY BOYS WHAT TO DO."

Silence fell. We all looked at Deliah, so small, so erect, so stern. I would never have expected such iron from so frail-looking a woman, and it was apparent that Mrs. G. hadn't either. Mrs. G. glared at Deliah with shock, anger, and indignation; but she was up against something deeper and more genuine. After locking eyes with Deliah for several seconds, she looked away. She fussed with her silverware, befuddled and shaken. I got the impression that nobody ever told Mrs. G. what to do, either, and she didn't know how to deal with it.

"As I was saying," Bierce broke in, and continued whatever lie he had been telling Mrs. G. Good old Bierce to the rescue again. Mrs. G. turned to him like a thirsty lioness to an oasis. We at the peon's end of the table turned back to our own meals. The boys stole sidelong glances at their mother with awe. Juan leaned over to them, a co-conspirator.

"Boys," he said in a stage-whisper. "It really is *muy rrrrrico.*"

Jerome and Henry smothered snorts of laughter in their hands. Deliah, who looked both resolute and embarrassed by her outburst, visibly relaxed and even laughed a little herself.

"Go on, Jerry, Henry," she said to her sons. "Eat up that *rrrrico* bird."

The boys set to with gusto and the room became filled with the clink of silver on china and the muffled sounds of satisfied mastication.

"Thank you, Juan," Deliah said across the table.

Juan shrugged. "I got t'ree little brothers of my own," he said. "They don' like *mole* neither, but they eat it." And he tipped her a wink before returning to his own meal.

The wine flowed, bearing the food and our little party on down the evening on an easy, companionable current. Bierce did his usual solid job at draining the bottle, but for once he was bested. Juan and his usual bottle of tequila were constant companions, and though he only allowed himself the thoroughly Mexican *"chiquitito"* each time, they added up. By the main course he was tipsy; by dessert (a delightful flan with cinnamon powdered on top), merry; and by "brandy and cigars," boneless. Bierce and I lugged him to his stateroom—the furthest, of course, from the dining car—made him comfortable on his bed, and returned to finish our own wine. The women and children had departed with great tact and forbearance while the food was being cleared. Bierce and I had the car to ourselves.

"Well," I said, once again ensconced in a leather easy-chair, "what next?"

Bierce took a long, contemplative draw on his cigar and let the smoke drift from his mouth.

"The center of the web," he said. "Mexico City. I hope that we may depend upon the local knowledge of our colleague"—he pointed the cigar toward our staterooms and the comatose Juan Romero—"to get us around the metropolis, or at least to orient us there. Failing that, we may rely upon Dr. Navarro, I'm sure. I sent him a telegram from Torreón apprising him of our approximate arrival, and it is to him that we must first repair, at any rate, to learn 'the lay of the land.'"

Bierce smoked; I sipped my wine.

I said, "How extensive do you think this conspiracy is, Bierce?"

"Very. That we should stumble upon two cells of it in our travels without much conscious effort indicates to me that we should encounter it wherever we stray in Mexico. And the City, being both the modern capital and the former site of the ancient Aztec capitol, would naturally be its epicenter."

"You mean to tell me that what we have seen thus far has just been outliers? That we should expect far worse in the City?"

"Yes and no, Amos. Yes, in that the cult's central organization is very probably there, with a concomitant concentration of its members; and no, because it is the City and the most cosmopolitan area we will have yet encountered. They must be more circumspect there, I believe . . . I hope. Less the gunfight than the stiletto in the alley."

I swirled my wine and pondered this.

"If that was meant to be reassuring," I said, "it wasn't."

"Nor was it meant to be, my boy. I want you on tenterhooks all the while we are there. Our nemesis is cunning as well as brutal. We cannot afford to let our guard down." He paused to mouth his cigar and look out the window at the passing blackness. "We are, in effect, putting ourselves into his very hands."

11.

We continued chatting on lesser things for a while. At last the river of wine he had imbibed took its toll upon Ambrose Bierce, and he lurched heavily to his feet. When I offered him an arm to steady him, though, he waved it off, thanked me, bade me good-night, and wove his way back toward our state-rooms. I remained with the lees of my wine and a headful of speculations, most of them dire.

At what point she appeared I cannot say. I was letting the time ratchet by on the rhythm of the locomotive's tracks, and all I know is that it was late. One moment the doorway was empty, and the next she stood in it, somehow filling the frame with her diminutive form like a beauty from some Sargent painting. She had the same unmoving grace of those Boston lovelies, if not their long, willowy form; yet even in her plain black widow's-weeds, she outshone them all. I rose to my feet.

"Mrs. Gadbury," I said.

"Mr. Littlefault."

She walked slow into the car, unconsciously compensating for the lurch of the vehicle with smooth arcs of her hips. I thought of well-oiled cams in silk, of a panther's haunches in stride. She walked up to the chair opposite mine, the chair lately vacated by Bierce.

"May I?"

"Please."

We sat.

"A pleasant evening," I said.

"An amusing evening," she said.

I said, "I must apologize for Juan's bibulousness. We have been under a fair amount of strain recently."

She laughed—those pretty birds took flight again.

"You must certainly *not* apologize for Juan, Amos. Without his aid I would have despaired of my boys eating their meal."

They had, in fact, eaten every scrap, punctuating chews with cries of *"Muy rrrrrrrico!"*

"It is I," she said, looking down at her hands in her lap, "who should apologize. I needn't have blown up at Mother that way."

"You were entirely within your rights," I said. "They are your children and yours to direct. Or so I judge."

"Do you have children, Amos?"

"No. No. It was a decision I made long ago—selfish, I suppose. But I felt my work precluded any children or wife. I felt I wouldn't have the time to devote to them that they deserved."

"That strikes me as far from selfish. Quite the opposite, in fact. Children do demand a lot of one's time. And yet"—and she smiled at something I could not see—"they repay it a thousand-fold."

We sat back in the silence of our own thoughts for a couple of minutes. She looked out the window as Bierce had done.

"I wonder just what kind of night it really is," she said. She rose like a wildflower unbending toward the sun and walked to the window. I stood and followed her. Standing by her side, all I could see in the window was the pale reflection of our two faces against the night.

"There is an observation platform at the end of our car, Deliah."

She turned and looked up at me. "Do tell?"

"Yes."

"Show it to me, please."

I stepped back and waved her on before me. We walked down the length of the dining car and on through the Pullman car, where her mother-in-law and sons slept; on through the loud gap between the cars and into the sudden silence of our own sleeper/observation car, all dim in the softened lights. When we drew nigh the compartment where Bierce and Juan slept, Deliah turned and, with an impish wink, put her finger to her pursed lips. I smiled back and guided her on with a hand to the small of her back. She did not pull away from it.

At the end of the car, the end of the train, in fact, I opened the door and let in a gust of night air full of sound and motion. Deliah put a hand to her hair but otherwise seemed undeterred by the commotion. She exited the train and I followed, shutting the door behind us.

The observation platform on the train's end had the usual roof over it; handy for farewells and campaigning politicians at whistle-stops. But by standing at the rail one could lean back and see past it to the stars. Deliah walked right to the platform's rail and leaned upon it with both hands. Below and before us the landscape of the state of Zacatecas rolled away in dimness, bisected by the train-track that stretched north from us to the horizon. The Sierra Madre, our constant companion, pushed its rocky shoulders into the sky. And the sky . . . Deliah and I leaned back and looked up upon a panoply of stars scattered broadcast from horizon to horizon.

"It's gorgeous!" Deliah said over the shuttle of the tracks. Her face, tipped back and blue in starlight, was luminous with joy.

"Yes, it is."

I wasn't looking at the stars. When she turned and looked at me, her joy softened; it did not die, but mellowed into something warmer, closer and more intimate.

"I——" she started to say, but I put a finger to her lips. Then I gathered her little form into my arms, bent and kissed her on those soft lips. She did not pull away, but with a faint cry from deep in her throat pressed into me and put her arms around my neck and kissed me back. I tasted wine and something sour, but not unpleasant, and I crushed her to me, ravenous for all of her.

"A-*HEMM*."

We jumped. Holding on to each other for dear life, we looked up and back, further back over the lip of the roof, and beheld a Federal soldier sitting cross-legged upon the car's roof. He was silhouetted against the stars, but I could clearly see the long shadow of his rifle sticking up from his huddled form. And, as he tipped his hat to us, I thought I could see the outer curve of a smile on his shadowy face as well.

We laughed, still caught in our embrace. Hatless, I tipped him a salute from the forehead, which he returned. Of course they had a guard on the train; the countryside to the north was threshed and torn with war. With a final exchange of nods, Deliah and I turned to go back inside.

Just shy of the door she stopped me and said, "Amos, please show me your stateroom."

No fourteen-year-old fresh from a first kiss ever floated eager and dizzy as I did that wonderful night. I got us back into the yellowed quiet of the car and down to the door of my compartment. I unlatched it as quietly as I could, holding the doorknob and sliding the door as if they were hoarfrost glass, and stood aside to let the lady enter.

I came after and slid the door to until it clicked.

"Leave off the light, please, Amos." Her voice came from close and all around me in the blackness of the compartment. A rustle of long skirts, a tug and soft clatter of the window shade being lifted; and against the blackness opened a square of blue starlight. And from out that velvet blue, the shape of Deliah.

Without another word we began undressing each other. I remember an endless array of small buttons from her collar to her waist; her hands on mine to guide me through the intricacies of female wardrobe. And her quiet laughter as she undid a network of pins to let loose her hair in a rolling cascade to her hips. She smelled of honeysuckle and the natural warm hayfield scent of her skin, and I thought I should die of desire for her right then and there.

In the starlight she stood back from me, naked and revealed. Her clothes must have bound her cruelly, for she appeared to blossom once free from them; a fuller, more feminine shape, no longer a stiff Sargent portrait but a luscious Renoir nude, ghostly against the midnight black, soft curves of light and shadow. I stood alike naked and hoped I presented to her as pleasing an image. For a moment we stood thus, facing each other, appraising each other. Our breathing was hoarse, hungry, the pant of beasts close upon their prey. Then we rushed at each other and fell to my narrow bed.

What would Mrs. G. have thought? In those last, dragging days of the Edwardian era, before the Great War, before flappers and bathtub gin and "Makin' Whoopee," what would *anyone* have thought? Even I would have been scandalized to think of such a tryst, just a few weeks before. But grief and desire have their own rules, and the constraints of "civilized life" mattered not at all to us that night, racing south to the capital of a war-riven country. I bore no shame for it, nor do I now. The next morning the whole train could have been blown to smithereens by a howitzer shell. She was there and I was there, and the night held us close in its comforting arms.

Later, spent from our lusts not once, but twice, I lay upon my back with Deliah's head cradled upon my chest, and I looked at her. She slept; her small torso filling and relaxing against mine with each breath, and I thought the starlight upon her face the most beautiful thing I could imagine. She must have felt me looking at her, though, for her black lashes moved, fluttered, and she lifted her head to regard me with those sad, mysterious eyes.

"Hello."

"Hello."

She put her hand to my cheek and kissed me. When she pulled back, I could see a tightness in her features.

"What is it, my dear?" I said.

"You mustn't—that is, you must think me a complete wanton."

Now I put my hand to her cheek, smiled, and shook my head.

"I should be the basest of ingrates for doing so," I said, and kissed her on the forehead. "You have let me love you, know the delights of your body. We are both adults and alone . . . who is there to judge us?"

She sighed and lay her head back upon my chest.

"Society," she said, as if it were the most dreary thing in the world. "Other men. My mother-in-law."

"Well, they will never hear it from me."

I felt her smile against my skin.

"You are a good man, Amos. One of the nicest men I have ever met."

"Thank you, dear. And you are one of the finest, sweetest women I have ever known."

Deliah pushed herself up and turned to face me.

"What exactly *are* you, Amos?"

The question was said openly, ingenuous and curious. I looked into those wide-open eyes and saw no cant or deceit, and decided to be as honest to her as she was to me. I took a deep breath.

"I am Ambrose Bierce's personal assistant," I said. "Not to be confused with his secretary, Miss Christiansen, who no doubt sleeps well tonight in Washington City."

She shook her heavy mane of hair.

"That I was able to deduce. But what brings you here, to the heart of Mexico, in such a time?"

And I related to her how Bierce's daughter Helen had sent me after him; how I had found him and Juan in Laredo, learned of the modern cult of Aztecs and our mission against it; of our adventures with Villa's army, and our subsequent fleeing from them; our trek across the desert; and our most recent fracas in San Andrés Tecolotzán. I left out nothing. She let me reel it off in a watching silence. She was no doubt looking for the dissimulation she must have heard from other male "adventurers" in her past. But she heard none. I told her all and I told her the truth.

When I was done we lay looking at each other a long time. The coach rocked us as in a giant's crib. The tracks *shuck-shuck, shuck-shucked* beneath us. At last she reached over me to my left arm, lifted it to her lips, and kissed the round scar Don Máximo Golón's cigarette had made. She sighed, set my arm back gently, and lay her head back down.

"So much pain," she said. Her voice came to me from a still, empty room somewhere far away. "So what will you do now?"

"Follow the cult to its fountainhead in Mexico City. Bierce is determined, he has given his word he will help, and I am duty-bound to aid him."

"To protect him, you mean."

"If need be. But the old buzzard is far tougher than he may look. But for him, I would be lying in a ditch outside Ojinaga or somewhere on the Hacienda Golón." Her arm, lying across my body, grew taut and hugged me. I had to swallow a lump in my throat before continuing. "And so I go."

"But what can the three of you do? If this conspiracy is as large as you say, I fail to see what possible good you could achieve. Wouldn't you be better served going to the authorities, letting them handle it?"

I hugged her to me and said, "That might have been so if there were authorities to go to. Mexico is in such flux now that today's government may be tomorrow's outlaws. And until we know better, we must assume that even the authorities that exist are complicit. As for our puny numbers, it is Bierce's theory that we may benefit from that; that we can achieve by stealth what would fail through force."

She was silent then, digesting these ideas. I hugged her closer to me. This time was precious, a glint of sunlight thorough the wrack of storm-clouds, and I would savor it to its full.

"Come with me," Deliah said suddenly, jolting up to face me. "With us, I mean, back to the States. Leave this horror to the Mexicans—it is theirs to own, surely."

I looked at that earnest, excited face, still young and lit with the glow of the future. I reached out and stroked the smooth cheek.

"Would that it were that easy," I said. "If I thought that the Mexicans could deal with this and destroy it, then yes, I might agree to quit the field of battle. But Professor Navarro called in Bierce specifically. There are few, precious few the world 'round, who can do what Ambrose Bierce does. Carnacki in Britain, Dyson in Wales, John Silence on the Continent—but none in the Americas, and no one who does it as well as Bierce. And to halt this particular menace, his peculiar talents are needed.

"And this is more than just a Mexican problem. If the professor's conclusions are accurate, then the enemy means to change the very order of the planet, to plunge us all into a worldwide bloodbath overseen by ancient and heartless gods."

I stopped and gazed at her. My last words hung in the air, fantastic, melodramatic, absurd even to my own ears. I tried to read Deliah's reaction in the scant light, but all I could see were the dark pockets of shadow over her eyes and the still shape of her mouth.

"You don't believe me," I said. "I don't blame you—it sounds ridiculous, even to me. What did Juan call it? A *'cuento de hadas,'* a fairy tale, something to tell recalcitrant children to make them behave."

"It isn't that I don't believe you; I *can't* believe you. That such things should exist in a normal world . . . I keep seeing the interior of our Congregational church up home, the rows of pews, the airy windows, the minister's pulpit, all clean and orderly. This is what I was raised on, Amos. Do you see? There is no room for monsters in that world." She paused and the shadows deepened on her face. "None of a supernatural variety, anyway."

I pulled her back down to me again. So soft, so warm, and so small. How she had come through all she had already without the world chewing her up completely, I did not know.

"Then accept that there are human monsters," I said. "You know that better than I. And Mr. Bierce and I are committed to destroying them before they can destroy the rest of us." I lifted her face up to mine. "There is nothing I would like better than to go with you, Deliah. But we can't leave this to other hands. There are no other hands. Bierce must see it through, and I must go with him."

She nodded—a bare dip of the head. Then she lay her head and her long, auburn locks on my chest, and we said no more.

*

Much later, so late that it was early, I heard through the muffling curtains of sleep a soft shift of fabric on skin; the click of the door-latch; and the door slowly, slowly opening and closing. As I drifted back down though slumber to true sleep, I felt the train bearing me onward like a headlong hearse, as if I were plunging feet-first into a black and unknowable void.

12.

"You slept well?"

Ambrose Bierce looked at me over the Mexican newspaper he was pretending to read. His eyes were clear, questioning, nothing more.

"Yes," I said, putting my napkin on my lap. "Very well, thank you. And yourself?"

"Fairly well." He returned his gaze to the paper. "Though the train is full of noises, ghosts. We accumulate them as we go, I fear. An old man such as I has a clamoring horde of them." Then he really looked at me. "Even the young should beware of burdening themselves unnecessarily, especially when embarking upon a particularly hazardous enterprise."

I put down the fork I had lifted to attack my breakfast.

"This from the Romeo of San Andrés?" I said.

He put up his hands in a gesture of appeasement.

"*Pace*, son. I am not here to judge, only to caution."

I sat back, the wind taken out of me, and said, "Sorry, Bierce. Were we that obvious?"

"Only to the astute . . . and those in the stateroom next to yours."

"Thank goodness. I wouldn't have the lady's reputation tarnished."

"Nor would I, Amos. I wouldn't have mentioned it at all but that I need your senses clear, clearer than even before as we come into the City."

"Point taken. And thank you, Bierce—thank you."

He made a face and disappeared behind his paper again.

I caught movement from the corner of my eye and beheld Juan lurching into the dining car, shirt half tucked in, hair any way, a picture of personal disaster.

"Spanish lesson for today, Bierce," I said, and spread a hand toward Juan. "*'La cruda.'*"

Bierce looked up, frowned, and said, "I thought 'drunk' was '*boraxo.*'"

"'Borracho' is 'drunk.' Juan is demonstrating for us the aftermath, the hangover."

Juan punctuated the lesson by falling into the chair next to mine and almost into my lap. He put his arms on the table and his head on his arms. "*La cruda,*" he moaned. "More like *el tren. Ay, que viene el tren, cabrónes.*"

Bierce folded his paper into precise quarters.

"I expect that that is an explanation of your condition, Juan. Just a note for the future: gentlemen may get drunk, downright hilarious if need be, but never hung over. It is bad form."

Juan gurgled something in response. We were saved from more bilingual drunkenness by the arrival of the women, the boys following in solemn procession. We arose, even Juan, although with him it was more of an upward fall.

"Good morning, ladies," Bierce said.

"Good morning Mr. Twain, Mr. Romero, Mr. Littlefault." Deliah gave me the slightest ghost of a smirk.

"Ladies." I bent from the waist.

Juan said, "Señoras," and swayed in what might have been a nod of respect.

"Whatever is wrong with Mr. Romero?" said Mrs. G. Senior.

Bierce hooked his thumbs in his vest.

"Juan had an unfortunate collision with a distillery. We are still awaiting word on the distillery, although predictions are not optimistic."

Mrs. G. looked gentile poison at Juan but said nothing. We all sat then and the waiter brought food for the newcomers.

"So, Mr. Twain," said Mrs. G. once she had slaughtered her bacon and eggs, "what are your plans once we reach the capital?"

"We have an appointment with an academic, dear lady," he said.

Mrs. G. let her fork drop to her plate.

"Really? We know some truly important people in the capital. Perhaps he moves in the same circles . . . ?"

Bierce flapped his hand as if it were of no importance.

"I sincerely doubt it, Mrs. Gadbury——"

"Ethel, please!"

"Ethel, of course. I really don't think Señor Navarro runs in the same circles as your friends. In fact, I'm convinced that he doesn't run in circles at all, but approaches his responsibilities in a straight line."

Titters of amusement. Of course she got the joke. Deliah rolled her eyes and I winked at her.

After breakfast, Deliah and her family retired to some couches to play games. Bierce seemed intent upon his journal and Juan was chatting with a waiter. Left to my own devices and with nothing else to do, I sat and watched the countryside flit past.

We were rising now, ascending what I was told was the *"altiplano,"* the great central plateau of Mexico: the heartland of the Aztec Empire. The scenery became more dramatic, ridges and valleys, and the flora grew to include deep deciduous forests and pine. I feared how we would do in the higher, rarer air, Bierce especially with his asthma. But thus far I noticed nothing untoward. From the shade of the heavier trees, the whitewashed adobe and brick of small towns peeked at us; a church-tower with Rococo flourishes, the local Alcalde looming like a stone cliff over the central square. Roads and railways alike were neat and well maintained. Here was the handiwork of the *Porfiriato,* that extended Indian Summer of the late dictator Porfirio Díaz. A brutal man, but also a man who brought the modern world to Mexico. Looking at it all, the stately government buildings and hotels alongside adobe hovels, I had the impression of a country trying to emulate its giant neighbor to the north, like a younger brother who both idolizes and despises his older sibling. There was no doubt that Díaz and his minions had brought Mexico into the twentieth century; but at what cost? I recalled our hosts, the Martínezes, arguing over that cost. These days I'm reminded of that brute Mussolini and his dreaded black-shirts in Italy. They say he makes the trains run on time. They also say his enemies fill the dungeons and shallow graves of despotism.

But back to a cool, sunny day in the Mexican highlands of 1914. At last we attained the full height of the *altiplano*. Prickly-pears and organ-pipe cacti reappeared. The countryside, once relatively flat, began heaving and mountains appeared across the southern horizon. Zacatecas, Aguas Calientes, Leon . . . At Salamanca we changed from the Mexican Central to the National Railroad of Mexico, and our coaches improved. Onward through the crumpled countryside. Celaya, Maravatio, Toluca . . .

Then the mountains drew back like the curtains on a gigantic stage. The landscape opened up before us in a vast, flat valley—the Valley of Mexico. And taking center stage, like a mottled carpet of geometric design, Mexico City itself, the Tenochtitlán of the Aztecs; the mighty heart of the Mexican nation.

I tried to imagine what Cortés and his men must have felt when they first beheld the ancient metropolis four hundred years before. Back then, according to Bierce and the few histories I had read, the city spread in the middle of an enormous lake. Of that lake little remained now; centuries of urban growth, draining and filling had reduced it to a dirty, shrunken reflection of its former grandeur. I caught the glint of waters beyond buildings to the east, but little more.

At first there was little different in style from every other town and city we had passed through—the ubiquitous adobe and stucco—but it was the scale that impressed me. Everything felt increased, more intense; even the blue of the sky was deeper here. And something about the city's position, sitting on the broad dish of that huge valley, ringed by stern, snow-capped mountains, seemed meant to impress: Behold the beating heart of Aztec Power.

PART III
MEXICO

1.

The train descended into the valley gradually; our point of view flattened, spread; *ranchos* and villages dotted the landscape, melding slowly into an urban pattern. Now we were shuttling between mean houses of cracked adobe. People watched us pass as if we were an apparition out of a future they would never see. The neighborhoods became denser, the streets closer and more frequent. Larger buildings rose up before and around us. As if the density of the city made the very air thicker, the train slowed in its onward charge. Slowed, slowed—and came to a hissing, squealing stop.

"*¡Mexico, Mexico!*" called the porter. "*No se olviden el equipaje.*"

Don't forget your baggage, he said. We had little enough of it at that point, our original kit lost and scattered across the length of northern Mexico. We gathered what little we did have and stepped down onto the platform.

The scene at Torreón was repeated, but tenfold. Boys with impossible burdens on their backs hurried by; passengers in suits, uniforms, and the white pyjamas of the peasant gushed from the train's many doors to meet and mingle with awaiting crowds. Conductors stalked down the length of the train calling "*¡Mexico! ¡Mexico! ¡Salgan aqui pa' la Ciudad!*"

Mexico. Not even Mexico City, just Mexico. The fount and distillation of the entire nation, whence so much of its history and culture had derived. Mexico. The psychological weight of it loomed over me and left me breathless.

Juan, veteran of the capital that he was, pushed a path for us through the mobs to a quieter, open area around the corner of the station.

When we got there I suddenly remembered Deliah and her family and looked quickly around for them. I needn't have worried: Mrs. Gadbury Sr. was cutting through the crowds like a galleon under a full press of sail. Deliah, her sons, and a train of porters bearing their luggage followed serenely in her wake. They plowed a trail straight to us.

"Well, Mr. Twain," Mrs. G. said when they reached us, "this has been a most edifying experience, meeting you and your, *ahem,* associates."

She extended a lavender-scented hand that Bierce, ever the gentleman, ever the rake, lifted to his lips and kissed. Mrs. G. giggled.

"Madam," said Bierce, "the pleasure has been all ours, I assure you. I pray that we may cross paths with you ere we cross swords with you."

Again that disconcerting titter from the Yankee matron.

"Really, Mr. Twain—may I call you Mark? Your wit is so—cutting!"

Delighted with her own *bon mot,* Mrs. G. crumbled into a gale of full laughter that she tried ineffectually to smother in a handkerchief. Bierce smiled indulgently at her as a weary adult might smile upon a clever, if not very bright, child.

Invisible in the glare of these two luminaries, Deliah and I stepped apart and made our own farewells.

"Where are you staying in town?" Deliah asked me, looking up into my eyes.

"I don't know. I am assuming our contact here, Professor Navarro, has lodgings of some sort or knows of some we may use."

"Why not stay with us at the Imperial?" Then, thinking she had been overbold, added, "I would feel safer if I knew fellow Americans were nearby."

I smiled at her but shook my head.

"Bierce's purse seems bottomless at times, but I don't think even he could swing an extended stay at a grand hotel. But knowing you are there, I will be sure to let you know just where we land."

She put her hand out to me and I took it. No ostentatious slobbering over her digits as Bierce had done with Mrs. G., but a brief, chaste clasp of hands. And if we held to each other's hands a few seconds longer than was necessary, nobody appeared to notice.

Juan was already at the curb and calling up a taxi, so the time of farewells was brief. Tired and dusty but gentlemen still, we let the Gadbury clan and attendant baggage take the first car. As the taxi pulled away into the chugging, honking traffic, I caught Deliah's face looking back at me from the rear operawindow of the vehicle. There was affection in that glance, to be sure, but something more. Concern? Worry, even? I thought of Miss Smalls back in Laredo and her woman's intuition. What was it those ladies saw that we did not?

The taxi that Juan flagged down for us was the most decrepit, unsavorylooking flivver I have ever seen still moving. Holes had been patched with unrolled tin cans affixed with screws and prayer, and rope held the hood from flying off of the engine. I watched a Laurel and Hardy short recently in which the flivver they were riding in fell apart upon stopping. It wouldn't have surprised me to see this contraption do the same at the curb. But our *taxista* was service personified, rushing around the front of his vehicle once it had shuddered to a stop, to pack away our valises in a rack on the machine's rear end. Juan quickly rattled off the name of Navarro's university to the driver, who bobbed his head in understanding. Then Juan turned to us.

"I'm 'fraid I have to leave you here," he said. "I been away from my family too long, an' I must go home."

Bierce looked shocked, affronted.

"I was depending upon your knowledge of the city to guide us through its more worrisome parts, Juan."

Juan looked at the pavement and shook his head.

"*Lo siento, Mayor.* I like to help you, and you are okay Joes. But my family needs me."

Bierce nodded. The two shook hands. I saw the corner of some folded bills in Bierce's hand but said nothing. When he withdrew his hand it was empty.

"*Mucho gusto,* Juan," said Bierce. "Many thanks for all you've done for us. I dare say it would have been impossible without you."

"And my thanks as well," I said, taking Juan's hand in turn. Then remembering our anger at the Golón hacienda, I added, "No hard feelings, I hope."

He shrugged and smiled that odd, down-turned smile of his.

"*No hay de que,*" he said. "Think nothing of it. Water over the bridge."

"'Under,'" both Bierce and I said automatically. Juan shook his head and chuckled. He mouthed something as he turned away, something that sounded like "sheep," and I thought he had probably had enough of these *pinches gringos* and their impossible language.

We boarded our erstwhile coach and lurched into traffic. The driver took delight in tempting accidents, but to his credit he avoided every one. In and out of the endless flow of wagons, ox-carts, horse-drawn trolleys, and other primitive engines of destruction we weaved and scuttled. At one point we hit a loose paving-stone and the left front fender of the taxi flew up and clattered to the pavement. Without a pause in our headlong career, the driver reached down and plucked the fallen fender from the road and tossed it into the seat next to him.

"Spare part," he grinned at us in his mirror.

Much of Mexico City, I learned later, is laid out in a grid, yet we turned and wove so many times that I quickly lost my sense of direction. A headlong, heedless plunge across a wide, airy boulevard—"*¡Paseo de la Reforma!*" yelled our driver over the wheeze of the engine. Looking down one side-street on our left as we flew by, I caught a flash of tall, green trees in a park.

"La Alameda," the driver said back to me as though reading my mind. At the moment, though, I really wished he would keep his eyes on the road. I glanced at Bierce and, veteran that he was of the Battles of Shiloh, Chickamauga, and all those unsung tangles he and I had had with the supernatural, his hands clutched the back of the driver's seat in a white-knuckle grip. For myself, I kept my right foot rigidly pressed down on an imaginary brake-pedal. The driver began singing "La Cucaracha."

Judging by the sun I knew we were headed mainly due south, or as nearly south as our zigzag route led us. We finally came to a jarring halt before a stately building made of dressed stone, a survival of the Emperor Maximilian's ill-fated reign back in the 1860s, I judged. A carved granite lintel over the front door proclaimed it to be the UNIVERSIDAD AUTONOMA DEL ESTADO DE MEXICO. We had arrived.

Prying ourselves from the taxi, we stretched out our tensed muscles while the driver detached our luggage from the rack. Bierce was already occupied with inspecting the university, so I paid the driver and even added a fair tip. For all the thrills of the ride, he had gotten us there quickly and safely. With a grin and a heartfelt "¡Muchisimas gracias, Señor!" he heaved the crank at the front of the Ford, jumped in, and sped off.

"Quite a 'university,' isn't it, Amos?"

Bierce stood, fists on hips, staring down the building before us. I lugged our bags up beside him and said, "Don't judge a school by its façade, Mr. Bierce. You're the one who vouched for Señor Navarro's credentials."

He humphed at me and strode up the steps. Bags in hand, I followed.

The interior of the building was as stately as the exterior. Walls of a soft green were offset by baseboards and door frames of dark, polished wood. The frosted glass on each door bore the titles of their inhabitants—Prof. Jimenez, Música Antigua, Lic. Salazar y. P., la Arcitectura Pre-Colombiana—or sometimes just room numbers. The hallway stretched the depth of the building and intersected with other hallways of equal length—I guessed. They all yawned far back beyond sight. And, I had noted, the building was four stories tall.

"Where to start?" Bierce said softly.

"Right here," I said, and turned to a young man who was hurrying past, laden with books.

"Excuse me," I said in Spanish. "We're looking for Professor Navarro's office. Could you tell us where it is?"

The youth halted, juggled his books, and pointed back down the way he'd come.

"Sí, Señor," he said. "Second floor—go straight and turn left. It's the third door on the right."

I thanked the youth, who nodded and lunged on toward the street door. I motioned to Bierce to follow me and headed down the hall.

"You sure you understood that?" he said.

"'Oh, ye of little faith,'" I replied. "We'll find out soon enough."

But my Spanish still held. We found the door the boy had indicated and, sure enough, the door was inscribed "Prof. Navarro y M. Arte Anciana." Bierce knocked on the glass panel. A surprisingly young voice from within called out, "*Sí, ¿quién está?*"

"Ambrose Bierce, Professor," Bierce proclaimed in a voice that shook the glass in the door.

"*¡Gracias a Dios!*" came the young voice again, followed by hurried footsteps. The door was pulled wide and framed within it was a gentleman as surprisingly young as his voice. He stood a trifle shorter than I, had an erect, straight-shouldered carriage topped by a well-proportioned head. His hair was dark and cut severely short with a pronounced widow's peak. The nose was straight ("What can one say about a nose?" Bierce once wrote), the eyes dark and bright and full of energy. His gaze was direct, curious, intelligent—the gaze of a lawyer. His well-lipped mouth was framed by a dark goatee. He wore the trousers, vest, and tie of a dark suit, but had shed the jacket and stood before us in shirtsleeves rolled up to the elbows. His eyes went from me to Bierce, and when they alighted on Bierce, their glow doubled.

"Señor Bierce!" he cried, and took Bierce's hands in his own. "*¡Qué milagro!* I have been worried sick. Please, please, gentlemen, come in!"

He stepped aside and spread his arm wide in a gesture of welcome.

"And you . . . ?" he said to me.

"Amos Littlefault," I said, "Mr. Bierce's assistant."

"He knows of our mission, Señor," said Bierce. "He's all right."

Navarro smiled and we shook hands.

The first thing I noticed upon entering Professor Navarro's office was the smell. Formaldehyde, wax, floor-polish, and a dusty scent of age all competed for olfactory dominance. The cumulative effect was actually pleasant, reassuring, just how a professor of antiquities' office should smell, I thought. The second thing I noticed was the amazing clutter of the place. We couldn't help but notice, as we had to step over and thread our way between a rigid crowd of Pre-Columbian statues and artifacts. One knee-high sculpture goggled at us out of wide, circular eyes as we stepped gingerly past.

"Don't mind old Tlaloc," Navarro laughed. "He stares at everyone like that."

In the center of the room was a long table, also populated with artifacts. A desk sat in a corner under one of the room's two windows. Sunlight leaned in and sparked on dust-motes. The view was of similar buildings to the one we were in; but beyond and between them loomed a green hill topped by a broad, squat palace or mansion. Seeing my attention diverted, Navarro came over to me.

"Chapultepec," he said. "'Grasshopper Hill'—an odd name for the home of an Aztec emperor, no? Then again, they called bloody wounds 'the flowers of war.' A curious people, our ancestors, part poets, part killers. But please, please, sit."

He waved to a couple of chairs that had been invisible before, so heaped with papers and the detritus of history. I set our bags down and we carefully cleared the chairs and sat. Navarro, energy personified, ran to the door and threw it open.

"Tomás!" he called. *"Tres cafes, por favor."* Then he shut the door and returned to us, sitting in the wheeled office-chair behind his desk. He grinned at us as if we were a late dinner finally arrived.

"So," he said, "at last we meet. I am so grateful for your coming all this way—this work we have before us is very important."

"And I am grateful for your knowledge of English," chuckled Bierce. "I do fairly well with your *español*, but it's far easier for me to use the good, old mother-tongue."

I smothered a smile. Navarro nodded in a courtly manner. "Of course."

There was a knock on the door.

"Ven," said Navarro, and a thin, nervous-looking young man came in, bearing a tray of mugs, coffee-pot, and pastries. He set it on a rare clear space on the central table and stood by, fidgeting, until Navarro shooed him out.

"Tomás is a good lad," he said as soon as the young man was gone. "But he has big ears. That is both a blessing and a curse, as you shall see."

Navarro stood and distributed coffee and pastries—delicious flaky things he called *"cuernos"*—to all. He sat again and we took preparatory sips and nibbles.

A cloud passed over Navarro's features. The happy energy in his eyes drained, and a deep crease formed between his brows. He leaned forward with his hands clasped between his knees.

"Manos a la obra," he said. "Time to get to work. The situation is dire, worse than I had expected. I did not know the conspiracy was so widespread until I got your telegrams from the north, Señor Bierce."

"Nor did I," said Bierce. "The knowledge was imparted to us in a brutal way. Amos here nearly lost his life to agents of the conspiracy ere we got the upper hand."

"*¿ Verdad?*" said Navarro. "I am sorry. I did not know you were in such peril. If you please, relate to me the details of your encounters with these agents."

And so we did, starting with the discovery of the sacrificed soldiers in Ojinaga and on through the battle at the Hacienda Golón. Navarro listened intently, fixing us with that lawyer's stare except when he made notes upon a pad. When we were finished, he sat back and sighed.

"Golón," he said, looking over his notes. "Him I did not know. But Bendiga . . . can it be?"

"Then you know of him?" I said.

"Perhaps, yes. I know of a Señor Bendiga, and it's an odd enough name and the likelihood of coincidence is so small . . . You tell me he is a soldier, yes?"

"A captain in the employ of Villa," said Bierce.

"The gentleman I know—well, know *of*—he has the bearing of a soldier, to be sure."

I said, "How do you know him?"

Navarro sighed again and ran a hand over the bristle of his close-cut hair.

"It goes to the beginning of this story," he said. "Two years ago, I was occupied with research on the great Aztec Sun-stone. You have perhaps heard of it, or seen a photograph? It is a very large stone carving, and it is displayed at the Museo de la Histora here in Mexico. I spent many hours there, copying the symbols on the stone, looking for patterns and meaning in the designs. Some days I noticed another gentleman looking intently at the stone. It is not unusual for people to examine it—it is one of the great monuments of our Aztec past. But few truly understand its significance.

"One day, just to be sociable, I addressed him.

"'Impressive, isn't it?'" I said. He nodded, his eyes fixed upon the carvings.

"'The whole cosmos in a circle,' he said to me. I was startled. The average person knows nothing about the symbolism, and even many of my learned colleagues mistakenly call it 'the Calendar Stone,' thinking it is a representation of the solar year. But not this fellow.

"'You impress me,' I said to him. 'Not many people know the true meaning of the carvings.'

"'Isn't it clear?' he said, and he approached the massive stone. 'Here,' he said pointing to the carven head of a jaguar. 'The *tigre* that ate the world. And here'—he indicated the fanged face of our friend Tlaloc, there, the rain-god—

'the rain that drowned the world.' Then he pointed to the great face in the center of the stone, and his voice became quiet, almost reverent. 'Our Lord Tonatiuh the Sun, who feeds off the hearts of men.'

"I didn't know what to say to that. His knowledge was impressive, but did not seem scholarly exactly. *Me entienden, amigos?*"

"Yes," I said. "We understand. Please go on."

"Wanting to draw him out, I said, 'Are you with a university?' But he merely smiled and said, 'No.' I could get nothing more about his affiliations, but we remained cordial. Many times we saw each other there, traded *'Buenos dias,'* and went about our studies. We traded names, too, and I learned that he was Bendiga—'bless' in English, but a command form of the verb. As I say, an odd name, not one I would forget. This Bendiga that you met—is he young, straight, a little tall?"

Here Navarro held up a finger a little over his head.

"That fits him," I said.

"And he has a *cicatriz?*" Navarro ran a finger down his cheek approximately where Bendiga had a scar.

"Just so," nodded Bierce. "Although many men could fit that description, the chances of two with such a feature and in such circumstances appear small. Pray, continue."

Navarro shrugged.

"There isn't much more to tell. Bendiga continued coming to see the Aztec stone and other artifacts for as long as I was there, longer still, for all I know. We had a few good conversations touching on *el mundo azteca,* and it was clear he was a scholar of some sort. But I always felt that he was testing me or drawing information from me."

"How so?" I said.

"It is hard to put into words." Navarro pondered. "*Bueno.* One day we were talking about the *ollin,* which is the central symbol of the stone. It is not an obvious symbol; it just looks like an odd frame around the face of the Sun-god Tonatiuh. But Bendiga knew it was there.

"'A powerful symbol,' he said to me. Then he looked at me like a fox. And he said, 'You know what the *ollin* means, don't you?' as if he would teach *me* about it.

"'Of course,' I said. 'It is the date on which the world would end, but for the human sacrifices the Aztecs made.'

"'Ah, yes,' Bendiga said. 'Every fifty years, they say.'

"'Every fifty-*two* years,' I corrected him, and something in the way he nodded made me think, *He just tricked me into saying that.* It was nothing I could prove, but I still believe it. Other times he just asked me honestly about this or that detail of Aztec life. But sometimes that fox would look out at me, and I would get that feeling that he was trying to steal information or find out how much I knew. You see?"

"Yes, we see," said Bierce.

"*Bueno.* This kind of thing happened so much that I decided to find out more about the mysterious Señor Bendiga. But he revealed little about himself, his interests. He always turned the conversation back to Aztec studies. When I asked him about himself, he said he was just *un chilango humilde,* a humble man of the city, interested in his heritage. A hobby, you would say.

"But I still didn't believe him. At first I wondered if he was a spy from another university, trying to steal my discoveries. So I sent my own spies to watch him."

"*Your* spies?" Bierce's face was a study in amazement.

Navarro laughed and shrugged again, a gesture of humility.

"*Pues*, sort-of spies. You saw Tomás, who brought us coffee? He is one of my 'spies,' and a good one. That is what I meant about his 'big ears'—in the right situation, a good thing to have. Most people look at him and see an eager, clumsy *varón,* a typical student with too many books and not enough sense. But he hears everything, I tell you, and his very clumsiness makes him invisible. Who would suspect that bumbling *fulano* of anything? I have several such 'agents,' students of mine who earn extra grades by running my secret errands."

"And are they effective?" said Bierce, pouring himself a cup of coffee.

Navarro took a bite of pastry and said between chews, "Very effective. I won't tire you with all the details, all the facts and observations that meant nothing, but added up to a very big Something. Best let me try to summarize it.

"For months my spies brought in this information, which I wrote down and tried to put together into a whole picture. It was like the meaning of the Sunstone: taken separately, each detail meant little; but when you stood back and saw them all together, voilà—*la verdad.* My young men watched and followed Bendiga and saw him attend meetings in a building north of the Palacio Nacional. Other men—always men—came to these meetings as well, and my spies followed them, too."

Navarro stopped and let out a long breath.

"When they told me where these men went after the meetings, and *who they were,* I knew that this was much bigger than just a rival professor trying to steal my notes. The men they followed were important men. Dangerous men. Men in government, in the army, and, *válgame Dios,* even in the church. Bendiga didn't seem to fit. Who was he, just another *chilango,* as he said, and what was he doing with these powerful men?

"Then we had luck. One of my spies, Guillermo is his name, was following one of these big men from a meeting one night. Mexico City is not safe to walk around at night, *mis amigos,* you should know, and sometimes not even in the day. So this man was walking home when a gang of *rateros,* robbers, attacked him.

"Guillermo was following at a distance so he was safe; but he was close enough to see what happened. He said the man, a colonel in the army, was strong and brave, and beat off his attackers at first. But there were too many of them. They were beating him and Guillermo saw one of them pull out a knife.

"It was then that the colonel shoved the *rateros* away from him, put up his arms, and called out in a loud voice. Guillermo said he couldn't understand what the man said, said it was gibberish, not Spanish at all. But when he told me, I thought I knew what it was."

"And . . . ?" Bierce leaned toward Navarro. Navarro rubbed his chin.

"Understand," he said, "this is second-hand and translated also. But he said part of it sounded something like 'wal-pilli.'"

"'Wal-pilli'?" I said. "Now I don't understand."

"Neither did I at first. Again, this was from a scared young man, little more than a boy, repeating something he heard at a distance under difficult circumstances.

"It was what happened next that gave me the clue.

"Guillermo says the thieves stopped their attack on the colonel when they heard this. He says it was as if they were frozen. But it only lasted for a moment or two. Then they rushed him.

"But he wasn't there. In his place—and again, please understand this was a very scared young man—"

"Yes, yes," said Bierce, fairly champing at the bit. "Go on, we understand."

Navarro said, "Guillermo said that in the colonel's place now stood an eagle."

Bierce and I exchanged looks.

"An eagle," Navarro repeated. "But not a real eagle, not like a normal eagle. It was like the shape of an eagle, but cut out of the night. *Ay, caramba,* this is difficult. I don't know if I make you see. And he said it was much bigger than any eagle or bird he had ever seen. It towered over the thieves. Its eyes burned like suns, and it fell upon the *rateros* and killed them all."

Navarro looked down at his hands. We stared at him, waiting for something more.

"'In the midst of life,'" I said.

"'Can such things be?'" finished Bierce.

Navarro looked up at us. His gaze was less that of the lawyer and more of the defendant.

"Then you believe me?" he said.

"We've seen worse," Bierce said. "Even on this little jaunt through your lovely country."

Navarro nodded as if we had just affirmed something he had believed all along. He said, "This is an old country, Señores, terribly old. They say people have been living in Cholula, south of here, for more than five thousand years. We have had a long time to dig the secrets out of this land, to pull the veil from Nature herself. She is not always the beauty we expected to see. Do you know of Coatlicue, Lady of the Serpent-skirt?"

We shook our heads.

"There is a sculpture in the museum of her—you must see it. It is enormous, three meters high, and carven by a genius artist of the Old World. But he must have been an artist with dark dreams; for how else could he picture that double-snake head, or the necklace of human hearts and skulls, or a skirt of woven rattlesnakes? She is nightmare itself, and she was the mother of Aztec gods. That is the Nature our ancestors saw."

"And that word that Guillermo heard," I said. "'Wah-pilli'?"

Navarro sat back and said, "As I say, it was the colonel's *change* that gave me the clue to the word. Guillermo is a good student, but his knowledge of Náhuatl, the Aztec tongue, is limited. What he heard can be rendered more accurately as 'cuaupilli,' and it means 'eagle-lord.'"

Silence again—a silence as deep as the history all around us. Finally Bierce, face crushed in to a frown, said, "You say you got lucky that night. Is there more to tell?"

Navarro rubbed his face vigorously with his hands.

"Guillermo, he waited until the eagle, or whatever it was, was done with the thieves. After the thing had flown away, he approached the scene of the fight. There was little left of the thieves. Guillermo wouldn't give me details, but I guessed that the eagle-thing had not only torn them apart, but had *fed* upon them as well."

"And nothing was made of this?" I said. "The newspapers, the police . . ."

"This is a nation at war, señor. Bad things, very bad things happen, ¿y qué? I was here during the *Docena,* that sad time when battle raged in these streets of Mexico. The bodies lay in the streets for days. What could you do? And I suspect that the conspiracy may have agents in the police as well. I never saw a word about this killing in the newspapers.

"But to answer your question. Yes, we did have luck that night. While Guillermo was looking at the dead *ladrones,* he noticed a paper lying in the mouth of an alley nearby. The colonel-eagle, spirit, whatever, must have dropped it and not noticed it. Guillermo picked it up and read it, but it didn't make sense to him."

"Like 'wah-pilli,'" I said.

"*Exacto.* It was written in Náhuatl, and not what *los indios* of today speak, either, but a classical Náhuatl such as the codices of Sahagún and de las Casas are written in. Guillermo couldn't read it; but I could."

Navarro turned and reached back to a drawer in his desk. He produced a key from his pocket, unlocked the drawer, and drew forth from it a single sheet of paper. He handed it to Bierce and me. It was covered with lines of neat handwriting, evidently a schedule or minutes to a meeting, to judge from the careful lay-out of the text. Bierce and I puzzled over it, but it looked like nonsense to us. One corner was obscured with a spatter of dark brown spots. We handed it back to Navarro by our fingertips.

"It's a record of their meeting," he said, replacing the paper in his desk. "The meeting of the Eagle-knights of Tenochtitlán, the old name for Mexico City. It contains the names of the men attending—and it tells what they are planning to do in the near future." He paused. "It is not a good thing."

"We have seen enough of their works to be assured of that," said Bierce. "The question now is, what do we do about it?"

Navarro spread his arms in surrender.

"I was hoping you could tell me," he said. "Word has reached us, even here, about your skill in fighting *los horrores.* Is there nothing you cannot suggest, Señor Bierce?"

Bierce took a sip of his coffee, crossed one long leg over the other and sat back.

"We know," he said, "that they are susceptible to good old powder and ball—in their human forms, at least. We may have injured that *onza* up in San Andrés—"

"It still looked pretty healthy to me," I muttered.

"But remember, Amos, its human form was wounded. And nobody got up to contest my marksmanship when the shooting was done."

He didn't need to remind me.

Bierce said, "Where do they meet, Professor?"

"Teobaldo, please, or Teo my friends call me. I will show you."

He rose and walked over to a rack of perhaps fifty cubby-holes set in one wall. He reached up and without a pause plucked a paper roll, identical to every other roll in the rack, and took it to the big table. He quickly but carefully grabbed up all the statuettes, shards, codices, notes, pencils, rulers, notebooks, masks, stones, and feathers with which the table was strewn, emptying a broad bare spot in the center.

"Here," he said, handing me an odd-looking paddle or bat. It was about two and a half feet long, six inches wide at its widest, narrowing to a rounded handle like the handle of a baseball bat. The edges of the thing were inlaid with wide shards of black volcanic glass.

"What on earth is this?" I said.

"A macahuitl," Navarro said. "Or, rather, a replica of one. An Aztec 'sword' or war-club. Bernal Díaz, Cortés's old campaigner, writes that he once saw a warrior use one to decapitate a horse with one blow."

"A horse?" blurted Bierce.

"One blow?" I said.

"*Sí.*"

I merely touched one of the razor-edged shards of obsidian and opened a long, red line on my thumb. I quickly set the weapon down against the wall. Bierce was observing all this and let out a very audible sigh.

"You're hopeless, Amos," he said, and handed me his handkerchief to stanch the bleeding.

"That's why I am such a perfect companion for you."

I wrapped the kerchief securely around my thumb. Navarro never looked up.

"*Cuídate,*" he said. "That obsidian is sharp."

"Thanks for the warning." I saluted him with my bloody pennant. But he was intent upon the map that now lay unrolled upon the table. The impressive breadth of Mexico City now stretched before us in ink lines and pastel colors.

"*Miren,*" he said, and pointed to a grid of streets drawn upon the map. "Here we are, in Colonia Juárez. Over here is the *Plaza de la Constitución,* what we call the *Zólalo*"—he pointed to a large square decorated with idealized tree-tops, tiny rumpled green balls—"and here, here is where the Eagle-knights meet." He thumped his finger into a block north of the Plaza, and stood erect with a look of triumph on his face. Bierce leant over the map until his nose was almost pressed to it.

"Hmm," he said. "So perhaps fifteen blocks away. A good stroll, wouldn't you say, Amos?"

Navarro looked at us in horror.

"You don't intend to just walk there," he said, "do you?"

"It's not so far," said Bierce, straightening up to his full height. "Even for a *viejo* like me."

"It is not the distance I worry about, Señores. It is who may see you, if you go. Broad daylight . . ." He waved at the windows.

"Point taken," Bierce said. "Then we shall go at night."

Navarro sank down on a chair as if all the strength had gone out of him.

"Have I said nothing that you understand?" he said. "I don't think you truly appreciate the forces you are dealing with. *Fíjense, Señores:* they plan to drown the world in blood, to bring back the terrible gods of the past. When the first Aztecs dedicated their great temple, they sacrificed eighty thousand people to keep those gods sated. *Eighty thousand.* The priests dressed in the skins of their victims. This is the kind of philosophy we are treating with. If they have their way, this awful war you see around you is only the prelude to a worldwide slaughter."

"With all respect, Teo," I said, "we have had more direct experience with the conspiracy than you have." I pushed up my sleeve and showed him the scab on my wrist. "A present from Don Máximo Golón, and only the start of his generosity. But for the quick action of Mr. Bierce, I would no doubt now lie in a shallow grave somewhere out in the *monte.*"

Navarro looked at us, and there must have been something in the set of our expressions that impressed him.

"All right," he said, nodding and rising. "I did not call you all the way down here for a mere lecture on the archaeology of Mexico. I can see that you are men of action, and action is what is sorely needed now."

2.

So there, in the cluttered, scholarly office of Teobaldo Navarro, we began our plotting. The morning wore away, and when we got hungry, Teo—for so he insisted we call him—ordered sandwiches brought in. The details and back-

and-forth of our conversation is unimportant; but the upshot of it was that we knew we had to cut off this conspiracy at its fountainhead. That it was here in Mexico City, we had no doubt. Where else would it be but in the ancient Aztec capital? And the presence of those "big men" Teo spoke of indicated the proximity of the center of power. As terrible as the deeds and men we had already seen had been, they were mere outliers—the skirmishers, to use Bierce's analogy—to the main body of this evil. What we would do when—and if—we finally came on that awful heart of mystery, we couldn't say. For what could an aged writer, his middle-aged companion, and a bookish professor of archaeology do against such forces? Yet we must try.

But our immediate needs were more prosaic. When we reached a natural end to our discussion, Bierce asked about lodging. "I'm sure you can recommend a hotel that combines economy of price with sufficiency of hygiene," he said.

But Teo shook his head and waggled his index finger at us.

"No," he said. "I won't hear of it. Shuttle *el muy estimado* Señor Bierce off to some *nido de cucarachas?* Never. You will stay with me."

And man of action that he was himself, Teo leapt up, grabbed coat and hat from the rack by the door, and led us out of the college.

It was early afternoon and that period of siesta one hears about in the States. The busy clatter and rumble of the city had quieted; not stilled completely, but hushed in respect of that ancient, practical, and attractive custom. This mild February day in Mexico City, we were three of the few people still up and abroad. Those few others we saw were to a man courteous and friendly—a tip of the sombrero and a smiling *"Buenos tardes"* from all. They moved a bit more quickly than their brethren in the country, but not too quick for a touch of courtesy. Cooking smells, rich and spicy, wafted from open windows, accompanied by the clink of silverware on crockery.

"This is the hour of *la comida,*" Teo said as we walked along. "We have a meal, then rest. Later we will return to work."

"A very civilized custom," Bierce said, nodding his approval.

Teo smiled at him and said, "I'm so glad you approve. Else we'd need another *revolución* to change it!"

The scenery about us changed in subtle ways from the larger, more official-looking buildings near the city's center to streets lined with more modest rooming-houses and private residences. The small stores that occupied the first floors of many buildings were closed and shuttered, their awnings folded up and their

windows dark. It was an odd sensation for a *gringo* like me, so used to the constant bustle of cities such as San Francisco or Washington City. Although the
scene was peaceful, there was something eerie about it as well; as if all the people had been cleared off the earth, leaving behind their houses and heavy busi-
ness-blocks to be opened and occupied never again. Then we would catch the
gentle notes of a guitar or the click of dominos and men's laughter from some
hidden patio, and the illusion would fade. The city was dead no more, simply at
rest.

The walk from Navarro's office to his home was not a long one, yet by the
time we reached his apartment I was thoroughly winded. What is the matter
with me, I thought. I looked at my companions, and while Navarro strode
along at an easy pace, I did notice that Bierce was puffing a bit more than usual.

"The altitude," Navarro said without looking back at us, as if he had read
my mind. "You will grow used to it, but it will take time. *Paciencia, amigos.*"

My vanity was reassured by this. I had been proud of how I had borne up
under the rigors of war and the desert in the north, and would have been disappointed to find myself, suddenly old and tired on a level city street.

But I worried about Bierce. In addition to the altitude, he bore the twin
burdens of old age and asthma, and even the most iron constitution must wear
down eventually under such influences. Then I recalled our time in San Andrés
and said to Bierce, "A cup of Doña Huitzil's tea may be in order when we reach
the Professor's rooms."

Bierce bobbed his head once and wheezed out what might have been a
"Yes, Amos."

The professor's accommodations proved tasteful and comfortable. His
building, a neat, four-story affair of dark, volcanic stone, wedged among almost
identical neighbors, was well kept and quiet. Teo's rooms occupied much of the
third floor, and on the stairs I again worried for Bierce's comfort. But he irritably
waved away my offers of help, even refusing to relinquish his grip to me.

Teo unlocked a large, dark paneled door and threw it wide.

"Bienvenidos, compañeros," he said. *"Mi casa es su casa."*

We nodded our thanks and entered. Bierce found a chair and collapsed into it. I followed suit—the stairs had been the last straw—but Teo bustled into
the kitchen to put on tea.

While he was gone, I inspected our new digs. The room itself was as neat
as the rest of the building. In many ways it duplicated the décor of the university building, but made homey by heavy and well-used furniture, comfortable

castaways from the shipwreck of the Victorian age.

And there was a cat. Movement caught my eye among the divans and chairs, and I saw a pretty, all-white cat leap up onto one of the chairs with silent grace. She looked back at me with an air of curiosity and mild indignation. Teo returned just then, bearing a tray with tea cups and a steaming pot.

"Ah," he said. "You have met Toni!"

"Toni?" I said. At the sound of her name the feline soundlessly flowed across the room to reappear on my lap. I scratched her ears; she purred her thanks.

"Tonantzin, properly," said Teo. He set the tray on the low table before our chairs. "An Aztec goddess, of course. Toni puts up with my eccentricities only if she can be a goddess."

"And so she is." I scratched some more and she pushed her wedge-shaped head into my palm.

But if I thought I was the great charmer of our company, I was sadly mistaken. Bierce had been resting his eyes but opened them upon hearing our voices. When he saw the cat he fluttered his fingers in a light castanet-like rattle. Immediately Toni's gaze turned to him. In another second she was purring to his caresses and kneading at Bierce's lap with gusto. I sighed.

"The ladies always did prefer you," I said.

"The patience of age again bests the passion of youth," he said. Toni purred like a lioness.

By tacit agreement all talk of our mission was put off for the nonce. We were just too tired. After tea, Teo showed us our bedrooms—one for each of us, an unexpected and welcome luxury. After showing them to us, Teo said, "I will leave you to your rest. I will be working out here whenever you feel ready to visit." And with an oddly old-fashioned but courteous bow, he left us.

I can't speak for Bierce, but I was asleep as soon as my head hit the pillow. The physical and emotional toll of the past few days seemed to crest and crash upon me all at once, and my sleep was profound. If I dreamt at all, it was lost in the halls of slumber.

I awoke refreshed, retrieved my pants and shirt from where I had dropped them over a chair, and pulled them back on. As I buttoned up my shirt I first heard the low sound of voices. Bierce must be up already. For a seventy-one-year-old asthmatic, he still sometimes put me to shame. Hurrying on my socks and shoes, I opened the bedroom door and went out into the apartment's main room.

I blinked at the yellow glare of the hanging ceiling-lamp. Bierce and Teo were seated in the same easy-chairs we had vacated some hours before. They leaned toward each other in attitudes of deep conspiracy. Each held a glass that I was certain did not contain tea. They both looked up at me and smiled when I entered the room.

"Amos, my boy!" beamed Bierce. "Proof that the dead do rise! Come join us with some of this excellent tequila."

Teo got up from his chair and offered it to me. I sat opposite Bierce, and a glass of tequila materialized in my hand. I sipped and savored the liquor's burn down my throat.

"Been up for long?" I said to Bierce.

"No, not long." Behind him I saw Teo roll his eyes.

"Did you sleep at all?" I asked Bierce. He took a sip of liquor and made a face at me.

"Sufficient for my needs," he said. "Stop mothering me, Amos. The role doesn't suit you."

Teo returned with his own glass and pulled up a chair to face us.

"Bueno," he said. "So we are gathered. You slept well, I hope?"

I said, "Very well, thank you. You are a perfect host."

Again, an old-fashioned bow.

"You kept siesta like a true Mexican, Amos. Time for work. While you slept, I made a list of our enemies and tasks. Look at it, please, and tell me if it lacks anything."

He handed a sheet of paper to Bierce, and I shifted over to read it with him:

Eagle-knights Size of cult?
Bendiga   Center of power—D.F.?
Golón   How to fight them?
                         How many?
                         Where?

"'D.F.'?" I said.

"Distrito Federal," said Navarro. "Like your District of Columbia. This city."

Beneath Golón's name were the names of several powerful men, familiar to Bierce and me through the newspapers. It was a daunting list.

"These are men who were seen in the same place as Bendiga?" I said.

"*Exacto.* We have some powerful enemies, I fear."

Bierce tapped the paper.

"I think we may safely answer your one question in the affirmative," he said. "Mexico City is surely the center of their power; they would not deny themselves either the concentration of resources here, nor the symbolic value of the city."

Navarro nodded. "*De acuerdo.* I feel the same. To the Aztecs themselves, some places were always sacred; temples were always built atop older temples to absorb that power. And too many big men have been seen here in Bendiga's company. And there was what Guillermo saw . . ."

A pause. Then Bierce: "They seem to thrive on violence, Teo. We saw evidence of that both in Chihuahua and San Andrés. This begs the question: how widespread is the violence?"

Teo sighed and rubbed his hand over his bristling hair.

"Everywhere," he said. "There is war in the north, war in the south. When the armies can't find an enemy, they fight each other. Now I hear Villa and Obregón, once allies, are fighting."

"Some of this can be put down to human beings' natural factiousness," said Bierce. "Our own Civil War was a good example of that. We had won it long before but for inept boobs such as McClellan and his feud with President Lincoln."

I jumped in to thwart a long lecture on the late War Between the States.

"Very well, then, so the Eagle-knights are based here. But where, exactly? And once we find them, what then?"

"*Pues,*" said Teo, "that building my students saw Bendiga visit. I am sure that that is their base."

Bierce made a seesawing motion with his hand.

"Perhaps. Not to impugn the abilities of your 'spies,' but I find it a little too convenient that they were able to find the creatures' nest so easily."

I set down my glass.

"I agree. If this conspiracy is both as widespread and as dangerous as we think, I feel its agents will be more careful in their movements."

"Possibly," said Teo. "And yet, maybe they are so confident that they don't fear being seen. Where better to hide than in, *cómo se dice,* plain sight?"

Bierce said, "Then it is clear that some further and more serious observation is merited. We are fortunate that Bendiga is occupied far to the north—Amos and I can move about without fear of detection. And you, Teo, would any of these men recognize you?"

"No. I am just another dusty *profesor* to the public."

"Good. Let it remain so. Amos and I can act as observers, spies, if you prefer, whilst you can stay safely in your office and interpret the information we bring you."

Navarro nodded at this and the relief on his face was clear.

"Now," said Bierce, pouring himself another tumbler of tequila, "to means and tools. As far as the average conspirator goes, Amos and I are 'well healed,' as we say in the U.S. Both of us are proficient in the use of firearms and will not hesitate to use them.

"However, that still leaves the Jaguar-knights to contend with. We had a brush with one in San Andrés, but our experience has shown that more than mortal arms are needed when dealing with the supernatural."

"Your experience?" said Teo. "Then you have fought with such beings before?"

"Once. You recall, don't you, Amos?"

"Irene Marlowe," I nodded. Happy will be the day I can forget that case; at once one of our most deadly, and poignant, cases. I took a long draw on my tequila.

"A shape-shifter," Bierce continued. "Like your *onza,* except in Miss Marlowe's case there were hereditary forces at work. What we seem to be dealing with here is witchcraft of a sort, but many of the same fundamentals should apply."

"A *nagual,*" said Teo, nodding. "A sorcerer who can change into an animal."

"One thing," I said. "We were able to wound that *onza* in San Andrés with a gun. His human form needed a crutch to walk afterwards."

"We certainly did wound him, Amos. But I don't think we should depend upon such force in the future. I get the impression that young Golón was a neophyte, a mere dabbler excited about his new access of power. The men we are going up against now will be more committed—and hence more dangerous."

Teo, who had been lingering on our every word, now interposed. "But how do we defeat them, then?"

Bierce leant back in his chair, the glass of tequila flowing gold in his hand. Here we go, I thought. The Lecture.

"In our experience," he said, "revealing the creature's true nature to itself has been half the battle. To that end I had fashioned a special mirror, composed of elements gleaned from old alchemical texts. It has proven most effective. Once exposed to its own image, the creature becomes susceptible to more mundane weapons."

Teo rose and said, *"Un momentito."* He walked into another room—his own bedroom, I assumed—and returned with a large, crumbling folio volume in black covers. Twine held the whole flaking mess together. Teo set it down reverently upon the table before us and undid the twine.

"Your talk of mirrors," he said, intent upon his task. "It reminded me of something."

The twine parted and Teo carefully lifted the cover and several brittle leaves of parchment. The manuscript was constructed in one long continuous sheet, folded accordion-wise into separate pages. I saw that each page was illustrated in a flat, stylized manner, a chronicle of warriors in bright costume and conquistadores in silvery armor. The simple style and colors reminded me of Sunday color supplements back home, Little Nemo or the Yellow Kid; but Sunday comics drawn by an hallucinatory.

"*A ver,*" mused Teo as he lifted and folded back the ancient pages. He stopped and sat back.

"The Codex Genovese," he said. "Written in 1527, 'As Told to Fray Diego de la Cruz by the Indian Juan-Carlos.' One of the earliest accounts of Aztec life and its customs, written by a former attendant of the great Cuautémoc himself, last emperor of the Aztecs."

Bierce and I leaned forward, fascinated.

"Does the university usually lend out such texts?" Bierce said.

Teo smiled sheepishly. "Not usually," he said. "I have my especial, *digamos,* benefits as a professor."

He turned back to the text before us. "Here," he pointed. "What I wanted to show you."

We looked. Upon the page, in the middle of the page and taking up most of it, was a very odd and ornate figure. It was human in basic form, but so adorned with colorful symbols and extrusions that the figure itself was nearly lost in them. A flat profile typical of the Aztec artist was striped horizontally half-blue and half-yellow. From out the midst of this visual hurricane looked one half-closed eye. The mouth was open and lined with teeth. It looked as if the figure were about to speak—or bite.

"Yayauhqui Tezcatlipoca," Teo said. "The Aztec god of War. You can't see from this picture—the symbolism is very complex—but the name means 'Smoking Mirror.'"

We stared at the image: it stared right back.

Teo poured himself another tot of tequila, took a sip, and sat back in his easy-chair.

"There were four main Tezcatlipocas," he said. He held up one finger. "First there was the red Tezcatlipoca, called Tlatlauhqui, also Xipe Totec, 'the Flayed God.' He represented the renewal of Spring. Second"—two fingers went up—"white Tezcatlipoca, who was also called Quetzalcoatl. He was god of learning and *Lucero,* the Morning Star. A kind god, he was banished from Mexico but vowed to return one day to reclaim his kingdom. He was said to be a white-skinned man with a beard. When Cortés landed, the Aztecs thought he was Quetzalcoatl."

"That must have made Cortés's task much easier," I said.

Teo nodded. "*De verás.* He and his men were honored—until the emperor Moctezuma was killed. Then things went bad."

He held up three fingers.

"Then there was Huitzilopochtli, the Left-Handed Hummingbird, or blue Tezcatlipoca. He was the god of war, sun-god, and tutelary god of the Aztecs."

Teo stopped to sip his tequila and ponder. Then he held up four fingers.

"Finally," he said, "there was black Tezcatlipoca. The Smoking Mirror. He was arch-sorcerer, god of night, the jaguar, darkness, and magic. He was supreme among the Aztec gods."

"Wait a moment," I said. "You say that Tess-cat, Tess—"

"Tezcatlipoca, yes."

"Right. You'll have to write these down for us. My Spanish is poor enough, never mind my Aztec."

Teo smiled.

I continued: "You said that Tezcatlipoca was god of war, yet so was Huitzilopochtli. And you named a different sun-god on the Calendar-stone."

"Tonatiuh, yes. I know, it is confusing. We here in Mexico have not sorted it all out either. But consider: the Holy Church tells us that God is one, but God is three—Father, Son, and Holy Spirit. Is this no less confusing?"

"In mystery lies power," mused Bierce.

"*Exactamente.* Four, but One, and of the four, Black Tezcatlipoca was the most terrible. The most honored sacrifices were given his identity, given feasts and women and taught to play the flute. He lived like a prince. At the end of a year he was led to the temple, and as he walked up the long steps he broke his flutes. Then the priests blew dust in his face to dull the pain—"

"A narcotic of some kind," I said.

"Just so. And then the priests cut his heart out. It was considered a great honor."

Bierce let out a low whistle.

"All things considered," he said, "I think I'd rather be given a handshake and a certificate of appreciation."

Teo smiled.

"As would I, Señor Bierce. But to *los aztecas,* it was a priceless privilege."

"Were all their sacrifices so special?" I said.

"No. Most were quick, bloody, brutal. The Aztec Empire waged what they called Xochiyauyotl, Flower-Wars, in which they fought against their ene-mies—and allies. It was a war to, *cómo se dice,* take tribute?"

"A levy," Bierce said. "Like the tribute the Minoans demanded of vassal-states, virgins and youths for the Minotaur."

"Just so," said Teo. "The called it a 'war' to make it look like an even con-test. But the Aztecs almost always won. Then the defeated warriors were taken to the temples for sacrifice."

"You say a 'war,'" I said. "How many men were sacrificed at a time?"

Teo sighed. "Hundreds. Thousands. As I mentioned before, at the dedica-tion of the Great Temple of Huitzilopochtli alone, eighty thousand are said to have been slaughtered. This is probably exaggeration, but still . . . The temple steps are said to have run red with blood."

We all sipped our tequila in silence.

At last Bierce said, "From what we have seen, the modern killings are done by flying squads of men. They have to be—one man alone could not overpower a group of five or ten."

"They beat down resistance, then the knife appears," I said.

"And not just a knife," Teo said, and bent to leaf through the Codex. "There"—pointing to a picture of a temple. Atop the temple was a group of figures, disproportionately large for the setting. Four of them held a fifth man spread-eagled over what looked like a post or pillar of stone, so that his chest was exposed and arched upward. From a neat cleft in the chest, red streaks ra-diated out like rays of the sun. The four other figures holding him down, and a sixth who wielded the knife, were robed in black. Black paint covered the up-per halves of their faces, recalling the god Tezcatlipoca, and their thick, snaky black hair reached to their ankles. The one with the knife also held aloft a styl-ized heart dripping cartoonish gouts of blood.

"What is wrong with their hair?" I said.

"They matted it with blood," said Teo, as matter-of-factly as if he were dis-cussing the latest fashion. I wrinkled my nose.

"That must have made them very popular at soirées," I said.

"That is nothing. The priests of Xipe Totec wore the flayed skins of their victims to resemble the god himself. They wore the skins until they rotted off."

"Cheery," muttered Bierce into his tequila.

Teo said, "But *miren*, amigos, the knife." We looked back at the illustration. Even at such a small scale, the artist had achieved a remarkable amount of detail. The handle of the knife was carven into the shape of a crawling figure. The figures' head emerged from what looked like the gaping beak of a large bird, and the hands grasped the base of the blade. Where it wasn't smeared with red gore, the blade was green. That struck me, somehow, and I said to Teo, "Why is the blade green?"

"It was made of obsidian, volcanic glass. Sometimes it was flint, but the more valuable of blades were made of obsidian—black, or, *lo más especiál*, green."

"So, to sum up," I said, "there are the two kinds of sacrifice: one of the special victim, and the other of mere captives."

Teo waggled his finger at me.

"No," he said. "More than that. Women sometimes, even children were killed. The rain-god Tlaloc was especially fond of *los niños.*"

"'Fond' is a curious word to use in this context," Bierce said. "So pampered victims, war-captives, women, and children—does that cover all the sacrifices? I wonder that there was anyone left alive to greet the Spaniards."

"One other kind," Teo said. "When a great warrior was captured, he was tied to a large stone by his waist. That way he couldn't escape. Then he and his captor were given the *macuahuitls,* the Aztec swords, to fight to the death. The *macuahuitls,* remember, are edged with obsidian, deadly sharp. But the captive's sword was not edged with obsidian—it was edged with feathers."

"'The Aztecs almost always win,'" I quoted Teo. "Why was this sacrifice so different?"

"The Aztecs wanted to capture the strength of the great warrior. He had to die fighting, even if it was, *digamos*, pre-ordained?"

"The deck was stacked," I said.

"'The Aztecs almost always win,'" said Bierce.

"It's very sad," I said. "Your country seems to keep trying to devour itself, Teo."

He nodded.

"*Verdad.* We have a saying, each sixteenth of September, our Independence Day—'*Viva México, ¡lindo y bravo!*' Long live Mexico, the beautiful and the wild!

Note that—the beautiful *and* the wild. We know that there is a black place in our hearts that we keep trying to cut out."

"An apt metaphor," said Bierce. "But I shouldn't shoulder the sins of all humanity just yet. In the U.S., our own treatment of the Negroes, not to mention the Indians and the Chinamen, is scarcely any better."

"But they are *'el otro,' ¿me entiendes?* The other, different. Not to excuse it, but people often instinctively dislike the 'other.' We look in the mirror and there is Moctezuma—and there is Cortés. Both. We *are* the other."

"Philosophy aside," I said, "what do we do now?"

Teo took a deep breath and let it out.

"Bueno," he said. "We know where they meet. We must see if there is a way we can get in there. Or follow and capture the men who came there."

"And do what to them?" I said. "We're not the police, and I don't relish the thought of cold-blooded murder, even for such as they."

Teo said, "You mention a special mirror, Señor Bierce. I don't suppose—"

"As a matter of fact I do," said Bierce.

I stared at him.

"You have that mirror with you, Bierce? How would you know that we would need it?"

"From Teo's initial query to me. His talk of 'Eagle-knights' and 'Jaguar-knights' immediately made me think of our old friend Irene Marlowe."

It seemed a stretch, but I knew that Bierce had a remarkable instinct for such things—which, sadly, was balanced by a certain blindness to some social niceties.

"That's all very well and good," I said. "But using it requires getting fairly close to the creature. With Miss Marlowe it was a single entity, and even then it was touch and go. We may be faced with a gang of such things."

"True enough, Amos, but we may have little choice in the matter. A confrontation is inevitable; we must needs ensure that the balance of power tips in our favor, with whatever tools we may employ."

"And are we just to go on a rampage, then, assassinating any Eagle-knight we come across?"

"Of course not, Amos. As we've seen, the cult is too widespread. However, being here, at the fountainhead of the cult, I hope that we can at the very least thwart or destroy the organizers of it, and that subsequently the rest will scatter in disarray and confusion."

"A high-priest," Teo nodded. "A man who is both war-leader and holy man. A man who watched for omens—Moctezuma was such a man. He saw the comet and the coming of the white men. I would search for a man such as that."

My stomach took that moment to growl like a dog.

"Not to abuse your hospitality," I said to Teo. "But I'd like to search for some food, if I may."

Teo slapped his forehead.

"¡Idiota!" he said, standing up. "Of course—a thousand apologies, gentlemen. I will prepare food immediately."

He bustled off to the kitchen, and half an hour later the three of us (plus a rather impertinent Toni the cat, reaching a long paw up to take morsels from Teo's plate) were enjoying a simple but delightful meal of meat, rice, beans, and tortillas. I complimented Teo on the fare, but asked why he didn't employ a maid.

"My house, my habits," he said. "I am a complete *soltero,* bachelor, and my hours are often unusual. And I couldn't stand a stranger handling my things."

I thought of the priceless codex in the other room and nodded understanding.

3.

Despite our naps, we retired directly after supper. Full stomachs, the tequila, and residual fatigue from travel conspired to bring us down; and I, for one, did not resist. I fell asleep to the sound of the city at work.

In the morning, clear, clean sunlight flooded the rooms. I arose, bathed and dressed, and joined my fellows in the small dining room.

"Good morning," I said. I sat, took the white napkin off my plate, shook it out, and lay it across my lap.

"Good morning," said Teo. He reached out and ladled some scrambled eggs from a pan into a plate and gave the plate to me. Bierce, scowling at a newspaper, said nothing.

"Interesting reading?" I asked him.

"Eat your eggs and don't be impertinent," he said without looking up. "I am trying to gauge the mood of the city."

"By reading the funny-papers?"

Bierce sighed, slapped down the paper on the table, and glared at me.

"I read more Spanish that you give me credit for, *young man,* and one can divine a lot from mere pictures."

I swallowed. "Such as?"

"Such as our esteemed President Huerta is throwing a gala."

Bierce handed me the paper, and damned if one of the headlines didn't read, "The President Is Pleased to Offer a Grand Fiesta to High Society." Accompanying the article was what looked like a stock photograph of Huerta himself. Even the uneven half-tone print couldn't obscure that close-shaven bullet head, the gray bristle mustache, or the imperious gaze through wire-rimmed spectacles. He looked as though he were about to whip someone—if he didn't fall asleep first. I read some of the article.

"The cream of the regime will be there," I said. "Officers, gentlemen and their ladies, high men of business . . ."

I stopped reading and looked up. Bierce and Teo were watching me.

"A good time," I said slowly, "to investigate certain buildings."

"Precisely," said Bierce. "I imagine that most if not all of Teo's 'big men' will be in attendance at this shindy."

"They dare not attend," added Teo. "The request of *el Chacál* is an order."

I looked back at the paper.

"The day after tomorrow," I said. "It gives us little time to reconnoiter, plan."

Bierce said, "It shouldn't require excessive planning, Amos. A neat break-in, a look around, and out."

"Assuming that no one is there."

Bierce smiled and patted his coat pocket.

"Mr. Colt will be accompanying us."

"In the meantime," I said, "I should like to contact Mrs. Gadbury again. Teo, can a telegram be sent to the Metropolitan Hotel?"

"*Cómo no,* Amos. It is the most simple thing. When we go to my office, I will send one of my students."

We finished our breakfast and cleaned up. By nine o'clock we were out the door into a clear, beautiful day. The *chilangos,* for so the residents of Mexico City call themselves, were up and about and brisk upon their several businesses. Peasants in their white *calzones* swept the sidewalks with vigor. We walked among crowds of well-dressed men and women; the former in their suit-jackets, bowlers, homburgs, and even top-hats, the latter graceful in long dresses of black or brown and short bolero jackets. The ladies had adopted the extravagant hats of their *yanquí* sisters, so one often had to duck aside to let them pass. In the streets, an unending parade of drays, motors, trolleys, and carriages jostled one another. The trolleys were usually packed to the limit, sometimes to the point of bearing extra passengers clinging to their exteriors like barnacles on some aquatic monster.

We had seen little of the city the day before, what with the rapidity of our taxi ride and revelation upon revelation first at the university and later at Professor Navarro's apartment, so we were glad to get an uninterrupted look at the town now. Teo led us back the several blocks to the school and up to his musty office. There I composed a quick telegram to Deliah. I told her we were safe at Teo's flat, gave her the address, and asked when I might see her. Then, considering that her mother-in-law might intercept the message, I replaced "I" with "we." She and I could sort out the hidden meaning of it all later. Teo called one of his students—Tomás, I think it was, he of the Great Ears—and dispatched him with the message to the nearest telegram office. Then we grabbed our hats again and set out to discover Mexico City.

As I mentioned before, the college was near to the center of the city and the edifices of power. The buildings loomed up on each side of us, stern in their stone or stucco fonts. Many of the older residences had charming iron balconies jutting from their upper stories. It didn't take much imagination to picture the mantilla-shaded beauties of the Viceregal Period fanning themselves coquettishly upon those balconies; nor to see their gentlemen-suitors in flat, broad-brimmed hats and capes, strolling along the pavements.

And then we emerged from one such deep flume of architecture upon a vast open space. The Plaza de la Consititución spread wide to the sky, the very heart of Mexico City. It is contained by the National Palace, the national cathedral—hell, for all I know, the National Confectioners as well—and by many of the offices of government. Familiarly it is called the Zócalo. Every city and town of Mexico has a *zócalo* around which to gather of an evening; but there is only one Zócalo. Within its acres-wide expanse, there were lines of trees, a phalanx of street vendors, and lines of trolleys gathering or disgorging their passengers. There was a merry din of commerce; the clang of the trolleys, the occasional hoot of an outraged jalopy, the calls of the vendors: *"Camotes, camotes y camotes," "¡Tamales, frescas y calientes!" "Mangos, duraznos y platanos hoy. ¡Cómprelos antes de que me voy!"* A mouth-watering scent of fruit, fried meat, and warm tortillas wafted through it all like a spell. And looming over the two sides of the plaza like ornate cliffs, the cathedral and the National Palace. It was breathtaking, exhilarating.

As crowded as the sidewalks were, it was worth your life to step off them

into the streets. Neither coach, automobile, trolley, nor even the occasional
ox-cart yielded so much as an inch in their race around the sprawling circus that
was the Plaza Mayor. But Teo expertly led us safely through the traffic and
crowds. In the very middle of the Zócalo, I paused and looked up. The largest
flag I had ever seen hung on a royal ship's mast of a flagpole, red, white, and
green fabric coiling and uncoiling in the breeze. I am in the very heart of the
city, I thought, the very heart of Mexico. For a second I could feel the psychic
and historical weight of the ancient city around me. It was a little frightening,
that titanic presence, but thrilling as well.

And then an odd thing occurred. As I scanned the pale skies of Mexico,
they seemed to darken—but not with clouds. A deep, sinister twilight purpled
the sky, as if layers of atmosphere had been skimmed off to reveal the Void beyond. And it had a sheen to it, an inner light as if glowing from within. But
within *what?* Any moment now it would resolve itself into clarity, and show us
a dark reflection of the world . . .

"Amos."

I tore my gaze from the sky with a start. Bierce and Teo were standing a
few yards away, staring at me as if I were possessed.

"If you are done woolgathering," Bierce said, "perhaps you would care to
join us."

I looked back at the sky, now just sky, and back at my companions. I wanted to tell them of what I had seen, to hear from them a normal explanation to
set my racing heart at rest. But the air was full of the voice of the city, and a
quiet voice within me said, *Not now.* I rejoined my friends and acted as if nothing were wrong.

"A touch of the vertigo?" asked Teo with a smile.

"It's all . . ." I started but could not finish. Teo chuckled.

"I know. I felt the same way when I first came here from Puebla. Come, I
have something to show you both."

He led us through the hurly-burly of the Zócalo and into a side street to
the right of the cathedral. The sudden quiet that descended upon us there after
the din of the Plaza was balm to my ears. We walked in silence for several
minutes. We came to a small café on the left-hand side of the street and took an
empty table upon the sidewalk. A waiter in clean, white shirt and apron appeared.

"Tres cafecitos, por favor," Teo said, holding up three fingers, and with a curt
nod the waiter went to fetch them. Teo had managed to seat us facing the op-

posite side of the street, and now he nodded toward a building across and down the street from us.

"There," he said, looking back at us. "The nest of the Eagle-knights."

Bierce and I both sat up straight. But Teo continued facing away from the street.

"*Calma, amigos,*" he said. "They may be watching."

At that we relaxed—or feigned relaxing. There was a well-thumbed menu on the table and I picked it up and pretended to read it. Bierce reached into an inner coat pocket and produced a cigar. He took his penknife, cut off the end of the cigar, folded the knife and put it away, and set the cigar between his teeth.

"That is where Guillermo saw them gather?" he said around the cigar.

"*Sí.*"

I glanced up as if watching the passers-by and inspected the building. Dingy black volcanic rock, a pair of balconies on the second floor—nothing unusual about it, nothing to distinguish it from its equally neglected neighbors. Yet as I looked at it, the windows darkened in the same way as had the sky above the Zócalo. I looked back at the menu.

The coffees arrived and we busied ourselves in preparing them to our tastes.

"The building disturbs you," said Bierce as he stirred his coffee. "Why?"

I said, "When we were on the Zócalo, I thought I saw something in the sky." I paused. "No, not *in* the sky, the sky itself. It seemed to darken and deepen, as if it were about to show me something—"

"Like a mirror."

Bierce and I shot looks at Teo. He continued stirring and looking at his own coffee, but his brows were tight with tension.

"I have seen it, too," he said. "In windows, fountains, even puddles. You remember what I told you of Tezcatlipoca, 'the Smoking Mirror.'"

Bierce nodded. "He is manifesting himself in reflective surfaces," he said. "There is deep magic here, boys, 'from a wild weird clime that lieth, sublime, out of space—out of time.' We have our work cut out for us."

Remembering the sacrificial victim from the codex, I thought that an unfortunate turn of phrase.

We dawdled over our coffees as long as would appear natural, then paid our *cuenta* and left. I don't know about my fellows, but I was relieved when we turned a corner and were finally out of sight of that drear edifice, and its windows that may or may not have reflected another sky.

Teo proved an affable and informative guide. He led us to the green peace of the Alameda; across the dizzying river of traffic known as Los Insurgentes, with its golden Angel atop its pedestal; and to the great hill of Chapultepec. At its crest stood the castle, now a military academy.

"When your country invaded us in 1846," Teo said, "the cadets defended the school. Mere boys, some as young as fifteen years old, fought and died to stop *los invasores norteños*. We call them *'los Niños Heroes,'* the Boy Heroes."

We looked at the leafy hillside and the quiet stately castle atop it, and tried to imagine those bloody days almost seventy years past.

"General Grant was here as a junior officer," Bierce said. "General Lee, too, if you can feature it. Both on the same side."

"Both fighting to conquer our homeland," Teo said. "Our histories are bound together like the eagle and the snake on our flag: one dares not let go of the other for fear he will be bitten."

From Chapultepec we just wandered. Teo showed us the neighborhoods, rich and poor, the shops and *talleres* where artisans chipped and cut and hammered out their wares; the great Mercado, quiet now but flooded with humanity every Thursday. One thing I noticed: for all President Díaz's efforts to modernize Mexico, it still wore an Aztec mask. Its neighborhoods still bore Aztec names—Coyoacán, Chapultepec, Xochimilco—and the Mexicans themselves proclaimed their heritage with every glance and accent.

Teo also took us to the museum to see the relics there. There we came face to face with the mighty "Calendar Stone" with its sun-god face glaring out from the wheel of the cosmos; and the statue of Coatlicue, eight feet tall and every bit as terrifying as Teo had said. I fell silent at the sight of it—at the kind of imagination that could create such a thing.

We had lunch at a restaurant in the Zona Rosa, wedged among bookstalls and fashionable stores, then trudged our weary way back to Teo's rooms. None too soon: the weather that had started so cheerfully had deteriorated into a heavy overcast, and thunder could be heard approaching over the valley. We had barely stepped into Teo's front door when, with a blinding flash and a report like artillery right above our heads, the storm broke, and the rain came down in a deluge.

"Quite a storm," said Bierce.

"Curious for winter," said Teo, looking out at the pelting curtains of rain. We watched the downpour and the poor, soaked souls running through it to shelter.

When we had tired of watching the storm, we partook of siesta. Later, re-freshed, I went into the sitting room to find a telegram from Deliah awaiting me.

WOULD LOVE TO SEE YOU CAFÉ ARMBRUSTER 8AM MANANA?
DELIAH

"Do you know this Café Armbruster, Teo?" I said.

"*Sí*. It is not far, near to Los Insurgentes." He grinned. "You have a *dama* awaiting you, no?"

"I have a *dama* awaiting me, *sí*," I laughed.

Dama—lady. I liked that.

Teo said, "Would you like to use my telephone to call her?"

I would, and I did. The hotel concierge connected me to Deliah's rooms, but I was disappointed when another female voice answered. It was their maid, it turned out, and madam was resting. Would I care to leave a message? I told her just to tell madam that 8 A.M. was *perfecto*, and I would see her there.

After I hung up, I turned to see Bierce's vulture glare upon me.

"It's coffee, Bierce," I said. "A brief visit."

"The brevity of the tryst is not what concerns me, Amos. You responded and acquiesced to her summons with schoolboy-like alacrity."

"Bierce," I sighed, "have you never heard the expression, 'All work and no play makes Jack a dull boy'? Besides, you're hardly the man to criticize another for falling for a woman's wiles."

"I only counsel caution, my boy. Keep your wits about you—we are in deep waters here."

I smiled. "Noted and appreciated, Bierce."

4.

The following morning at 7:55 I was seated at a table at the Café Armbruster, surveying the moving crowds for a familiar face. Teo had drawn me a map to get there, and I was vainly proud of the ease with which I found the place. The morning was cool and I was glad it was an indoor café. I toyed with the silver-ware on the table; then suddenly she was standing in the café's doorway. There was a young Mexican woman with her whom I took to be her maid. They stood in the doorway, looking this way and that, and I took advantage of the moment just to admire Deliah. She had on her widow's weeds as usual, but a slightly more fashionable version of them; and a hat that, while not as ebullient as those some women were wearing then, was at least festive in its silk flowers and feathers. With the sunlight behind her, she looked ravishing.

I stood and waved to them. When Deliah saw me, the smile that blossomed on her face made my heart catch. *Love?* asked a voice inside me. I did not know, and I couldn't afford to address that question right then. For now it was enough just to see her and be with her.

"Amos," she said as she swept up to me. "How good of you to come."

She offered a black-gloved hand and I took it politely. Even through the black silk I could feel the warmth of her pulse.

"And this," she said, indicating the young woman with her, "is Rosabla, my maid." I nodded and smiled to her. The girl curtsied and giggled. It was hard to tell, what with her dark pallor, but I thought that she even blushed a little.

"Please," I said, pulling out a chair for Deliah. "Sit."

We all sat and I waved down the waiter. We ordered coffees and suddenly there was nothing to say. I found myself staring at Deliah and was happy to find her staring right back. This won't do, I thought.

"So," I said, "your hotel is comfortable?"

"Eminently so. And your rooms?"

"Very nice, thank you."

Another awkward silence. Then Deliah laughed—church-bells in a summer sky.

"What children we are," she said, and held my hand on the table-top. "Rosalba is the soul of discretion, I assure you." She turned to the girl and said a few words in Spanish to her. The girl nodded, said *"Sí, Señora,"* rose, and left us. At the door of the café she turned and gave us an arch smile.

"I told her to find me some breath pastels," Deliah said. "That should occupy her for a while."

We sat holding hands and just looking into each other's eyes for long, delicious moments.

"I've missed you," I said.

"And I you," she laughed. "It's been, what, all of two days?"

"Two long days, mind you. In that time I have received a thorough education in Aztec mythology and history. Would you care to hear about it?"

"No, thank you. I'd rather hear about you."

I took a deep breath.

"I am well," I said. "Teo—our host, Professor Teobaldo Navarro—is generous with his time and accommodations. I find the altitude here tires me more easily than I am used to, but I'm sure I will adjust."

She squeezed my hand and looked more closely at me.

"No, dear," she said. "How are *you?*"

I looked into her wide, earnest eyes and sighed.

"Scared," I said. "In a word, terrified. Bierce and I have been up against some fantastic and dangerous forces before, but nothing this widespread or powerful. The scale of the conspiracy is daunting, and is pushing toward a wholesale reshaping of the entire natural order. It is hard to know where to start, but we have some clues."

"Is the danger to you immediate?"

"No, not at the moment, anyway. I fear, though, that as we probe into it more closely, the danger will grow. I feel as if we were about to swat a hornet's nest with a stick, then stand around to see what happens."

For a brief, sharp moment I saw a jar full of moving, venomous jewels, and I started. I pulled my hand from Deliah's; but when she reached for it again, I gave it to her. The warmth of her touch soothed me. Our coffees arrived and we sipped in silence for a minute.

"Is there anything I can do?" Deliah said.

"No, dearest. I would not have you involved for the world."

"It saddens me to see this weighing upon you so. I wish——"

She stopped and looked startled. Then she reached down and set her purse, a small, black reticule beaded in jet, upon the table.

"I can't believe I forgot," she said. She rooted around in the reticule for a moment, and pulled forth a neat, folded card. Her face beamed triumph.

"'Your presence is requested,'" she said, and set the card upon the table in front of me.

> Su Excelencia El Presidente José Victoriano Huerta y M.
> Les Invita a Una Gala
> Palacio Nacionál
> Plaza de la Constitución
> México, D.F.
> R.S.V.P.

I stared at the card.

"It came for Mamá just yesterday," Deliah said. "She says I may come, and I think she is hoping 'Mr. Twain' will be there as well. And, of course, I will need an escort, if you know of anyone . . ."

She looked at me with sly meaning, the minx. I just continued to stare. Deliah's smile faltered.

She said, "I know you're no great admirer of General Huerta, but—"

"No, no," I hurried to say. "That isn't it. And I can think of no more delightful way to pass an evening than in your company." I took the card and looked at the date. "That's the day after tomorrow, isn't it?"

"Yes."

"Well, there are complications. . . . I must think."

I sat back and sipped my coffee. Bierce would not be pleased if I backed out of our planned raid on the Eagle-knights' hideout to go dancing. On the other hand, it might give me a chance to spy on some of the "big men" included in the conspiracy (who, no doubt, would be in attendance upon *el Presidente*). How real the elder Mrs. Gadbury's connection to General Huerta was was suspect; I'm sure she made more of it than there really was. Yet she had received this invitation, and I was certain that not many *gringos* had. In the end it seemed like a golden opportunity to gain some knowledge. And if I had to spend the evening in the arms of Deliah Gadbury to do so, so be it.

I set my cup down.

"I would be delighted," I said, and was rewarded with a smile from Deliah that warmed me to my heart.

*

"I will be damned, drawn, and quartered."

Bierce stood at full parade attention before me as I returned to Teo's house. Teo was at classes, so we had the place to ourselves. I could have wished it otherwise.

"Bierce—" I began, but he raised a hand and shut his eyes.

"I warned you about the distractions of the flesh, Amos," he said.

That got my dander up.

I said, "I hardly think you're the man to call me on that, Bierce. And haven't we had this conversation before?"

"Then it bears repeating, apparently. Your attraction to the younger Mrs. Gadbury is understandable, forgivable, even. But we have important work to do!"

"And I intend to pursue it! Did you not hear what I said? Some of the most important Eagle-knights may be at this gathering."

"'May' is an indeterminate verb."

"Don't play English prof with me, Bierce. This is an opportunity that won't be offered us again. If there are members of this cult close to the president, we need to know about it. How else are we to get close to them, I ask you?"

I had scored a point and I could see it. Bierce's arms remained folded across his broad chest, but for the moment he had no rejoinder. That alone felt like a victory.

A "victory." I didn't want to beat Bierce; alone in this strange city with each other, we were all we had. I sighed and let the anger leak out of me.

"Look, Bierce," I said, more pleading than arguing. "Honestly: when will we have the chance to get into such company again? Especially now, while nobody here knows who I am. You and Teo can teach me to recognize the members of the group and I can watch their relation to the president. You have to admit that they must have some support from higher up."

He continued to stare at me with those merciless blue eyes. But I could fairly see the wheels turning in his head.

"And I suppose," he said finally, "that you need my permission for this escapade?"

"No," I said slowly. "Nor even your blessing. Just your understanding and trust."

He stared for a few seconds more, but then his arms unfolded and he relaxed.

"All right," he said. "But I appreciate the level of, let us say, *distraction* you will be working under, even if you do not. You mustn't lose sight of our mission."

"Not for a moment, Bierce. I know how this appears, but I am in earnest about the possibilities of discovery. Consider: no one in the capital knows who I am nor why I am here. Accompanying the Gadburys will be the perfect introduction to this society."

"I dare say you will need decent attire for this shindig," he grumbled.

"Taken care of. Deliah said that she still has a suit of her husband's that would fit me."

At that Bierce actually chuckled.

"A dead man's suit," he said. "How apropos."

*

The rest of the day we spent in further acquainting ourselves with the city. Teo had warned us against wandering into the eastern slums beyond the National Palace—"A *pulquería* on every corner, a murder on every block," he quipped—but the rest of the city opened up to us in the bright winter sunshine like a vast, complex flower.

We ambled north from our quarters and returned to the Zócalo. We managed to dodge between the traffic with nothing worse than a few Mexican curses from passing *automovilistas* and a splash of horse manure on our pants cuffs. We took refuge on the long, tree-shaded center of the plaza. I gazed again at the coiling sail of the Mexican flag above me. When it spread sufficiently, we could make out in its center the image of an eagle atop a cactus, a writhing snake clutched in its talons.

"The national symbol of Mexico," intoned Bierce, pointing with the blunt end of his cigar. "Teo tells me that that is what the Aztecs saw when their wandering led them to the Valley of Mexico, six hundred years ago. By this they knew they had arrived at their intended home. A potent symbol, don't you think, Amos?"

I shielded my eyes with my hand and looked up at the rolling fabric. Its folds parted and closed around the image like a conjurer's trick.

"Many nations adopt the eagle as a symbol," I said. "Germany, Russia, Poland, our own United States. But I have never seen a variation such as this."

"Neither snake nor eagle durst release the other for fear of destruction. The Aztecs were unknowingly prescient in their choice of symbol: the rich and poor of this land, white and Indian, coil and grip each other, simultaneously dependent upon and destructive to the other. Here we see the seeds of this terrible revolution, Amos—and of our own especial peril."

It was odd to speak of revolution in that hurrying but peaceful scene. Memories such as the fierce battle of Ojinaga, the outrages of the Rurales, revolutionaries, and *federales*—even our adventure in San Andrés Tecolotzán— felt distant, otherworldly, fictional.

But the weight of the teeming city around us was palpable. I could feel it stretching out in all directions around us, from the ancient space of the Zócalo to the distant snow-capped peaks of Itztaccíhuatl and Popocatépetl; the mighty City of Mexico, ancient and modern, primitive and advanced.

"History is deep here," I said. "Its weight bears me down."

I fear I must have said this in a rather dreamy, stilted manner, for Bierce turned twinkling eyes upon me and said, "Why, Amos, the nascent poet in you awakens. Come, let us move on before it has a chance to gestate into something truly obnoxious."

We avoided the National Palace—no sense in alerting any potential foes to our presence—but ducked into the cathedral instead. Its stony, cyclopean bulk towered over us, and within was a centuried darkness relieved only slightly by begrimed stained-glass windows and the twinkling candles of the faithful. The lights glinted off a fortune of gold-leaf cherubs, saints, and Baroque floral eruptions that only accentuated the heavy darkness around them. We did not stay long.

Outside again in the free air, we turned west—and were delighted to walk into a cloud of heavy, sweet scent. Along the west side of the cathedral, peasant women sold flowers from heady banks of carnations, roses, and marigolds. Their blazing colors brought new life to the cathedral's gray stones. I bought Bierce a carnation from an ancient dame in a black rebozo. Her toothless face squeezed itself into a smiling mass of wrinkles at the few centavos I paid her.

"Here," I said, slipping the red flower into Bierce's buttonhole. "Now you look like a gentleman."

"Heaven forfend," he muttered; but I noticed that he didn't take it out.

From the Zócalo we wandered farther westward. Here was Avenida San Francisco, familiarly called "Plateros," a wide street running along the southern edge of the green-shaded spaces of the Alameda. The chaotic bustle of the Zócalo was here replaced by a stately if no less lethal parade of wealthy *chilangos* in their conveyances. No ox-carts here; long, dark limousines purred by; open calashes and broughams filled with stern-faced *gentilhombres* and *damas;* highstepping horses drew black-lacquered coaches adorned with gilt armorials. I had no doubt but that some of these family crests had survived all the way from the time of the tough Spaniards of the Conquest. The grim faces that looked out at us from these coaches seemed to bear this out. Despite the starched collars and gleaming top-hats, those faces would have looked equally at home beneath a Spanish morion or at the head of a company of horse. Their drivers, toughs clad incongruously in the sombreros and silver-studded pants of rural *charros,* yielded for neither pedestrian nor vehicle in their headlong charge down the avenue. The coaches were often accompanied by mounted bodyguards who carried brutal-looking carbines openly upraised or laid across their saddles.

"I am reminded of the London of forty years ago," said Bierce as we sidled through the crowds. "The hurry toward the future, the passion for ostentation—at least among the ruling classes." He paused and reached back suddenly. He was holding the arm of a ragged-looking *pelado,* and the fellow was holding Bierce's wallet. Bierce glared at the man; the man smiled back with several teeth. Some of those remaining were edged with silver. His white pyjamas and sombrero were grimy; one ear looked as if a cat had been chewing on it.

"*No,*" said Bierce. Whether English of Spanish, the *pelado* got the message. He shrugged, handed the wallet back to Bierce, and turned to go. Bierce sighed heavily and yanked the man back to him again.

"*Y el dinero,*" he said. "*Por favor.*"

Again that sheepish, gapped smile and the thief handed a wad of crumpled bills to Bierce. Bierce took them, flipped through and stuffed them into his pocket. His hand emerged with one bill, which he held out to the *pelado*.

"Here," said Bierce. "Next time, just ask."

The fellow took the bill, smiled that cracked smile, and Bierce released him. Despite his tattered white clothes and leather sandals, he disappeared among the elite as if he had never existed.

"We should have hailed a policeman," I said.

"To what end?" said Bierce. "Even if we could find one in this hurly-burly, we would have to hold onto the miscreant till the officer got here. And then what? They consign the poor wretch to the dungeons of the police, subject him to beatings, torture, or worse, and all for a fistful of specie that I got back anyhow? I would rather concentrate upon the bigger felons in our sight, Amos. Besides," he said, tilting his face to the sun, "it's too nice a day for such drama."

We continued our tour of Plateros. Jewelry stores and ornate restaurants displayed their wares and bedizened patrons through spotless plate-glass, while the occasional staircase dropped from the pavement down to the doorways of the caretakers' humbler quarters. I was amused to see chickens, turkeys, and even the odd pig or two in these impromptu sunken yards.

"Not difficult to see why this country is in a revolution," I said, pointing out the urban livestock. "Quite literally the rich live above the poor here."

Bierce glanced at the subterrene enclosure we were passing and nodded.

"The only mystery is why this revolt didn't happen sooner," he said. "President Díaz must have had a powerful grip upon both the fears and affections of the Mexican people. I fear that, for all the bloodshed, this revolution will accomplish little. Behold the rich even now, busy upon their selfish peregrinations while the poor on both sides of the conflict are slaughtering one another across the countryside."

"Was it always thus, Bierce?"

"From what I understand of Mexican history, yes. While you were making cow-eyes at Mrs. Gadbury, Teo lectured me upon the customs of the Aztecs. One of them in particular was especially brutal and cynical. You may recall him mentioning it: how the Aztecs led their people into so-called 'flower-wars' against other poor saps, convincing them that the others were the true enemy, then involved them in the ritual slaughter of the prisoners on the temple peak. 'It's all for you, to keep the sun shining'—yet the emperor still lived in his palace and the peon in his hovel."

"Then what is the point of our adventure here, Bierce? If this conflict should continue despite what little we can do."

"You mistake both our goals and our abilities, Amos. We are not here to reform the Mexican financial system; with luck and wisdom, the Mexicans themselves will do so in time. We are here to destroy a particular threat that is using this dreadful conflict for their own, more dreadful aims. 'What little we can do' will be sufficient—it has to be. Brace up, man. You are stronger than you think."

We found a café along the way that had a couple vacant chairs outside. We purchased sandwiches and sat and watched the ceaseless parade of the wealthy while we sipped our *cervezas* and pondered what to do next.

Bierce stood up.

"I need to stretch my legs," he said. "What do you say we amble into the *colonias* to the east?"

"Teo warned us to stay away from there, Bierce."

"Exactly why we should go. Come, lad, on your feet!"

Despite my misgivings—or because of them, not wanting to let Bierce wander into danger alone—I rose and followed.

If the contrast between rich and poor on Avenida San Francisco had been surprising, the gulf between the *colonias* and the *barrios*—the slums—was staggering. We walked from tree-lined avenues of tall, stately mansions to narrow, rutted dirt ways between the dingy *mesones,* where the peasants lived in noisy, crowded squalor. Between and beyond the more regular dwellings stood and leaned a motley assortment of shelters. The area was growing organically, throwing out swellings and growths of wood, sheet-metal, adobe, anything that could be cobbled together. Children and lean dogs careered through it all. And Teo had not been exaggerating: there *was* a *pulquería* on every corner. Bierce stood in statue-like contemplation of the first one we encountered—a tiny black room opening off the corner of a block of small stores. A hand-painted sign above the door declared it to be "Pulquería Los Ánjeles." Tattered decorative tissue-cuttings swayed lazily in the doorway.

"Walking is thirsty work," said Bierce, patting his belly. "Is it not, Amos?"

I looked at the *pulquería* and said, "You can't be serious."

"Oh, I am always serious where alcohol is concerned! Come, Amos. When will we have this opportunity again?"

"Hopefully, never," I said under my breath. But I followed him.

As it turned out, it wasn't as awful as I had pictured it. It was far simpler, for one thing; a plank across a pair of barrels served as a bar, and there were no chairs. At that hour of the afternoon it was also mercifully free of patrons. Two men in ragged calzones leaned in one corner, eyes half-shut, bowls of some white liquid I assumed was *pulque* held at half-mast before them. I got the feeling that if one of them moved aside, the other would crash to the floor. The man behind the simple bar, big as a bull in his upper body, with black hair oiled straight back from his glowing, tanned face, leaned both thick fists upon the plank.

"*¿Cuántas?*" was all he said, not "What'll it be, gents?" or "Good afternoon," but merely, "How many?"

"*Dós,*" I said, holding up two fingers to be sure. "*Por favor.*"

He reached under the plank and brought up a heavy clay jar and two wooden bowls, chipped and worn but tolerably clean. He unstoppered the jar and poured into the bowls the same thick, pale liquid that was in the other patrons' bowls. When they were half full he upended the jar, slapped the cork back into it, and put it back beneath the plank.

"*Diez centavos,*" he said. I put the coins on the counter. The barkeep swept them off the counter with a smooth, practiced motion. Bierce and I lifted the bowls, clacked them together, and said, "Cheers." Bierce began to drink his right off, but I stopped to sniff the liquid. A mistake—it was foul. I set the bowl untasted back on the plank. The barkeep smiled at me. Bierce, meanwhile, had drained his serving.

"An unusual vintage," he said, "but amusing in its own way. By your leave, Amos . . . ?" He looked at my untouched bowl and raised an eyebrow.

"Have at it, Bierce."

Bierce saluted me and drank. The barkeep, watching all this with a grim, said, "*El toro tiene mas conojes que el ternero, ¡de verás!*"

Lowering the bowl from his lips, Bierce said, "What did he say, Amos?"

"He said, 'Health and long life.'"

Bierce raised his bowl to the barkeep and drained off the last, milky dregs of the stuff. The leaning pair in the corner broke into song:

> *Sabes que pulque*
> *Es un licor divino?*
> *Es bebido por ángeles*
> *En vez de vino.*

Bierce nodded to them and they raised unsteady sloshing bowls in return.

"Never met a gringo who could hold his *pulque* like that," the barkeep said in Spanish. He stuck out his hand to Bierce and said, "I am Báltazar de los Ánge-les, the owner of this humble place, and it is an honor to meet you."

I translated for Bierce. He gripped the other's proffered hand.

"The pleasure is mine," said Bierce. Their eyes met and there was such a frankness and immediate bond between them that I actually grew a little jeal-ous. Except for translating, I might not have existed at all. It never ceased to amaze me that Bierce, in spite of his long-standing and ingrained misanthropy, could make friends so readily. As chagrined as I was, though, I was glad to see him make a new friend; he had cut ties with so many in recent years.

So," said Báltazar de los Ángeles, "you gentlemen are tourists in our fair city?" He spread a magnanimous hand that encompassed the room, its patchy walls, its dusty floor.

"Tourists, yes," I said. "We are staying with a friend in the city." More than that I was chary to divulge.

"Well, now you have *two* friends in *el De Efe*. You must come and dine with me and my family."

I translated for Bierce who put his hand to his breast and bowed like a gent.

"*Tu casa es mi casa,*" quoth he. Báltazar looked confused, angry—then burst out laughing.

"Just make sure to bring the calf"—he pointed to me—"with you! He can at least speak Spanish better than you!" And he guffawed hard enough to make the planks rattle like a marimba.

We stayed only long enough to hear Báltazar's description of local sites we must see ("Have you seen the canal? You *must* see the canal!"), with directions to them that I only half-understood. Then, with a stiff and titanic dignity, buoyed up by a small lake of *pulque,* Bierce led us out into the afternoon.

Our tour was necessarily brief, as the sun was already westering. But we were able to pass through a couple small plazas laid out around parish churches. They were far more humble than the Zócalo at the city center, yet more devout in their way. The rough casas and *mesones* of the area presented a cleaner face than their fellows on the side streets, and the churches themselves seemed to radiate a calm and dignity that precluded any ugliness in their presence. It was the hour of siesta, and aside from a couple men silently sweeping the pavements, all was still.

"The peasants' religion sustains them," I said to Bierce as we passed through one such space.

"As does that of the Eagle-knights," he replied.

I frowned at him—cynical old buzzard.

"A poor comparison," I said. "The Eagle-knights, like the Aztecs they idolize, use their religion for their own aims. The peasants here draw strength from their church—"

"As do the Eagle-knights from their debased form of Aztec worship," Bierce said with professorial emphasis. "All religions offer an illusory hope to their adherents, a balm for a difficult world. The Eagle-knights at least worship something that has an objective reality."

"As awful as that may be."

"As awful as that may be."

We continued on as far as the canal Báltazar had recommended to us. This, despite its reduced and fouled state, intrigued me greatly. "'The Venice of the New World,'" said Bierce as we stood above the canal's stone-walled flume. "So Teo referred to the Aztec capital of Tenochtitlán, upon which Mexico City was built. A veritable jewel of a city built upon the face of the lake and intersected by a network of canals that served the Aztecs as roads. All that, reduced to this." He pointed down at the turgid waters with his cigar. "They seek to revive the wrong things, Amos. These self-styled Eagle-knights and Jaguar-knights, striving to bring back some age of glory, while the descendants of actual Aztec kings live in this squalor." I looked around at the cracked walls crowding the canal in its dark, narrow flume; at the empty waters once alive with the commerce of an empire, and sadly, had to agree.

Yet even as I ruminated on this dreary state of things, a glow as of a rising sun approached us from the canal to the south. As it drew closer we saw that it was a broad, flat-bottomed boat, being poled upstream by a lone *muchacho* in spotless white pyjamas and modest straw sombrero. The deck of the boat was freighted with thousands of marigolds and carnations and roses—shoals of them, showers and hillocks of them—the flowers destined for the markets and the sellers we had seen by the cathedral. The orange-red glow of the flowers reflected off the canal's waters and off the drab stone walls. It filled the canal and the air above it with scent and color and cheer, and for a few minutes this vision turned the stinking barrio into the seat of empire again.

"Behold, Amos," Bierce said with a smile. "The Spaniards stole the wrong gold." We watched the boat glide past us and tipped our hats to its pilot, who smiled and responded, *"Buenas tardes"* in a soft sing-song.

When it was past, Bierce looked up.

"The day wanes," he said. "We should be clear of this place before night-fall."

We turned back toward the center of the city. Neither Bierce nor I had taken much notice of the streets by which we had arrived. It would have done us little good anyway; most of them were unmarked or their signs removed or defaced. However, we knew that if we kept the sun before us, we should arrive back near the city center without too much confusion. That the streets here, as rough as they were, had been laid out in a grid, further aided us.

But what did concern us was that the streets were again coming alive. It must have been the end of siesta, for people were emerging from their houses to pass others coming in from the city proper. Whereas before we had walked unnoticed, unmolested, almost alone, now we drew stares. Still, the several people to whom we tipped our hats responded in quiet and friendly tones.

But there was a residue of the crowds that did worry me. They were men, mostly young men, congregating on corners or by doorways, often adjacent to the nearest *pulquería*. Bierce appeared unconcerned by them—veritably uncon-scious of them, in fact—until he muttered sidelong to me, "Keep your eyes ahead, Amos, and your step firm. Act as if we have a goal in mind, and that we may actually attain it."

I did as he bade, matching, as well as I might, his long, easy, and imperturba-ble stride. The wind fairly whistled as his legs swept onward. With difficulty I kept my eyes ahead, too. Even so, on the periphery I noticed some of the hom-bres talking and laughing to each other as we passed. It gave me a bad feeling.

But Bierce was as good as his word. We strode straight out of the *colonias* and into a region of governmental buildings glooming up just south of the Zóca-lo, just as the sun sank behind the mountains. We regained the Zócalo, and from there it was an easy walk to Teo's rooms.

5.

The following day we spent in trying to track down the Eagle-knights listed on the paper Teo's student had found. It wasn't as easy as it sounds; the city directory was not all-inclusive, and some of the military men may have been staying in barracks. Still, Teo sent his "agents" out to all corners of the city, and by judicious questioning and perseverance they managed to track down most. I did what I could while Teo and Bierce "held down the fort" at Teo's university office, visiting some of the area's churches to find a couple priests on the list. I don't mind saying that tracking these men to their lairs, among the very congregations that would have been outraged, had they known of their other lives, was a touchy and at times nerve-wracking business.

When I returned to Teo's office, many of his students had already returned as well; and we were able to assemble our information together. Teo marked the knights' locations on a map of the city he affixed to the wall.

"A varied and scattered bunch," Bierce observed. "It will be difficult, given our numbers, to get them all without alerting the others."

I looked up at him. "'Get' them? In what sense of the word do we have to 'get' them, Bierce? Kidnapping? I'm pretty sure that that's a crime here in Mexico as well as in the United States."

Bierce and Navarro both sat back and looked at me in stony silence.

Bierce said, "These are rough times, Amos. And they require rough measures."

I stared at him. "I hope I mistake your meaning."

"There is little room for mistakes, my boy."

"Then what you're considering is murder, Bierce, cold-blooded murder. I know I haven't your experience in war to bolster me up, but this—this isn't war."

"Isn't it? Do you think that these people"—he slapped the list in his hand—"would hesitate for an instant to slay us, given the chance? You surprise me, Amos, you, of all people, knowing what this gang is capable of. And beyond your own scruples and safety, there is the peril to the greater world to consider."

"Yes, but—" I said, searching for some argument to counter Bierce's. Unconsciously I touched the burn-scar on my wrist, gift of the late, unlamented Don Máximo Golón. *Kill them all,* a voice said in my head. *Bierce is right—kill them ALL.* I shook my head, tugged my sleeve back over the scar, and faced Bierce.

"Look," I said. "Indiscriminately killing these characters will achieve little. It is their leader we should be hunting."

"And how, pray tell, should we do that, Amos? It seems to me that yanking the tiger's tail, so to speak, will bring the head around. The byword of this gang is secrecy, and I'm sure that their leader isn't marked out for all the world to see."

"Can you be sure, Bierce? What about their eagle tattoos?"

"Are you volunteering to disrobe these men as soon as we locate them, Amos? Rather impractical, I should think, what with knives and guns in play."

"All right, a poor idea. But there must be some way to isolate him, to separate him from his warriors and bring him into the light."

"There's torture."

Bierce and I looked at Teo. He shrugged.

"You gentlemen are well versed in these supernatural phenomena," he said. "but I know the culture these men spring from, or what they aspire to. They will only respond to force. And I also know the nature of the entities they are trying to invoke. The massacre of millions will be only the beginning of the horror they bring. It seems to me that the pain of one or two men is a small price to pay to prevent this."

We continued to look at Teo. His calm brown eyes looked from one to the other of us, a mild-mannered college professor coaxing an answer from two dense students.

"It doesn't work," Bierce said. "The answers you would squeeze from them would be suspect. A man will say anything to stop the pain."

"Never mind that it's immoral," I added, hoping that Bierce might catch the implication from his own scheme.

We lapsed into silence for some minutes. Three of us, just three of us, and even in that small a group we had three conflicting approaches to our problem. If we couldn't agree on that, how did we think that we could defeat this conspiracy? Three of us, I thought. How pitiful, how quixotic, how foolish.

As if reading my mind, Bierce said, "We need reinforcements."

Now it was Teo's turn to look shocked.

"Not my *estudiantes*," he said in horror.

Bierce waved off the idea as if it were a troublesome fly.

"No, no, Teo. Never fear—as efficient spies as they have been, I wouldn't trust them not to shoot off their own feet. Amos and I have other resources we can call upon."

I said, "Those are equivocal resources, Bierce."

"Do you have any better ideas, Amos?"

I shook my head. I owned that I did not have any better ideas, nor did I have the stomach for killing that Bierce was suggesting. Yet at that moment, it seemed a choice between evils.

The decision, at the last, was put off by mere practicality. We still hadn't found the locations of several of the rest of the men on the list, and, as Bierce himself pointed out, a premature attack on one might drive the rest underground

Or worse. It would alert the gang to an enemy's presence, and none of us doubted that they could find us easily, if prodded. A grand, all-encompassing scheme was needed.

Later, while Teo was attending to his professorial duties, Bierce and I talked.

"Bierce," I said. "I admit that I still don't have a viable plan to fight these killers. But those 'other resources' you mentioned, they come with a very high risk."

Bierce lit a cigar and puffed for a few minutes before answering.

"Our friend Carnacki in Britain has invoked them with success," he said.

"Yes, but at great peril to himself and others. We need to weigh the benefits and dangers in all this."

"We do, indeed, Amos, and to my reckoning it is worth the risk."

"We don't have Carnacki's equipment."

Bierce scowled at his cigar. "An excellent point. I wonder how quickly he could ship it to us?"

"From Britain to a country in wartime? I doubt we'd see it in a month, even if the Navy let it through."

Our own U.S. Navy had been partially blockading Mexico to hinder President Huerta's forces. Since Huerta's bloody rise to power, he had been no friend to our President Wilson. Just the other day, Wilson had lifted an embargo on arms shipments across the border to Villa and Carranza, Huerta's sworn enemies. But Huerta was still in power, and there were even rumors of his seeking aid from the Germans. Ships were still being searched, and God knows what the swabs would make of one of Carnacki's supernatural devices.

"Very well, then," sighed Bierce. "We will have to make do on our own."

*

Making do, I was pleased to see, meant doing nothing for the moment. Teo's agents still scoured the city, when they weren't at classes; and I took advantage of the lull to visit Deliah. It was the morning of the Gala, and Deliah had sent me a brief but suggestive telegram:

MAMÁ HAS TAKEN BOYS TO ZOO. ALL ALONE. D.

I wasted no time in sending an answer. It was scarcely out the door when I finished my morning toilet and prepared to leave. Bierce looked up from his newspapers.

"Going out?" he said.

"Yes, and you know where. I'll be back by noon."

He huffed with heavy irony.

"Cherchez la femme," was all he said, though, before submerging himself in the paper again.

Like a schoolboy to his tryst, I took a taxi rather than spend the time walking to Deliah's hotel. The Imperial faces that grand avenue called Reforma at an angle, cutting across the pavement like a dreadnought out of President Roosevelt's Great White Fleet. I scarcely had time, however, to admire the brilliance of its white walls set against the pure azure of a winter sky before the taxi pulled up in front. As soon as we were stopped, I threw the *taxista* his fare, a *gracias,* and I was out and through the hotel's front doors.

Some time later, I lay relaxed and still in the arms of Deliah Gadbury. Her room was blessed with tall windows, and as it was on the highest floor and higher than anything nearby, we lay naked and unashamed beneath the big sky on her bed as the sunlight dried the sweat from our bodies.

"A penny for your thoughts," Deliah said, swirling the hair on my chest with her finger. I smiled.

"A penny? Am I that cheap?"

She tugged at the hair. I yelped in pain and wrestled her back onto the mattress. We kissed, but she stopped me.

"No, dear. I'm in earnest. What are you thinking?"

"Besides the obvious?" I gently brushed some of that beautiful dark hair from her forehead and looked into her eyes. "All right. I'm thinking that Mexico City is a dangerous place for a *gringa* to be these days."

She considered, searching my face.

"It is a dangerous place for everyone these days, Mr. Littlefault. And I do hope this is not the prelude to a farewell."

"I want nothing less, Deliah, except for harm to come to you."

"Then don't send me away. I could not be safer than where I am now, at the top of the most exclusive hotel in Mexico City. I am fairly sure the management pays a healthy *mordita* to the police to keep it that way. And we are Americans, after all, of the upper crust. Nobody would dare risk an incident with the United States now. They all have too much to lose."

"You have thought it out with your usual intelligence, dear, and under normal circumstances, I would have to agree with you. But these are not normal circumstances. The people Bierce and I are dealing with have no scruples, no mercy, and no fealty to any cause but their own. They care not a whit for U.S. interventions. They would probably welcome it, if it brought more bloodshed, which it surely would."

Deliah gently pushed me away and stared at me.

"I see you have given this much thought as well," she said. "And have you considered the vanity of your case, Amos? Three men, one a septuagenarian, arrayed against this vast invisible conspiracy you warn me of? For pity's sake, Amos, if anyone is in danger, it is you!"

"But can't you see that you are in danger, too, just by association? I cannot leave, my love, but you can. I have to see this thing through, but you could be safe back in the States. And I surely don't have to remind you of your boys."

I felt Deliah stiffen against me.

"No," she said in a cool, level tone, "you do not need to remind me of my boys. And I will send them home with Mother as soon as may be. Does this satisfy you?"

I took her hand. "Dearest, nothing—*nothing,* believe me—would make me happier than to have you by my side. But not at the cost of your safety. And if this is not reason enough for you to leave, then consider: your being here gives the enemy a potential lever to use against me."

She stared at me, mouth open in shock. "What manner of men are these?"

I sighed and flopped onto my back. "Scarcely men at all, if I understand them completely. Changelings, shape-shifters, neither one thing nor the other. This is what makes them so dangerous, besides their superhuman strength— they just don't care. As they see it, this world is just some cheap theatre-set they must strut through toward the Real World. What does it matter if a few more dozen, hundred, thousand people die along the way? I can't have you be a victim of such violence, dear, not if I can help it."

She settled onto her back, too, and stared at the ceiling.

"I know you are telling me the truth, as you see it," she said slowly. "And I like to believe that I know you well enough to know that you are a good man. But I also know the tangles of this world, of this life. Even if—" She stopped. I looked at her and saw that she was biting her lip.

"Even *when*," she corrected herself, "you return to the States, what guarantee do I have that I will ever see you again? I have my heart, Amos, but I have my dignity as well. I don't want to become just another foreign adventure to you, something you laugh and wink about at the club."

I'm afraid I laughed then. I turned and took Deliah in my arms, though her face registered shock and irritation.

"Deliah," I said, "dearest. First of all, I don't even belong to a club, and if I did, it would not be the kind where self-styled 'gentlemen' brag about their conquests. Secondly, you could not keep me away from you. Here." I reached around her and pulled off the gold ring I wore on my left pinky. "This belonged to my grandfather—a dour old squarehead, fresh from Darmstadt and stubborn as a post. But he was my Opa and I loved him. I want you to take this as a loan. Someday, sooner rather than later, God willing, I will come to you and retrieve it. If you doubt my love, then at least believe in my greed."

She made a face at me, but took the ring and slipped it onto her index finger.

"I like wearing your ring," she said. Her eyes sparkled.

"Then perhaps I will buy you your own one day."

"Perhaps I will wear it."

*

"It's one."

Bierce was standing in Teo's living room. His back was straight, his gaze hard, and his voice had an edge to it. I looked at him and sighed.

"Bierce," I said, "you'd really make a very good father."

The words were barely out of my mouth when I regretted them. Both of his sons had preceded him to the grave, and I knew that, beneath all the bluster and confidence, he blamed himself for their deaths. I braced myself for the tongue-lashing that I deserved; but instead he just took out his watch, jabbed it with his finger, and said, "We agreed you would return at noon."

Inwardly I thanked the gods for sparing me the Biercian wrath. Aloud I said. "I'm sorry, Bierce. The time got away from me."

"We cannot operate properly with 'time getting away from us,'" he said. Then, fiddling with his watch he said more softly: "We didn't know if the worst had happened."

Navarro was nowhere around. The "we" was clearly Bierce, and just as clearly, he had been worried about me.

"I'm sorry, Bierce," I said again. "It shan't happen again."

I walked up to him and put my hand on his shoulder. With a pang of sadness I felt the bones of his shoulder right through his clothes. In the work we pursue, Bierce and I have learned to trust what many call "omens" or "signs." Very often they are merely echoes of one's own mind, interpreting something as a symbol for a truth one already knows. Sometimes they are something more. Whether Bierce's and my ability to see this outré residue is a blessing or a curse is a matter of debate. But at this moment, on a sunny morning in Mexico City, my ability to see the tall skeleton in Bierce's clothes felt like the worst curse of all.

"What ails you, Amos?"

I blinked and it was Bierce again. That frosty scowl, that edge of annoyance in his gruff voice . . . I could have kissed the old buzzard.

"Nothing," I said, patting him on the back. "I am due at the palace at eight. What can we get done before then?"

We spent the next couple of hours poring over our city map, locating the homes and haunts of the Eagle-knights as best we could. We would need Teo's expert knowledge to refine it, we knew, but we did a pretty good job.

"You will notice," said Bierce, "a preponderance of sites to the north and west of the city."

"Chapultepec and environs," I nodded. "The wealthy neighborhoods—not a surprise there."

"No, but it could make our operation more difficult."

I looked up at Bierce. "Are you still set on this course of murder, Bierce?"

"It isn't murder if one is defending oneself. You of all people, my boy, should understand that."

My boy, I thought. Yes, Bierce, you would make an excellent father.

"I waste no love on those creatures, Bierce, believe me. But if we go shooting them peremptorily, then how are we any better than they? In fact, we may be playing into their very plans by doing so. Bathe the land in blood. I'm sure that the topmost leaders of this conspiracy wouldn't scruple to lose some of their own to further their aims."

Bierce straightened up from his crouch over the table and stretched his back.

"A fair point," he said. "As for the morals of it all, 'War is all hell,' as General Sherman once said. Nobody gets through it with clean hands. But the possibility of aiding this plot, however unintentionally, is a troublesome one. Have you any suggestions?"

I was pleased to be asked for my opinion by Bierce; pleased, moreover, to see that my ideas might carry weight with him. But I was also suddenly very tired.

"God, Bierce," I said, "I don't know. If we just knew who the ringleader of this bunch was . . . There has to be a guiding figure at the top, as you say. Planning a massacre by committee doesn't sound all that practical."

Bierce humphed a laugh.

"No, indeed, Amos, regardless of the members of that 'committee.' I have seen enough of such gaggles of stupidity to know better. But say we identify this ringleader of yours. Would you be agreeable to his assassination, if it meant the dismantling of the entire gang?"

"A choice of evils, again, but yes, if his death led to the end of the conspiracy." I paused and looked over our map. Twenty or so Xs on it, each denoting an Eagle-knight. "It really is a dirty business, isn't it, Bierce?"

"It truly is, and I would spare you from it if I could. Ironic, isn't it? That we should come this far, having given battle to entities that would freeze the blood of your average citizen, and yet the hardest battle should be with our own species?"

Teo returned to the apartment around five. We showed him our map of the city and he nodded his approval—while correcting the three or four mistakes we had made.

"*Bueno,*" he said. "Our plan of attack takes shape."

"One thing troubles us," Bierce said. "There must be a leader to this conspiracy, above even the twenty members of this elite group. Our fear is that we may destroy the limbs without killing the head, if you see what I mean."

"Yes," nodded Teo. "The Aztecs had their *tlatoani,* their priest-king, who directed war and conquest. At the time of the *Conquista,* it was Moctezuma II—an ineffectual man, really, when it came to handling the Spaniards, but beloved of his people. Since these new *guerreros* think of themselves as Aztecs, it makes sense that they would have their own *tlatoani.*"

Bierce picked up the list of conspirators.

"I count two majors, five priests, and a general on this list," he said. "Who would they take orders from? Another general? The archbishop?"

"Dios lo evite," said Teo, and crossed himself.

"We can't rule it out," said Bierce.

I looked at my watch and swore.

"You'll have to excuse me, gents," I said. "I still have to eat, bathe, and dress before this shindy tonight."

"I will make dinner," said Teo, and we scattered to our appointed tasks. Bierce, I noted as I dodged to my room, lit a new cigar, sat in an armchair, and watched the smoke coiling up with deep interest. Toni the cat took advantage of his languor to leap into his lap. Once she was settled, man and cat looked as if they had always been there—and always would be.

At dinner Teo produced some newspapers.

"These," he said, spreading them upon a vacant place on the dinner table, "have photographs of some of our foes. I regret that I cannot provide more."

I smoothed the papers with my hand. When I had finished chewing my food, I said, "This is excellent, thank you. I see some of the military men. Some of them will surely be at the gala tonight."

I hope so, and yet . . . I hope not, if you understand me."

"I do indeed. May I cut these pictures out for reference?"

"Por supuesto."

Teo rose and walked into the other room, returning with a pair of scissors. I cut out the pictures of the Eagle-knights, and a fierce and daunting rogue's gallery they made, too. I secreted them in my wallet.

I bathed after dinner and dressed in the suit Deliah had lent me (the "dead man's suit" that so amused Bierce), and sat to try to still my mind before leaving. A thousand things raced through my brain—the faces of the conspirators, Deliah, glimpses of my visit to Hacienda Golón that made me flinch—until I thought I should go mad. Bierce, established again in the armchair with Toni purring thunderously on his lap, noted my agitation.

"Be still, Amos," he said. "All will be well."

"How can you be sure? It isn't you going into this nest of devils."

"I think I have visited enough devils in their nests to speak with some authority—and yet here I remain!"

He spread wide his arms and grinned. He presented such a vision of himself, black suit, white, self-contented cat, foolish grin and clouds of cigar-smoke, that I couldn't help but chuckle.

"Here," he said. "This will cheer you up:

> "Down among the sainted dead, many years I lay;
> Beetles occupied my head—moles explored my clay.
> There we feasted, day and night, I and bug and beast.
> They supplied the appetite, and I supplied the feast!"

I stared at him for a moment and burst into laughter. He put on an expression of mock-indignation and said, "Amos—you cut me to the quick! I consider that to be one of my best!"

But that devious smile was spreading beneath his mustache, and in a minute we were both guffawing like fools.

Teo's face appeared around the edge of the doorway.

"*¿Que pasó?*" he said, and the look of confusion on his honest face set us off into more gales of laughter. He frowned at us a moment, muttered something about "*norteños chiflados,*" and ducked back into the kitchen.

6.

The gala was held in the large, rectangular courtyard of the National Palace itself. Electric lights had been strung all around the courtyard from second-floor galleries; but while the desired effect may have been Modernity and Progress, the bulbs painted everyone's faces in a flat, merciless light that made us all look like photos of the recently dead.

At the entrance to the party I was confronted by two soldiers who looked about as comfortable in their dress togs as two pigs in suits. But I handed them the invitation Deliah had given me, and they were suddenly all manners and respect. "*Pásele, Señor*, and have a lovely evening," one of them said as he touched the peak of his cockeyed cap.

Standing in that milling, disparately festive crowd, one could not only believe that people such as Villa, Zapata, Madero, and their precious Revolution were far and insignificant, but that they didn't really exist at all. A small orchestra occupied a corner of the space and whined out sentimental ballads and Strauss waltzes. There was something odd about them, and when I got closer to them I saw that they were all blind, nodding and swaying to their own music in complete absorption. Somehow it seemed very appropriate that we should all be led by a blind orchestra. Huerta and his officers held court in their dark dress uniforms, shaggy gold-braided epaulets, and sabres, far down at the other end of the space. Women whispered across the tiles in long, *fin-de-siècle* dresses with ancient cameos at their throats or ropes of pearls upon their bosoms. Their consorts smiled too much, laughed too loudly. I felt like the imposter I was and waited every moment for some stiff-necked major-domo to take me by the arm and throw me out. But the currency of the Gadbury name was still good here, and I remained unmolested. I sipped my champagne and nodded and smiled at the passing parade—and kept my eyes open.

As I wandered among the elegant people, my eye was caught by one particular fellow who sat alone in a corner. He had an open book on his lap and a pencil in his hand. He kept looking up at the crowd and back down at the book, where he appeared to be making notes with furious haste. The haunted palace romp all around was a separate world from him: he worked and they danced; neither acknowledged the other. What with Huerta's stranglehold on the country and security worries, I wondered that no one had confiscated the fellow's notes. Curiosity inflamed, I walked over to him and stood by his shoulder. He looked up at me, eyebrow cocked.

"May I?" I said, motioning with my champagne flute at his book.

"Como no."

He lifted the book for me to inspect. There, reveling, dancing, and cavorting across the pages, was a host of well-dressed skeletons. They laughed and bowed and overall aped the living in the room around us. But every one had the unblinking face of a skull.

"Maravilloso," I said. "That's wonderful."

The man abruptly rose, snapped shut the book, and extended his hand.

"Posada."

"Amos Littlefault. *Mucho gusto.*" We grasped hands. His were muscular and thick, but I was pleased and surprised at how gentle and sensitive his grasp was. He was a sturdy man with the barrel torso of the Indian, a formidable mustache, and direct, incisive gaze. Thick black hair swept back mercilessly in an oiled wave over his great head. He was dressed as formally as I was, but I instinctively knew him for a fellow imposter in this charade. I liked him immediately.

"Quite a fiesta," I said.

He chuckled. "*El General* is bound and determined to push back the forces of the twentieth century," he said. "Let the *villistas* burn and conquer up in the desert, let Zapata run his peasants ragged in the south. Here, in *el De Efe,* let the music play and the champagne flow—all is right with the world."

He sat back down, opened the book, and began drawing again. I pulled up a chair and watched, fascinated.

"That really is wonderful," I said. "I can't draw a straight line."

His body rippled with mirth again.

"Not many straight lines here, amigo. The whole *palacio* is crooked."

Posada's pencil quickly, expertly drew a bald skeleton in uniform. Its shaggy gold epaulets danced as the figure brandished a sword.

"Isn't that a little—dangerous?" I said. I looked around to see if anyone else were watching Posada, but nobody was. He could have been part of the decorations for all they cared.

"Yes and no," he shrugged. "It looks like a certain general, it acts like a certain general. But if someone asked me, I'd just tell them it's a silly *calavera*. Dancing skeletons, *no más y no más*."

"Yet anyone looking at it could see—"

Posada gave me a mischievous grin and a wink.

"Exacto."

"Brilliant," I said. "Are you published around here? It seems a shame to keep such things to yourself."

"Yes, I used to print quite a lot, in fact." He levered his stocky body to the left, put his hand in his pants pockets, and withdrew it with a small white card. "Here," he said, handing me the card. "I have a *taller* here in the city. Come by any time. If I'm not out front, ask for Posada. I'll probably be out back with the presses."

I looked at the card:

> José L. Posada,
> Impresor.
> Calle St. Inéz, México.

"I will do that," I said, and pocketed the card.

I sat beside him and watched him draw. He quickly added lines of shading to the Huerta-skeleton's arms and legs, making it in a few deft, assured moves more solid, more real. I said, "It amazes me that he has achieved as much as he has. Although he's brutal, he doesn't strike me as a great strategist."

Posada scratched a few more lines and held the drawing out to judge it. He frowned at it like a parent at a froward child.

"You know the General, then?"

"Gods, no. I'm only going by his actions."

"Don't be fooled, amigo. Despite appearances, he is a vastly cunning man. It is perhaps his greatest strength—to appear stupid while being clever." He nodded toward the far end of the dance floor. A momentary break in the parade of grandees and their dames revealed the crowd of darkly uniformed figures; and in their midst, diminutive but somehow dominating all else, stood the president of the República Mexicana. Even at that distance I could see him sway a little as if in a wind that only he could feel.

"He's drunk," I said.

"And who doesn't like his *mezcalito* once in a while?" Posada set down his pencil and book and raised a small, crystal glass of clear liquid. "*Salúd.*"

"*Salúd.*"

I tipped my flute of champagne and took a sip. Posada tossed his back, set the glass down, and resumed drawing.

"Stuff'll be the death of me," he said. "But . . . As I was saying, not a stupid man, el Señor Victoriano Huerta. Did you know that he graduated with honors from the Academía Militar at Chapultepec?"

"No, I didn't."

"*Pues, sí.* Astronomy and mathematics were his specialties. He was still a *profesor* there when Madero made the mistake of making him his general. Fancies himself the emperor of a new Aztec Empire, but he is really *el Gran Brujo*— the Great Sorcerer, making his charts and spells and watching the stars for the right moment." He added a dash of pencil to his drawing. "Like Moctezuma waiting for Cortés."

"You make it sound as if there were someone else really pulling the strings."

Posada seesawed his hand.

"*Así así, puede ser.* Huerta is certainly in charge of the armies and the Congress—those he hasn't thrown into prison or had shot. But the destiny of the country is in other hands."

Posada concentrated upon his drawing again, eyes intent upon the page; and though his hand moved in a languid, almost lazy fashion, an image formed.

He drew an eagle.

I looked up quickly and met his iron gaze.

"You have my card," he said. "Come see me."

"Mister Littlefault—*there* you are!"

I looked up to see Ethel Gadbury descending upon me like a hurricane of

purple silks and steel-gray bouffant. In her wake, as usual, and outshining the
grand dame with her quiet beauty—also as usual—Deliah. She wore a long
black gown that left her shoulders bare so beautifully that she would have put
all the debutantes of Washington to shame. Posada and I rose to our feet.

"Mrs. Gadbury," I said. "And Mrs. Gadbury." Deliah gave me a sweet smile
behind her mother-in-law's formidable back. Mrs. G. never acknowledged Posada's presence beside me. This irked me, but Posada merely hitched up his
trousers and sat back to his drawing.

"My dear boy," Ethel said in tones that turned heads. "We are so very glad
that you could make it—aren't we, Deliah?"

Deliah opened her mouth to agree but Ethel gushed on. "But I don't see
our Mr. Twain," she said, looking over my head, her smile starting to wither.
"Surely he was able to attend . . . ?"

"He told me to relay to you his regrets. The rigors of travel have worn him
out, and he wanted to catch up on his writing." True enough, as it went. But it
didn't appease the lady.

"But he simply *must* be here! I have told the general all about him."

Something cold raced down my back.

"The general? Do you mean General Huerta?"

"Is there any other one? Of course! He will be so disappointed." She pursed
her lips, looked at me as if I were a specimen. "Well," she said at last, "I suppose there is no helping it now. But *you* must meet the general."

I looked to Posada for help, but he just shrugged and smiled.

"Hasta entonces," he said.

"Hasta entonces," I replied, and the women swept me away in gusts of feminine drapery. When I looked back, Posada was already intent upon his drawings
again.

As we bustled through the dancing couples, Mrs. G. Sr. said, "El general really is the most charming of men." She pronounced the title as *el henerul*. "The opposition says such terrible things about him! But they have never met him at a
soirée." And you, I thought, have never seen the bodies his soldiers leave behind.
Anent his enemies, Huerta had been quoted as saying, "I will hang them like ear-
rings from the trees," and he was true to his word. Aloud I said, "I really wouldn't
want to impose, Mrs. G. After all, the general must be a very busy man."

*"Non-*sense! He is never too busy to see *me.*"

The crowds parted before us like waves before a cutter. Over their heads I
could see the carefully oiled pates of Huerta's staff officers; and in the center of

all, the bald, slightly pointed head of the man himself. I had a bad feeling about this meeting. Was I such a slave to propriety that I would allow this woman to bring me face to face with this murderous dictator? Or was it my own curiosity that let me be led there like the lamb to the slaughter?

The last layer of dancers broke before us and I was suddenly in front of Victoriano Huerta, President of Mexico, General of All Federal forces; the Usurper; the Jackal. My initial impression was one of disappointment. He was short, shorter than I; a nearsighted old man peering at us through prissy-looking steel-rimmed spectacles. His hands were clamped behind his back. He stood at rigid attention, as if it would make him taller.

"General," said Mrs. G., reverting to the English pronunciation. "May I introduce to you a friend of ours, Mr. Amos Littlefield?"

I let the mistake stand—no need to extend this interview more than necessary. The bald head swiveled on its frozen shoulders like the turret of an iron-clad. The eyes looked from Mrs. G. to me, and I suddenly, fearfully, knew why this little man—Villa's derisive *"borrachito,"* the little drunkard—was so feared across his country. Huerta's black eyes drilled right through me. The nerves at the back of my neck tingled like a galvanic charge.

"Li'l fea," he said in a quiet voice that cut through the music and gaiety like a cold wind through Summer. He brought his right hand around to offer to me. I had to force myself to take it. It was cold, inanimate, dead as a stone.

"M-mucho gusto, General," I managed to say. He gave my hand one quick, hard pump and dropped it as if it were a throttled fish. Mrs. G. said, "Mr. Littlefield is an acquaintance of Mr. Mark Twain, that I told you of."

The stony gaze turned slowly to Mrs. G. and back to me.

"Tweng."

"Yes, Mr. Twain, you do remember, don't you?"

And that awful stone face smiled at that good woman. I wondered that she didn't fall down in a swoon right there; but perhaps ignorance is bliss. Her concerns were so concentrated upon the surface of things—what will look good, who will know she was there with "the general"—that the awfulness, the hateful, soulless awesomeness of that expression just passed over her like a vulture passing high above a party. To me it looked like a rock smiling. I have had nightmares about that smile.

Mrs. G. was prattling on.

"Mr. Twain so wanted to come here tonight and meet you, General, but was unavoidably detained. He sends his very best regards, doesn't he, Amos?"

"Yes, his very best."

"*Tweng.*"

The carven head turned from one of us to the other. Then, thank God, it swiveled away to regard the fiesta behind us. Mrs. G. faltered.

"Well," she said, "we shan't bother you more, *Señor Presidente.* Come, Amos, Deliah."

I had been so absorbed in Huerta's presence that I had forgotten Deliah standing right behind me. When I turned the sight of her was balm to my soul. I let out a long breath. As we walked away Deliah said, "Are you all right?" She put a hand on my arm.

"Of course he is all right!" Mrs. G. fluffed and fussed. "Meeting the good and great always makes an impression."

"Yes," I said, unsure. "I'm fine."

Deliah, however, caught more than I was saying. She frowned at me but said no more. I was looking idly over the crowds, the tuxedos, uniforms, and gowns, when I stopped short, staring.

Deliah said, "What's wrong, Amos?"

"That man," I said, pointing. "I know him."

She stood on tiptoe, trying to peer over the crowd. "Where?"

"That man in uniform," I said. "Against the wall."

"I don't—oh, yes, I see. Colonel Águilar."

I looked at her. "You *know* him?"

"Why, of course. He is part of the general's circle. We met him in Torreón after it fell."

"But you call him 'Águilar'?"

"Yes, Colonel Águilar. Why?"

"Because I know him by another rank and name." Indeed, there could be no mistaking that lean face, so sharp it looked as if the winds of war had carved away all the flesh from it. There could be no mistaking that scar, either. Lieutenant Bendiga had made the party. I turned toward Deliah so that my back was to him.

"How well do you know Ben—Águilar?" I said to her.

She shrugged. "Well enough to speak to, no more." She smiled a sly grin at me, looking like some mischievous kitten about to pounce. "Why? Are you jealous, Amos?"

I could barely speak.

"Jealous? Deliah, jealousy is about the last thing on my mind right now. You remember that business that Bierce and I are involved with?"

"Of course."

"That man, whom we know as Lieutenant Bendiga, was with Villa's troops not a month ago. And he is deeply involved in our mission here."

She frowned at me. Turning, she dared a casual glance towards the wall. Turning back she said, "Are you sure?"

"Positive. Like your general, he makes an impression, and like your general, it is usually in blood."

"But if he was with Villa, what on earth would he be doing here?"

"An excellent question. But I feel that he is really on neither side in this conflict. His allegiances are beyond the petty alliances of parties—or he may be playing the one off the other. I must see Bierce."

She caught my arm before I could turn.

"Now?" she said. "Right now? Because the ball is still in full swing."

I gave her a puzzled look.

"That is," Deliah continued, "it might look awkward for you to leave so soon. Conspicuous. Suspicious."

I was about to object—the crowds would cover my departure—when I saw a glint of something else in Deliah's eyes. It was a pleading, almost a sorrow. Around us, the elite of the Huerta regime swirled in gorgeous extravagance. If such as they, the overfed, blood on their manicured hands, could dance and be gay, why shouldn't this beautiful woman enjoy herself, too? We had shared intimacy, but she needed more; she needed a public display of our closeness; a happy whirl across the dance floor without shame or regret.

"I suppose I don't have to go quite yet," I said. "Madam: may I have this dance?" I took her hand in mine and led her onto the floor. And there, beneath the tawdry lights and among the grinning corpses of that gruesome company, I danced with the most beautiful woman in Mexico.

*

It was very late by the time I left the gala. I stayed, in fact, until the very end, so lost was I in Deliah's company. At the same time I had remained acutely aware of the presence of the venomous Bendiga, or Águilar, or however he styled himself now; and the combined effort of dancing and of keeping an eye out for Bendiga, while remaining hidden myself, told on me. I was ragged.

Fortunately, the presence of so many luminaries ensured a fleet of carriages and taxis for the departing guests. After bidding Deliah and her mother-in-law good-night, I found a vacant and battered Tin Lizzie on the outer tier of taxis. The driver, a young Indian who appeared to know as little Spanish as English, did know the city streets. He returned me to Teo's rooms in safety and blessed silence. I relished the quiet to collect my thoughts. For all the guile I had expended watching and avoiding Bendiga, the man had just vanished at some point. I had built some idea of following him when he left—but that too, of course, disappeared with him. I was relieved, but I knew Bierce would not be pleased. I had had an opportunity to track Bendida/Águilar to his lair, and I had lost it.

I was still mulling over the best way to break it to Bierce when the taxi pulled up in front of Teo's building. I paid the silent Indian, who nodded his thanks and drove off. I dragged myself up the two flights of stairs to Teo's floor. To my surprise, yellow lamp light fanned out from under his door, and I could hear soft voices in conversation. The door was locked, however, so I rapped upon it.

Silence. I checked my watch—2:15 A.M. Then, *"¿Qíen hay?"* Navarro's voice, dulled through the door.

I said, "It's me, Amos. Let me in."

"Ahorita vengo." The quick patter of footsteps, the creak of a board, and the bolt clunked back. The door swung wide and Teo stood before me, beckoning me in. I stepped past him, blinked in the sudden light, and saw Bierce standing at Teo's dinner table. He glowered above it like some giant in shirtsleeves and vest, contemplating which buildings to crush first. He looked up at me from under his snowy brows and smiled.

"So," he said, "the Prodigal Son returns."

"Hullo, Bierce. I'm surprised to see you still up."

He nodded to the table before him and said, "Teo has been educating me on the intricacies of Mexico City's byways."

I stepped closer and looked. Spread upon the table was the same vast map of grids and angles and green spaces we had consulted before—Mexico City, reduced to the size of a table-top. A grand version of the tourist-map Bierce and I had used before; but like it, now starred with Xs showing where our enemies lurked. As I sidled up beside Bierce, he turned to me, frowned, and sniffed.

"What a delightful perfume you're wearing," he said.

"Thanks." I was too tired to be baited. That I had spent the evening in Deliah's arms was undeniable. Let him make of that what he wanted.

"You had a pleasant outing?" he said, when he saw his jibe would go nowhere.

"Just peachy," I said. "We shut the joint down."

Bierce flinched. He hated slang and more, hated his protégé using it. Too bad, you old buzzard. He straightened up and, with a bit more starch, said, "Did you see anything of interest? Beyond the obvious, of course."

"Bendiga is in the city."

That brought him up short. Bierce and Navarro both stared at me.

Bierce said, "Can you be more specific?"

"Sadly, no. I saw him across the dance floor. Thankfully, I don't think he saw me."

"You don't 'think'? Did you 'think' to follow him, by any chance?"

Bierce's color was rising so I chose my words carefully.

"Of course I did. But he slipped out when I wasn't looking."

Bierce turned full to face me.

"I dare say you were distracted," he said.

"I dare say I was," I answered. "And for that I won't apologize."

"Need I remind you, Amos, of the gravity of this mission?" Bierce's voice was dropping to that dangerous quiet that presaged a storm.

I said, "No, Bierce, you need not remind me of the gravity of our mission. Nor need you remind me of my deficiencies as a spy. On the other hand, I'd like to see you, all six feet of ghastly skin and hair, keep an eye on an enemy in a crowded room while remaining invisible."

We glared at each other for several moments. Then Bierce, harrumphing and moving some pens and pencils carelessly over the map, looked away.

"Well," he said, "I hope you at least learned something further to aid us."

"I think so. You may appreciate this, in fact: Bendiga calls himself Águilar now, and he's an officer in Huerta's circle."

At that Bierce and Teo (who had been looking as if he wanted to disappear) snapped their gaze on me.

"*¿Con Huerta?*" Teo said. "That jackal?"

"The same," I said. "Bendiga now wears the gray of a Federal officer, and I have it on reliable authority that he is close to Huerta."

Bierce said, "And what authority, pray, is that?"

"On the authority of my 'distraction,' the widow Gadbury. Her mother-in-law is on speaking terms, if not as companionable as she pretends, with the general himself; and Deliah tells me that they met Bendiga during their stay in Torreón."

"Huerta," said Teo. "So we have found our *tlatoani*."

Teo's whisper filled the room. He slowly lowered himself onto a chair and stared off into nothing. Bierce cupped his elbow in his hand and rubbed his jaw with the other.

"Troubling news, indeed," he said. "Hard to say what Bendiga's game is— playing Villa and Huerta off each other? Or something deeper?"

"He and his lieutenants may be prolonging this war by inflaming its two greatest contestants. Blood and pain seem to be meat and potatoes to the Eagle-knights. What better way to get them than to set the country at its own throat?"

"This may be so," said Teo from his seat. "But Huerta, he is nobody's fool. I think maybe Bendiga is working for Huerta."

We all mulled these thoughts over in silence for a long while. The implications were frightful: if Huerta was with the Eagle-knights—if he were their *tlatoani,* their leader—then they had access to men, machines and materiel: the whole organization of national power in Mexico. My head began to throb.

"And you fellows," I said. "How did you fare with the Eagle-knights' nest?"

Bierce and Teo looked a little embarrassed.

"Truth be told," Bierce said, "it was a bust. The place was empty, deserted."

"If they did meet there," said Teo, "then they took all their things with them." An uncomfortable gloom settled on us all.

"I'm going to bed," I said. "Huerta and his ilk can wait for morning."

"An excellent idea," said Bierce. "We'll achieve more once we're rested."

I was almost to the bedroom door when I remembered.

"One more thing," I said, turning back to the others. "I met a most remarkable gentleman tonight who may prove an asset. He's an artist and printer here in the city. He seems to have his hand on the pulse of the country. José Something. Porrua, Posito—"

I felt in my pocket for the card Posada had given me. My questing fingertips touched something thin and stiff, and I pulled out a piece of withered palm-leaf.

"What in blazes?" I muttered.

"Posada?" Navarro said.

"Hmm?" I said. "Yes, that's it. José Posada. Stocky gentleman, forthright, decent fellow. Do you know him?"

Teo looked drained of color.

"Señor Posada was a very popular artist. *Was*—he died a year ago."

7.

Looking for a ghost may not have been the first thing on most people's minds the day after a dance, but most people also do not actively seek out cults of murderers. Given a choice, the former appealed to me more than the latter. Thus we found ourselves outside a dingy storefront on Calle St. Inéz, a small but busy street just behind the National Cathedral, on a dreary winter day. Above and between the two, narrow doors before us, J. G. POSADA— TALLER DE GRABADO was painted in large red letters. But the paint was flaking and the stucco chipped, and the windows were half-blind with dust.

I walked up to the door and knocked anyway. We waited. Behind me, the life of the city rumbled and hooted and jittered. But the door remained shut, silent.

"There can be little doubt as to the veracity of his address," said Bierce, nodding to the sign. "Perhaps spirits don't respond to knocking."

I gave Bierce a sour look, but tried the doorknob. It was unlocked. The door swung easily open with only a sigh of unoiled hinges. Within, all was dark but for two pale rectangles of light thrown by the door's windows upon the floor, like two pale rugs. My shadow was silhouetted in one, Bierce's in the other. We entered the silent shop and shut the door behind us.

The silence within was complete. It was, in fact, too solid for the circumstances; not a whisper of the great life of the city behind us. I felt my senses grow sharp in response. Sweet scents of inks and solvents, the vinegary smell of acids; a dry stillness to the air bespeaking abandonment. As my eyes grew used to the darkness, a counter appeared before us, and behind it the suggestions of heavy machinery. Posada's presses, I assumed. And then directly in front of us, a V of white floating in the air. A shirt-front, contained by dark jacket and vest, and bisected by a black cravat. The shape of the cravat reminded my uncomfortably of the hourglass stain on a black widow spider; but though I felt presence near me, there was no threat.

Now a dim, pallid smudge in the gloom above the hourglass. Black pits of eyes, a big black handlebar mustache, heavy jowls. Posada. He moved forwards toward us, his suit coalescing out of the dark as if cut from the darkness itself. He was nothing more than that face, those great, sensitive hands, hanging from the sleeves, a shine of shoe-leather, the glint of buttons. When he came within the fall of light from the windows, part of him vanished. His legs swung into the light and ceased to be. He stopped six feet from us, a man only from the thighs upwards.

"You are a ghost," said Bierce. It was not a question.

"Just so."

Thunder drummed in the distance. It sent a hum of vibration through the floor and into the soles of my feet.

"Does it matter?" said Posada. He spread his arms wide and his white cuffs rose like doves in the darkness.

"Not to us it doesn't," said Bierce.

"You have seen my like before."

"Many times. I am only wary of your tribe when I have reason to be."

Posada let out a deep sigh and smiled.

"My 'tribe,'" he said. "Once my tribe was artist, *chilango,* Posada. Now I am one of the *fántomas* I once drew."

Rain pattered on the windows; the thunder rolled closer.

Not knowing what else to say, I said, "How long—"

"Have I been dead? A year and some. Something to do with my *panza*—" He put a hand gently, gently to his belly. "Maybe the food, maybe the drink. No one was around to tell me."

Drink will be the death of me—his words echoed lonely in my mind. I swallowed and said, "We often find that spirits linger because they have a task left to finish."

"*Verdad.* The Eagle-knights. They are why I asked you here. I sensed a kindred soul in you, an amigo, perhaps, who could help me."

I put my hands out before me.

"*A sus órdenes,*" I said. "At your service."

"As am I," said Bierce. "Ambrose Bierce, friend and mentor of this young man, and searcher after phenomena." He put his hand to his heart and bowed. "*Mucho gusto, Señor.*"

"*Igualmente.*" Posada dipped his head. "You must stop them, these so-called *aztecas.* What they do—what they plan—reaches far beyond this country, beyond your world, beyond *my* world. Already their crimes change the Other World. The dead flood this place, and they are uneasy dead. Scared, confused, angry . . . They make poor company."

In spite of the circumstances, I smiled. Bierce must like this man, I thought. They share a distaste for injustice, and a talent for understatement.

"They roam," continued Posada. "In drifts, in crowds. The angry ones flash like fireflies, like heat-lightning." He paused, seeing something I wished never to see. "This is the House of Dust, *mis compadres.* It is not a happy place, but the presence of these miserable spirits makes it more terrible still. They thrash and cry out, and throw themselves against the walls that surround us. They yearn to get out—to get *back*."

Bierce cleared his throat. "These walls," he said. "Are they tall?"

"*Sí,* and long, longer than sight. But they are not without cracks."

I shivered. As if in response, a peal of thunder crashed down the city streets.

"But it is not those *inconsolables* you should fear," said Posada. "The universe will absorb them—in time. No, the real *terrores* are on your side of the wall, amigos. Our President Huerta has allied himself with some very bad forces, very old forces."

"*El Gran Brujo,*" I said.

Bierce turned to me. "Come again, Amos?"

"'The Great Magician,'" I said.

Posada nodded.

"Someone who knows the stars and their language. Joined with the Eagle-knights, he makes a formidable enemy. But not invincible. They can still be beaten, but it must be soon, and it must be you and your Señor Bierce who do it."

"Why us?" I said.

Posada spread his hands again, but this time in a gesture of helplessness.

"*Soy espíritu,*" he said. "My powers are limited in the land of the living. I can wield no weapons, drive no vehicle. But I can spy for you and guide you."

"And why now?" said Bierce.

"The equinox approaches, when the priests of old sacrificed to renew the earth. The blood they shed will initiate the *Sexto Sol,* the Sixth Sun, a new world of terror. There is tension between the worlds, a feeling of doom about to topple, and it will begin here." He paused, and his heavy, spirit face grew heavier with sorrow. "*Mi México pobrecito,*" he said. "My poor, dear Mexico. When I was alive, I made fun of the crooked politician, the greedy and the base. But all, all will be swept away by this conspiracy if it isn't stopped. There will be a slaughter and a revival such as would make those old *aztecas* blanch."

Bierce cleared his throat again.

"We may help each other," he said—"and in so doing, prove stronger than our nemesis. Lacking numbers, our strength lies in stealth, and in this at least you have an advantage over the living."

Posada sighed. "But what can we do, Señor Bierce? The dead walk quietly, but without purpose. We know not where to aim our blows, such as they are.

There is Huerta, but he is protected by strong magic, magic so old it scares even me. And we do not know who his henchmen are."

"Ah, but we do, Señor Posada, and their names we will share with you."

Posada thought for several moments.

"Names are good," he said, "but not enough. We must have their faces. Can you bring these to me?"

For a chilling moment I thought Posada wanted their actual faces. Then I thought of the newspaper cuttings I still had in my billfold from the previous night.

"I have some of them with me," I said, and started to pull my wallet out. But Posada held up his hand.

"Wait," he said, "until you have them all. Then bring them here, to me, and burn them. Their smoke will travel; their faces will be known in dark places, amigos, I assure you."

"And then?" said Bierce.

"And then the restless Ones, the angry Ones, will have a purpose and a target. Cracks in the wall will be made just a little bit wider"—Posada held thumb and forefinger a hair's-breadth apart, and used the charming, oh so Mexican diminutive, *"un chiquitito"*—"not much, but just enough. Who knows what may escape into your world?"

The retreating storm emitted one final, sullen rumble, and I shivered. Posada became quiet. He stared down at the ink-stained floor, then looked back up at us. "My task done," he said, "I will be free to leave this House of Dust and to be at peace with *mi querida* María again. Bring me the faces of our enemies, and look for my messages on the walls of Tenochtitlán."

Then, still watching our faces, he stepped back and became one with the darkness again.

*

Bierce gently closed the door behind us and we walked in silence down the street. I noted with little curiosity that the pavements were dry; that, in fact, the sun was beginning to emerge.

"Let's find a drink," I said.

"My thought exactly."

Over beer in a small café off the Zócalo, we brooded and drank and pondered. At last I said, "Bierce, do you have any idea what we are doing?"

Bierce sipped his beer, set it down and licked the foam off his mustache.

"Not exactly, Amos, but sufficient for our purposes. Or so I fervently hope."

"Is hope enough, though? Can we gauge the extent of the forces Posada may loose upon the world?"

"Can they be any worse than what the Eagle-knights plan to unleash? As in many conflicts, we must choose the lesser evil. It does, at least, absolve us of any direct guilt in what may happen."

"I must admit that that appeals to me, regardless of how self-serving and myopic it feels." I sipped my beer and watched the strings of bubbles twinkling up through the amber liquid. "Still, can we be sure that Posada's allies, his 'angry Ones,' will cease once they have fulfilled their missions?"

Bierce stared into the far nothing.

"I believe—I am sure, rather, that these spirits will focus entirely upon the victims given them. We have had our adventures with such tormented beings, Amos, and they are usually put to rest once their purpose is fulfilled, much as Posada himself longs for release to join his wife. It is further to our advantage that many of these poor souls may be in their present state due to the outrages of the Eagle-knights themselves. What better incentive than revenge?"

"I just fear for the innocent."

Bierce smiled. "As few of them as there are in this world. But I take your point. If it makes you feel better, we will extract some promise or reassurance from Posada when next we meet."

"And when will that be?"

"'In thunder, lighting and rain?'" quoted Bierce. "As soon as may be. Posada indicated that the equinox is some kind of deadline for our enemies, and that is scarcely a month away. Our next step is to obtain images of the remaining conspirators and get them to Posada as quickly as possible."

"And then?"

"Then, wait and see, my boy. Wait and see."

8.

The task of obtaining pictures of the remaining Eagle-knights took longer than expected—longer, certainly, than either Bierce or I wanted it to. Some of the conspirators were wary of photographers, some just hard to find. One of Teo's students barely escaped a beating and jail when he took a Kodak of one police captain, by claiming he was just taking a picture of a nearby building. Even so, his Kodak was taken from him and smashed to splinters on the cobbles. It took a more careful and circumspect approach (a shot from a window overlooking the captain's station) to get that particular portrait.

But by the end of February we finally had all the pictures we needed. In the meantime we had copied and re-copied the original list of conspirators and se-creted them in diverse places in case the originals were lost—or stolen. The very idea that the Eagle-knights might learn of and raid Teobaldo's apartment put dark bags of worry under his eyes.

"I don't ask you to hurry, Señores," he said to us one day, "but please hurry."

We were all on tenterhooks during this time. I, at least, had the comfort of Deliah's presence. Even this, however, ultimately added to my worry. She continued to refuse to leave me in this mess, despite my entreaties. I would tell her to please go, she would answer yes, she would, and nothing would happen. Then I would sigh and fall back into the fool's paradise we had built around ourselves on the top floor of the Imperial Hotel.

And things might have gone on like this for weeks, until one day when I arrived to find a very different Deliah. Once within her rooms, I embraced her and kissed her, and immediately knew something was amiss. Her smile was tight as if she had to pull the corners of her mouth forcibly into shape; her embrace of me was perfunctory, distracted. I disengaged myself from her arms and held her away from me.

"What is it, dear?" I said. That staged, tense smile again, her eyes anywhere but on me.

"Nothing, Amos, I just, well . . ."

She turned and walked away from me to one of the towering windows. The sun and endless blue sky shone down bland and beautiful; Mexico City moved below us like an anthill. I followed her and put my hands upon her shoulders.

"I had a visitor," she said without preamble. She huffed out a cheerless laugh. "A suitor, actually. Someone you know, in fact."

My scalp tightened—blood ran roaring through my head. I turned her to face me.

"Bendiga?" I said. "Here? When?"

"Just this morning. He was quite charming, actually." Again that unhappy laugh. "He was a perfect gentleman, Amos, really. He even brought a chaper-one—some dreadful old woman, Doña Inez Lechuga, Lechuza, something like that." She laughed harder now, an edge of hysteria making it ring horribly.

"'Lechuga'—imagine! Lady Lettuce! Isn't that a pip?" Her laughter grew and caved in upon itself into loud brays of crying. She fell forward into my arms and I held her tight as if to keep her from all the horrors of the world.

"My God, Deliah," I said softly into her hair. "Why didn't you call me?"

"I didn't want—you're in danger, you said it yourself . . . That Lechuga woman, she said, she said, 'As a mother I know *you* know what it would mean to—to lose your children. Better to lose a friend, a lover than—'"

I gave her one more squeeze and gently pushed her to arm's length.

"Where are your boys?"

Deliah swallowed and pressed her handkerchief to her face.

"With Mother," she said. "They are visiting the gardens at the Alameda." Sweet Jesus—at least it was a public place. Deliah stared at me. "Amos," she said. "My boys—they wouldn't—"

"Get packed," I said, "and pack something for your sons and mother-in-law. I will get a cab and we will pick them up en route. Just essentials—you can send for the rest later. No, no arguments, no delay. These people are playing a deadly game, Deliah."

Deliah looked at me from her tear-wet face.

"En route to where?" The question was more than curious; it bordered on hopeless.

"The train station. We'll find the quickest, soonest train to get you out of the country." I began dialing Teo's number from Deliah's room telephone.

Deliah watched me for a moment, amazed. I have to admit that, though I can dither and procrastinate to a criminal extent when my own well-being is concerned, when it comes to those I care about a stronger, more businesslike Amos emerges.

"Pack!" I said to Deliah, and she ran to do so. The 'phone buzzed for a damnably long time. "Come on, come *on*." Finally there was a click, a pause; then Bierce's voice, hesitant and unsure for once.

"Uh, hallo? *Buenas dias?*"

"Bierce," I said, "it's Amos. You must come quickly—the Imperial Hotel, Room 822."

"Amos, what—"

"It's Bendiga. He's been here—to see Deliah."

"Are you heeled?"

"No, I didn't—"

"I'll take care of it. Stay there."

Bierce has his own tendencies to argue and debate, but like me he knows when to drop everything and come running. He must have heard it in my voice.

With Bierce on the way and Deliah packing, I called the hotel's front desk and asked whether they had a schedule for trains. Deliah and Mrs. G. certainly knew where to stay; the manager was helpful to the point of being obsequious. He would have a list of departures sent up in minutes, and would be happy to call and arrange tickets for the Señora and her party.

In the meantime I did what I could to collect and pack the Gadburys' varied belongings. Deliah had already packed her own valise, so I concentrated upon the boy's things—knickerbockers and dress shirts for a couple of days, a pull-toy shaped like a train; a teddy-bear with one ear chewed lovingly half off. Within a few minutes we had most of it stowed away, completely if not terribly neatly, and stacked by the door.

My heart nearly stopped when there was a knock at the door; but my query was answered only by a cheery, *"Su horario de ferrocarríl, Señor."* I opened the door, took the schedule from the smiling bellboy, and gave him probably too large a tip. Shutting the door on his puzzled face, I scanned the schedule. There was a train for the coast in an hour. I yanked the door back open and called to the bellboy, now more puzzled than ever. "We need help with the Señora's bags and a taxi, *muy pronto,*" I said. The lad touched his cap and said, *"¡Inmediatamente, Señor!"* and ran down towards the elevator.

In five minutes more Deliah and I were in the hotel's lobby. I stationed myself within sight of the front door, looking out for Bierce and any potential assailants—though without my gun, what I thought I would do should they choose to appear, I didn't know. Deliah settled up their bill and approved the train tickets the manager had selected for her. He was still on the telephone with the station when Bierce appeared. The taxi bearing him had not even stopped before the back passenger door opened and one of Bierce's long, black-clad legs angled out, followed by the man himself. I jogged out to meet him.

"Where are the Gadburys?" he said, breathless, as he slipped me my gun.

"Deliah is inside, settling her accounts. Her mother-in-law and the boys are at the Alameda."

"Damn!" Bierce looked all around the lobby as if searching for an outlet for his frustration. "What do you need me to do?"

I could have hugged the old buzzard.

"Stand guard out here and hold a taxi while I wait with Deliah."

Bierce gave his lapels a tug, adjusted his hat a millimeter, and stood by the curb like Leonidas at Thermopylae. When he straightened his coat I caught a glimpse of his revolver at his hip, and honestly, I worried more about anyone who should challenge him than about the old man himself.

As quickly but as calmly as we could and trying our best not to alarm the hotel staff ("We have to hurry, sick aunt at home, a lovely stay"), we strode out to where Bierce stood holding open the door of the jitney. The bellboy and bags followed.

"We'll be wedged in tighter than sardines in a can," Bierce said, "once we get the elder Mrs. G. and the boys. I'll jump off at the Alameda."

"Bierce," I said, "please come with us. We'll sort it out, but I want all the firepower we can muster if Bendiga comes back for them."

He nodded once. Deliah was already in the cab; I joined her in back while Bierce sat up front. The driver didn't look very comfortable to have the elderly *pistolero* at his side, but said nothing. Once we were moving toward the Alameda, Bierce turned around.

"What did Bendiga say to you, Deliah?' His eyes were direct on her but not unkindly. She swallowed.

"Nothing, really. He had seen me at the gala and recognized me from Torreón, and wondered whether he might take the promenade with me one evening."

"I dare say he saw me as well," I said. Bierce gave me an exasperated look but said nothing.

Deliah said, "It was more in the way he said it, as if it were a *fait accompli,* regardless of what my wishes might be. I told him that I was already spoken for"—here she gave me a watery smile and a squeeze of the hand—"but it didn't seem to make any difference."

"Did he mention either me or Amos by name?"

"No, and neither did I, certainly. Even when he asked the name of my *novio,* I said nothing. Again, it wasn't so much what he said as how he said it. And what he didn't say. It was as if he were trying to get something from me, information or a promise or something, trying to draw me out. And all the time that horrible woman was sitting there, silent, glaring at me, as if Bendiga needed protecting from *me!* It was awful."

She bent her face into her handkerchief. I took her hand, but looked to Bierce. I mouthed one word to him—*Golón*—and he nodded once.

When we arrived at the Alameda, Bierce again volunteered to stay with the taxi while Deliah and I searched for her family. The Alameda is not an intricate park; it is merely a large rectangle, divided by two main paths that describe an

X through its center. But it is large. Deliah and I exited the taxi and looked around, despairing.

"All right," I said. "I will go east on the north sidewalk, then down to the southeast corner. You go south from here and along the south side of the park, and we'll meet at the southeast corner. If neither of us has seen anything. We'll go together up the diagonals."

"Very well," she said. She reached out and touched my hand. "Thank you, Amos. I don't know how to express it sufficiently."

I smiled at her. "Don't thank me until I've gotten you safely on that train."

And with that, we began our search.

I walked briskly, turning my head this way and that to scan the crowds. It shouldn't be hard to find an elderly American woman and two rambunctious boys, I thought, especially during a weekday. But we had started our search right before midday, and people were flocking to the park to escape the confines of their offices and workplaces. I must have made a spectacle of myself as I pushed through them all, lunging along with my eyes wide and my hat in my hand. *"Desculpe—perdón—perdóneme"*: I rolled out every polite word of excuse I could remember. I nearly tripped over one of the eternal sidewalk sweepers and his long broom, but continued on.

I reached the northeast corner of the park and had seen nothing. Right down the east side, jostling the suited businessmen, shoeless *pelados*, vendors hawking tamales and cool drinks. A hundred faces, a thousand—but no Ethel Gadbury or her pale grandsons. I arrived at the southeast corner breathless, and a moment later Deliah, panting and disheveled, arrived too.

"Anything?" I gasped.

She put her hand to her bust and took a couple deep breaths. "No. Let's try the diagonals."

I nodded and took her hand. Headway was easier here, away from the streets and the throngs. Tree-shadows flashed over our eyes, making the world flicker. Top hats, garden hats, flat caps; faces of bronze, tan, coffee, mahogany. But no Gadburys.

"There!" cried Deliah. She pointed off to the left of the path. Some thirty feet away and seated upon a bench were Mrs. Gadbury and her two grandsons. They had paper bags in their laps and were tossing something to a crowd of busybody pigeons gathered at their feet.

"Mother! Jerry—Henry!" Deliah picked up her skirts and ran to them. I followed, watching all the time for Bendiga or one of his creatures to emerge from the greenery.

"Deliah!" said Mrs. G., rising from her seat and brushing peanut-shells from her skirts. The pigeons took flight with a clatter of wings and petulant coos. "Mr. Littlefault—what are you doing here?"

Deliah hugged her two sons to her as if to absorb them. "We have to leave now, Mother," she said to the elder Mrs. G. "Immediately."

The older woman's face was a study in dull indignation.

"But why?" she cried. "It is a lovely day, the boys are enjoying the sunshine and the pretty doves—"

"I'm sorry, Mother, but we really must go. I have packed some things for you and the boys and a taxi is waiting."

The look of incredulity on Mrs. G.'s face deepened until her eyes and mouth formed perfect O's in her white face.

"My—the boys? But what is the meaning of all this?"

Deliah shot me a pleading look over the shoulder of her older boy.

"Mrs. Gadbury," I said, "word has reached us that your lives are in danger. The political situation has shifted and all American nationals are urged to leave Mexico directly." To amplify my words, I took her by the elbow and began leading her away from the bench. Deliah and her sons were already clopping quickly down the diagonal path to our taxi.

"This is terrible," said Mrs. Gadbury as I hurried her on. "Dreadful! Will we not even have a chance to say farewell to the general?"

Leave it to Ethyl Gadbury to worry about manners when her life was in danger. The very thought of looking up General Huerta at that moment made the bottom fall out of my stomach.

"I'm sorry, Mrs. G., but there really is no time. Perhaps you can send him a telegram once you reach the States."

"At the very least. After all, he was good enough to purchase our train tickets and arrange for our safe passage."

Now it was my turn to be flummoxed. I stopped us in the middle of the path, the busy people of Mexico City flowing around us, and stared at the woman.

"General Huerta?" I said. "He arranged for your voyage?"

"Why, yes, of course General Huerta! Is there any other? We may take the train to Vera Cruz at any time—I have the documents in my reticule." She began to rummage through her little bag, but I stopped her.

"That's wonderful," I said, "but not here. Hold onto them until we reach the station."

From her look at me it was clear that she still did not appreciate, or even believe, the gravity or our situation. And who could blame her? All around us the sun shone, people strolled arm in arm, chatting and laughing; somewhere a guitar and violin were making the air gay with sweet music. Yet behind and between every pair of happy faces I expected any second to see the soulless, avid, cruel faces of the Eagle-knights.

I took Mrs. G.'s arm again and led us back to the corner where the taxi, Bierce, Deliah, and her boys awaited us. Once again, Bierce's mere presence saved the day. When Mrs. G. spotted him standing at parade-rest by the taxi, she clapped her hands with joy.

"Mr. Twain!" she exulted. "I should have known that you were behind this. I could scarcely believe that we would be in any danger, what with the protection of the general. But if *you* tell me we must leave, then leave we must."

Bierce, who was holding the door open while Deliah packed her sons into the back of the taxi, gave me a quizzical look.

I said, "I told her about the State Department's call for all U.S. citizens to leave, 'Mr. Twain.'" He registered the deception immediately, nodded to Mrs. G. in a businesslike manner, and said, "Quite so."

What with six passengers and the *taxista*, there was not an inch of room left in the cab. In fact, once everyone else had gotten situated, there was no room for me at all. I hooked an arm through the car's two passenger windows and, standing on the running-board like some Chicago hoodlum, held on for dear life while we negotiated the busy streets to the train station.

I nearly lost my hat at the first intersection; so, not wanting to lose another, took it off and plunked it onto Deliah's younger son's head. He laughed as it sunk down over his eyes.

"We're on an adventure, boys," I told the two lads. "You've got to stay close to your mother to protect her!"

The younger one tipped my hat up so he could look at me, giggled, and let the hat fall back over his eyes. The elder one, grave as a judge, gave me a proper salute. Deliah mouthed the words *thank you* to me.

Ten windblown minutes later, we heaved up in front of the railroad station. Porters appeared in competing squads, dickering for our custom; and while "Twain" dealt with them, Deliah, Mrs. G., and I ran inside to settle the tickets. I knew Deliah's Spanish was far better than mine and the pass from Huerta would probably smooth over any difficulties; but it is a failing of many men that they don't take a situation seriously unless another man is involved.

To that end I played the part of "the man of the house." On the way to the window I told Deliah about the general's gift to them. She threw a puzzled look at me but was too intent upon our mission to stop and ask.

Deliah led the charge up to the ticket window. It was a good thing I had decided to accompany her as "the man of the house," for, despite her obvious wealth and haste, the clerk took his own time in examining the documents that Mrs. G. handed him. He frowned at them turned them this way and that, looked back over his shoulder for guidance from some imaginary associate, turned them over, and pushed them back towards Deliah.

"Lo siento, Señora," he said in a heavy *chilango* sing-song. "I don't have the authority to approve these papers."

"Look," said Deliah, pushing them back to him, "it's very simple: General Huerta has already signed these papers as safe passage to the coast, free of charge. The tickets are good"—she brandished them at him—"what is the problem?"

I could see the clerk taking in a big breath, steeling himself for a long explanation to this loud, stubborn *gringa* all about the parameters of his duties. Giving my lapel a good tug, I stepped forward.

"It's all right, dear," I said. "The gentleman is just doing his job. I assure you, sir, that these documents are valid and that the general will be most displeased if his good friends here are not on the next train to Vera Cruz." Here I pushed the tickets back at him, leaving a ten-peso bill on top of them as if by magic. *"Most* displeased."

He looked back down at the papers. Then, leaning out to the side of the ticket window, he called, "Sargento Flores! A moment of your time, *por favor.*"

An upright soldier in spotless Federal uniform strolled up.

The clerk said, "These ladies are the personal guest of our noble *Presidente* Huerta. See that they and their luggage are safely placed on the next train to Veracruz."

I pulled out my watch. The train was scheduled to leave in five minutes.

"And please hurry," I said to the sergeant.

"¡De prisa, varón!" added the clerk, and the sergeant saluted and trotted off to a group of soldiers loitering by the wall. Within moments they had hustled out to the taxi, scattering the competing porters, and had brought Bierce, the boys, and the luggage through the station and out to the train. The ladies and I followed.

The big engine's oily angles and wheels gleamed as it chuffed out drifting clouds of steam. People hurried to board. There was a quiet urgency to the scene, bordering on desperation. Doubtless many people were just trying to flee Huerta's regime of terror; regardless, it served us well. Mrs. G. looked around at the harried faces of her fellow travelers and said, "My goodness! How fortunate we were able to make this train!"

She made her farewells to us and led the boys aboard. At the last moment young Harry Gadbury lifted my Stetson off his head and handed it to me.

"Thank you, Mr. Littlefault," he said in careful English.

"Not at all, Harry. Perhaps I'll let you wear it again someday."

He gave me a solemn handshake and ascended into the carriage. I was suddenly alone with Deliah and Bierce; and Bierce said, "I seem to be late for an appointment with my cigar," and walked down the platform. I took Deliah's hands in mine.

"No words," I said.

"No time," she said.

"Someday."

We nodded. I leant forward and kissed her—Mrs. G. and her propriety be damned. Then we embraced like two drowning people clinging to the last bits of flotsam in the whole dim ocean. Without a word or a backward glance, she pushed away from me and ran up the coach steps. A conductor walked down the length of the train, calling, "¡Abordo, abordo! Express train to Vera Cruz is leaving." The engine's whistle gave a long, high scream, the chuffing grew louder and the whole contraption began to move. I stepped back and watched as the cars ticked past me, slowly at first, but gaining speed. I waved a couple times at pale faces behind the train's windows, but no one ever waved back.

"They are safe now, my boy."

I turned and found Bierce back at my side. The cigar smoked lazily in one hand; the other was in his coat pocket. Like me, he watched the train slide past; but as to whether my face mirrored the iron resolve in his, I doubt it. I felt as if the last ray of sunshine had slipped beneath the horizon, and we stood upon a darkling plain, alone.

9.

Bierce and I repaired to a nearby restaurant for lunch. While we waited for our order, Bierce sipped his cerveza and I pushed the cutlery around the tablecloth into precise, geometric patterns.

"What I don't understand," said Bierce, "is why Huerta should want to give them passage."

He was trying to draw me out of my funk, I knew. But I wasn't having it.

"I don't know," I said to the tablecloth. "Perhaps he's in love with Mrs. G."

Bierce huffed a laugh.

"Perhaps he is. I cannot see the attraction myself, but the general *is* a notorious drunkard." Bierce sipped his beer and when he spoke again his tone was more thoughtful. "Though truth be told, I have not been immune to the charms of a widow myself upon occasion."

This was one of the chinks in that dense Biercian armor—widows. And here we had been in the company of not one but two widows for the past weeks. His elevated expressions of gallantry and protection were explained. I sighed and nodded, and offered my own glass in a toast.

"To widows, then."

We clinked glasses and drank. We meditated on the virtues of widows for a silent couple of minutes.

"It puzzles me, though," I said at last, "that Huerta should do this while Bendiga was trying to insinuate himself with Deliah."

Bierce shrugged. "Who can say? Huerta may have issued the pass before Bendiga thought to approach Deliah. Or Bendiga's interest in Deliah may have been purely coincidental and had nothing whatever to do with us. Or the right hand may have not known what the left was doing. This could well be to our advantage."

I nodded. "Huerta strikes me as a man who is long on cunning but short on planning. He thrives on shows of violence, but the long view is beyond him."

"Yes. He is a very dangerous man, but perhaps just a tool for the Eagle-knights. Theirs is a long view, indeed, and reaches beyond the petty greed of a dictator like Huerta. He serves his purpose as their—what did Teo call it?—*tlatoani,* high priest, yet there is someone who is beyond him still."

"That would explain why Bendiga did not deign to tell him about his interest in Deliah, whether it involved me or not. He simply felt it was none of Huerta's business." I drank and thought. "Could Bendiga be the head of it all, Bierce?"

"He may well be, Amos. We have seen him in the company of both Villa and Huerta, and it's an unusual man who can maintain two such associations. There is, too, the rather disturbing notion that he may be following us."

"But how? I can't see that anyone followed us from Ojinaga. The natural assumption would be that we scampered back across the border to the good old U.S. of A. I thought we were pretty careful about leaving no tracks."

"Except for those left in blood at the Hacienda Golón."

"Mm. Deliah's description of that old woman, for what it's worth, tallies with that of the Señora Golón. Of course, it may be a different woman entirely, but we should act upon the assumption that it was the Señora and that our enemies are hot upon our trail. Considering that, I suggest we repair to Teo's rooms immediately upon finishing our meal."

As if on cue, our plates arrived and we set to. Afterward we hailed a cab and were back at Teo's rooms by 1:30. Teo was not in, being at class; but he had left us a small stack of photographs and cuttings on his work-table. Bierce picked up a note from atop the pile and read it aloud.

"'Here are all the pictures of the people that you need. Good luck, Teobaldo.'"

"His students have been busy," I said.

"Indeed. We should take advantage of their industriousness and meet with Señor Posada."

I started to rise from the chair where I had settled, but sank back before I had gotten halfway up.

"I'm sorry, Bierce," I said. "This morning, the rushing around, leaving Deliah . . . I'm spent. Would you allow me a brief siesta before starting?"

"Of course, Amos. Take your rest and I will awaken you when it is time to go."

With a nod of thanks, I stumbled off to my bedroom. Within moments of hitting the pillow, I was asleep.

I awoke in a complete limbo of twilight. I checked my watch and stared stupidly at the face—5:30. Was it morning? Was it evening? And where was I? San Francisco? Washington City? Harrisburg? The possibilities floated above me in the dimness like inchoate tatters of fog. I heard someone moving about in another room, and as I looked toward the door everything fell back into place. This was the guest-room in the apartment of Teobaldo Navarro, Mexico City. Finding my place in them and space gave me a good feeling of security, and I lazed in it. But the next moment it struck me: Bierce—Posada—the photographs. I had slept the afternoon away. Had Bierce left without me? The thought of Ambrose Bierce alone in Mexico City in the twilight sent me into a panic. I jumped out of bed and strode to the door—only to stop and hang my head. I had left my blood in my feet and felt on the verge of blacking out.

"*Buenas tardes,* Amos."

The voice came through muffled by the thickness in my head. A gray fog blotted out everything for a moment. Breathe, I told myself. Relax. A hand settled on my shoulder.

"*¿Estás bien, amigo?*" It was Teo, and as the grayness faded I saw his face, pinched with concern, learning close to me.

"I'm all right," I said, straightening up. "I got up too quickly. But Bierce—"

"Señor Bierce is resting himself. He said not to disturb you, but when you awoke I was to give you this."

He handed me a thin sheaf of papers. It was dim in the half-light from down the hall, but even so I recognized Bierce's precise handwriting. I snapped on the light in my room and read:

THE PRINTER'S DEVIL,

BY

AMBROSE BIERCE.

> For Amos, with apologies. I once swore never to pick up pen again, but the circumstances were impossible to resist.

"Get comfortable in the living room" said Teo, "and I will find some food for us."

Teo disappeared into the kitchen while I retired to the parlor. I sat in the deep easy chair I had reluctantly quitted hours before, poured myself a couple fingers of tequila, and read.

> During a trip through the ancient metropolis of Mexico City recently, I had occasion and leisure to see something of its marvels. The more obvious of these—Chapultepec Castle, the National Cathedral, the gardens of Xochimilco—having exhausted their allure upon me, I asked of an acquaintance what more I could see.
>
> "You must see Cajón," said he, with a peculiar amusement in his eye. "He is our most famous artist—a man of vision and imagination."
>
> When I had voiced my desire to see this Cajón, my acquaintance gave me the artist's address. I gave him my thanks in return and set out to find this marvel.
>
> The address proved to be on a narrow dingy street lined with narrow, dingy buildings. Each contained a business or workshop—*taller,* in the local parlance—advertised with such symbols as the owners saw fit to display. In the case of Sr. Cajón, the advertisement was plain: above two

narrow and pealing doors were lettered the words, "J. Cajón, Impresor. Illustrations and Engravings." Thus assured of my destination, I entered.

The interior of the *taller* was dark and close. (I will not grace it with either the epithet of "narrow" or "dingy." Repetition breeds boredom.) It was redolent of the ink and solvents that paid for its existence. No bell apprised the owners of my entry; no sound at all, in fact, disturbed that sepulchral silence. I should have expected the workshop of "our greatest artist" to be deafening with the thunder of presses, the shouted instructions of the printer and the frantic questions of the printer's devils. In fact, except for the presence of this author, no devil was in evidence at all.

But of inhabitants there did soon prove to be at least one. Despite the paucity of warning bells, my presence had been noted. A man stepped from the gloom before me. He was dark and barrel-chested; "solid" is the euphemism usually employed for such corpulence, and yet I felt that if I stared at him long enough I should see the massy, iron limbs of his printing presses right through him. He stepped to within a couple yards of me and stopped. In the half-twilight of the shop I could see little of his features save an enormous black mustache and a pair of bleak eyes that regarded me with a tired but not unfriendly gaze.

"I am Cajón," he said, proffering his hand. I took it in mine and felt the muscles beneath the cool flesh. "May I help you?"

"You may," said I, relinquishing his hand. "But whether you can is another question. I am told you are one of the marvels of the city."

He shrugged with honest self-deprecation. I liked him.

"I am Cajón," he repeated, "no more and no less. But I am at your service."

The expression *"a sus ordenes"* is as common and as threadbare a greeting in Mexico as is its English equivalent in the States; a courtesy having long lost its original, more sincere meaning. Your average American, not to mention your average Mexican, is not truly offering his servitude to you, but the offer remains.

"I am told that you are Mexico's greatest artist," I said.

Again he shrugged and laughed lightly.

"Perhaps I once was. Time casts his changes over us all, Señor. But you may see for yourself."

He motioned toward the walls, and for the first time, owing either to my inattention or to the adjustment of my vision to the dark, I saw that the walls of the shop were adorned with dozens of printed papers. Some were on rough-edged, smudged stock—printer's proofs, I assumed; most were merely tacked to the walls, and a few, more finished works were installed in frames. Upon closer inspection, I found that all depicted skeletons in the attitudes of the living: skeletons dancing, skeletons drinking, skeletons laughing, skeletons weeping.

"The dead are active here, it seems," I said.

"They are indeed, sir."

Despite, or perhaps because of the prints' unique subject-matter, the high quality and workmanship of the art was undeniable. I owned that I had, truly, discovered one of the marvels of Mexico City.

I said, "You are justifiably praised, Señor Cajón. I am pleased to have made your acquaintance. And as for your previous assertion of being 'at my service,' I will make bold to hold you to it."

He nodded. "How may I help you?"

I reached into the inner pocket of my jacket and withdrew the several papers I had carried there for long, trying weeks.

"My business in Mexico is with the law," I said. "Or rather, with those who defy the law. I am a United States Marshall, and I am on the trail of these gentlemen."

I unfolded the papers and smoothed them out severally upon the shop's counter. There were seven in all, wanted posters given me by the U.S. Government with the injunction to find and return the men portrayed to just and certain penalties. As to their mortal condition upon delivery, that was up to my discretion. The Government is generous in its choice of evils.

Cajón studied the hard, brutal faces on the seven sheets of paper for long minutes. The faces were a record in flesh of a history of train robbery, bank robbery, assault, and murder that was well known to all citizens of the western United States. Their names were synonyms for savagery, their lives object-lessons in the stern injunction that "the wages of Sin is Death." To Cajón, however, lacking the perspective of his northern neighbors, they were faces, nothing more.

"You wish to reproduce these notices," said he.

"I do. In Spanish for the enlightenment of your fellow *mexicanos*. How much would you charge for, say, a hundred of each?"

Cajón rubbed his great chin and jowls with a meaty hand.

"You wish to catch these men?" he said.

"Dead or Alive," I said, and pointed to the very words upon one poster.

"Muerto o vivo," Cajón mused. Looking me straight in the eye he said, "I may have a better solution, Señor—if you do not care whether they are dead or alive.

I shrugged. "I am not picky."

Cajón nodded. He reached beneath the counter and brought up a drawing-pad, an inkwell, and a fistful of pens. Turning the poster around so that they were right-reading to him, he pulled up a stool, sat, and, hunching over the pad, began drawing. I noted that the ink in his ink-well—the ink that quickly, without hesitation or error, began to assume familiar lines, was a rusty red in color.

"Do you always draw in blood?" I said, shocked.

Cajón smile at me. "It is a special ink I reserve for special jobs."

He returned to his drawing.

Another man might have checked his watch, might have questioned the wisdom of a drawing-lesson at such a moment. Time, and criminals, after all, wait for no man. But there was something in the assurance with which Cajón ran his lines over the papers, something in the intense concentration he brought to the task, that forbore any criticism or hurry. I let him draw, and I marveled. Upon the page there soon took shape the faces of some of the most wanted men in my country; accurate down to the finest proportion and shade, and down to the most negligible crease and smile. When Cajón finally sat back and turned the paper toward me, the desperadoes—not their mere image, but the hated men themselves—looked up at me from the vellum.

"How is that?" Asked Cajón simply.

"It is marvelous," I said. "You have captured them perfectly."

Cajón nodded. "That is what I wanted to hear."

He reached again under the counter and brought up a wide plate or bowl—its depth was in odd proportion to its breadth—made of some material that resembled jade. Around its curved edge were carven the images of skulls and animals and plants in a flat, archaic style familiar to me from local museums.

"That is Aztec," I said.

"It is."

There was a mutter of conversation, voices in tense, subdued argument, from the walls around us. I looked around, but it must have been from the neighboring buildings—not a soul was in evidence. I then noted that the deep center of the dish or bowl was blackened as if by fire. Cajón took his careful drawings of the desperadoes, crumpled them into a ball, and set them in the bowl. He then produced a box of ordinary kitchen lucifers—the term gaining significance from the circumstances—struck one, and to my horror applied it to the edge of one of the pages. Before I could snatch the papers away, they had blossomed into bright, yellow flames. The muttering voices around us grew in volume and consternation. There seemed to be a debate and a warning, and all in a language that had no living analogy. It hurt my ears to even hear it. The fire in the bowl flared, dwindled, sputtered, and finally died. Among the blackened shreds, glowing worms of fire prowled and curled, seeking out the last unconsumed edges of paper. Smoke rose from the wreck to vanish in the darkness above, as if snatched away by ghostly hands. The sullen voices in the air withdrew and faded away in concert with the dying flame.

"There," said Cajón. "It is finished. Your chase is finished, your prey destroyed."

I could not fathom how this had been accomplished, yet knew as surely as the sun rising in the east that my quarry was, in fact, destroyed. I would not insult my host with pointless and unanswerable questions as to the agency for such a deed. Instead I merely said, "My many thanks, Señor Cajón. What do I owe you?"

"A votive candle in memory of José Cajón, lit in the Cathedral."

And with that he stepped back into the darkness and I did not see him more.

Postscripts can be tiresome, but this tale requires at least a modicum of elaboration, lest the "loose ends" return to throttle the author.

I ran into my acquaintance from the beginning of this tale the following week. When I thanked him and told him that I had sought out the amazing Cajón, he eyed me in the way a warder at a madhouse might regard one of his patients.

"Surely," he said, "I meant only that you should seek out Cajón's *work*. The man himself is a year in his grave."

To this I could offer no argument; its truth was self-evident.

Within the next two weeks I received word that all seven of my fugitives had met Death in a variety of guises. Some had met with "accidents" that were notable for their variety as well as their gruesomeness. One fell under the wheels of a train; another, apparently in the act of cleaning his pistol (the only eyewitness to the "accident" is unavailable for verification), shot himself; yet another fell down a flight of stairs in a bawdy house where he had been hiding for months, months in which he was never known even to stumble upon those same steps. Whether accident or ill luck, in future days' time the entire gang was wiped from the face of the earth.

My schedule thus freed from obligations, I took time to light a whole bank or candles to the memory of José Cajón.

*

"Does it meet with your approval?"

I started and dropped the written pages.

"My God, Bierce, you're like to have given me a heart attack!"

Bierce was standing across the low table from me, hands in pockets and smiling.

"I will take that as a critical success, then," said he. He sat opposite me and produced a cigar from his coat. I bent down and collected the scattered leaves of his story, rapped them into neat order upon the table-top, and set them down.

"It's tremendous," I said. "And produced so quickly."

Puffing his cigar alight, he said, "I must admit to having a ready supply of material."

"This, then, is what happened when you met with Posada this afternoon."

"More or less. All stories are lies, but the best are lies that illuminate a truth. The ritual portrayed in the story is accurate, as far as it goes. Whether its results will be as effective as those in the tale remains to be seen. But I trust Señor Posada and I trust in his abilities. He really is quite an artist."

Teo appeared and called us to the dinner table. Meals come and go, and I cannot at this point in time remember everything that I ate in Mexico. But this night and this dinner remain clear in my memory as being one of the happiest we spent on that adventure. Teo had outdone himself. When we sat at the table I expected nothing more than the tamales he often bought down the street, or one or another variations on the tortillas he produced. But this night he appeared with a platter of meat slathered with a dark, spicy, pungent sauce.

"Mole poblano," he proclaimed, and set it before us. "The national dish of Mexico—¡Buen aprovecho, chamacos!"

Teo set small plates of tortillas beside our larger plates, and I for one was not remiss in using them to wipe up every drop of that sauce. Teo had brought out a bottle of white wine for the occasion, and it was a merry time. For once our talk was not of cults and murderers and Aztecs, but of the homey details of our lives. Teo regaled us with stories about his native Puebla, a day's ride over the mountains to the south. It is a very old city, watched over by its dark, towering, stern cathedral and the twin fortresses where the Mexican army so thoroughly trounced the French invaders on May 5, 1862—henceforth sacred to Mexican memory as "el Cinco de Mayo." He told us of nearby Cholula, a city older than even ancient memory, and its church upon a hill that was not a hill at all, but a pyramid that predated even the Aztecs. The intricate layers upon layers of Mexican history were laid bare to us, revealing a panorama beside which the Patriots of 1776 and even the stalwarts of the *Mayflower* were like yesterday's parvenus.

Bierce and I responded as best we could. I recounted my quiet, nay, boring life in rural Pennsylvania, my German forbears and the paths that led me to Ambrose Bierce. He, in turn, told of highlights in his long life, some amusing, some grievous. Again I heard how he and his brother Albert, as rascally boys, had tied a burning branch to the tail of a horse and drove it through a Revival meeting. That frightful first morning at Shiloh, Tennessee, dawned again, when the Confederate army ran yelling into the Union camp, bayoneting the sleepy Northerners in their tents; and again Grant led the hard-fought victory back from the banks of the Tennessee River. But if Teo had been paying broader attention he might have noticed that Bierce said nothing about his family. Except for his daughter Helen, they were all gone now, and I knew Bierce was not proud of his behavior toward them; regrets that would now have neither object nor resolution. These were ghosts that Ambrose Bierce durst not disturb.

And perhaps it were better so. After all our travails, and with yet more ahead of us, we needed this "furlough," as Bierce called it, a rest between battles. The wine flowed and the talk rambled on, and if our laughter grew louder, there was none to complain of it.

10.

To our mixed relief and consternation, our "furlough" stretched well beyond that night. Having sent images of the Eagle-knights "across the borderland of conjecture," as Bierce once put it, it was out of our hands. In whose hands the responsibility now lay, I endeavored not to think. For us, now, it was a period of waiting and observing. We "holed up" in Teo's apartment for days at a time, improving our Spanish, extending our knowledge of Mexican history, and scouring the newspapers for signs of the actions we had set in motion.

We did not have long to wait. What the dynamics of travel and communication between the worlds of the living and the land of the dead are, I cannot say; but they must be efficient. Two days after our glorious dinner, Bierce opened the day's paper and a flyer fell out.

". . . the Devil?" said Bierce. He grunted as he bent to pick up the flyer off the floor.

"What is it, Bierce?" I said. He was reading it or trying to read it. At last he snorted a laugh and handed it to me.

"Our friend Posada has been a busy man," he said. "He not only unleashes the angry dead upon the land—he advertises it!"

I took the flimsy from him and looked at it. There could be no mistaking that stark, woodblock style—Posada. The image depicted a skeleton, one of his wild-limbed "Calaveras," in Federal uniform, being knocked into the air by a truck—driven by another calavera. Arms and skull and legs all flew willy-nilly. Beneath the image was the following:

> *El Coronel debía mirar el escalón*
> *Antes de abordar el camión.*

> The Colonel should have watched the curb
> Before getting on board the truck.

It was printed in red ink and was so fresh that a reverse image of the flyer had been imprinted upon the newspaper page opposite it. By coincidence—or not—the skull had reappeared just above an article entitled, "Colonel Padilla Dead. Personal Confidant of the President." I shook the paper back into shape and translated the article for Bierce.

"'Coyoacán, D. F. This quiet neighborhood was greatly saddened this morning to hear that one of its most illustrious residents, Colonel Inocente Padilla y F., 36, had been killed in an accident just last night. Eyewitnesses to his demise state that the colonel was walking down his street, taking the evening air, when he suddenly was possessed by some kind of fit. Witnesses insist that there was nothing to see, but the colonel stared and began stammering something unintelligible, as if addressing an unseen person. He then began backing away, and, despite warnings from passers-by, he stepped off of the sidewalk and into the path of a truck. The colonel was killed instantly. Police have questioned the witnesses and truck-driver, but have ruled out any conspiracy of assassination. Investigations continue.'"

"Ha!" Bierce slapped his knee. "As well they might. So it begins, Amos! The die is cast, the Rubicon crossed, and the ball begins. 'Cry havoc, and let slip the dogs of war!'"

I'm afraid I could not share Bierce's enthusiasm. I felt stunned, even a little sick at the news. The efficiency of our new allies was clear; but would they stop when the task was done? Bierce saw my expression and frowned at me.

"For pity's sake, Amos, don't look so dour. You knew the nature of these entities before they acted. And you cannot say that many will mourn the passing of this Colonel." He reached into his coat and withdrew his copy of the list of conspirators. He unfolded it and placed it upon the table. Uncapping his fountain-pen, he crossed out a name on the list with an ornate flourish.

"One down and nineteen to go," he said, as gleefully as a boy who had just won a handful of marbles. "The Eagle-knights will soon feel the strength of our arm."

"Then why do I feel guilty?" I said. "A man is dead because of us—indirectly, it is true, but at our bidding."

Bierce slowly capped his pen and returned it to his pocket.

"So must a general feel upon seeing the carnage he has instigated. Yet it must be so, Amos. The alternative is beyond consideration."

"I know, Bierce. But up till now all our opponents have been supernatural or at least unnatural. These are mortal men such as we, and regardless of their actions I can't help but feel that human link."

"It's a bad business, my boy, but you at least have the advantage of distance. Imagine the crush of bodies in battle, the sickening 'splat' of rifle-balls striking flesh; the cries of the wounded and the dying . . ."

He was staring at some place and time far away; a battlefield in Tennessee or Georgia in the lost years of the last century. Abruptly he snapped back to the present.

"Your pardon, Amos," he said. "But it can't be helped."

"I know it, Bierce. That doesn't make it easier."

"Consider this, then: the men marked for destruction by Posada's agents would not have scrupled to put young Mrs. Gadbury to the question, even unto death."

This did put a better light on it all; and, in fact, it became easier with time to accept what was being done in our name. Notices from the phantom printer came with eerie regularity—Father So-and-so, crushed beneath a stone during renovations to his church; Lieutenant So-and-so accidentally shot himself; Captain So-and-so fell down the steps of the pyramid at Teotihuacán . . . We crossed off name after name until there were more names deleted than remaining. Some days there were two notices, sometimes one, but always accompanied by Señor Posada's pithy flyers. The appearance of these flyers was as mysterious as the rest of the business, as we knew from others who also bought the paper that we were the only people to receive them. The manner of their dispersal was of a piece with their arrival; soon after we read them, they would undergo a transformation. The ink would fade and the paper would become brown and brittle. After only a few minutes we were left with nothing but sere, brown flakes that stray breezes carried away we knew not whither.

I found myself in the odd position of feeling guilty about *not* feeling guilty. Bierce, on the other hand, set his jaw and crossed off names without a trace of emotion. Captain so-and-so of city police, shot by his own men after a "fit" in which he shouted about "*los pendejos* who wouldn't stay dead." Señor C., *muerto* after a fall from the terrace at Chapultepec Castle; and so on. February ended and we slipped into March, and still we watched and waited. The list of conspirators dwindled from twenty to fifteen, fifteen to ten, ten to four. Four names, and Gonzalo Águilar was one of them. Though his picture, a particularly arrogant studio portrait in full uniform, had been burned in effigy along with the rest, day after day he evaded death. Whatever protection Huerta or whoever afforded him, it was very strong, strong enough to deflect the hands of the dead.

As the gang faded away and Águilar/Bendiga remained at large, his threat to us became more palpable, more real. Deliah had sent me telegrams upon her arrival both in Vera Cruz and later from Galveston, so I knew that she had escaped. And the nature of the "accidents" that struck down the Eagle-knights were such that all could be explained away as pure chance. But by now it would be clear to even the most primitive of Águilar's subordinates that something was stalking the gang with deliberate and lethal intent. Thus far we had depended upon our anonymity and hiding out among the city's teeming crowds for safety. But we knew it could not last. Bendiga's courtship of Deliah began to look less and less like a coincidence and more and more like part of a plan that stretched back to the dusty streets of Chihuahua City.

To prepare ourselves for Bendiga's inevitable assault, we reduced our few belongings even more and kept our bags ready for swift departure. Our pistols, too, we regularly oiled and checked, and never went abroad without one fully loaded.

One day Bierce reached into his valise and brought out a small, flat object wrapped in heavy chamois.

"You will recognize this, Amos," he said as he unwrapped it. He handled it with a care most men would reserve for family heirlooms or fine crystal. When the final layer of fabric was laid back, an oval mirror about the size of one's palm was revealed. Its frame was of silver and etched with what at first appeared to be random scratches, but which upon a second look resolved into a form of writing, not unlike Runic or cuneiform. I did indeed recognize the item immediately, and knew that the writing was unknown to even the greatest of linguists. It was the alphabet of the Dead.

"Irene Marlow," I said quietly. Bierce nodded.

"The Soul-Mirror that spelled her doom. We may have need of it again soon."

"God keep us from that eventuality."

Bierce snorted. "Had we been relying upon *his* mysterious ways, we would have been worm-meat long since. But I take your meaning and agree with the sentiment. That Golón-creature we encountered in San Andrés was as yet only half-formed—a novice monster, as it were. Bendiga will be a master of the art by now and, with his confederates falling all around him, a nervous and dangerous creature in any form. We must prepare, mentally as well as physically, for anything he may throw at us."

"There is the solstice to think of, too."

"Yes. No doubt the Eagle-knights have something especially delightful planned for that date. We should work to resolve our business before then."

Given that we were virtually prisoners in our rooms, I wasn't sure how this could be done. But I relied upon Bierce to plan for it, and resolved myself to be ready when he gave the order to charge.

Outside the quiet walls of Teo's apartment, the world was making its own plans. The favors of heaven—read, the United States—were as fickle as ever. At the beginning of February, President Wilson allowed war shipments through to Villa, Carranza, and the other Constitutionalists; but just a week into the month Villa made the colossal error of murdering a British national on the man's own ranch. In Villa's vanity, or assurance in his invincibility, he even claimed that it was in 'self-defense,' although how a lone Briton could take on the entire Division of the North is up for debate. The "Benton Affair," which broke late in February, looked to thwart Villa's efforts. It seemed that one man might actually take on the Division of the North—and win.

There was a strange stasis hanging over the country. This is not to say that people weren't dying every day—they were. Rather, it felt like a time of regrouping, reshuffling. The Constitutionalists split into three armies: Obregón's in the west, Villa's in the center, and Carranza's in the east. Soon they would begin their inexorable move south toward Mexico City, rolling up Federal opposition as they came. Meanwhile President Huerta continued doing what dictators do: getting bonelessly drunk and hanging the few of his opponents left alive.

This may be the wisdom of retrospection, but it all felt inevitable and wearisome and I just wished that it would get done. The utter pointlessness of Huerta continuing his doomed, brutal regime grated on me. And just as we worried about what the elusive Bendiga/Águilar would do when cornered, so I worried about what Huerta might do when Villa rode into the Valley of Mexico.

"Flee," said Bierce.

The three of us were relaxing after a late dinner. It was early March, a windy night rattled the windows and sent shadows scuttling down the streets.

"Flee?" I said.

"Flee. What else can he do? With Villa in the north and Zapata in the south, he's caught in a pincer. Lee faced the same fate when Sherman drove him into the arms of Grant. You either fight, flee, or give up. Huerta is not the quitting kind, and not many will have the stomach to fight when those two hellions get here."

"Villa and Carranza are hardly the best of friends," said Teo as he stared into his glass of wine. "I cannot see them maintaining this alliance for very long."

"They both hate Huerta," I offered.

"Who doesn't?" shrugged Teo. "But two men of power like that, somebody has to be *el jefe* and the other has to be the good soldier."

"I hear Obregón is Carranza's creature," said Bierce.

"More so than Villa, but he is his own man, too. In a pinch he will side with Carranza, *no cabe duda*. But right now I think he is more concerned with crushing Huerta."

I turned to Bierce. "And how does this affect our own little battle?"

Bierce sipped his wine and stared through half-lidded eyes at nothing.

"I feel that we have had a hand in the ultimate defeat of Señor Huerta," he said.

"That's awfully grand, Bierce. I didn't know we were so powerful."

"We have had some tactical successes, which count for more than all the artillery in the world, Amos. Huerta may still maintain control of the Federal armies, but much of his power resides in his ability to inspire fear. The ministers of that fear have been the Eagle-knights, and by eliminating them we have undercut his power. He has backed the wrong horse and that horse is about to kick him. Hard."

"I can't help feeling," I said, "that the conspiracy will do something more before they are done. Teo, you said that the Aztecs held a certain festival on the solstice. What can we expect from them then?"

"If they are true to their ancestors," said Teo, sitting up, "then it will be the Feast of the Flayed Man. It is to honor the god Xipe Totec, the god who wears a man's skin the way the new corn wears its husk. It is a rite of spring and fertility. You recall: a captive, a great warrior, was tied to a stone and fought a duel with an Eagle-knight. They both used the macahuitl, but the captive's club was edged with feathers and the Aztec's with obsidian blades."

"Yes," mused Bierce. "Quite a tradition."

"That was not all. The loser of the fight, always the captive, was sacrificed to Xipe Totec. He was skinned and the priest wore his skin until it fell apart off him." Teo shivered. "I can think of more comfortable ways to die."

"To me, it sounds like the culmination of their efforts," said Bierce. "The capstone of all this bloodletting. We must stop it. In particular we must locate and dispose of Bendiga. He cannot remain at liberty any longer." Bierce turned to Teo. "Have your students maintained their watch upon the Eagle-knights' rendezvous?"

"Sadly, no. Our semester has become busier as we near the year's end."

"Then we must do it ourselves." Bierce turned to me. "The task devolves upon us, Amos. We have relied upon Teo and his students too much already— it is time we took a more active role."

I nodded, but within me I felt as if time had become a vortex and was funneling all the days and nights down to right now. It was a dizzying and disconcerting feeling.

And I liked it less when Bierce and I found ourselves hidden in a doorway opposite the gang's meeting-place in the middle of the night. Teo had helped us as much as he could, giving us old clothes and sombreros to wear so that we might pass as a pair of poor *chilangos* just looking for a place to flop. Bierce wore an ancient frock-coat that would have been in style in Victoria's reign, and a straw sombrero that looked as if the chickens had been at it. I sported a sombrero and a serape of thick, lumpy cotton done in strips of blue and green. All our attire looked as if it had been dragged through the street. The one thing our vestments had in common was that they were dark. Underneath it all, we kept our hands to our pistols.

For two long, cold nights we kept vigil on that lonely Mexican street, warmed only by the brandy flask we passed back and forth and our ardor for justice. We watched from after the dinner hour until the weary hours of the morning, when the only lights were the rare starlight, and the lanterns the police set at every intersection. In case we in turn were being observed, we moved from place to place, affecting a shambling, drunkard's gait. After a couple of hours sipping the brandy, it wasn't a hard act for me to perform. Bierce, of course, took it all like a face of granite. But whether we were observed or not, we could not tell. Once a policeman stalked by. He ran his gaze up and down our unsavory costumes and said, in the time-honored speech of his kind, "Move along, move along." A small donation to the policeman's personal fund ensured that he did not bother us again in our new spot.

We spoke but little, not wanting our voices to carry in the still night air; and thus the hours dragged by without relief. We gave up around two each morning.

On the third night we were again in our doorway. I shifted one leg to the other.

"I'm stiff," I said.

"You're bored," said Bierce. "I have never known a more impatient person. You would have made a terrible sentry."

I gave him a quick, sloppy salute. "Yes sir, Lieutenant, sir."

"*Major,* if you please." He looked out at the street, suddenly as tense as a cat on the prowl. *"Wait."*

Across the street a man walked swiftly toward the door of the hideout. Darkness and distance made it hard to be sure, but something in that stiff, assured stride left me little doubt. As if to confirm my suspicion, Bierce said in a whisper barely a breath, *"Bendiga."* The man walked to the door, looked sharply around the street (I was glad for the depth of our doorway hiding place), then reached to the door's lock. A couple moments of his hands working over the lock; a sharp click, audible even at our remove, and the door opened. Bendiga entered and closed it behind him without a sound. Bierce let out a pent-up breath.

"Now we wait," he said.

"Oh, joy," I said. "Just when I was getting tired of all this action."

"Oh, shut up, Amos."

Our wait, thankfully, was shorter than I feared. When Bendiga had first appeared I had just checked my watch—almost one-thirty exactly. At one-fifty-five the door opened like a knife of darkness across the building's front, and our man reappeared. He held an umbrella under one arm and looked absurdly like some British banker, about to go home for tea. He pulled the door shut behind him, gave the street another quick look. He pulled his hat low over his eyes and walked away. We watched until he reached the next intersection, where he turned left and was lost to our view.

"*Now* we hunt," said Bierce. We left the doorway and trotted diagonally across the street toward the intersection. The police-lamp burned bright and lonely upon the pavement, but from across the way we could hear the snoring of the policeman himself where he sat on a doorstep. After a quick glance around the corner to be sure of our quarry, we rounded it and headed east.

Bendiga moved quickly, and we were hard put to it to keep him in sight. It worked in our favor, though; at that distance we were far enough behind him that he was unlikely to see us. Onward he strode, ever eastward. We left the precinct of the National Palace and passed through a region of dark, ponderous buildings of negligible upkeep. I felt a tingle in my feet and imagined these structures erected to hold down the resurrection of the past. How old was this place? There had been tribes here even before the Aztecs, ragged and half-savage, had appeared out of the north. This place had then been a vast lake, spreading across the Valley of Mexico. I remembered a story of Teo's about how the local tribes gave the Aztecs an island in the lake on which to settle. The island teemed with rattlesnakes, and the local chiefs thought that would be the end of the uncouth Mexica. When, to their surprise, the Aztecs came back from the island to trade, the local leaders asked if they had not seen any snakes.

"Oh, yes," said the Aztecs. "They were delicious."

There is humor in this tale, to be sure, but a warning as well. Within a couple generations the Aztecs had risen to dominate the whole valley and had begun the bloody rituals that would make their name infamous down through history. Those were the kind of men we had now set ourselves against. This was the kind of man we were now trailing into the meanest *colonias* of Mexico City.

The buildings around us shrank. Business blocks were replaced by adobe and rough stone hovels. On we followed, Bendiga just a tiny black figure in the distance, sometimes only visible as he passed through a streetlight's glow.

"I don't like this, Bierce," I said. "We should confront him or call it off. We're too far from help and too far into his own territory." When he didn't answer I thought of a military term that might drive the point home to him.

"Supply lines, Bierce. We're stretched too thin." Bierce was puffing from the effort of hurrying after Bendiga. He took a deeper breath and nodded.

"Just—just another minute," he said, and plunged onward toward the receding figure. I followed. What else could I do? I certainly would not leave Bierce alone in that place.

Bendiga had turned down a side street on the right. When we reached the corner and peered around it, we saw him walking swiftly out the other end of the street into a church plaza. We waited until he was halfway across the plaza before following.

"At least his pace is slowing," I said. Bierce didn't answer. His twin bull's-eye gaze was locked upon Bendiga. That man, I thought, has no idea of the implacable hunter he has on his heels.

Bendiga reached the other side of the plaza and entered an alley next to the church. We followed along the right side of the plaza, keeping close to the buildings and as far from the meager streetlights as we could. Not as hard as it sounds; streetlamps were far more rare in that part of the city than elsewhere. With a start I realized that we had not passed any police-lanterns either, or their attendant officers, in a long while. I stared ahead at the black alleyway where Bendiga had gone. It radiated a menace that fairly made the nearby walls vibrate. Halfway down the plaza's side, I had had enough. I grabbed Bierce by the arm.

"I really don't like this," I said. "We've done all we can tonight, and I feel we are pushing our already threadbare luck. Let's go back."

Bierce, eyes still locked on the alleyway, strained at my grip like a hound denied his prey. Just then I noticed a flimsy sheet of paper affixed to the wall at our side. I walked up to it. Even at a yard's remove there was no mistaking the manic woodblock style. In true Posada fashion, a skeletal eagle swooped screaming at a running skeleton with long, white mustachios.

"Look at this," I said to Bierce. He came over and peered at it in the uncertain light.

"You're right," he said. "Another day."

We turned and began walking back toward the west side of the plaza. In the distance there was s shout—sharp, short, like a dog's bark in human voice. A pattering of footsteps beyond the north side of the plaza, and down the side streets to the south. I glanced down the next one we passed and thought I saw something running. I took Bierce by the arm again.

"Hurry, Bierce."

We trotted across the plaza. The laughter of a man, echoing off adobe walls. More running feet, beating a tattoo down deserted streets. By the time we reached the other side of the plaza we were running. I looked back and saw Bendiga and two or three others emerge from the alleyway. Two more came running from side streets to join them. The lone streetlight glinted and slid off blades in their hands.

"Jesus," I breathed. Bendiga still held that ridiculous umbrella; but even as I shot a glance back at him, he held it at arm's length and shook it, and it fell away to reveal a long paddle edged with shining black shards. What had Teo called them? *Macahuitl*—the deadly Aztec sword, which could decapitate a horse in one stroke. I looked forward again and ran as I hadn't run in a very long time. Bierce, despite his age, asthma, and the exertions of the night, kept pace alongside me. His long legs swung, his arms pumped. His hat flew off. Something glittered in his right hand—his ancient Colt. I looked down and found that I, too, had unconsciously drawn my pistol as I ran.

We pounded into and down the first street we came to heading west from the plaza. All the windows were dark, all the doors shut and bolted. Our quondam prey, now pursuer, could not have lured us into a more desperate place. Even Teo did not know where we were. We shot out of the street and I risked a look behind. Bendiga and his gang were coming after us, but not in any kind of hurry. They trotted easily along as if they had all the time in the world. This worried me more than anything.

"This way!" shouted Bierce. He was running toward a narrow alley between two cracked and stained adobe walls across the street. It looked like the mouth of a trap to me.

"What?" I gasped. "No, Bierce! Wait! Dammit!"

Out of the corner of my eye I saw a figure race across the street to our left, disappearing into the gap in the walls parallel to our path. They were cutting us off. Too late—Bierce and those long, goddamned legs of his had charged into the alley. My heart in my mouth, I followed.

The alley was scarce five feet in width, the adobe walls enclosing it to a height of ten feet. Above us was a narrow strip of sky, pulpy and swollen and dimly glowing from the city's lights. It was the view from the bottom of a grave. The ground rose slightly here so that I could see the opposite end of the alley beyond Bierce's heaving shoulders. Then I wished I could not: black shadows of men appeared there and filled the alley's end.

"Bierce—" I gasped, but he said, "Shut up, Amos, and check your weapon." He slid to a halt on the alley's unspeakable surface and looked to his own pistol. I stopped and wheeled, my own gun out and cocked. Bendiga and his men were just crossing the last street. He had his macahuitl held high and the streetlight ran liquid silver along its edges. At his back followed the other three men, and they all held knives and they all smiled.

"Back to back, Amos!" roared Bierce. "They can only come at us one at a time—make every shot count, for God's sake!"

Suddenly I saw the reason for taking this alley. Bierce had known we were cut off; we needed some way to even the odds. Now we defended a space where only one could come at us at a time. Bringing my pistol up in both hands, I prayed that the tactic would work.

Bendiga charged into the mouth of the alley. Even in the dark I could see his eyes wide with delight, his teeth locked in a ravenous smile. He screamed— a sound that shot up through all the registers a human voice is capable of and into a region of airless heights and alien desires. He charged—he *grew.* He flung his arms up in a broad arc on either side of his head and, like some stuttering after-images, they duplicated themselves into a fan of shining, black feathers. His grinning, maniacal face pulled into a long triangle—the beak of a bird of prey. The Eagle-knight had come.

The vision was so strong, so terrible, that I stood frozen for a couple of precious seconds. Only the explosion of Bierce's gun at my back jolted me out of my daze. The Bendiga-thing filled the alleyway from side to side and towered against the clouds. Its wing-tips snatched sparks off the adobe as it rushed toward me. I stiffened my arm and fired—*one, two-three,* deafening in the close space, a counterpoint to Bierce's fusillade. I might have been throwing spitballs at the thing, for all the effect they had.

On came the creature. I gritted my teeth—"Come *on!*" Bang—bang—and it was upon me. The wind it pushed before it nearly knocked me down. I looked up into that awful face, neither man nor bird-of-prey nor anything; a blasphemy against Nature, merely a long triangle of some bony substance pierced by two black eyes the glittered with an awesome, unfathomable hunger. Already one wing, broad as a cape and scattering light like black glass, was swooping down toward me. Without thinking I threw up my left arm to fend it off. At the same moment, I slipped and fell—a fall that surely saved my life. Pain like a bolt of electricity from my wrist to my elbow—a slap of liquid hitting the ground. I hit the earth with a jolt, still staring up at the thing's non-face.

"HALT!"

It was Bierce. Shock was settling over me and his words came muffled through it all, but still I heard them—the Words of the Dead. I looked over and saw him standing, torn and bloody but erect, his smoking Colt in one hand and that soul-mirror held up in the other. The words, I knew, were the same as those inscribed around the edge of the mirror; words, mercifully, not known to more than a handful in the world; words not spoken nor meant to be spoken since man first shambled out of his caves. They thundered out in Bierce's voice and filled the low, narrow space with their power.

In a deepening haze of shock I looked back up at Bendiga—now no more the bird of prey out of nightmare, but a man, just a man, looking crazed and frozen. The light from the mirror held his face; he did not move as the frightful Words rolled over him. From his right hand dangled the *macahuitl,* the obsidian blades painted red with my own blood. My blood. The sight awoke something in me. My right hand fell in the muck of the alleyway, crabbed around until it met familiar metallic edges. I gripped it, raised it without aiming, and fired. A neat red hole appeared in the underside of Bendiga's jaw and blood and matter shot into the air above his head. Still staring like a madman at Bierce, the only man ever to have beaten him, Bendiga toppled over across my legs. I let hand and pistol drop back to the ground.

A ringing silence settled over all, and gun smoke drifting like ghosts down the alley's depth. I looked down at my left arm and was almost sick. The sleeve of my coat hung off it in a long black pennant. An oblong of flesh, like a cutlet of meat, connected to my elbow by a strand of flesh, lay across it. From the welter of blood that was my arm a length of bone, blue-white in the twilight, stared out.

Bierce pocketed the mirror and stumbled over to me.

"Amos, my boy," he said, breathless. "My God, Amos, are you with me?"

The shock was settling in throughout me, and the pain in my arm was like the story of someone else's pain far away. Still, I managed a smile.

"Always," I said.

He pocketed his big Colt and looked at my arm. He tore away the sleeve and used it to bind the flesh back onto my arm. I watched all this with a stupid, detached interest.

"We've won, Amos, we've won," he said. He looked around and actually chuckled. "You're a better marksman that you know: all three bullets you put through Bendiga made short work of his troops." I looked down the alleyway and saw it was true. Three bodies were sprawled in various poses of death down the alley. One of them had silver-framed teeth: Bierce's one-time pick-pocket. Looking past Bierce, I saw two more bodies. It was a charnel-house.

"We won," I mumbled. But the words meant nothing to me. I was swiftly pulling away from the world, settling like a leaf down through lightless spaces of peace. In the moments before I blacked out completely, I saw a long, dark motor roll across the end of the alley behind Bierce. It rolled until the rear seat was level with the alley and stopped. An old man—did I truly see this?—an old man in the uniform of a general of the Federal army sat there and turned obsid-ian-lenses toward the carnage we had made. Immobile, unreadable, he regard-ed the scene for a few moments. Then his bullet-head turned forward again, and the motor rolled silent into the night.

PART IV

THE BLACK-GLASS GOD

here on earth there is
heartache
worry
fatigue
a wind blows
it is obsidian
it is sharp
it is cold
—Aztec poem

1.

Deliah Gadbury and I were enjoying a picnic. Sun fell broken and cheerful like weightless golden coins upon us through the shade of an oak tree; a stream chattered gaily nearby. My head was upon Deliah's lap and she was combing her fingers through my hair.

"This is lovely," she said, "but you really must wake up."

I frowned. End this sunny day? She smiled sadly.

"Despiertese, Señor. Tiene que tomar su medicina."

I blinked, and Deliah and the sunny day disappeared. In their stead were the tall white walls and beds of a hospital. Slanting light, whether afternoon or morning I could not tell, fell in soft sheets down the wall across from me, bright banners of peace and quiet and healing. I turned my head and saw a nurse in white dress with a small white cap balanced upon her black hair. She held a dark green bottle in one hand and a spoon in the other. She was young, pretty. She smiled when she saw me look at her.

"Where am I?" I said.

"The Hospital de Jesús in Mexico City. You have been here for four days, Señor. The doctor will be pleased you are awake."

She uncapped the bottle, poured some reeking, dark, syrupy fluid into the spoon, and held it to my mouth. Now that I knew how long I had been unconscious, I was ravenously hungry. That on top of the foul smell of the medicine made my stomach lurch; but like a good boy I swallowed the stuff. It was not what I would have chosen for a first bite after a coma, but it pleased the nurse—and that pleased me. She gave me another smile and walked away down the aisle between the beds.

A tall figure clad in black appeared from behind her. It walked slowly down between the beds until it came to parade rest at the end of my bed.

"Mr. Bierce," I said, "you look like death warmed over."

Bierce smiled. He had bandages on his neck, hands, and just about everywhere that wasn't hidden by clothes. It made me wonder how many more there were that I couldn't see. But otherwise he was the same old Bierce, right down to the carefully combed mustache and black suit.

"At least I am warm," he said. He pulled up a chair and sat beside me. "How are you, Amos?"

317

The question hadn't really occurred to me. Now I looked down the length of my body with some interest. I was lying on a hospital bed—no surprise there—a sheet pulled up to my chest. I was clad in a flimsy nightgown and my left arm was wrapped from wrist to elbow in bandages. Somewhere under those yards of fabric, an ache was crying to be felt.

"Not bad," I said. "Just peachy."

He made a face but it couldn't hide his pleasure.

"You had us worried—you took a bad blow to the arm."

I looked at my arm again and tried lifting it. The cry of pain within it rose to a shriek. I must have winced because when I looked at Bierce again his face was a study in worry. *How old he is,* I thought.

"Not to worry," he said. "Time to rest."

"Who is 'us'?" I said.

"'Us'?"

"Yes, you said I had 'us' worried."

He sat back and fussed with the button of his vest.

"Why, Teo, of course, the doctor—and I. Yes, I was concerned, but I knew you would pull out of it."

It was a lie and I knew it; but I'd let him save face. His affection for me was plain. I wouldn't have survived that alley without it.

"Thank you, Bierce—and my thanks to the doctor, of course."

"Not at all, Amos. Why, I see the very man now. He must be interested in your progress."

I turned to the right and saw a small but intense man in the white lab-coat of a doctor approaching. He was, I guessed, in his fifties, with close-cropped dark hair and beard shot with silver. A pair of pince-nez perched upon his patrician nose. His eyes were very dark, and at the sound of Bierce's voice he looked up from the clipboard he carried and looked at us. There was an expression in those eyes I despair of describing. Determined? Strong? Haunted? All these and something more. They were the eyes of a zealot. Had you replaced the doctor's togs with the armor of the Middle Ages, he could have been a Crusader at the gates of Jerusalem.

He walked to the right side of my bed and extended his hand. "I am Doctor Muñoz," he said in a deep and hollow voice. His English had the direct and careful diction of long instruction, and he pronounced his patronymic as "moon-YOTH," betraying the Hapsburg lisp of Spain. I shook his hand and was surprised at its coolness. He must have recognized my reaction from habit, for he added, "Poor circulation—a problem of mine since childhood. Let's look at that arm."

Bierce made way for the doctor while he moved to the left side of my bed. I tried to relax, but even his soft, deft touch sent nails of pain up my arm. I suppressed a grunt and he looked sharply at me.

"Can you move your fingers?" he said.

"I'll try."

I bent my first and middle fingers a half an inch or so.

"Good," said the doctor. "Very good. Now the others."

I tried to move my ring finger and pinky, but there was a break somewhere between the intent and the action. All I could manage was a twitch of the ring finger that pulled another shard of pain through my arm. The pinky would not move at all.

"Hmm," said the doctor. "Well. It will take time, but I feel sure that you will eventually have use of most of your hand."

"'Eventually'?" I said, fear creeping into my chest. "'Most of'? Doctor, is there nothing more that you can do?"

Bierce leaned forward. "Now, now, Amos, the doctor has already performed miracles on you."

Doctor Muñoz nodded.

"In all modesty, your friend here is right. Your extensor carpi brevis, extensor digitorum communis, digiti quinti propius, and extensor carpi ulnaris were all severed. I could not have done it more neatly with a scalpel." I thought of the obsidian blades and swallowed hard. "In addition, you picked up a particularly virulent infection from the ordure in that alley. You are lucky to still have an arm at all."

The doctor set my arm back down as gently as if it were made of glass.

"I will keep you here for observation for a couple of days more to ensure that the infection does not return. Beyond that, I have done all I could."

"Thank you, Doctor," I said. "I consider myself fortunate to be under your care."

Doctor Muñoz picked up his clipboard, stood, and bowed.

"In my non-professional opinion, you are more fortunate in your choice of friends. It was Mr. Bierce who sought me out and settled your bill."

And with that he turned on his heel and walked away. I looked at Bierce.

"What did he mean, 'sought him out'?"

"Well." Bierce pulled the chair back over, sat, and made a great show of smoothing out his pants legs. "The good doctor is not a regular employee of this hospital. He is studying here on loan from Madrid, I believe, and I just happened to hear of him."

Bierce did not "happen to hear" about anything. He sought things out and proved them or disproved them to his satisfaction.

"How much did you pay him?" I said.

"A nominal fee."

"How much?"

"He is paid, Amos. That is all. Do you think I could leave my trusted amanuensis to the ministrations of some quack? Whom would I get to carry my bags?"

There were volumes of unspoken feelings behind his badinage—love, sorrow, gratefulness, and guilt. It pained me to see how he could not express it all, but it is the way of most men. It is "unseemly," "womanish" to bare our souls, even to those we most trust. I hated especially to see his guilt. He could not have known we would be ambushed like that; but for his quick thinking, we both would probably be dead by now. But I would only make him uncomfortable and even angry to drag it out of him.

"What makes you think I'll carry them now?" I said, and was rewarded by a grudging smile from the old man.

Bierce's own wounds proved to be superficial. The wounds of someone defending himself, nothing mortal. This was one of the many things that puzzled me about the whole affair. Everyone knows the old saying, "Don't bring a knife to a gunfight"—yet that is just what the Eagle-knight and his thugs had done. Did our enemies not know that we were armed? Did they not care? For Bendiga the question had been moot; he had been impervious to normal weapons, and if not for Bierce's Soul-Mirror and spell, he would have made a hash of us. His fellows, however, had charged heedlessly into the very muzzles of our guns. An image of Cortés's Spaniards, armed with their heavy harquebuses, firing into a charging crowd of Aztec warriors, came unbidden to my mind. And here we were, four centuries later, re-enacting the same scene.

And though I was younger than Bierce by twenty years, I had come off the worse for the attack. In one sense, of course, I was glad. I could not have borne seeing Bierce cut down in some miserable alley like a common thief. Was it just chance that put me in the way of the Bendiga-thing rather than Bierce? I could not believe I was held in such esteem by the Eagle-knights that they would seek to slay me first.

It was at this time, too, that I first learned of the details of our rescue. Despite the innate caution of the *colonia*'s residents, some few did emerge to see what all the shooting was about. As luck would have it, one of them was our quondam bartender, Báltazar, armed with a heavy cudgel. He and a few others helped Bierce and me out of the alley, Bierce walking but leaning upon Báltazar shoulders, and I carried by the others. We were transported to Báltazar's *pulqueria* where our wounds were laved in the strongest tequila the good man had at hand.

None of this I remember. I remained unconscious until waking that sunny morning in the hospital bed. As Báltazar saw to our wounds, the first alarm given by the police sounded outside. Their tardiness in coming, even after the racket of all our shooting, is something that gave us pause. As it turned out, it served us well, as it gave us time to get away from the slaughter before they arrived. Yet their lateness in coming was more than convenient for a getaway, whether ours or someone else's.

All this Bierce and I discussed at length during my stay in the hospital. Bierce, with his lesser wounds, was free to go as he pleased but opted to stay with me instead. Teo had been apprised of our situation and location, and came in the first day I was conscious. He entered looking pale and nervous, wiping his palms on the legs of his pants, but he came.

"Amos," he said and shook my good hand, "so good to see you awake and—well."

"Good to see you too, Teo. All is well with you?"

"*Pues sí,* everything is fine. Oh, here." He dug into this jacket pocket and too out a small, square parcel wrapped in blue ribbon. "A present."

I was touched. Unwrapping it was more of a challenge than I had anticipated. The loss of the use of one arm creates complications you never imagine. Finally, with a modicum of grunts and gasps, I pulled the cover off the box and looked within. Lying on a bed of cotton was a small pendant shaped like a seated skeleton, its knees drawn up and clasped by its long, bony arms. I looked at Teo—he shrugged.

"Fight fire with fire, fight magic with magic. It is authentic, I assure you—an image of Mictlantecuhtli, Lord of the Dead. I found it on an excavation near here. May he watch over you, *mi amigo.*"

I shook his hand again. "Thank you very much, Teo. I will put it on right now."

With my right hand and Teo's assistance I looped the cord over my head and let the pendant drop against my chest. It had the rough and solid feel of something that has been made to survive the centuries. It may have been my imagination, but I immediately felt safer with it on.

"Well," said Teo, rising, "I will leave you to rest. Señor Bierce? A word with you, *por favor*."

Bierce and Teo walked down to the far end of the room and huddled together in conversation for several minutes. I lay back and watched the evening deepen from blue to indigo to a purple-black in the hospital's tall windows. Was there yet a subtle tinge of obsidian in it? When the two men had concluded their conversation, Teo left and Bierce rejoined me at the bedside.

"Teo," he said, not looking at me, "has asked that we find other lodgings."

This was something of a shock but not a complete surprise. I nodded for Bierce to go on.

"He feels it is becoming too dangerous—for himself, of course, but for his students as well. We have become a magnet for evil, it seems, and he cannot face it any more."

"I don't blame him, Bierce. He has been more than generous with us, and I wouldn't put him in danger for the world."

"Nor would I. And he is being kind enough to us to let us stay in his apartment until we can find rooms of our own."

I looked at the evening again.

"Do we really need to, Bierce? With Bendiga gone and his followers dead or scattered, I don't see any reason for us to remain. We won—remember?"

Doubt and concern roamed over Bierce's face like shadows of clouds.

"We have won the battle, Amos, but not the war. I feel that something more remains. Huerta is, after all, still in power, and the equinox draws near. I should like to stay here at least through that date, just to make sure."

"Little we can do about Huerta, short of assassination. Can we sic Posada's phantoms on him, do you think?"

For answer Bierce reached into his inner coat pocket and pulled out a sheet of flimsy paper. I knew the stock even before Bierce unfolded it: from the presses of José Guadalupe Posada. Bierce set it upon my lap. I looked down at an image of a skeleton, a somewhat corpulent skeleton, if you can imagine such a thing, astride a galloping skeleton-horse. The calavera raised his derby in farewell. The caption, in rusty letters, was simple:

ADIOS

It struck me as somehow very sad. We had made a friend, a good friend, and now we must bid him farewell. Perhaps it was the strain of the previous days catching up with me—but no. That cheapens the emotion. I considered Posada my friend, and I was going to miss him. I swallowed a hard lump in my throat.

"May I keep this?" I said.

"If it doesn't curl up and blow away."

It didn't; and today it hangs with pride above my desk as I write, the last creation of José Guadalupe Posada.

*

There is little more to tell of my stay in the hospital, especially when compared to its sequel. I slept a lot. Every time I awoke I found Bierce at my bedside, struggling through the daily papers. Whether he was always there or not he would not say and I was too tired to ask. But he was always there when I awoke. Dr. Muñoz reappeared once each day to examine my wound. On the day before my release he unwrapped the bandage to check on the healing. The smell coming off the bandages was foul—I had visions of gangrene—but the good doctor smiled and shook his head.

"If it were rotting, you'd know it."

He removed the last bandages, and I looked at the new form of my arm. It was red and bloated, and the skin over that portion that had been nearly severed from my arm looked inflated. It pulled at the stitches that held it together. As if reading my mind, the doctor said, "The swelling will go down."

I nodded and looked back at my arm. It was hideous but, as the doctor had said, I was lucky to still have an arm at all. Compared to Bendiga and his henchmen, I was in very good shape.

The pretty nurse was back and handed Doctor Muñoz a fresh roll of bandages. He took the roll and gave her the old bandages to dispose. After applying salve to the wound, he wrapped my arm in the fresh linen. It felt tight but secure, and the calmness in the doctor's face did much to reassure me.

When he was finished he said, "I will not see you again. I have, I fear, obligations elsewhere. But I will instruct one of my fellows, Dr. Salazar, to observe you from time to time. *Adios, Señores, y que vayan con Dios.*"

He gave Bierce and me a neat, curt bow and walked away.

"What an extraordinary fellow," I said. "I'm sorry that he won't be attending me any more."

Bierce said, "Not to diminish your importance in the cosmos, Amos, but I'm sure that the doctor has more illustrious patients to attend to."

Late that afternoon, I was released from the hospital. Bierce and I limped out, arm in arm (my good arm—the other hung in a sling) to the waiting taxi, and rode in silence back to Teo's rooms. I felt drained of strength, emotion, even the ability of simple thought. Glancing at Bierce I could see that he was similarly exhausted. It would be good to relax and bask in Teo's erudition and friendship for a while, as short as it might be.

We arrived at Teo's building, paid the cabbie, and trudged up the long steps to our rooms. Bierce had to stop twice on the climb.   "I—miss Señora Huitzil's . . . tea," he gasped out.

"I didn't know that you still took it," I said.

He nodded. "Best med—best medicine I've ever taken."

After a minute's rest we continued on up. Even before we arrived at the landing outside Teo's door we knew that something was amiss. The door was ajar, sunlight lay quiet across the hallway rug, and raw, pale wood showed on the doorjamb where the lock had been forced.

"Torn out is more like it," said Bierce as we looked at it. Pushing the door slowly open, we beheld a scene of chaos. Books, papers plates, cushions, all the minutiae of Teobaldo Navarro's scholarly life, were thrown together in a shin-deep mess across the floor. Cabinets gaped open, emptied of all within. Glass crunched underfoot as we entered the flat.

I was too stunned to speak. Bierce advanced into the wreckage, bent down, and picked up a small piece of paper—a telegram, from the look of it. He glanced at it and pocketed it.

"They were looking for something important," he said quietly. "This was as much a search as it was a threat." We looked at each other—Teo. I ran to the kitchen, my arm crying pain with every step, while Bierce dodged back toward the bedrooms. The kitchen was a wasteland of shattered crockery and spilled silverware; heady fumes of wine hung over it all. But there was no one, nobody, there. I turned and went back into the sitting room. Bierce reappeared.

"Anything?" I said.

He shook his head.

"Nothing. And the telephone line is cut." He held up Teo's candlestick by a severed wire.

"We've got to try the neighbors," I said.

Bierce dropped the telephone and we left the apartment. I closed the door behind me—out of habit, for all the good it would do—and we went to the next door down the hall. We pounded on the door for five minutes, but no one ever answered. The same happened at all the other doors we tried on that floor and the floor below. Whether the occupants were at work or, more likely, within and too scared to answer, our entreaties and demands came to nothing.

"No use," gasped Bierce after a couple minutes of this. "We've got to get to . . . college."

We hobbled back out of the building to the street. It was beginning to get dark and, with the daily siesta blanketing the city in quiet, it was several minutes more before we secured a cab. Fortunately—if I may apply that word in the light of future events—we were not far from the college. The ride was swift and silent.

We arrived at the college amidst pandemonium.

From the doorway of the university building, students were shoving, scrambling, running, frantic to be out, while stolid policemen in blue-black uniforms strode in past them like dreadnoughts through a flurry of sailboats. Out front, police cars hugged the curb as if on parade. As we passed through the crowd I noticed some men in their midst who were not policemen, exactly, but were certainly not students. Men in cheap suits and dark fedoras pulled halfway down to their badger eyes. As we passed one of them, I heard a muttered *"ese gringo viejo y su fulano"*—that old gringo and his fool.

We muscled through the log-jam of bodies at the door and followed the file of policemen up the stairs. I don't know about Bierce—perhaps his war experiences made him more stoic in such situations—but I know that I was still holding out a hope that whatever had happened here had not happened to Professor Navarro.

But the trail of policemen led inevitably, tragically, to Teo's office door. It hung slantwise open upon one hinge. We slowed. More police stood in the hallway, and they eyed us with professional suspicion and disdain. Closer and closer to the doorway . . . and around the doorjamb, I looked into a room of nightmare. As in his apartment, Teo's precious papers and artifacts were scattered in heaps and shards upon the floor. Stretched upon the great table from which they had been swept lay a figure. Sunlight pouring in the windows spotlighted it—dark, glistening, inert. A smell rushed upon me from the room, and I was again in the room of sacrifice in Ojinaga: the iron stench of blood.

And something more—a pungent but sweet aroma. Flowers. Marigolds. I glanced back at the horror and the splash of burning yellow where the mouth would be. His mouth was stuffed with marigolds.

I felt my gorge rise suddenly high into my throat, threatening to spill out and fill the hallway with vomit, and I put my hand to my mouth and turned away. I shut my eyes to block out what I had seen, but the image of it—the dead meat in the sun—only burst forth in all its hideous detail behind my eyelids. When I opened my eyes I saw Bierce standing, arms folded, facing the wall opposite to the door. He was as still as if cast in iron.

A hand gripped my upper arm—my good arm, thankfully. I turned and saw a tall man in tweeds, one of the plain-clothes policemen.

"Espere," he said to me. "Did you know the deceased?"

Did I know the dead man? I glanced at the unholy mess in the room. How could you tell who it was? It scarcely looked like a human being at all. I swallowed a lump of brick.

"¿Quién fue?" I said. *Who was it?* I knew damned well who it was, lying in Teobaldo Navarro's private office in Teobaldo Navarro's college; but I felt that just the act of asking might negate the fact. The policeman had a notebook in his hand and he flipped back a page or two.

"El Profesor Teobaldo Navarro y Morero," he read, slowly and carefully as if unsure of his own notes. He looked back at me, hard. *"Did* you know him?"

"Yes," I said. "We knew him."

The policeman glanced at Bierce, still staring down the wall. "How?"

"Pardon?"

The officer sighed as if all the air were being let out of him. "How did you know him?" he enunciated at me.

"We were—colleagues, doing research on Pre-Columbian art. My friend"—I nodded toward Bierce—"is a writer and was doing research—"

"You said that," said the officer, and jotted something in his notebook. "What are your names?"

"Halpin Frayser." Bierce's voice. It seemed to come out of the air.

"Peyton Farquhar," I said, taking my cue from Bierce, and produced my counterfeit passport. I prayed that the officer, detective, whatever, had not read any of Bierce's fiction. Apparently not. He copied my information from the passport as if it were Gospel and never batted an eyelash. Somewhere in Mexico there is a very odd note appended to a murder case.

"And can you tell me," he said without looking up from his writing, "where you two were this morning?"

Blast. Our alibi was rock-solid: we had been in the hospital. But then the officer would want to know why. As I searched for a credible lie, Bierce saved me the trouble.

"We were in the Hospital de Jesús," he said. "We were recovering from an accident."

"And the name of your physician?"

"Lázaro Muñoz."

That stopped the detective. He looked up sharply from his note-taking and studied Bierce. Bierce hates a lie and I, for one, can tell when he employs one. He wasn't lying now, and though a stranger to Bierce, the detective could clearly see that he was telling the truth now as well. Something in the doctor's name, though, had made him pause.

While he wrote I observed him. He looked solid, trustworthy; a straight nose and firm mouth, ringed by a fashionable goatee. His manner was brusque but, given the circumstances, understandable. He looked like an honorable man—but who could tell in those days? I wondered whether he had any tattoos.

"And where are you staying?" he said, addressing me.

"At Señor Navarro's rooms," I said, and told him the address. He wrote. The scratch of his pen on paper was the only sound in the building. Finally he shut the notebook with a snap and handed me back my passport.

"*Bueno,*" he said. "We will look into this and contact you when we need you." He started to turn away (*you are dismissed*), then turned back. "Don't go far."

I knew I had been dismissed, but I had to ask one more thing.

"*Perdóname,*" I said, "Señor, but—but how did Professor Navarro die?"

He turned again to me. "*Desollado.*"

It took me a moment. Not a common word, but then it came rushing up into my consciousness. *Skinned.*

"And they cut his heart out."

And he turned away for good. From the room, that cursed, hateful abattoir, came the sound of laughter. One of the policemen—what did he look like? Did he possess an eagle tattoo? And what in God's name could be so funny in such a room?

2.

The college closed. Its students fled to their various homes, and the building was shuttered. For how long, none could say. It was a crime scene, only officials could decide when it might be re-opened—if ever.

And which officials? Who were these people? I pictured the bureaucracy of the Huerta regime like an impenetrable tangle of roots. Splitting and bifurcating, linking and growing together into an unravelable web of power.

And it was, you'll pardon the pun, academic anyway. There was nothing left for us at the college. With nowhere else to go, we returned to the disaster of Teobaldo's rooms. His cat Toni, I was heartened to see, was unharmed and emerged from whatever secret place where she had hidden herself. We straightened up as much as we were able, cleaned and set back up enough furniture to sit in, and collapsed upon two of the vacant chairs. We were spent.

"Well," I said.

"Well," said Bierce.

We let that stand for several minutes. There was little else to say. We had struck the Eagle-knights, and they had struck us back. And here we were, the survivors, two wretched, maimed older men, pitted against God knew how many bloodthirsty warriors. It was worse than hopeless—it was insane. Bierce took a deep breath.

"We must regroup."

I stared at him in dumbfounded amazement.

"'Regroup'?" I said. "'WE'? Have you looked around to see how many left 'we' are? And 'we' aren't the 'we' of even a month ago, Bierce. I can scarcely use my left arm, and I have no idea how you are even still on your feet." I leaned forward and put out my hands in supplication. "We're beaten, Bierce. If we stay any longer we will end up like Teo. I'm not even sure why we're still alive at all! All I can think of is that somehow Mrs. Gadbury got into Huerta's good graces on our behalf. But the Gadburys are, thank God, far away now, and that means any swing we might have had with these monsters is gone with them."

Bierce observed me in silence for a time.

"I'll admit," he said slowly, "that things appear dark—"

I snorted at that and sat back.

"—but we are not beaten," he finished. I continued to stare at him. Those pale blue eyes were as direct as ever.

"We *cannot* be beaten," he said. "There is no choice in this, Amos. If our adversaries win, then they win all. This is not merely about us but about civilization—the whole world."

I shut my eyes and rubbed my temples. He was right and I knew it; but just then I just wanted to climb into bed, roll over, and go to sleep.

"I——" I started, then stopped. "I know you're right, Bierce. But I'm tired. I don't feel as if I can go on, never mind do battle with sword-wielding thugs."

Then Bierce smiled. It was a slight smile, and a sad one, but a smile nonetheless.

"Of course you can, my dear boy. You can not only go on, but you can fight and beat these creatures. You need rest—we both do. And we need to think. So we will take that time to rest and think, and plan what we are to do next. We are, as you say, not the 'we' we once were; but that can be our strength, too. They won't expect us to rally."

I sat up then. Perhaps it was just the old man's irresistible strength, flowing over me, raising my spirits. Perhaps it was hopeful delusion. But either way, I felt the weight of despair falling off of my shoulders.

"Very good, Bierce," I said. "Then beat them we shall."

Bierce and I sorted through Teo's things and found the address of his family in Puebla. Teo's body, what was left of it, was in the city morgue and his family arrived two days later in a creaking cart to reclaim it. A more pitiful, hang-dog group of people you have never seen. None of them spoke English, and by their patchy Sunday clothes I guessed they were all laborers and poor. A couple of the more ancient *abuelas,* wrapped head to toe in black, conversed in what I was sure was Náhuatl. Teo must have been their pride and joy, the one member of the family who had educated himself and risen out of the dust of the country to success in the city. And now this.

They roomed with us at Teo's apartment; they could not afford a hotel room. We had put the apartment in some semblance of order before they arrived, and fed and comforted them as best as we could. They were noble people, proud, quiet, respectful, and grateful to us for what we were able to do for them. When the body was released to them, Bierce generously paid for it and the whole family to be transported by truck back to Puebla. The very thought of them riding for two days over the mountains with Teo's mangled remains was intolerable to the old man. He even paid for the remains to be packed in ice, not an inexpensive gesture.

When the family and we had exchanged our sad *despedidas,* they shuffled out of Teo's rooms and his uncle, last in line, pulled the door shut behind him.

The silence they left in their wake was suffocating. Bierce and I busied ourselves with putting the rooms back in order: washing dishes, stripping beds, sweeping floors. Anything to keep our minds off the ominous days ahead.

When we had done all we could, we prepared a simple dinner and sat down to eat.

"I have sent word to Juan Romero."

Bierce's words rang like distant church bells in the silence. I thought for a couple chews.

"I don't want to offend you," Bierce added when the silence stretched out. "Your Spanish is admirable. But Juan speaks it like, well, like a native. What's more, he has the local's knowledge of the city. That can be invaluable to us."

"Do you think he will come?" I said. I didn't look up at Bierce.

"I have already had a reply." He pulled a crumpled telegram from his coat and smoothed it on the table between us.

VERY SAD TO HEAR OF SR. NAVARRO. WILL COME MUCH SOON
AS POSIBLE—   JUAN

"Well," I said, "at least we can count on his grammar being the same."

Bierce huffed a laugh. "He is coming from a place called Malinalco. Do you know of it?"

For answer I rose and walked to the sitting room. From our cleaning, I now knew the identity and location of most of Teo's books, and readily found his atlas of Mexico. I returned to the table and opened the book to the index.

"Here," I said, putting the atlas onto the table between us and pointing at a map. "A day's journey to the southwest. When did he write to you?" I looked at the telegram again; it was dated March 12, the day before.

"He should be here in the morning at latest," said Bierce. "We must arrange our plans before he arrives."

I sat back, sighed, looked at Bierce. "I can't say I'm any more sanguine about our mission," I said, "with Juan or without him. But what did you have in mind?"

Bierce leaned toward me.

"Their meeting-place. It is the one location we know of where they gathered."

"But didn't you and Teo already go through it?"

"That we did, but that was a couple of weeks and many adventures ago.

Call it an instinct, intuition, a 'hunch' or what have you, but I feel sure that some of our answers lie there." He sighed and collapsed back in his chair. "Besides, can you think of anywhere else we should look?"

I considered mentioning Huerta again, but didn't. The president was all but unassailable to us, doubly so now, no doubt, since we had decimated his fellow conspirators. The newspapers, moreover, were full of the general's reverses and defeats. He would be even more nervous and on guard than usual. That way, clearly, was a dead end.

"Very good," I said. "I am your man, Bierce. And I hope that Juan proves to be up to it as well."

We spent the rest of that day and most of the following day doing as little as possible. The doctors had relieved Bierce of his sling, but his left arm was still sore and healing. Mine was all but worthless. Doctor Salazar, a quiet, grave man with wavy hair and thick mustache well streaked with gray, arrived on that first afternoon and tended to our wounds. He unwrapped and redressed my arm and gave me a jar of salve to apply to it. He held the jar up to the light and squinted at it.

"I have no idea what my esteemed colleague put into this," he said. "But it works."

It did indeed work, and I noted improvement almost immediately. The pain lessened its grip upon me, and my fingers grew more responsive. The improvement in my physical being lifted my spirits as well.

News from the greater world cheered us also. Villa and Carranza were having a spat up in the north, so their progress against Huerta was stalled. Even so, other rebel forces were on the move. In the south, Zapata had taken the city of Cuautla and promptly executed every Federal officer he could find. It seemed bloodthirstiness was not the sole property of the *federales*. I wondered how many Eagle-knights rode with Zapata.

"Cuautla is only thirty miles from here, Bierce," I said. "Seems the trap is about to close on the good *presidente*."

"Don't underestimate our dear general, Amos. There is nothing more dangerous than a cornered jackal. And you have, I take it, been watching the skies at twilight?"

I nodded. "That blue-black shade," I said. "In pools and fountains as well. *El Gran Brujo* is still weaving his spells."

"And his henchmen still slay and fill some unseen reservoir of blood for their gods."

I touched my wounded arm.

"Considering the wealth of blood we've contributed, it should be over-flowing by now."

Juan arrived the next afternoon. He walked in with his battered cardboard suitcase in one hand and his crumbling hat in the other.

"I'm so sorry, *mis compadres*," he said. He shook hands with Bierce, both of the old man's pale claws gripped in his strong, brown paws.

"*Y tu,* Amos." He shook my outstretched hand firmly. "I am so sorry. *El Profesor* was a good man, a good man." He shook my hand firmly with each "good."

"We have set aside the professor's own room for you, Juan." Bierce motioned towards the bedrooms. "Once you are settled, we can discuss our plans."

Over dinner (rice, beans, and tortillas, all our bachelor talents could produce), we brought Juan up to date on our mission. We did not educate him on the theology behind it all, just told him that we were still on the trail of the same group who had attacked us in the north. When we had done, Juan blew out his cheeks and sat back.

"*Diosito mío,*" he murmured. "The same people, the same *pandilla.* I don' know, señores—I must think of my family, my safety . . . " He held up his hands as though weighing the dangers versus the possible benefits.

"If it makes it any more agreeable," said Bierce, "I intend to compensate you generously for your trouble."

Juan looked at me. "*¿Mande?*"

I translated Bierce's words and Juan nodded.

"You are *muy generoso,* Señor Bierce," he said. "But the money won' protect my wife, my children, won' bring in the harvest from the *milpa* to feed us."

"I can be *mas generoso,* Juan. As much as you need. We need you and your help—there is no one else we can turn to."

Juan gave him a long, sideways, green look from his cat's eyes.

"'*Sta bien,*" he said. "You give me enough to live now, and if I die, for my family."

"Done."

They shook hands on it.

We were all tired—Juan from travel, Bierce and I just from getting through the day—and by mutual assent we all retired for the evening after dinner. Juan was good enough to wash the dishes while we made his bed.

"Do you think he'll stick with us, Bierce?" I said once we were alone.

"Like glue, Amos. We have offered him compensation he values too highly to refuse. More than that, and if I know my man as I am sure that I do, he is a creature of honor and dedication. Once set upon a certain path, he will not deviate from it. You will see."

We had determined to search the Eagle-knights' nest after dark, so the next day was left for preparation. Not much we needed to do; Bierce and I checked and rechecked our guns (rescued and kept by the reliable bartender, Báltazar), while Juan went out to purchase a weapon of his own. We checked and rechecked our maps and our notes as well, trying to understand the Knights and their motivations and methods from Teo's works on the Aztecs. Even after all we had been through, this study sent fresh chills down my back. The sheer bloodthirstiness of them, the inhuman inventiveness of their savagery . . . If the modern Eagle-knights were one-tenth as brutal as their predecessors, then we had to leave nothing to chance.

Juan reappeared mid-afternoon bearing a stained cloth bundle.

"*Miren,* amigos," he said, swept his hat from his head and tossed it on the divan. "Took some lookin', some *lana,* y'know, but I got me a pistol." He set the bundle on the table and unwrapped it. Upon the grease-stained burlap lay a large, black pistol. Bierce picked it up.

"A Colt Dragoon," he said. "Probably worth more as an antique than as a weapon."

"If it doesn't fire," I said, taking it from Bierce, "you can always throw it at them. Ye gods, but it must weigh twenty pounds."

Juan laughed. "*Verdad.* But yes, it shoots—I tried it."

The afternoon unwound slowly. I was too nervous to be hungry, but Bierce insisted we eat.

"We cannot say when we may be near food again, Amos." He set plates of rice, beans, and tortillas—our quondam dinner—in front of Juan and me, and one at his own place setting.

"I cannot say the prospect of meeting these animals gives me much of an appetite," I said.

"I agree with you; but yet we must maintain our strength. Eat up."

Juan, I saw with some chagrin, was devouring his meal with fork, tortillas, and hands. How he could have such an appetite at such a time was beyond me. I sighed and bent to my own repast.

*

Darkness descended. Mexico City, halfway through its daily siesta, slumbered. The sky between the blocky ornamented buildings deepened from blue to indigo to purple. Did it have a black shine to it? I couldn't even tell anymore. I felt a hand rest upon my shoulder. Bierce.

"It is time, Amos."

I nodded. I retrieved my pistol, holster, and belt from where I had left them on my bedside table. I strapped the gunbelt on, holster on the right. I tugged the gun from its leathern sheath, snapped open the gate, and spun the cylinder with my thumb. Six copper shells winked out at me as they rotated; six yellow eyes with raised irises. When I had counted all six, I twitched the cylinder back into place with a snap and re-holstered the gun. I pulled on my coat, slowly first over my wounded left arm, then shivered my right arm in, and shrugged until the yoke settled comfortably upon my shoulders. I took my hat and electric torch from the wardrobe, and went out.

Bierce and Juan awaited me. Nobody said a word. Bierce opened the door, motioned Juan and me out before him, then pulled it to. The new lock snicked shut behind us, like the period on a long and convoluted sentence.

Down the darkening staircase, three sets of boots thudding neat and quiet in the echoing gloom. The glow of a streetlight through the glass panels in the door; then open to flood the foyer with sad, anemic light.

A lone taxi rolled up in front of our building, as long, as silent, as irrefutable as a hearse. We walked down the steps and across the pavement three abreast, our footsteps synchronized, simultaneous. Bierce took the front seat, we climbed in back. Bierce gave the driver the address and the car slewed onto the street.

We rode in tacit silence. The heavy blocks of our neighborhood gave way to sterner commercial and then government buildings. Of a sudden the Zócalo opened before us like a breathtaking night-blossom, stained with lights, open to the plunging heavens. Across and through the muted traffic. The national cathedral rose up to our left; the National Palace stretched away to our right. Up the side street, buildings closing in again. Behind the cathedral, a glimpse of Calle Santa Inez, where Posada's shop dreamed printed ghosts in the twilight. Another couple of blocks passed, and the building that sheltered the most dangerous cult in Mexico drew up on our right. Bierce had the driver continue past it to the next corner to avoid our being seen. The car snugged over to the curb and stopped. Bierce paid the man and we opened the doors and got out. We stood facing back down toward that dark, waiting building while the putter of the taxi grew faint in the distance.

"Are you game, lads?" said Bierce.

"Yes, Bierce."

"Sí, Señor."

"Then let us proceed."

Like a general before his troops, Bierce led us down the sidewalk. The city watched and waited. The sidewalk leading back to the gang's meeting-place seemed to stretch to the horizon; yet all too soon we stood before the dark door. Bierce stepped forward, gripped the doorknob and twisted.

"Damn. Locked."

"Did you expect a welcome mat?"

Bierce glanced venom at me.

"A ver," said Juan. He stepped past Bierce. He hunched over the doorknob in the weak light and worked at the door; and in half a minute we were rewarded with a faint but sharp *click.* The door swung wide of its own volition. Bierce took a deep breath.

"'Once more unto the breach, dear friends, once more,'" he said, and led us within.

Once in the actual building, we stopped and waited. Nothing happened. No half-animal warriors charged screaming at us, no blood-smeared priests drove their volcanic glass knives at us. Nothing. The hallway opened only onto darkness, complete and still. It smelled of old rugs and dust and dry-rot. It smelled of age.

"A light, Amos," said Bierce in a hushed voice. I stepped up and the darkness reached out and around me, dimming not only what I might have seen before me, but all the world behind me as well. I fumbled out the torch and pushed the button on its side. In that last half-second before the light went on, the darkness before us *solidified*—that is the only way I can describe it. A sheen from the streetlights slid along one sea-green edge . . .

Then the light snapped on and illumined a sudden scene of dusty boards and stairs, climbing into the darkness. To the left of the staircase a hallway ran back into the building's depths in ever diminishing rectangular frames. It could have gone on forever for all that I could tell. Doors in dark thresholds marched down the left-hand wall and away. I moved the torch to my left hand and drew my pistol with my right.

"Lead on, Macduff," I said.

"It's 'Lay on,' you Philistine."

But lead on he did. He sidled past me, keen as an axe-head; his big pistol, his arm, his black-suited body. His black hat was low on his head and his eyes shone like blue fire from beneath the brim. He looked like something out of the Hole-in-the-Wall Gang. Holding the torch high to light the way, I followed him. I heard the door close as Juan pulled it to and fell in behind us.

Bierce led us up the stairs. The steps creaked and complained beneath our weight, but held. Up on the second-floor landing we met with another hallway, a twin to the one downstairs. Bierce stepped noiselessly to a door. He raised his finger as if to point—then let it fall. He stepped to the next door down the hall and pointed at it.

"Here."

Juan and I stepped up behind him, guns at the ready. But the door was not even locked. Bierce turned the handle and pushed the door wide and we entered into more gloom, more silence. Across the breadth of a wide space there were two windows. Their quartered light was thrown upon the ceiling in eight, pale squares. The floor yawned gray and empty as a desert but for a plain wooden table and several chairs. The chairs sat at all angles around the table as if pushed back in haste. The table itself stood contrary to the room's walls—nothing was square or aligned. My torch only accentuated the grey of walls, floor, ceiling. *The house of dust.*

Guns held out, we three walked into the room. We wandered, aimless, leaving meandering trails in the dust. We were all searching, but we knew not what for. Aside from the askew furniture, the room was bare. It felt as if it had been deserted not weeks before, but centuries, millennia before.

"You're sure," I began, but Bierce cut me off.

"It was here." He pointed at the floor. Our voices echoed once and died in the flat air.

We shuffled through the dust, our eyes never resting in their search for something. Juan approached the table.

"*Mis compañeros,*" he said. "*Aquí.*"

Bierce and I walked to Juan's side from opposite corners of the room. Juan pointed to the dust on the tabletop; to the one word in the dust on the tabletop:

debajo

"'Below,'" I said. Juan nodded slowly.

"Does this place have, *como se dice,* a *sótano?* Cellar?"

Bierce rubbed his jaw and clenched his brows in thought.

"We never looked. The gang was meeting up here—that was all that was pertinent."

Without another word Bierce led us out of the silent room and back down the stairs. Around the newel post at the stair's end and down the first floor hallway; more doors, a monotonous prospect of doors leading on forever. Along the right-hand wall, below the staircase, other doors. I tried one; a tight space cluttered with brooms, a mop standing out of a bucket like a shaggy-headed scarecrow, dusters and rags.

"Just like new," I muttered. "Not that they ever got any use . . . "

"Hush, Amos." Bierce held up an admonitory finger. He opened the next door down and Juan was at the one beyond that. Bierce barely had his door open when Juan hissed, "Amigos! It's here!"

Bierce and I hurried to join him. Juan had the door wide now and pointed with his pistol at the first of many steps descending into blackness. Bierce clapped Juan on the shoulder.

"Well done, Juan."

Bierce held out his hand and I placed the torch in it. Holding the torch before him, he began to descend the stairs. Darkness gathered at our backs as the torch's beam poured down the paint-chipped brick walls and fading stairs, going ever down, down. Bierce walked in silhouette against the light; just a black paper Bierce cut-out.

I looked at Juan and saw the sheen and sparkle of perspiration on his dark face.

"Después de tí," he said, motioning me ahead of him. I nodded "gracias" and followed Bierce.

If I was expecting a descent into the Underworld, I was disappointed. The rickety staircase brought us down in twenty steps or so to a cluttered cellar. In one corner stood a gang of tall, metal cylinders—the boilers for the building's various floors—and between them and us was a wasteland of broken chairs, tables, an armoire half-draped in a soiled sheet, half-empty cans of paint, broken tools, piles of ledgers, a sink. We moved into the clutter—and someone moved with us. We all jerked up our pistols, hammers clicked back—and the strangers did the same. Bierce let out his breath and lowered his gun.

"That deadliest of enemies," he said. "A mirror. 'A vitreous plane upon which to display a fleeting show for man's disillusion given.'"

"Please don't quote the Devil in such a place," I said. He grinned at me. Juan turned a puzzled look at me. "He's quoting himself," I said. Juan nodded slowly as if not quite sure of the joke.

Again, as in the room upstairs, we divided and searched the cellar. Bierce set the torch atop the armoire to give us all a little light at least. We pushed the abandoned furniture around, peeked behind the cold, sweating bulk of the boilers, lifted sheets, and disturbed spiders at their work, but found nothing. I was back under the stairs, prodding a box with my toe in the doubtful light, when Juan called us.

"Señor Beer? Amos? I think I find something."

I left the box, and Bierce crossed from the other end of the room, grabbing the torch as he came. Juan was standing opposite the end of the staircase. The maintenance man or whoever governed such places had propped old doors against the wall there. They had been stripped of hardware and stood several deep in places, tall, forlorn, and somehow menacing. *Doors to where?* Juan had slid several of the doors aside in one place, revealing yet another door. At first I thought it was just another cast-off; then Bierce shown the torch more directly upon it: it still had a doorknob and hinges. Like the doors that had hidden it, it leaned at an angle against the wall; but unlike those others, a narrow bulkhead of stone and mortar had been built up behind it. It was like a more upright version of innumerable cellar bulkheads I had seen back home. So why should I have to swallow down a hard lump and still the shaking of my hand? I glanced at Juan and in the light reflected up from the door's cracked varnish I saw that he, too, stared with fear at the portal. The whites of his eyes shone like those of a spooked horse.

Bierce, made of sterner stuff, stepped up to the door and gripped the knob. Again a door refused his advances. Again he turned to Juan.

"Juan," he said. "If you please."

Juan nodded and pocketed his pistol. He wiped his hands on his pants and bent to his work once more. Subtle clicks and scrapes; tumblers slipping back into hidden cavities. Bierce bent forward with the torch.

"Do you have enough light, Juan?" he said.

"*Sí, sí, Señor, basta,*" Juan said, and as if to prove it, he hunched closer over his work like a predator over his prey. Another click and Juan stepped back from the door, drawing his sleeve across his brow. "Is unlocked now."

Bierce stepped forward again and turned the doorknob. With a soft grating sound the door opened toward us. Within, a blackness even deeper than what had greeted us upstairs; it was the difference between dusk and a hopeless midnight; a darkness more profound by factors of hundreds, the breadth of an entire spectrum more stupendously *black* than anything I had ever seen before. Just looking at it, I felt as if I were plunging headlong into it.

Bierce must have felt the same for I saw him brace himself against the crude stone jambs of the opening. Juan leaned away from it, still staring. Bierce took a couple deep breaths (thank you, Doña Huitzil, I thought, for your potions and teas) and shone the light down into the doorway. The ancient blackness withdrew, reluctantly, and disclosed walls and stairs of dressed, volcanic stone. Bierce took another gallon of air into his lungs and said, "A good general does not lead from behind," and stepped into the doorway.

I almost grabbed his shoulder, pulled him away from that awful abyss; turned him toward the staircase, outer door, outer world, and safety. But I didn't. How different things might have been is a subject for the gods and dime-novel writers to debate. Not I. Bierce was an intensely stubborn man. Even if I had succeeded in dragging him away from that door, he would have continued to get back to it again and again, until his fate was fulfilled. He would have reminded me of our duty to thwart those monsters, those hybrid half-men of terror, regardless of risk—and what could I have said in response? No, Bierce, it is too dangerous; let the Big Wheels of the Universe turn, let the bodies pile up, the blood fill the maws of the Unspeakable . . . In all honesty it was an argument I could not even make to myself. This *had* to be done. The best that I could do, the only thing I could do, was stand by Bierce and help him, and hope that I could protect him. Bierce took two hesitant steps down the abyss; and I followed.

But just before I left the upper world, I saw from the corner of my eye a lone, faded sheet of paper affixed to the nearby wall. Upon it, a skeleton in black clothes and black hat, a familiar white mustache, a pistol held before him, crept towards a black doorway. One word was printed below the image:

Cuidado

Caution. I blinked and it was gone.

The torch illuminated only a short section of the passage before us. I noted that the roof began with that eminently useful invention of the Romans, the arch, carried to the New World by their Spanish inheritors; but after a few step it was replaced by crudely dressed plinths of stone; later still by raw slabs of the same material. Bierce's silhouette before me, Juan's excited breathing behind me, I felt as if we were descending into deep Time itself. The steps continued on down, ever down. We must be in the very bed of old Lake Texcoco itself by now, I thought. Even as I did so, the light flattened out before Bierce on a rock-strewn dirt floor. The staircase ended and the passage led away before us, flat and still. Bierce paused briefly to pass the light over our new surroundings. More walls of pocked, volcanic stone, a ceiling of heavy stone slabs, the earthen floor—nothing more. Once again that feeling of the weight of Mexico City, past and present, six hundred years of piled up history, bearing down upon us.

But Bierce paused only for a moment. Out duty beckoned. The only sound, our shoes crackling softly on the earth beneath us. Further down that hateful tunnel, further . . . And then the sound of running water, at first just the merest trickle, but growing to a continuous, burbling song in the darkness. A smell—the dusty air of the tunnel violated by something rich and foul and cloying.

"Mierda," muttered Juan at my back. No need to translate that for Bierce, I thought. He covered his nose and we did the same. Past Bierce's shoulder I saw the light break and glitter on the floor ahead. As we approached it, sound and smell grew, and I saw I was a steam of sewage flowing out from under the right-hand wall and way under the left. In the paltry light the water was gray and lumpy. Fortunately a pair of planks had been thrown across the foul stream. We crossed it one at a time, carefully lest we upset them and drop ourselves into the filth.

A few yards beyond the sewage, the passageway's walls suddenly vanished, and we emerged into an open space so wide that its walls were lost in the shadows all around. Then, as my eyes adjusted, I could see more steps climbing toward the heavy ceiling to our right. Broad, long steps, such as you would see out front of a government building—or climbing to a temple. And tall: each stone riser must have been almost two feet in height. One would have had to climb sideways up them. And no government building I knew of could boast of such guardians, crouching stone jaguars that snarled in timeless, mindless rage from the bottom steps. In the wavering light from the torch, shadows reared over them as if the creatures were preparing to spring upon us.

"A pyramid," said Bierce, "buried beneath the modern city."

I nodded. Once he said it, the structure took shape in my mind. On either side of the stairway the stepped nature of the edifice itself, what Teo had called *"talud y tablero,"* likewise climbed up into darkness. Free of the confines of the tunnel, we spread out again. Bierce walked slowly toward the gaping blackness to the left; I went straight ahead; and Juan approached the pyramid. The reek of the sewage still tainted the air, but a new scent began to insinuate itself in my nostrils. It was equally foul—and familiar in a way I wished it weren't. Flowers and decay. I breathed through my mouth to avoid it. Something moved in the black distance before me.

"Amigos," said Juan. I turned and saw him bent over something on the bottom step of the pyramid. "Come quick."

Bierce turned and came back to us and with him, the light. As he turned, it flashed across the darkness before me and yes, there was something moving back there . . .

"Bierce," I said, but he had already joined Juan at the pyramid. I walked to them, keeping my eyes on what I thought I had seen, what was now approaching. I gripped my pistol more tightly; my sweat made the grip slick.

"Bierce," I said louder. But he was leaning over toward Juan. Juan had found a small bowl of red earthenware. He lifted it in both hands—his own pistol lay forgotten on the stone step. He turned slowly to show us—"*Miren.*"

I looked past the curve of Bierce's back and now saw a naked man coming slowly toward us out of the blackness. I cocked my pistol, the sound loud in the low space. It brought Bierce out of his preoccupation. He turned to me, saw my look, and snapped his head around to see what I was watching. At the same moment Juan held the bowl up before us—it was filled with a rusty-colored powder—and blew into it. The powder flew in suffocating clouds over our heads and faces. I blinked at it, coughed at it, heard Bierce coughing, too. I gasped in a breath and felt the powder drawn into my throat. As though a plug had been removed at the base of my spine, my mouth and tongue went numb, and the strength drained out of my limbs. The pistol fell from my hand, thudded to the ground a million miles away. I dropped to my knees like a rock to the ground. Blinking desperately at the grit in my eyes, I saw Bierce at my side on his hands and knees, hacking and hawking and coughing. And beyond him, coming closer now, the naked man. It was Teo, Teobaldo Navarro, back from the dead. But no. As the stench of decay enveloped me and my vision blurred and dimmed, I saw that it wasn't Teo at all. It was someone wearing Teo's skin.

3.

I walked in the fields of Carcosa, or Aztlán, or Lyonesse—one of those deathless realms that never really did exist, yet never die, and strolled among the standing carvings of forgotten gods. It was twilight and all was stained in shades of gray. There was no sound but a low vibration that began in the earth and grew up through the souls of my feet and into my very bones. It swelled in volume and climbed the scale until it was a rough, full-throated, one-note dirge—open-mouthed, like the unending first syllable of an "amen." If you can conceive of stone throats singing, then you will have some idea what it was like. Just as I thought this, I looked up at the double line of antediluvian carvings looming over me, and saw that their mouths were wide open. The statues sang. They all sang the same note, deep and timeless and awful. The wave of voices veered sickeningly down the scale again into thunderous depths of sound that shook the earth. My spine rattled; my skull ached.

The rumbling voices resolved into one growling voice, a mindless mechanical voice, the shaking into an uneven bumping against my back and head. I opened my eyes to musty darkness. I blinked and, as my eyes adjusted, I could make out heavy, dim figures seated around me, towering above me. The singing stones, I thought. I felt hard wood at my back. When I tried to move myself to a more comfortable position, I found that my hands and feet were bound. The hard surface beneath me gave an unusually large lurch, and the darkness behind the seated figures suddenly parted like a drape, admitting a weak light. It lasted for only a second, but just long enough to show arches of metal, a roof of stretched, dirty fabric, and the limned edges of bulky shoulders and heads. I was in the back of a truck in the company of several large men. And my hands and feet were tied.

Suddenly I thought of Bierce. I yanked my head to the side and got a bright spasm of pain down through my head and neck for my trouble. But there he was. He was bound hand and foot as well, just a pale, woolly head and two pale hands lying there nearby. His black suit blended seamlessly with the darkness. It reminded me uncomfortably of Señor Posada of blessed memory. When I had stretched my neck and blinked back as much pain as I could, I said, "Bierce. Bierce, wake up, please." The pale head rocked with the rhythm of the truck. "Bierce," I said a little louder. The leonine head just rocked a little more. But was there just a notion of purpose to it?

"Se despierta," said someone in a meaty voice behind me. Another voice responded, "Sí, lo veo, Beto." The was something familiar about the second voice, like that of a friend one knew in childhood, but grown. I turned my head that way (oh, pain) but could see even less than before; shadows moving over shadows. Then there was a sharp click and light bleached the scene. I squeezed my eyes shut against the glare for several moments. When I dared open my eyes again, I saw the dusty interior of a medium-sized truck. The canvas roof, rippling in the wind of travel, was held up by hoops of metal set in the truck's sides, Conestoga-wagon style. Along the sides of the truck-bed were benches, and upon these benches sat four men, two on Bierce's side and two on mine. One of the men on my side held an illuminated electric-torch. It was Juan Romero.

It was Juan Romero, but not the Juan we had traversed the wide desert of the north with; nor even the Juan Romero who had walked at our side, leading us into the bowels of Mexico City. This Juan sat up straighter, and radiated a confidence and easy strength in his new posture we had never seen before. His eyes, which were always looking for the angle or how to help our mission, now gazed coolly down upon me out of a face more composed than I had known— again, Juan, but not Juan. He even seemed to have grown and become more muscular than the last time I had seen him. The last time I saw him . . .

"You are feeling well, Amos?" he said in perfect English. I did not know how to reply; it was as if a total stranger inhabited the flesh of a friend. And with that thought came the other memory from before, and I swallowed bile before I had to vomit. Juan turned to his companion and said in Spanish, "Beto, our guest looks uncomfortable. Be so good as to set him and Señor Bierce in a sitting position."

Beto, all two hundred and more pounds of him, grunted and got up. He leaned down and, grasping me under the armpits, lifted me up until my back rested against one of the side-benches. Then he did the same for Bierce, who, I saw with mixed relief, was starting to wake up. I also noted with chagrin that Bierce had been lying on a mattress while I had not. Naturally, his first instinct was to complain.

"You could have chosen a more commodious mode of transportation, Amos."

"You're one to talk, Bierce," I said. "You and your mattress. Besides, it wasn't really my choice. Look around."

He did look around, then, at the worn surface of the moving truck and the stone-fixed faces of our captors. He sighed.

"We seem to repeat this scene ad nauseam," he said.

Satisfied that we were upright and awake, Juan/not Juan hung the torch on a hook at the back of the truck's cab and smiled at us. Just visible in the torch's fan of light were the head and shoulders of the driver up front, as dark and still and monolithic as if carven from granite. Juan leaned his hands upon his knees and faced us.

"We do indeed seem to return to this scene," he said in English. "Twice before we have had one or the both of you in our grasp, and yet you flitted away. But 'third time is the charm,' isn't that how the saying goes?"

Bierce stared hard at him.

"My, Juan, how your diction has improved," he said.

Juan smiled his odd, downturned smile and sat back.

"Do you like it, Mr. Bierce? Or should I say, 'Señor Beer'? Perhaps you would you prefer *el tonto Juan*, the caricature from your gringo comic pages, 'jus' 'nother *estupido mexicano*'?"

"I do not deal in stereotypes, Señor Romero—or whoever and whatever you are. They are the short-cuts of the unlettered and bigoted. And is it still 'Juan'? I assume that was a dodge as well."

"It will do," shrugged Juan. "The original owner of that name no longer needs it."

"So I deduced. Lying in some ditch, no doubt. For what it's worth, I pierced your disguise long ago."

I turned to look at Bierce (oh my blessed neck), and said, "You *knew* Juan was part if this? When were you going to tell me? Once I was stretched on the sacrificial stone?"

At this Bierce looked down at his bound hands.

"I'm very sorry, Amos. I could not continue the fiction of our ignorance with you knowing. You have many worthy talents, but dissimulation is not one of them—you wear your thoughts upon your sleeve, so to speak."

"And you knew that Juan was keeping pace with us, keeping track of us?"

"As I was of him, Amos. I had a feeling that he was an important cog in this infernal engine of theirs. One watched the other."

"The Eagle and the Serpent," smiled Juan. "In eternal grapple."

"One durst not release the other for fear of being destroyed."

"You will forgive me if I take the guise of the nobler creature and leave to you the role of serpent."

"I've been called worse."

"Perhaps I can help you understand," said Juan, turning to me. "I assume you know something of our religion; Professor Navarro must have told you about it, even just to aid you in hunting us."

At the mention of poor Teo, I swallowed again. Rage and terror rose tangled within me.

Juan continued.

"Ours is an old, a very old religion, predating your Christianity by millennia. It is said that our ancestors brought it down out of the north, and out of Asia before that in dim ages past. It passed down through the different cultures of the aeons—the Olmec, the Maya, the Toltec, and the Teotihuacano—the names and sculpted faces changing, melting one into another through time like clay in the sculptor's hands, always different yet always the same, always that same basic clay of Truth.

"And yet we nearly lost the Old Faith, when the *pinches conquistadores* came. They were canny, those old Spaniards; they knew how to destroy, but they also knew how to steal. And they stole our gods and put new names on them and stripped them of power. Perhaps you know of the so-called Virgin of Guadalupe—actually our own beautiful, brown-skinned Tonantzin, draped in your Christian rags. Or San Andrés Tecolotzán, Saint Andrew of the Place of Owls. For example."

I could have ripped that smile from his face.

"But not," Juan continued, "our Lord Tezcatlipoca. He was too strange, too different for even the Spanish priests to capture. For how do you dress a god, a *true* god, in human form? And so Cortés and his butchers shoved the gods' statues down the temple steps and broke them with their massy hammers, and put our priests to the sword. But just as they could not cast the Smoking Mirror in their own, syphilitic image, neither could they destroy Him. He is beyond human touch, of so different a substance that men cannot truly see Him, must less destroy Him. Only through the guise of the Smoking Mirror are we granted a glimpse of His Wonder. He is death to see, but deathless. And we are restoring his reign on earth—and you will help us."

"In a pig's eye," I said.

"'And the power and glory shall be thine, now and forever, amen," said Bierce. Beto bent his doughty form toward us and stuck a finger up in front of Bierce's face.

"Fíjate, gusanito," he said in a low, menacing voice. "You do not speak to our Lord Ocelotl like that, *¿me entiendes, Mendez?"*

Juan put a hand on Beto's shoulder; and though the latter looked as if he could break Juan in two, he immediately sat back and gazed at Juan with a deference bordering on fear.

"Cálmate, Beto," said Juan. "Señores Littlefault and Bierce are our honored guests, remember? Señor Bierce has an especial place in the rites to come."

Bierce nodded. I looked from Bierce to Juan, each of whom had locked

eyes with the other and who clearly had some deep, silent understanding between them.

"What does he mean, Bierce?" I said.

"He means that I am to be given the privilege of dying like a warrior for the
honor of their black-glass god."

"Exactly," nodded Juan. "The sacrifice requires a great *guerrero,* a killer of
many men, a champion of many captives. Only such accumulated power will
satisfy *Him.*"

"So you lured us all the way here, just to kill us for your cult?" I said.

Juan shook his head sadly.

"'O foolish people,'" he quoted, "'and without understanding; which have
eyes and see not; which have ears and hear not.'"

"Jeremiah," said Bierce. "Now I am impressed."

Juan ignored him. "It is not for our 'cult,' as you call it, but for the Entrance of the Gods. Each day we feed the gods the blood They need to thrive;
but to bring Them to Earth, a special gift is required. Your Mister Bierce, your
Major Bierce, has lived a long life and absorbed the lives of many. His blood will
set in motion the Great Entrance, and the world will begin its new, glorious
Sixth Age."

"'World without end, amen,'" said Bierce. Beto looked as if he were about
to pounce on Bierce, but Juan again put a restraining hand on his shoulder.
Still, even Juan looked annoyed at Bierce's levity.

"You do not take this seriously," Juan said, "but you will. Soon."

And he sat back and would say no more.

"Bierce," I said softly. "Bierce, I—I don't know where to begin."

Bierce stared out into space.

"I know, Amos, I know. And again, I am deeply sorry. My intent was never, ever to put you in any danger—or any more than I thought we could over-
come together. But it was vital that Juan and his confederates not suspect that
we were honing in on their fountainhead. I did not suspect Juan at all until Ojinaga, when I chanced to take a sip from his bottle of 'tequila'—that bottle he
kept so closely to himself, you will recall. It was water, Amos, just water. I had
to ask myself why Juan would pretend to drink; and, further, pretend to be inebriated. Obviously he intended to keep a clear head whilst yours became
muddled."

I noticed that Bierce exempted himself from the legion of the drunk; but
let it pass.

"The unfortunate Teobaldo clarified this deceit further, when he told us that the Eagle-knights were teetotalers. I expect it's a rare *mexicano* who never touches alcohol. Then there was that nasty business in San Andrés. It was clear to me, as it was to you, that Juan had put you in the hands of Don Máximo's gang, thinking that you would never survive them."

"He little counted on your bravery, or that of the townsfolk," I said. "Thank you again, Bierce."

He squirmed a little in his bonds and looked away.

"Saved you then and again in that alley, just to lead you to the pyramid and the slaughterer's knife."

"You couldn't have known that Juan would have that powder. It must be that same narcotic the Aztecs used to drug their sacrifices."

"My own thoughts exactly. They have researched their roles as thoroughly as Teo did. He, too, learned of the fake 'Juan,' just before his death."

"That telegram . . ." I said, remembering the paper Bierce had picked up after Teo's apartment had been ransacked.

Bierce nodded.

"That telegram. The real Juan's family wrote to Teo, asking him where he was; this a couple weeks after our 'Juan' had supposedly departed for home. You will remember that he left us at the train station—"

"—before Teo could see that he was an imposter," I finished the thought. The drug Juan had blown in our faces was wearing off; but in its place was a confusion that almost made me dizzy. That this "Juan," whoever or whatever he might be, had deceived us—me—for the past couple of months was disturbing enough; but that Bierce had allowed it to go on hit me more than I could say. I sought to distance myself from that hurt.

"And what of Villa?" I said. "And Don Máximo, Huerta, and Bendiga?"

At mention of the last name Juan and his men turned as one to glare at me.

"Lord Águilar was a great loss to us," Juan said in a hard voice. "He was an adept, a prince among the Eagle-knights. But he sits by the throne of Tonatiu now, and his death at your hands will only serve to make your soul a more worthy sacrifice.

"As for *Pancho* Villa"—this said with a derisive snap of the fingers—"just another blunt tool to further our conquest. Don Máximo? A good captain, but replaceable. *El Presidente* himself may outlive his usefulness—the tide is turning against him even now. For did not the Eagle-knights and Jaguar-knights of old continue the fight, even after Moctezuma was slain?"

"*El Borrachito,*" grunted Beto, and he and the others snorted a laugh. "*El Gran Brujo,*" I said, and was rewarded with another sulphurous glare from Juan and his thugs.

"How do you know of *el Gran Brujo?*" said Juan. There was a threat in his voice; but considering the circumstances, I wasn't impressed.

"Professor Navarro had it figured out," I said, "possibly even before you left for the north."

Juan continued scowling at me for another couple beats, but shrugged and looked away as if it were nothing.

"*No vale nada,*" he said. "Navarro paid for his snooping, and even *el Gran Brujo* can be replaced. The power lies with us." He raised a clenched fist and his followers nodded approval. I thought to remind him how few his "us" were at this point—the five of them in the truck, perhaps a couple more in the city—but thought better of it. I knew that they had recruited far and wide, and that many of their "knights" probably still held positions in the various armies sweeping across Mexico. Our hope was that we had so hollowed out the center of their organization badly enough that the rest would ultimately fall apart. That we very likely would not live to see that dissolution made it a bittersweet hope, but a hope nonetheless.

All the while the truck had been bumping and jostling its growling way through the night. I noticed that the floor of the truck had been tilted for a while past; we were headed uphill and, from the distance traversed, far uphill. It was still black as pitch outside, and now it was becoming colder. Were we on a mountain? I hugged myself together as best as I might to stay warm. It was poor commons. I looked to Bierce and saw that he was sitting back, eyes closed, rocking softly with the motions of the truck. Asleep? Trance? Dead? Something inside me cautioned me against waking him. *Necesita su fuerza,* said a voice inside me—he will need his strength. Was I thinking in Spanish now? We had been there long enough that it was possible. But something in the accent of that quiet voice told me that it wasn't mine. Posada, I thought. Out of the night, out of the depths of my consciousness and as if from a great distance, came the reply:

Vaya con Dios

Go with God. If I could have believed in a god at that moment, after all we had been through, I would have been a devout man indeed. Instead I believed in the friendship of a dead artist, and that buoyed me up. *Y contigo, tambien,* I thought into the silence.

How long we rattled over that washboard of a road, I do not know; but when we at last came to a halt, and the monotony of the motor ceased, the only sound was a cold wind blowing.

Without a word Juan and his minions arose. One threw down the gate of the truck. Two of them grabbed Bierce and me and set us on our feet outside. As they bent to undo the bindings on our legs, I looked around. We were on a vast, tilting slope. To our right it soared up, black, naked, rocky earth, into a starry sky. At the very edge of space the mountain was highlighted with pale snows that glittered in the starlight; and above that, smoke rolled out of the peak in dim, muscular clouds to thwart the constellations. On our left the slope plunged down hundreds, thousands of feet until it vanished in a furred darkness of pine forest. Below that, a league or more, the slope met the floor of a valley, many miles wide and wider still in length. Far across the valley was a lacy grid stitched in lights—a city. Mexico City. It made me dizzy just to think that we were so high up; it reduced that busy world to just a patch of frost. Through my pain, weakness, and drug-addled brain, I estimated that we were at least twenty miles away from it and perhaps two miles above. Beyond the city and ringing the valley were mountains, no doubt fellows of the mountain where we now stood, black against the deep blue of night.

"*Ven.*"

Juan stood before us holding a long parcel wrapped in fabric of many-colored cotton. He beckoned to us and the other Eagle-knights took us by the arms and led us around the truck. My left arm pulsed with pain at their touch. I turned my attention to the ground so as not to trip, and saw the dirt track we were on, little more than a pair of faint ruts running parallel along the side of the mountain. The air was cold, piercingly cold, and so clear that the stars, just above us, seemed to throw out shadows at our feet in shades of blue.

We walked that narrow, desperate track around the curve of the mountain. The cold was so intense that I even took comfort from the warmth of my captor's body by my side. Bierce walked ahead of me, and I could see his back heaving as he struggled to get the thin air into his lungs. It was a struggle for me, and I ached to think of his battered lungs straining to draw it in. Yet he walked on and held his head up. I recalled a scrap of poetry:

My head is bloodied but unbowed.

Bierce, I'm sure, would have scoffed at such rank sentimentality; but he was the very picture of such defiance. His head of white hair, tousled in the cold wind, rose above the pates of his warders, and his very posture was a rebuke to their cruelty.

On we trudged. I looked up again at the peak of the mountain far above us, the clouds of smoke pouring up from it in an endless river. Juan caught my glance.

"Popocatépetl," he said. "'Smoking Mountain'—is it not beautiful? And yet more lovely is the sleeping maiden he watches over, Lady Ixtaccíhautl." Juan waved out at the darkness falling away to our left and I could just see a long, heaving ridge of white stretching away towards the north. Even as I looked I thought it grew clearer, the pristine blue snows of the peaks paling toward white beneath the skies. I looked ahead and saw that the sky was less dark there as well. Dawn was not far away. I did not take this as a good omen.

Two lesser peaks stood silhouetted against the heavens before us. Out captors led us toward them, and I saw that one was a natural hillock that had been shaped by human hands into a crude pyramid. Stone steps let up to the peak, where a lone post stood stark against the stars. Further up the mountain to our right was a smaller structure, but higher than the other by virtue of its position nearer the mountain's peak. It was only three tall steps high and circular in shape, like a stack of millstones. But there were no mills here; only five killers, their captives, the mountains, and the wind. And soon, the sun. In a flash I remembered where I had seen such a structure. In one of Teo's books on the Aztecs, the gladiator's stone to which the captive warriors were bound to fight their final battle.

"No!"

I struggled with my guards, but they tightened their grip upon me. The one on the left grabbed my left forearm and the pain dropped me to my knees. Bierce was led by Juan and the other two thugs up the slope to the millstone structure. Halfway there Bierce stumbled and he, too, went to his knees. His guards reached down to grab him again; but Juan, who had turned around at Bierce's fall, said something that was lost as cold vapor on the wind. Bierce's guards stood away from him. Waited. At last Ambrose Bierce, Civil War hero, champion of the just and nemesis of uncounted threats, supernatural and otherwise, put one foot to the earth and pushed himself from the dirt one final time before his last battle. With unspoken respect, his guards stood back and let him walk the last few yards alone.

"Bierce."

Tears ran down my face. One of my guards grinned down at me.

"Don't worry," he said in Spanish. "Your turn to honor the gods is coming." He threw a glance up at the post atop the crude pyramid. I had seen one of these, too, in Teo's books—the stone over which the sacrifice was stretched to offer his heart to the sun.

I should have been terrified, but I was not. Not to give myself airs of nobility and bravery; rather, I was so devastated by the thought of my mentor, my teacher, guardian—my friend—Ambrose Gwinnett Bierce, going to a lonely and brutal death that I did not care what fate awaited me. I looked to the paling sky for succor, as if the black gods of chance and circumstance could offer me some escape or solution to this horror.

And there, riding the air in a high arc, was an eagle. As it wheeled above me, its outspread wings caught the glow of the rising sun that was still denied to us below, and I suddenly knew why such dark birds were dubbed golden. Was it "my eagle"? Was this my companion from the windy skies of Texas, dark against the evenings of San Andrés Tecolotzán and Mexico City? It leaned and dipped into a sharper curve, dropped out of the zone of sun and became black shade once more.

"AYA!"

I looked back up the slope. Bierce stood atop the gladiator-stone while one of his guards tied a rope to his ankle. The other guard received Bierce's coat, folded it neatly, and carried it off the platform. Bierce stood in his shirtsleeves, vest, and trousers, his body working to suck in the attenuated air. Beyond him, Juan stood apart, arms thrown up to the heavens. He called forth in a language I did not know, a language old when Cortés first stepped upon that Mexican beach. Yet I knew it; somehow, I understood it.

> The earth shakes; the Mexica begins his song:
> He makes the Eagle and Jaguar dance with him!
> Come to see the Huexotzinca:
> On the dais of the Eagle he shouts out,
> Loudly cries the Mexica!

In response the guards, Bierce's and mine together, raised their fists in salute. More worrisome, the very mountain beneath our feet shivered.

> The battlefield is the place
> Where one toasts the divine liquor of war,
> Where are stained red the divine eagle,
> Where the jaguars howl!

Juan crossed his arms before him, grabbed his shirt, and tore it upwards off his torso. No eagle tattoo, I thought desperately, no eagle tattoo at all upon his arms! He unbuckled his pants and let them drop to his ankles; and I saw upon his broad, brown back the bracketed spots of the jaguar. Muscles rippled and chased one another beneath the skin, making the spots dance. With every piece of clothing he shed, Juan grew. He stood upright and out of his pants and shoes, naked to the skies, growing larger as he shed the guise of a man: the Jaguar-knight stood revealed. Juan's odd downturned smile, the cleft in his upper lip—I saw it now. The "jaguar smile" Teo had pointed out in numerous pre-Colombian works; the split chops and fang-ringed maw of the jungle's greatest predator. Juan raised spotted arms to the black sky and howled in triumph.

The other knights stepped back from the stone quickly, leaving Bierce alone to face the thing. To call it a man would be inaccurate; but to call it a jaguar, any kind of creature at all, in fact, would be wrong, too. It was neither man nor beast, nor was it even an amalgam of both. It was fake, somehow, a counterfeit of something earthly as seen through the eyes of the Unnamable. It was nothing from this world—it hurt my eyes just to gaze at it. The sky behind it glistened and flashed like black glass. The stars blinked out in the growing light, but above the Jaguar-knight all was an obsidian blackness. The thing bent to the bundle it—Juan—had carried up the mountain, and pulled forth two long, wedge-shaped clubs. One it tossed to Bierce. Even at that remove I could see it was edged with soft white that fluttered as the macahuitl sailed through the air. The club was edged with feathers, as per the ancient rite. Bierce caught it easily; the handle slapped into his palm. The jaguar-thing whirled its own club and razor-edged obsidian flashed starlight like mad comets. It advanced upon Bierce. Even standing atop the gladiator-stone, Bierce had to look up into its face. But he never flinched, never backed away. By contrast, the guards were cowering back from the thing and half sliding down the slope in their haste.

The earth muttered. Scree and loose gravel skittered down the mountain-side. High above, smoke from the volcano lifted orange and salmon-pink in the new sunlight. It was pouring out of the volcano now in tumbling volumes and burgeoning fists of vapor. Near at hand a figure stepped before me. It was one of my own captors. Now he stood before me attired in a long red robe embroidered in cavorting figures of black. His hair was matted in long snaking locks down his shoulders and back. Even in the thin air, I could smell the blood worked into it. Black soot lay in broad bands across his face, making his staring eyes more terrible still. His arms hung bare from the robe, and in his right hand he held an obsidian knife. He breathed hard, open-mouthed, as if from exertion or ecstasy.

"Here is glory," he chanted in the Aztec tongue,

> In war songs
> In war flowers
> The sacred water
> The sacred fire
> Are refreshed with tassels of blood

He nodded at the other guard and the two of them began dragging me toward the hill-pyramid. I panted in terror, in oxygen-starved panic, my feet gouging uselessly at the volcanic sand beneath me. Looking over my shoulder, I saw the Juan/Jaguar-thing circling the gladiator-stone, lashing out with its club in swift, short arcs. Bierce turned with it and parried the thing's strokes—but not all of them. Already there were tatters hanging from his sleeves and red splashed on his shirt, pants, on the merciless stone. My left-hand captor gripped my left arm and I gasped at the pain. The other thrust clay flutes into my hands and twisted until the flutes broke and dropped in pieces onto the steps. The chosen prince had had his year of pleasure; now he must render up his heart to the Divine.

I threw my head back to scream—and saw the eagle again. Its curving flight had brought it down, down, to within a score of feet above us. We were halfway up the pyramid when it folded it powerful wings and went into a stoop—straight at us. Like an arrow it shot from out of the sky, talons spread wide, and crashed into the guard-priest on my right. He never saw it coming. The razor-pointed talons struck him full in the face, sank deep into his eyes. The shock of the blow sent him stumbling back. He gasped as if he would draw in the whole of the sky; but the eagle never loosened its grip. The bird's head darted down again and again, and tore strips of flesh and hair from the man's head. Golden wings hammered at him.

For several moments both the other guard and I stared in shock. Then I saw the obsidian knife the priest had dropped. I grabbed it up with both hands and slashed sideways. It caught the guard's forearm—he roared and let go of me. Blood appeared in a thin line on his arm, then blossomed and ran. He swore, grabbed at his arm with his good hand, and staggered back. I didn't wait for an invitation; I lit into him with the obsidian knife, slashing and tearing into his chest and belly before his backward steps found the edge of the stair and he toppled back and down and down in sickening thuds and crunches.

Turning back to the priest I steeled myself for the next fight. But his struggle was over. The eagle was just disengaging itself from the man's head, now a bloody ruin. When the eagle finally let go, the priest slumped back upon the stairway like a boneless doll. His head lay over one step and a steady stream of blood ran down it and raced in black rivulets toward the next step.

Bierce. Clutching the knife between my knees, I sawed the bonds at my wrists until they parted. I looked to the gladiator-stone, now at eye-level to me, and Bierce still stood atop it, bloody but unbowed. He matched blows and turns with the Juan-thing; but he was moving more slowly. His mouth hung open; he breathed in long, tortured brays I could hear above the wind. Without thinking I put my left hand down to push myself up off the stone step—and immediately regretted it. Pain flashed up my arm into my shoulder and stole all strength from my body. Swearing and praying, I heaved myself up with my right arm and began falling, stumbling, sliding down the pyramid steps.

"Bierce!"

The Thing looked at me. Its eyes—that same howling emptiness I had seen in Huerta's eyes, the same I see in nightmares to this day. It must have seen that its henchmen were dead or useless. Yet it *smiled,* swung the macahuitl in a flashing black arc and moved toward Bierce. Bierce stood leaning heavily on his knees *(four more steps,* I thought, I pleaded, *three more steps).* He panted and gasped, but he gave no ground. He glared back at the Thing. *Just two more steps*—I kicked the fallen guard's body out of my way. The Aztec sword was a shimmering wheel of death, an arabesque—the Jaguar-thing ducked and wove and danced toward Ambrose Bierce, and all the while the obsidian blades whistled and shrieked as they described lethal curves in the air.

One more step—and solid ground. I gathered my wounded arm to me, now seeping blood through my sleeve, and ran up the slope. I had no gun, no knife, not even the obsidian blade I had taken from the priest. I had nothing but my bare hands, but I would be damned if I would surrender Bierce to that Thing unchallenged. I pounded up the slope, but the ground slipped from under me in hissing cascades of black powder. I gained two feet and lost one. It was like running in water, in a nightmare. The macahuitl came flying out of the jaguar's dance and swept toward Bierce's head. At the last moment he held up his own club—his nearly useless club, edged with down—and deflected the blow. But the obsidian shore through Bierce's weapon as if it were butter. Half of it fell away to clatter on the platform. Bierce looked at it as if he had never seen it before—the Thing's club had cut it cleanly away at an angle, leaving Bierce with a short length of board cut into a point. Huffing clouds of vapor into the air, the Thing stood back and grinned. It lowered its own macahuitl and waited. Bierce, alone, wounded, fighting for breath, held the broken club before him.

"Dammit!"

I slipped to my knees again pushed myself up again. Again. Twenty feet to get to Bierce's side, but it might as well have been a mile. And then what? Die at his side? I didn't even consider it. My feet dug into the dirt; my good hand tore at it. And it all slipped away beneath me. I dared a look up and saw the Thing raising its macahuitl, closing in for the coup de grâce. Bierce watched, waited—and just as the Thing rose up to strike, Bierce spread his arms wide and began to sing. Or call, or whistle; a soft, gentle, flowing, rippling invitation. I stopped dead in my tracks. The Thing must have been as nonplussed as I, for it, too, stopped, deadly club held high against the obsidian sky. For there could be no doubt now; the sky had turned an unearthly black, an emptiness from between the lonely stars through which, with the end of the ceremony— with just the last of the blood of Ambrose Bierce—Lord Tezcatlipoca and His manifestations would rush and seal the fate of the world.

But now there were flickering lights against that unholy darkness. Bierce continued his chant, his call, and in response the lights swept down in clouds— birds, hundreds of them, small and bright. They came from all points of the compass; they whistled and whispered past me, down the mountain, up the mountain, from valley, scree and forest. They swooped toward Bierce and his nemesis. At the last moment they rushed like a storm upon the Jaguar-knight and enveloped him in a streaking, woven skein. The Thing broke from its stupor, howled defiance, and swung its macahuitl and its obsidian claws. But the birds banked and wheeled and came 'round him again, in faultless patterns. Again and again the Jaguar-knight slashed at them, but all his blows fell between the flight of the birds. They swarmed him and dazzled him; and when Bierce finally stopped his invocation and dropped his hands, the flock arced as one and raced into the growing dawn.

And what they revealed when they left was no otherworldly giant wearing the black stains of the jaguar. Instead, it was a man, just a man; Juan Romero, white-eyed and mazed, his club hanging loosely from his hand. And before he could regain his senses or his demon's shape, Bierce gripped his own abbreviated weapon in both hands, stepped forward, and drove the point of it up and into Juan's belly. Juan bent to the blow—a short *"uh!"* escaped his mouth. He hung there head down as if bowing to his opponent. Bierce took the obsidian-edged macahuitl from Juan's nerveless hands, and with one wide, arcing swing, swept Juan's head from his shoulders. The head bounced down the scree, followed by a swarm of pebbles, down and down the mountain into darkness. The headless body slowly tipped back and crunched to the ground. Bierce, panting, swung the macahuitl one last time to sever the cord around his ankle. Then he tossed the weapon clattering to the ground and sank down upon the stone.

I somehow found my footing and lumbered up the last yards to Bierce's side.

"Bierce," I gasped, and could say no more. He was seated upon the middle level of the gladiator-stone, leaning back upon the upper level. His hands, streaked and spotted with blood, lay inert in his lap. In short, abrupt spasms, his chest worked to draw in the meager air. His mouth hung open and he stared out across the airy heights. The "red tassels of blood" lay all over him. Rivulets of it ran down his arms; a gash in his face pulsed red streams down his cheek and neck. No one wound looked mortal; but taken together they were ghastly and demanded attention. I climbed up the platform and collapsed next to him.

"Bierce," I said again. "I—how are you?"

It was the stupidest thing in the world to say, but my wearied brain could come up with nothing else. Bierce must have appreciated the absurdity of it, for he coughed out a laugh and said, "Just—peachy."

"How did you"—I panted—"the jaguar-knight?"

"Nature," he gasped. "Not . . . mocked."

I inched closer to him. I had some idea of stanching his wounds, but where to start? When I reached up just to pull his torn shirt over his arm, he stopped me.

"Don't."

I let my hand drop. We both looked out over the steep pitch of the mountainside, over the dark pine forests below, down leagues of blue air and the lights of distant towns waking up, to mountains like a purple wall against the glowing face of dawn. It felt good just to sit, to breathe. But even as I thought this, the chill of the air gripped me. My body was slowing down. I began to shiver uncontrollably. When I felt Bierce shift beside me, I looked over at him. He had hitched himself to his right and was reaching under the tatters of his shirt. Just in the past five minutes he had shrunk and grown pale. His hands shook as if with palsy, and I realized both that he had little time left, and that there was nothing I could do about it. I looked back out at the growing day as my throat locked up and tears coursed down my face.

"Here," gasped Bierce. Like a magician he pulled a snake from under his shirt. Not a snake—his money-belt. When he had it clear of his pants he let it fall between us. It hit the stone with a clash of coins.

"'Nough to . . . you live," he managed between short breaths. With trembling hands I picked it up and set it on my own lap. He slumped back against the platform and said, "Cleared off." I looked up, too, and yes, that evil black stain had gone from the sky. One star shown overhead; all around it the heavens were paling as the curtain came up on a new day. Bierce eased his head forward and his face was flushed with ruddy, golden color. A smile spread slowly beneath his moustache.

"Day," he said. "Sun."

Or was it "son"? In those last moments, had Ambrose Bierce's lost, golden son come to take his father home? I'd like to think this was so. Of all the ghosts we had seen, Day's was the one he had been denied, and the one he had most wished to see. I looked the way he was looking and saw a head of fiery rays lift in blinding glory over the far mountain-wall. When I looked back at Bierce, his chin had settled down upon his chest. He was gone.

4.

I did what one always does in such situations: I felt for his pulse, his breath, the sunken murmur of his heart. But all was still in that great, bony house. The cold wind played with his white locks and tossed the torn remnants of his shirt. I sat and shivered and looked at him a long while as the sun climbed into the winter sky and revealed the wild, beautiful, tragic land of Mexico all around. I felt its warmth upon me, but I shivered nonetheless. I felt as if I would always be cold.

But go on we must, and go on I finally did. What woke me from my stupor, and probably saved me from freezing, was something simple yet profound, in its way. A shadow, swift as thought, passed across my eyes. Shielding my sight from the glare of the sun, I looked up. Far above me, farther than I thought possible, was a great bird of prey. It wheeled upon the hidden winds of upper space, flashed a blade of sunlight—and disappeared. I kept staring at where it had vanished until a particularly violent spasm of shivering shook me.

It really was cold there. We were below the snowline, but not that far. And I was certain that, as on that awful night in the *colonia,* I was going into shock. The prospect of this was serious: if I became disabled up there, exposed to the elements on that mountain, I would probably join Ambrose Bierce sooner than I wanted. I looked back at him.

"Still dead, I see," I stuttered out. "St-stubborn old buzzard."

I pulled the remnants of his shirt around him as best as I was able. God, I thought, *so many wounds.* It was a wonder he had been able even to stand up-right. He looked as though he would simply fall apart if I tried to lift him. And that led to the thought: how was I to get his body back down the mountain? I could not take it now; I'd be lucky to get off that volcano myself. But perhaps I could come back later with help. When I had done all I could to make him look respectable, I shouldered the money-belt and staggered to my feet.

"Farewell, Bierce," I said. "I—" And the words dried up in my throat. I looked around at the tired, fallen old man, the mighty volcano at our back, the dawn spreading like a flood of gold over the land below, and could add nothing to the scene that wouldn't feel sacrilegious. We had won—*he* had won. The story ends. I reached down and touched his shoulder one last time. Then I turned and walked down the slope.

On the way I found Bierce's jacket where the Eagle-knights had dropped it. That reminded me of the two men who had run. Had they taken the truck and driven off? Worse, were they lying in wait in some mountain ravine to slaughter me? I looked around again, but could see no one. But for the knights by the pyramid, Bierce, and "Juan," sprawled naked and headless across the scree, the scene was empty. I briefly thought of retrieving the macahuitl—the one with the volcanic glass edges—but recognized that even if I had it, I was in no shape to engage in a fight. Really, the thing I wanted most just then was warmth; so I put Bierce's jacket on over my own. I wormed my right arm in and hooked the jacket over my left shoulder so that I wouldn't have to put that arm through the sleeve. It was a clumsy arrangement, made more ridiculous by the disparity in Bierce's height and my own. The coat hung on me like a black tent. But it did offer warmth. I nodded my thanks to Bierce. At that distance he appeared to be dozing, dreaming perhaps, of good California wine and cigars under the redwoods. I hoped so, anyway.

When I had made my slow way down the track and around the curve of the mountain, I saw with relief that the truck was still there. Unless those two run-aways were hiding in it; or maybe they had been so panicked in their flight that they had forgotten it completely. At this point a novelist might say that I "approached it warily." I did not. I was so damned cold and so tired and so drained of emotion that I wound't have cared if the whole Federal Army had sprung out of that truck.

Nobody did. It was sitting just as we had left it however long ago. An hour? Two hours? Fifteen minutes? I looked back to judge the height of the sun, and as I did so the entire mountainside gave an enormous heave. Thunder cracked below the earth; smoke cascaded out of Popocatéptl, dyed an angry orange in the sunlight. Pebbles, sand, and rock rattled and bounded down the slope all around me. I steadied myself against the truck with my good arm and waited for whatever was coming. A long shadow appeared on the incline beside the pyramid-hill and gladiator-stone where Bierce still sat. It deepened, it widened. It gaped. With another fearful rumble, the mountain shrugged its titanic shoulders and swallowed the entire slope where Bierce had been reclining only a second before. The hill, the steps, the gladiator-stone, Ambrose Gwinnett Bierce—my mentor, my friend—all slid into that chasm and vanished. There was a gout of sulphurous smoke, the hiss of falling sand—then nothing. It was as if it all had never happened. Ambrose Bierce had really and truly vanished.

I blinked and turned back to the truck. The driver's side door was still open and I leaned in to find the crank. There it was, just under the seat. I adjusted the choke, carried the crank to the front of the truck, and inserted it beneath the radiator. I had done this a hundred times, but never, of course, in such a state. If I judged it wrong, the crank would kick back and break my arm—my right arm, my one good arm. Then where would I be? Walking God knew how many miles back down to some salvation that might not even exist, both arms hanging as useless as salamis. After I got the crank situated, I stood back up and took several deep breaths.

"Not going . . . start itself," I chided myself. All right, Littlefault—*manos a la obra.* I crouched before the engine and braced my knee against the bumper and gripped the crank. One good turn—nothing. *One good turn deserves a worse one,* said a smug, rasping voice in my ear. Shut up, Bierce. Grip, brace, and turn. The engine coughed, banged, and started. I sat on the bumper and leaned back against the radiator. Even that little exertion had set me back. When I had regained some balance and strength, I trudged back to the cab, tossed the crank in, and yanked myself in after it. I left the door open—I couldn't be bothered with it. Maneuvering the pedals, wheel, and gearshift with my three sound limbs, I managed to get the machine moving.

Now came the tricky part. The truck was pointed east, toward the scene of our fight. I needed to go the other way. And the track upon which the truck rode was not wide enough to turn around. I slowed the vehicle to a stop and looked ahead, looked behind. There, back the way we had come—was it a little wider there? There appeared to be a gorge up the slope from the track a hundred feet behind me, something like a small bay. If I could back into it, I could possibly turn the truck around.

I worked the shift and the pedals again. When I felt the gears grab the reverse drive, I took a firm hold upon the wheel and, eyes upon the small, round rearview mirrors on either hand, eased my foot off the clutch. Slowly, so pathetically slowly . . . The truck crept back down the road. I watched one mirror and the next. In one, the gray shape of the mountain; in the other, space and a prospect of lands thousands of feet below, still lost in the shadow of night. I thanked God and the angels that I hadn't had to do this in the dark. No doubt I would have ended up far below in the crown of some pine tree.

Slowly, now, Amos, slowly. The bay in the mountainside came closer. At last I was able to turn the wheel and snug the rear end of the truck into the bay. When the rear end connected with the mountain, I nearly stalled the truck. My feet crushed the brake and clutch pedals to the floor. After a nerve-wracking shudder, the truck's engine regained its rhythm. Deep, shaking breath. I was looking straight out now over the pitch of the mountain; the miles-long ridge of Ixtaccíhuatl, once so ghostly in the night, now blazed silver in the new sun. Away below and to its left was Mexico City in its broad valley. A city of thousands, the seat of a country at war—from that height, just a collection of children's blocks. I fixed it in my mind, eased the truck back into gear again, and turned it onto the road leading off the mountain.

I will not tire the reader with further details of that ride. Much of it was a monotony that faded from my memory once it was over anyway. But once I awoke, unaware that I had even fallen asleep. I was lying across the wheel of the truck and my chest hurt. The truck was canted at an odd angle to the right, and there was no sound from the motor. I sat back, massaged my chest, looked around. Through the windscreen I could see a ditch stretching away before me. The right front wheel of the truck was in it, apparently. Only dumb luck had kept me from pulling the same stunt up where there was no ditch, only the long fall off the mountain. Looking around me more, I saw that I was in a fairly level region of woods and fields. How long had I been driving? And how long had I been unconscious? And who was this anyway, staring in through the driver's side window? He looked in at me, brown face creased with concern. A straw hat, more holes than straw, a champion of a silver mustache, dark eyes as tilted as a Chinaman's.

"*¿Está herrido, Señor?*"

My mind fumbled through its chambers and drawers. Spanish—"Are you hurt, mister?" I could have laughed—perhaps I did, for the good man drew away slightly from me. I got a glimpse of a denim barn-jacket and canvas pants, all decorated with the refuse of a barnyard. Clearing my throat and blinking away the dust of the road, I said, "*Sí, gracias*. But more than anything I need to get my truck on the road." My Spanish must have been sufficient, for the man, a farmer no doubt, nodded once and withdrew. In another moment he reappeared with two gigantic oxen, drawing a deep cart on solid, six-foot diameter wooden wheels. The farmer clacked and muttered endearments to his beasts. Man, oxen, and cart all moved to a point down the road just beyond my fallen vehicle. The farmer took a coil of rope from the cart and tied one end to the truck's bumper. The rest he played out until he got back to the oxen's yoke, to which he tied the other end. With another whispered word of encouragement to his beasts, he led them down the road. The line went taut—the truck lurched. I turned the wheel to the left and the truck lifted out of the ditch. The farmer led his little parade on for a few yards further down the road, no doubt to make sure that *ese gringo estupido* wouldn't get himself stuck again; then halted the oxen and undid the rope. After coiling the rope over his arm and undoing it from the truck's bumper, he tipped his hat and began walking away.

"*¡Espere!*" I cried. "*Por favor.*"

The man stopped, looked back at me and tilted his head. *What now?* I could almost hear him thinking. I got out of the truck and limped to the front, crank in hand.

"One more favor, if you please," I said in my most careful Spanish. "The crank . . . ?" I held it out to him. He looked at my helpless left arm and smiled.

"*Cómo no, señor.*"

He squatted down to seat the crank in its place while I went back to prepare the engine. His face peeked around the radiator: "*¿Listo?*"

I nodded. He gave the crank one mighty whirl and the truck roared to life. When he came around the truck to return the crank, I dug into Bierce's money-belt and handed him a $20 gold piece. He stared at it in amazement; sunlight off the coin gave his face a golden glow. But he shook his head and handed me back the coin.

"No, I can't, señor. *Gracias, pero . . .*"

I put the coin back on his palm and closed his fingers over it.

"*Sí,*" I said. "Yes, you can."

He doffed his miserable hat and returned to the cart with a happy trot. When he got back to his oxen, the farmer showed them the gold coin in his hand and prattled to them in Náhuatl. Apparently, there still remained enough glamor in me from our adventure up on the mountain such that I was able to understand what he told them.

"Xóchitl," he said, patting their steaming noses, "Guerrero—look. That good man just paid for a new shed for you and shoes for the niños! May Our Lady bless him!" This last sentence was said in reverent Spanish, and I caught the word *bendiga*—"bless"—among the rest.

Bendiga—he and Juan and Huerta and all the rest—they got it all wrong, I thought. Here was the real Aztec, tending his maize, feeding his family, following his lowing beasts down the furrows of the centuries. Bendiga and his ilk had carefully chosen only those aspects of their Mexica ancestors—the bloody rituals, the dark magic of conquest—that suited their lower natures and ignored the every day beauty of life. The burly farmer had named his ox "Xóchitl"—"flower," in the Náhua tongue. Would Juan Romero ever have thought to name a gentle, lumbering creature such as that "Flower"? Never in a million years. I watched the farmer and his oxen and his creaking cart wobble down the road and away, and smiled.

PART V

VOLVER

I see eagles tigers I see glory
But I am sad leaving the friendship
That we have here

—Aztec poem

1.

I arrived at Mexico City in late morning. But for Reforma, the Zócalo, and a few other major streets, I still did not know the city well; but I did at least remember where the hospital was. The truck brought me safely there, gave one petulant kick, and died. I left it where it sat; and when I emerged from the hospital a day later, it was gone.

Doctor Muñoz was gone too, off to his more illustrious patients. But Dr. Salazar was in attendance. I can't say that he was happy to see me; in fact, he was cross with me for pulling several of the stitches Dr. Muñoz had so carefully used to put my arm back together. But he was a professional, and recognizing that I was also suffering from exposure, shock, and God knew what-all else, he took pity on me and did his best to repair my battered body.

His work was excellent. I was in good enough shape to walk out of the hospital by the next day, only to find, as I mentioned before, that the Eagle-knights' truck was gone. Whether it had been stolen or confiscated by the police, I never learned. For all I knew it had already been stolen when we were driven up the mountain aboard it. I hailed one of the ubiquitous taxis and gave the driver the address of the late Teobaldo Navarro.

I had nowhere else to go. Bierce, Teo, Deliah, and her brood were all gone in one way or another. But once I got to the professor's rooms, I knew that I couldn't stay. The place was alive with ghosts; one tall, stern one in particular. Everywhere I looked in that place I caught him smoking or reading or stroking Teo's white cat, or just staring at me with that inimitable mixture of exasperation and amusement. Amos, for the love of God, what *were* you thinking? After only a couple of hours there I could stand it no longer. Bierce had left me with more than enough to care for myself; so I gathered what meager belongings of mine and Bierce's that remained and dragged them back down to the street. A cab carried me to the Hotel Imperial, site of my trysts with the beautiful Mrs. Gadbury, and there I stayed on Bierce's dime until I could secure rooms of my own.

It turned out that I was in greater need of rest than either I or the doctor had known. Once I was ensconced in my new rooms—a humble but clean *departamiento* near to the Alameda—I collapsed and did not go out for days. My arm, despite the attentions of Drs. Muñoz and Salazar, still ached deeply and was good for little. More than that, though, I had sustained a heavy blow to my soul that would need time and quiet to mend. I had, fortunately, secured the services of a neighbor's son to fetch me food for a small allowance. This allowed me to stay hidden in my rooms—which I did, nursing my wounds both spiritual and physical.

When I did finally work up enough energy and equilibrium to emerge, I did so only for brief walks in the comforting green of the Alameda. The park was free of the dark memories linked to such places as Teo's apartment or the Zócalo and its environs. Even the memory of the frantic search for Deliah's boys in the park was tempered by the thought of her pretty face. And I passed happy hours there watching the *chilangos* at their recreations, or just absorbing the cool green of the trees.

I spent the remainder of March and the whole of April in this fashion. I might have stayed longer except that events beyond the walls of my little sanctum were moving swiftly toward some bloody conclusion.

On April 2, Torreón fell again to Pancho Villa. San Pedro de las Colonias fell immediately after, extending a line straight toward the City. The writing, as they say, was on the wall.

Then, on April 9, Huertista soldiers briefly imprisoned some U.S. sailors in Tampico on the Gulf Coast. The "Tampico Incident," like the "Benton Affair," backfired upon its author. It might have been just another misstep between two nations except that some blockhead of a U.S. naval commander decided that a formal apology wasn't enough. He demanded that the Mexicans fly the U.S. flag over Tampico and officially grovel before the great gringo nation. Diplomacy and bluster and pride went back and forth between Mexico City and Washington until April 21, when the U.S. Atlantic Fleet descended upon Vera Cruz, bombarding and invading the city. Some U.S. Marines and sailors, and some hundreds of Mexican defenders, were killed. We weren't at war with Mexico—not yet, at least—but we had taken Mexico's largest Caribbean port and given Huerta a black eye just when he needed it least.

On the heels of this came "the *Ypiranga* Incident," in which the *Ypiranga,* a German ship loaded with arms for Huerta's armies, attempted to land in Vera Cruz; this in direct defiance of President Wilson's blockade. Needless to say, the U.S. fleet turned them away. Meanwhile, Emilano Zapata and his wild-riding *charros* had taken complete control of the state of Morelos, only a day's ride from the capital. It seemed that General Huerta, bereft of both his overt and occult allies, was losing the entire country. His once-great power was gutted. The capital itself was so far untouched, but for how long? The Jackal was on the ropes, and, as Bierce had pointed out, a cornered jackal is the most dangerous kind. I decided it was time to leave.

I left Mexico City on May 2, taking the train north and praying I could avoid Villa's rampage. One might question my sanity in plunging straight into the heart of the war—no doubt Bierce would have. But it was partly because of Bierce that I chose that route. I detrained in Torreón amidst the same pandemonium we had seen back in February—soldiers getting on and off the trains, the vendors, the smells of cooking meat and fumes from the locomotives, cries of greeting, farewell, confusion. The only difference I could see was the different color of the uniforms on the soldiers: Villa's khaki instead of Huerta's gray. I pushed my way out of the crowds and found a livery stable in a nearby street. I hired a horse and saddle and rode northeast out of the city and into the peace of the countryside.

It was, of course, a deceptive peace. Pockets of *huertista* resistance still lurked in hidden places, and even the victorious Constitutionalists were not above some highway robbery on occasion. But I had bought a new revolver to replace the one Juan's gang had taken from me, and wore it prominently on my hip on a belt well laden with bullets. I may have lost a lot—so very much—in my travels, but I had gained a toughness that would see me through a lot.

It wasn't a long ride, anyway. I came to the main street of San Andrés Tecolotzán just as evening began to deepen. Bells rang lazily from the old whitewashed church; a pig and a chicken ambled down the street together, clucking and grunting the latest gossip. All was as I remembered it, with one important exception: There was no fear there. The shadow cast by the Golón clan was gone, and in its place was a sleepy calm.

Mamá Huitzil's place was just the same, too, but for a black wreath upon the door. Fearing the worst, I knocked on it and called out her name. It was a long, painful minute before my knock was answered; but when it was I was relieved to see the old curandera's wrinkled-apple face again. She was still dressed in black, and something in the added depth of her eyes and wrinkles made me think of winds crossing lonely graveyards.

"Está' muerto, ¿no?"

He's dead, isn't he? Her first words to me. In another situation I might have felt slighted; to have come all that way only to have her ask about the one who was absent. Then again, that was why I was there in the first place; and beyond that, I knew that her words were a statement, not a question. She had known already. The wreath made that clear.

Mamá Huitzil sighed heavily and stared at the ground.

"Come in, Amos, please."

She stepped back and waved me inside. The herb-heavy air was just the same—the drying plants and jars of God-knew-what, all the same. Yet a vitality had gone from it all. Mamá Huitzil walked slowly to her great rattan chair and lowered herself into it. I sat opposite her on a love-seat that had seen better days.

"Forgive my lack of hospitality," she said, passing a hand across her face. "I knew you were coming and I knew the news you bore. And yet, to see you there . . ."

I nodded. I felt that I understood now how soldiers assigned to notify a fellow's family of his death must feel. How she had known about Bierce I didn't ask; but she volunteered it anyway.

"A month ago, early one morning it was, he came back. He was straight and tall—such a beautiful man"—she used the word *lindo*, "beautiful," not *guapo*, more commonly used for "handsome"—"and he smiled down upon me. And then I knew—oh, my heart grew cold. But he reached out and touched my hand and said, 'Don't grieve, my little hummingbird. I am with you always.'"

She stopped, and I saw her produce a handkerchief from some hidden place in her gown and dab at the tears starting in her eyes. With little surprise I saw that the initials "AGB" were embroidered upon it. Almighty God Bierce.

"I knew that what he said was true. I felt it then, and I feel it now. He has a home in my heart." She put her hand to her withered breast and smiled. "But still, to know he will never walk through that door again, never puff up like some *sapo grande* again"—we both laughed. Bierce could indeed puff up like some great frog sometimes. Mamá Huitzil shook her head and looked smiling at her hands.

"He will never touch my hair again, he will never . . ." She shook her head vehemently, as if to negate all the sadness of the world. Her face collapsed in tears and I brushed a few from my own cheeks.

"That was when he died," I said. "When you saw him."

She nodded. "Did he die well, at least?"

"He did. He died like a warrior, like a man, never backing away from his fate."

"What were his last words, *m'hijo?*"

I tried to explain the confusion I had felt over Bierce's last words, but the pun of "sun" and "son" doesn't translate well into the Spanish. But her own knowledge of English stood her well, and her smile returned.

"His boy, his Day, came back to fetch his father. You can believe this or not, if it brings you peace; but I know this."

I nodded. "I felt it was so, but it is good to hear you say it, *abuela*."

She settled in to her chair, staring at a place on the floor. I did the same. I had said what I had come to say and there was nothing more to be said.

Then I remembered. "One moment," I said as I stood up. Mamá looked so alarmed at my rising that I hastened to add, "I will be right back."

I went back out to my horse, which was tethered near the shop. I undid my bag from the cantell of the saddle and carried it back inside.

"This," I said, unstrapping the bag and rooting though it with my one good hand, "is for you." I knew it when I felt it. Carefully, reverently, I took the dark bundle from my bag and unfolded it upon my lap. It was Bierce's jacket, the same one he had worn on that terrible last morning; the same one that had kept me warm all the way off the mountain. I had had it cleaned and repaired—he had not been easy on his clothes, those last days—and now I held it out to Mamá Huitzil.

When she saw what it was, her face lit up from within. Suddenly she was a young muchacha again, plump and wide-eyed and not yet worn thin by the world, and looking with wonder at what Father Christmas had brought her. She held out her small hands and took it from me. She held it as one would hold a baby and cradled it to her breast. Tears of joy coursed down her face.

"Thank you," she said. *"Thank you."*

I stayed only a little longer with her. Despite her entreaties, I wanted to see the Martínez family as well before I left San Andrés. She finally only allowed me to leave after I promised—after I *swore*—that I would return on the morrow and tell her more about her *"Ambrosio lindo."*

It was dark when I rode into the Martínez farm, but it was a gentle dark. They were overjoyed to see me and buried me in hugs, handshakes and questions, and a cup was put in my hand and I was ushered to a seat and it was supper time. Cabrito again, no surprise there, but done to perfection. The Señora beamed as I devoured it. José listened attentively and critically to all I could tell him of the political and military situation, and grew quiet when I recounted (minus a few incredible details) the circumstances of Bierce's death.

"Era un macho," declared José and raised his glass of tequila. *"Un caballero y un amigo. Le echaré de menos."* A gentleman and a friend—I will miss him. We toasted Bierce and sipped tequila. José's reaction to the duplicitous Juan Romero

was no less dramatic, if different in tone. He spat upon the floor and forbade the mention of *"aquel pinche pendejo"* in his house ever again.

We sat up late talking. When we finally tired of it, I was led to my old bedroom. A bittersweet moment: the last time I had been in that room had been with Bierce and Juan, my greatest champion and my greatest enemy, had I but known it. Back then we had been *compañeros,* united, or so I thought, against the forces of chaos and violence. I was glad when sleep came over me and blotted the world from my sight.

I had breakfast with the Martínez family, a hearty farmer's breakfast of cabrito, rice, beans, and tortillas with those good, honest country folk. Then I rode back to Mamá Huitzil's shop and spent the next few hours with her, sipping tea and telling her everything that I could not tell the others. Only she would believe; only she would understand. Despite having to test my knowledge of Spanish to the limit, it was a great relief to me to be able to tell it all without omission or editing. Mamá Huitzil had, of course, dealt with the supernatural herself; and it reassured me immensely when she agreed that the cult was probably broken.

"They did not just need the blood for their gods," she said, taking a sip of her tea. "They needed the belief and support of the people. Since most people did not even know they existed, when their leaders died, their plans disappeared like snow in the summer sun."

I nodded and sipped my own drink.

"I hope so," I said. "I am not in any shape to go fighting them again."

She set down her cup on the side-table. "Let me see that arm."

I couldn't refuse her—it would insult her—but I had little faith that she could help me at all. The wound was already more than two months old, and what was going to heal had probably already begun to do so. But I took my coat off and rolled up my sleeve, and let her hold my arm and squeeze it and mumble over it.

"Wait here," she said. She went into her back room through the curtain, the same room where she had first treated Bierce for his asthma, and returned with a bowl and strips of white linen. She pulled her chair up close to me and removed the bandages from my arm.

"This wound," she said, "was made by *piedra mala,* bad stone. A stone is neither good nor bad until a man or woman makes it so. Your 'Juan Romero' leaked evil from his pores. I can still smell it on you. But this salve will remove it." She placed the bowl on her lap and dipped her finger into it. It was green and lumpy, whatever it was, but smelled soothing—thyme and some wildflower, I think. When she touched her finger to the long loop of scar on my arm, I flinched; but it didn't hurt. In fact, it tingled where she touched me, almost a tickle. As she applied the salve she chanted under her breath. I had heard enough of Náhuatl, the language of the Aztecs and their descendants, to recognize it. But coming from this gentle old soul, it held no terrors. Her chanting became soft singing, and when the wound was all covered she took the strips of linen and wrapped them over and over my arm so gently that I did not even feel them. When she was done, she sat back.

"*En fin,*" she said. "It should start feeling better soon."

I gave my arm a tentative flex and was happily surprised at its renewed strength and flexibility. "How can I repay you, Mamá?" I said. She made a face and fluttered her hands at me.

"Repay," she said as if it were something shameful. "You have already given me much." She turned her gaze to the wall behind her where Bierce's jacket now hung on a framework of woven branches. A garland of herbs hung around the shoulders; the skulls of birds and small animals made a ring above it on the wall like a halo. Mamá looked at it with adoration and a profound, palpable sadness, like an added color to her complexion. Then, with a sigh, she turned and smiled at me.

I said, "One thing bothers me, Mamá. We destroyed most of the Eagle-knights, it's true. But what of *el Gran Brujo,* Mamá? What of Huerta?"

At mention of Huerta's name, Mamá Huitzil's face darkened and fell into lines of fury. The grieving Madonna was replaced by a goddess with a skirt of rattlesnakes. I quailed and leaned back from her.

"Leave him to me," she said. And she smiled a wicked smile, and we finished our tea.

I had planned to leave that day, but my talk with Mamá Huitzil lasted so long, and she was so insistent upon my staying, that I didn't have the energy to refuse. She made up the love-seat as a bed and we honored the siesta. I for one slept like a stone. The dim, quiet shop, redolent with herbs and ancient magic, quieted the months of fear, grief, and just plain excitement that I had been bearing. In the back room, Mamá Huitzil snored softly like some great cat purring. I closed my eyes. And when next I opened them it was dark outside. Mamá was puttering around her shop, lighting lamps and plumping pillows. I sat up and felt as if I had shed the weight of years.

I got up and helped her prepare a meal. Our talk continued over supper and into the evening—easy, friendly talk of everything and nothing. It was balm to us both, I think.

When I left the next morning, there were tears all around. We both knew we would probably never see each other again. It was *"adios,"* not *"hasta luego."* I hugged her and held her out by the shoulders.

"Que vayas con Dios," she said.

"Y que los Espíritus te cuiden," I answered.

We embraced again. Then I turned, mounted my horse, and rode out of San Andrés Tecolotzán.

Back to Torreón. I returned my horse and paid the balance of my debt to the hostler. Climbing on to the train later, I turned once to survey the city and the crowds. Torreón had been only a stopping-place on all my travels; yet I knew that, as with San Andrés, Mexico City, and Chihuahua City, I might never see it again; and as part of that last adventure with Ambrose Bierce, my departure from it was a milestone. I gave it a salute, sighed, and entered the car.

My voyage thence to the border was largely uneventful. For several miles one fellow, in a white canvas duster that looked as if it had never seen dust, gray suit, and, incongruously, a straw sombrero, sat next to me and tried to initiate a conversation. His accent was unplaceable—not Mexican, and probably not American—and he looked exactly like what he was trying not to look like—a spy. His talk was all hale-fellow-well-met—"Say, you look like a fellow American on the dodge!"—and was full of not too subtle probes into my history.

"That arm sure looks sore, mac . . . Coming from Torreón, eh? Boy, they had a dust-up there, didn't they? I heard Nuevo Laredo is a swell place . . ."

I nodded, smiled, and let all those fishing attempts fall gloriously flat. After a few, profitless minutes, he mumbled something about having a cigarette and wandered away to find some other rube.

At Monterrey and Nuevo Laredo, soldiers came through and gave my passport a stern looking-over. They were Constitutionalists now, of course, not the dreaded *federales*. Still, a uniform is a uniform, and can be daunting. However, if they thought to intimidate me into some kind of confession, they were disappointed. By then I was so tired of the war, so apathetic about anything less momentous than death itself (and even that had left me numb), that I gave them no satisfaction. Like the spy, they soon tired of the game and gave me back my passport.

2.

Laredo, Texas. The United States of America at last. Be it ever so imperfect, it was still my home. I did not drop to my knees and kiss the ground, but I did heave a long sigh of relief when I crossed the Rio Grande. Suddenly I no longer had to work at something as basic as speech, although I had been in Mexico long enough that many of my thoughts, and even some of my dreams, came to me in Spanish. For example: I passed a haberdasher's in Laredo that had a sign advertising a SALE in the window. I automatically read it as the Spanish *sale,* or "he/she leaves," and wondered, "Who is leaving?" It turns out that it was I who was leaving. I boarded the train to San Antonio and never looked back.

At the Alamo City I disembarked and sought out the Menger Hotel again. I wanted to see Avis Smalls, but despaired of finding her airfield on my own. Fortunately my good host Ernst was in at the Menger when I stopped by and, miracle of miracles, even remembered me as well.

"You're the fella gave the old campaigner that money," he said, and enveloped my hand in his great paw. "Sad 'bout him—dead a week after you saw him, though I do say you made his last days a mite easier. And what of your friend, there? Bierce, was it?"

"Yes. Gone, too, I'm afraid."

"Well, that's a right shame, Mr. Littlefault, it truly is." He reached under the bar and brought up a bottle that looked as if it had come over on the *Mayflower.* He brushed some dust and cobwebs off of it and smiled at the label he revealed.

"My Opa brought this from 'the old country,' as he'd say, back in '39. Seems like it's set long enough." He took two small shot glasses down from the shelf behind him and set them on the bar. Then he took a corkscrew, punched it into the cork in the bottle, and twisted it out. Immediately the aroma of bright, heady herbs saturated the air.

"Kimmelwasser," said Ernst. "Cures whatever ails you." He poured us each a tot and set the bottle down. We raised our glasses.

"Absent friends," I said.

"Absent friends."

Ernst did better than give me Miss Smalls' address; he telephoned her and a cab to take me to her airfield. I thanked him for the help and the Kimmel (something only a fellow Dutchman could appreciate), and left feeling, once again, that I was losing a friend.

The airfield looked identical to when I flown out of it months before, right down to the sun pounding the earth flat. Miss Smalls' aeroplane was sitting in the waves of heat like a large, dainty bird airing its wings. When my cab pulled up by the shed, Miss Smalls herself and one of her mechanics (Hap? Lamar?) emerged. She was clad in oil-stained coveralls and a flat cap held her auburn locks from coming loose in the hot wind.

"Why, Mr. Littlefault!" She smiled as she approached me, offered her hand. "What a pleasant surprise. I had hoped the Mexican fighting hadn't swallowed up you and Mr. Pierce, was it?"

"Bierce." I was flattered that she had remembered my own cumbersome name but not Bierce's. Got one up on you, you old buzzard.

"Bierce, of course. And how is he?"

"I am very sorry to say that he is dead."

She put her hand up to her mouth in what, despite the grease under her fingernails, was a very ladylike gesture.

"I am deeply sorry to hear that, Mr. Littlefault. What a gentleman he was, gracious and mannered . . ." She stared out across the plains as if to find him there. "And your other friend, Mr. Romero?"

"Gone as well."

"Well—well. It isn't proper to speak ill of the dead. Still, I shan't grieve over him as I shall over Mr. Bierce, poor soul."

I looked at her and remembered our meeting with Bierce and Juan in Laredo. Something about her attitude toward Juan back then had stuck in my mind.

"If you don't mind my asking," I said, "you did not care for Mr. Romero, did you?"

"No, I did not."

"May I ask why not?"

She crossed her arms over her chest and looked at me speculatively.

"The Mexicans have a saying, Mr. Littlefault. Perhaps you have heard it in your travels: 'Me cae feo.'"

"Certainly," I nodded. "We would say, 'he rubs me the wrong way.'"

"Yes, a vivid expression, but I've always liked the Spanish better—'he falls ugly upon me.' My translation is crude, but it conveys the sentiment exactly. Mr. Romero was deeply ugly to me."

"I could tell that he was, Miss Smalls. At first I thought that perhaps you just didn't like Mexicans, but—"

Her laughter, rising into the spring sky like a flock of birds, cut me off.

"Oh, Lord, no, Mr. Littlefault, *no!* There is no lack of people 'round here who do not care for the Mexicans, I assure you, but I am not one of them. I could scarcely do so when my own dear *abuela* was a Mexican! No, Mr. Littlefault, my problem with your Mr. Romero was with him alone his own self. There was something off about him, if you get my meaning; something hidden, yet I could see its teeth when I saw him off-sided." She paused, laughed quietly and self-consciously. "My goodness, such nonsense I spin. Forgive me, Mr. Littlefault. Call if 'woman's intuition,' if you like, but there was deceit in that man. I could feel it."

"You are more right than you know, Miss Smalls, and I just wish I had listened to my own intuition when you felt it back in Laredo. And yet, Mr. Bierce knew of Juan's duplicity early on and said nothing—not even to me. I dare say that things would not have turned out as they had if he had acted sooner on his knowledge—neither as well, nor as badly."

"You speak in mysteries, Mr. Littlefault."

"I fear that I do," I laughed. "Your pardon—the nature of our mission precludes my saying more, even now. And I think this Texas heat has addled my brain."

"Well, we can't have that, now, can we? Come on in to the shed. We have some delightful lemonade on a block of ice."

They did indeed; and I sat and enjoyed it with Miss Smalls ("Miss Avis, if you please!") and her mechanic, sitting among the odors of oil and sawdust and varnish, and speaking of trifles.

*

I loitered in San Antone for only a day or two after seeing Miss Smalls. Footloose and fancy free, as they say, I toyed with the idea of visiting San Francisco again. But any sentimental value the city may have had for me had faded. Without Bierce's good presence, it would feel like a stage-set long after the show had ended; the actors gone, the colorful backdrops lifted into the shadows to leave the stage stark, empty, lonely. Besides, others were waiting for me. I wrote Helen Bierce Cowden a brief note, telling her that I had found her father, but sadly, he had been killed in battle. I hoped that would be enough; she never responded. I also sent Deliah a telegram and waited only long enough to receive the response:

As soon as you can make it. We are looking forward to seeing you.

DG

I could almost feel Mrs. G. Senior's breath upon Deliah's neck as she wrote this. I wondered how much of our affair Deliah had revealed to her mother-in-law, if anything. It was, after all, still 1914, and not seemly for a young widow to be seen gallivanting with strange men. I did, however, hope she might reveal some of our feelings about each other to Mrs. G. before I got there. But it wasn't my decision.

The train voyage from San Antonio to Boston was just long enough to al-low for some reflections without being tedious. I had been so preoccupied with our mission and "putting things aright" upon my return that retrospection was not a luxury I could afford. Now it was all I could afford, and the ghosts came on at full gallop.

At their lead, of course, was Ambrose Gwinnett Bierce, leading the charge as was his wont; but in his train was a motley crew, beloved faces and dreaded faces. Posada, Villa, Huerta, Mamá Huitzil, Don and Doña Golón, the vicious Lieutenant Bendiga, Tomás with his elephantine ears—and Juan Romero. Juan, or the man who called himself "Juan," still haunted me mercilessly. A friend, a boon companion, our deadly nemesis—a mystery. Who was he? How long had he been an adept of the mysteries of the Jaguar-knights and their priests? He claimed to make his home in Malinalco, which, I later researched, was the site of a major Eagle-knight temple in pre-Cortésian days. But even that was ques-tionable. Up until the end, most of what that creature had told us had been lies. How could I trust anything the man had told us? Malinalco made sense, given everything else; yet it could just have been a taunt from a being who thought he was so superior to us that we would never put the hints together.

And we hadn't. Or, at least, I had not. Despite his keeping me in the dark for so long, I like to believe that Bierce would have succeeded but for that powder Juan blew in our faces down beneath Mexico City. We were armed, had our guns drawn, in fact; we "had the jump on Juan," as the dime-novelists put it. In his human guise Juan would have fallen to a bullet as quickly an any other man.

But these were might-have-beens. What had happened had happened, whether Helen Cowan or anyone else believed it. And we had won . . . *hadn't we?*

I read the newspapers obsessively on my long ride back east, with especial attention paid to our neighbor to the south. Villa, Carranza, and the rest of the Constitutionalists were quickly rolling up the entire landscape of Mexico. On the second of June, Villa took Saltillo; on the eighth, Obregon conquered Guadalajara. It seemed as though Mexico City would fall soon, Huerta would be in the hands of his enemies, and the war would end. That, surely, would spell the complete end of any remaining groups of Eagle-knight still out there. Even if they survived, their bloody cause would be lost.

Yet I still had my doubts.

Seeing Deliah again did not dispel those doubts so much as drive them into shadowy places in my brain. She and her boys were waiting at South Station in Boston when my train arrived. I saw them eagerly scanning the windows of the carriages even before we had stopped. I waved, but reflections must have hidden me. Afraid lest they might not see me and leave, I grabbed my bag and lunged for the door. I squeezed myself though the crowds in the aisles, down the stairs—and into the arms of Deliah Gadbury. She had seen me and was waiting at the bottom of the steps. We embraced each other as if we would never embrace again; we embraced tightly and warmly and completely. Tears squeezed out of my eyes. When I blinked them away I saw Deliah's older boy holding the younger one's hand just behind her. They were staring at us as though we had just shed all our clothes—a *scandal!*

When at last we released each other, we held each other at arm's length for a long look.

'You are lovelier than ever,' I said.

"You are—changed." Her arched brows drew together in concern. "Are you well, Amos?"

As if reminded by her words, my left arm began to ache. Mamá Huitzil's salve had healed it wonderfully and the scar was just a pale ghost of a line. But certain moments, moments when I forgot just how wounded I had been, brought sudden bolts of pain to remind me. So it did now, and I winced. Deliah pulled me close.

"No, you're not all right."

I smiled, disengaged her from me, and rubbed my sore arm.

"I am fine, Deliah. Truly. I was wounded but am mostly healed. And seeing you makes me feel better than I have in years. And you—your trip home was uneventful, I trust?"

She laughed. "If you compare it with our stay in Mexico, then, yes, I suppose you could say it was 'uneventful.' Nothing more serious than a near mutiny and a frantic hour while Jerry disappeared to explore the ship."

We looked at each other; we couldn't stop looking at each other.

"Mother," came a querulous voice at her back. "Are we having lunch soon?"

Then we both laughed and turned to her boys.

"Yes, yes, of course, boys. But first, you do remember Mr. Littlefault?"

They looked at me, this strange man who took such liberties with their mother, their four eyes steady and critical. The passage of a couple months can seem like the wearing of years to the young. Best to make friends.

"Hullo, boys," I shook their hands. "Do you know anyone around here who likes candy?"

That brought smiles. I dug into my pockets and gave them each a hard sugar skull I had bought at a stand in Nuevo Laredo. Their eyes blossomed, but they looked at their mother first.

"Really, Amos," she scolded. "You shouldn't have." The boys faces fell. "But, I suppose since you brought them all this way . . ." Like electric lights touched to current, the boys' faces lit up again. "But not until after lunch, boys!" called Deliah, as the boys took their candies and turned away, chatting to each other about whose skull was better. I picked up my bag. Deliah smiled and gently took my arm, and we followed.

"Honestly," she said. "You spoil those boys. What am I going to do with you?"

"I have a few suggestions."

Then she really laughed.

*

Of the dramatis personae of the last adventure of Ambrose Bierce, their fates were as varied as the people themselves. I have allowed ten years to elapse before committing this adventure to paper (I write this in the heady year of 1924), in the hopes that those affected by its chapters may be either beyond its consequences. Or, like Bierce, beyond caring.

In the meantime, Deliah Gadbury made me the happiest man in the world and married me not long after my return, and we live, quietly, in Waltham, Massachusetts, with her mother-in-law and sons.

The tale of Victoriano Huerta y Martínez, one-time president of the República Mexicana and Gran Brujo of the Eagle-knights, had a less than happy ending. After fleeing Mexico in July 1914, Huerta followed the traditional path of forced "retirees" from office and boarded a ship (a German ship, for those who were keeping track) for Spain. But a sleepy retirement was not for the old Jackal either. He soon hopped to England and thence took ship for the United States, arriving in April of 1915. He probably hoped to evade detection this way, but the U.S. Government was not to be deceived. Huerta made contact with a German agent in New York—where he also picked up a tail of a couple Secret Service agents.

It was at this point that Dr. Muñoz, sick of his illustrious patient's shenanigans and seeing the walls closing in, jumped ship and settled in New York. An acquaintance of mine from Providence saw him there not long ago. Meanwhile, Huerta worked his way toward the Southwest where he met up with his old crony, Pascual Orozco. Orozco had rounded up a group of disgruntled ex-Huertistas seeking to overthrow the Constitutionalists. Germany had already pledged money and materiel for the plot, hoping to open a second front against the United States there, and Huerta was eager to return to the fight. All the time he unknowingly led his little parade of Secret Service agents. They let him get as far as Newman, New Mexico, where they decided that he had gotten close enough to Mexico. There they arrested Huerta and Orozco and put them in Fort Bliss, Texas. Orozco slipped back into Mexico and was killed. Huerta was later removed to house arrest; and there, within sight of the country he once ruled, Victoriano Huerta died of cirrhosis of the liver on January 13, 1916.

Certainly *el borrachito* laid the path to his own death many drinks ago, and the desertion of Dr. Muñoz (and subsequent loss of his ministrations) can't have helped. But in Huerta's series of failed opportunities and thwarted attempts I seem to see the wizened hands of Mamá Huitzil at work. I like to think so, anyway. It was a fitting end to the old reprobate's career, more punishing it its way than "being stood up against a wall and shot to rags," as Bierce once famously predicted for himself. Sick, powerless, alone, nearly forgotten except as a bad chapter in a long war, Huerta probably died wishing he had gone out as Ambrose Bierce had done—facing the battle head-on. I can at least draw some solace from that.

And even with the death of el Gran Brujo, I still have my questions. Where did all the Eagle-knights and Jaguar-knights *go?* The summer after the death of Juan Romero, the Europeans began their own extravagant dance with Death in what was euphemistically known as the Great War. They outdid even the Mexican Revolution in slaughter, and it made me wonder how many of the Eagle-knights followed their *tlatoani* into exile. For the blood still flows down the temples of power across the world, and shows no sign of stopping. The violence is like a virus, flitting unseen from country to country, only showing itself when it is too late to defeat it. Did Huerta carry this sickness to Europe with him? Did the Legion of the Sun, survivors of an age-old cult, regroup and spread their poison through the august halls of Europe as well? Granted, war is nothing new to the Europeans, nor is violence exclusive to Mexico. Yet the appalling scale of death and savagery enacted upon the fields of France, Flanders, Germany, and elsewhere dwarfs even the bloodbaths of old. The Mexican Revolution swallowed 900,000 people; but this statistic pales in comparison with the millions lost in the Great War.

The skies are now clear above Mexico. The Black-Glass God sleeps again.

But for how long?

ACKNOWLEDGEMENTS

My thanks to George Arnold, Steve Behrends, the late Sam Gafford, S. T. Joshi, and David Schultz for their encouragement, unwavering support, critical advice and friendship during the writing of this book. And to my wife, Jackie, for her love and enthusiasm always. Love you, babe.

www.ingramcontent.com/pod-product-compliance
Lightning Source LLC
Chambersburg PA
CBHW060927030726
47503CB00003B/501